The Reluctant Savior

The Reluctant Savior

Paul Breer

Copyright © 2010 by Paul Breer.
Cover illustration by Analise Dubner
Author photo by Varouj Hairabedian

Library of Congress Control Number: 2010914605
ISBN: Hardcover   978-1-4535-8918-2
                 Softcover   978-1-4535-8917-5
                 Ebook   978-1-4535-8919-9

This is a work of fiction. Names, characters, places and incidents either are the product of the author's imagination or are used fictitiously, and any resemblance to any actual persons, living or dead, events, or locales is entirely coincidental.

This book was printed in the United States of America.

For information about the author's other works, go to PaulBreer.com.

MAR 1 7 2017

To order additional copies of this book, contact:
Xlibris Corporation
1-888-795-4274
www.Xlibris.com
Orders@Xlibris.com
81371

CONTENTS

1

The Crash

At the rim of the caldera, Rafer Alexander looks down into the crater where the tiny plane that left Kathmandu just days ago lies empty, its nose pressed against the rock and both wings askew, all glimmering in the mountain light like a crumpled silver butterfly. To the left of the plane lie four small, uncrossed mounds . . . catafalques of snow lovingly prepared and sheltered from the Himalayan winds by the spires of rock and ice behind. His eyes are riveted to the closest three . . . one for his mother, another for his father and the third for Jason, his older brother. A fourth grave, carefully separated from the other three, holds the stiffened body of the pilot, he who boasted they could escape the sudden winds by dropping to 15,000 feet and hugging the border between Tibet and Nepal. It was a decision based on hope, not reality. Within minutes the snow had come sweeping down from the peaks and trapped them in a shroud of white, obscuring the cliffs directly ahead. Helpless to see, they continued to descend only to fly straight into a caldera, a mammoth crater left eons ago when a volcano exploded then collapsed, drawing its molten lava back into the interior.

Rafer had survived with nothing more than a gashed cheek and bruised left wrist but awoke to find his parents, brother and the pilot all dead. For five days he moved about, alternately scanning the skies for help and digging graves in the snow. With his one good hand he built fires; he wrote messages in the snow; he used bits of metal ripped from the wreckage to mirror the sun whenever a plane appeared overhead; he spent hours trying to resurrect a smashed cell phone. Despite these heroic efforts, each a torturous victory over the gravitational pull of despair, there was no sign that he had been seen, no dipping of wings, no flares, no parachutes of food or clothing. Five days passed and he was still invisible to the world, locked away in a pit carved deep into molten rock and obscured from above by both shadows and snow.

Still standing at the rim now, his mind drifts back to the previous night where he lies bundled into the rear of the fuselage, only feet from the bodies of his family. With no company but an ebbing moon, he struggles to calm his fears and review his options. Thanks to an appetite depressed by grief and anxiety, he still has enough emergency rations for another four or five days, but is it wiser to spend that time waiting for a rescue that might never come or should he climb out of the crater and try trekking down the mountain to a lower elevation in hopes of finding help in a remote village?

As the cold of the night creeps under his makeshift covers, numbing his brain and tempting him with the promise of a life beyond this one, a life free of pain and struggle, he sits up, wipes the ice from his eyebrows and makes his decision. All signs say it is time to go. The caldera is too hard to see from above; the chances of being rescued are minimal and unlikely to improve. It is essential to leave before there are so few rations left that he'll lack the strength to trudge through the miles of snow and ice that lie between the caldera and civilization below. As he pulls the covers tight, a flurry of ideas, some ingenious, others impractical, begin peppering his mind. He can use the plane's seat cushions to fashion snow shoes . . . then bind them to his boots with laces looped through the leather covering. The emergency skis, although shattered beyond repair, can be split and used as poles for handling steep drop-offs. Shards of broken glass from the plane's windows could prove useful in warding off predators or cutting up meat if he should come across an animal frozen in the snow. The primary predator in the Himalayas, he recalls, is the secretive snow leopard . . . its main food source being the ibex, marmots and small rodents. Not too much to worry about there, he reflects . . . as long as he keeps moving.

His mind turns now to the snowy graves just outside the cabin. In pondering their frozen flesh, he is reminded of an old movie about a plane crash in the Andes, a true-to-life film that had left him nauseous at the thought of what the passengers did to survive. The same nausea returns now. After all, he reasons, three of the four bodies are his own family . . . how could he carve up their arms and legs and eat the very muscles that once embraced him? "But what about the pilot?," he asks. The answer comes in the form of an image: it is Ajo introducing himself at the airport, his smile as wide as the Tibetan plains, his hand soft and warm. Standing before his tiny Piper cub, he speaks the only two English words he knows, "You welcome." Rafer shakes his head violently. "It's too disgusting. How could I even think of it?"

His sleep is fitful, punctuated by recurring dreams of burial and suffocation. Rising just after sunrise, he hastily assembles his gear, then climbs up out of the crater onto the rim where he stands now, gazing upon the scene before him . . . snow, rock and ice stretching without interruption for miles both down and to the sides, erasing any hope of a straight line descent. The sight is both welcoming in its vast, unbounded beauty and frightening in its hostility to anything that breathes or moves. Not a single sign of life, not even a tree as far as the eye can see. What looms immediately before him is a wide expanse of snow bordered by a long, descending outcrop of rock and ice to the right. From his experience in the caldera he is aware how deep and dangerous snow can be when it is protected from the wind. On numerous forays from the plane, he had more than once fallen into drifts that were six to eight feet deep, making it impossible to go on and just barely possible to backtrack to safer ground. He is also aware that wide, steep expanses of snow are vulnerable to avalanches which can be started by something as simple as a loud noise or a sudden movement.

A plan comes quickly. The only realistic option is to stick to the windswept ridge on the right where the accumulation is limited to a thin crust, probably capable of supporting a human being. Stepping carefully through the fallen scree, it should be possible to follow the rock down as far as it goes. Such a strategy brings its own dangers, however, in that a ridge, seemingly gentle in its slope, can drop off without warning into a crevasse making forward movement impossible and backing up difficult.

As he turns now for a final look at the three graves where his family lies frozen, he is again assaulted by the torment of what he has done. Should he have buried them face down with their eyes and mouths pressed into the snow, forever cutting them off from the sun's healing light? Or should he have laid them there with faces up and made his farewells even as he covered their eyes and lips with a shovel? He struggles with a desire to go back down and lie next to them, to apologize for leaving them like this, for having suggested that they come to the Himalayas in the first place. Unbidden, the thought of remaining with them, of joining them in whatever afterworld exists, calls from the outer edges of consciousness. Frightened, he closes his eyes and turns back to the task before him.

Still musing and reluctant to start, his thoughts return to last Christmas when his parents first announced their gift. The trip was offered as a present for his reaching a goal first suggested by Mother in grade school then nurtured with ample doses of praise and support throughout high school and college . . . the goal of winning a Ph.D. from Harvard University, thereby matching the M.D. planned for his older brother Jason. This was to be his reward for years of dedicated achievement, a trip anywhere in the world he wanted to go. After weeks of private deliberation, he had chosen a plane trip over the Himalayas, starting in Kathmandu and tracing the highest peaks of the range from Dhaulagiri and Annapurna in the West to Everest and Kanchenjunga in the East, being careful to stay clear of the Chinese-controlled Tibetan plateau. It was to be two weeks of both ground and air exploration of an area that had fascinated him ever since he saw a picture book of the Himalayas in third grade. All of this was to happen right after June graduation, a month prior to his taking a highly sought-after job in the research department at Kidder-Homans, the oldest and biggest investment brokerage in Boston. To a tall, good-looking, healthy 26 year old man boasting a newly minted Ph.D. in economics from perhaps the best university in the country, everything was coming up roses. How could things have gone so wrong?

With a final sigh, he starts down the slope, veering carefully over to the ridge on the right. The air is warm . . . probably in the 80's . . . but the sun feels harsh enough to burn his skin. He tugs on his cap to shield his face. A passage from a travel book comes back to him: 'In the Himalayas the temperature at 15,000 to 20,000 feet above sea level can vary as much as 100 degrees in a single day . . . from +80 at noon to -20 at night.' The article goes on to warn of the severe headaches, even vomiting, that are common when hiking at this elevation. From what the pilot said when they were still in the air, Rafer figures that his present position is probably somewhere around 15,000 feet. The nearest human habitation could be somewhere around 8,000 feet, leaving 7,000 feet of snow and ice to descend and only four more days of rations to do it in. The numbers were not promising.

He gets no more than 100 feet down the slope before his boots slip out of the laces binding them to his snow shoes, the ones rigged from the plane's seat cushions. After two attempts to tighten and readjust the laces, he gives up and discards the cushions. One of the two ski poles is left behind as well, the remaining one preserved for situations where a third leg might be needed for balance. Soon after reaching the safety of the ridge on the right, he encounters snow no more than six inches deep. The walking is considerably easier here although some of the rocks are too big to step over. A hundred yards ahead, the ridge opens up into a V-shaped pass nestled between overhanging walls of ice-covered rock. There is less wind in the pass, making it easier to breathe, although at 15,000 feet his lungs are working hard to get enough oxygen. It occurs to him that the only reason he has any chance at all is that the trek he has undertaken is all downhill. Climbing out of the caldera in the opposite direction, over the peak behind the crater and down the other side, would have required more strength, stamina, and food than he could possibly muster.

His steps take on a slight bounce as he heads down into the pass and on into the open. The whole thing suddenly seems doable. With the next few hundred yards clear of any obstacles, his mind shifts from the exigencies of hiking to thoughts of the family he has left behind. Strangely, he feels Mother close by; she seems to be following from her icy grave. Her voice is still clear, still encouraging, no different really from what she has said over and over since early childhood. "Rafer, you can do it . . . there's nothing in this world you can't do." As her words return, he quickens his step and drives his stick into the ground. Her face is right in front of him now. She speaks again, as if they were still at the kitchen table back in Babylon, New York: "You can become anything you want . . . anything." His shoulders broaden at her voice, his lungs expand, gulping ever more oxygen. He can see her smiling as she enjoys the effect of her words. "This trip is going to be hard but you can make it." As he watches, she lifts her head in defiance. "Never give up," she adds, her jaw clenched against defeat. He nods his vigorous assent, unaware how strange his gesture must look . . . alone, here in the mountains with no one around for miles. His arms ache to hold her, to be held in return . . . but this has never been her way. She loves with her voice, not her arms or lips. This much he has learned in 26 years.

The pass ends now, as the enclosing walls merge to form a single narrow ridge extending sharply downward like the razor back of a long-tailed dinosaur. The walking is more difficult here since the ridge slopes both downward and to the left. After a hundred yards he is fatigued enough to sit and rest. Bending over, he scoops up some snow and presses it into his mouth, careful not to scrape his lips which are already feeling the effects of the searing sun. Unmelted, it does little to quench his thirst.

As he stretches out on a flat rock, fully aware of his aloneness, thoughts of life in Babylon, followed by an image. He sees himself as a fourteen year old, walking into his parents' bedroom and opening the top drawer of their dresser. From previous intrusions, he knows that the condoms are in the corner of the drawer, carefully stacked on top of each other in cellophane jackets. He picks up the top one and slips it into his pocket where it will remain hidden until sold to his friend visiting from Kentucky who plans to use it on a girl named Maggie. He has been promised 25 cents. In subsequent weeks he returns to the bedroom often to see how many condoms are left. On each visit he is surprised to find the pile unchanged . . . except for that one he took earlier. It would be several years before this discovery would reveal its meaning. That was the day Jason, his older brother who rarely told him anything interesting, confided that right after the wedding Dad was so frustrated that Mother wouldn't have sex that he walked out of the house and got drunk at a nearby tavern. Mother in turn got so upset that she ran home to her own mother who, sensibly, according to the aunt originally conveying this information, sent her back to her husband with the message that she should "learn to endure it."

One memory evokes another. On the day he was leaving for college Mother stopped him at the door for one last piece of advice. "Save it for marriage, Rafer. You'll be glad you did. It's not everything they say it is anyway." If he had been honest about the whole thing, he would have replied, "It's too late Mother. I've already slept with Marylou and two prostitutes, one down in Albany and another up in Saratoga Springs." But he said nothing. Why upset her now when I'm leaving home, he had reasoned at the time.

Still on the rock, he recalls the more recent dilemma of where to place the three family graves, particularly those of his two parents. He had considered placing Mother and Dad right next to each other, with arms or hands actually touching but changed his mind when he recalled that in 26 years he couldn't remember a single time when he saw the two of them kissing, let alone hugging. It certainly wasn't his father's fault. Once, several years ago, Dad had let it be known in private that at best he and Mother made love no more than several times a year. "Sounds like she's frigid," came the youthful response. "Sshh," he had whispered, "I wouldn't want her to hear that." Loyal to the end, he never stopped loving her, probably never even had an affair despite ample opportunities to do so.

Overhead the sun is falling now, already below its noon apex and ready to slip behind the jagged peaks to the North. He hurries on, conscious of the need to find a niche in the rocks that will shield him against the frigid air soon to descend on this secluded wilderness. Up to now his hands and feet have been cool but not uncomfortably so. That, he realizes, will change when the sun disappears. As he scans the rocky slope to his right, eyes squinting against the late afternoon sun, he suddenly becomes aware of an acrid odor in the air. "Cat piss," he murmurs, breathing deeply like an ibex desperate to locate the leopard's position before it gets any closer. He stops and looks up at the razorback to his right, straining to catch a glimpse of the giant cat. What he sees instead is a large opening in the rock, a cave, the very kind of place a snow leopard would pick for its home. A cave, he murmurs, a wonderful place to spend the night, away from the wind and snow . . . but not if it's already occupied by a predator capable of bringing down prey twice its size or more. He quickens his step now, eager to put as much distance as possible between the cave and whatever shelter he can find for the night. It is another two or three hundred yards down the slope before an opportunity presents itself . . . a rocky overhang jutting out from the side of the dinosaur's back . . . and under it a flat slab of stone free of both ice and snow. He sniffs the air for signs of leopard and finds none. Already weary from a day of trekking, he climbs up to the slab and sits down. From this position he can look out over the snowfield that lies spread before him . . . and plan tomorrow's move. "Stick to the side of the ridge as long as possible . . . that's the strategy. When the ridge ends and I have to make my way through the snow . . . well, I'll just have to hope it's not too deep." With that thought in mind he pulls out a small tarp rescued from the plane and crawls on top of it. Falling asleep on such a hard, unforgiving surface will not be easy, especially as the temperature falls below freezing. But he needs the sleep if he is to have energy enough for tomorrow's descent.

Gradually worries about the night give way to thoughts of his family back at the plane. Once again it is Mother who provides the memories. Yes, she shied away from physical contact with her husband and even with her children, but she more than made up for it with her voice. To hear her answer the telephone was electrifying. There was nothing matter-of-fact about her "Hello." It was more like a gasp, the kind of response that made you think she had been sitting there all day waiting for you to call. And this was before she even knew who was calling. Once she knew it was one of her own flesh and blood, the gasp gave way to a semi-hysterical outburst more appropriate for a call to the intensive care unit. "How **ARE** you?"

And this was no occasional thing; she always answered the phone that way. She probably reacted the same way to his brother Jason, but he couldn't be sure since he and Jason rarely talked about anything personal. Shifting his weight on the cold slab now, his attention turns to the image of Jason lying rigid in the snow, eyes closed and glazed over with ice. The thoughts come quickly. "What I remember best about you," he murmurs, looking up toward the plane "was all the fighting we did in the car and at the dinner table. That's a terrible thing to say, I know. I wish I could think of something more positive; maybe I will later . . . (*pause*) . . . The warmest memory that comes to mind right now is the time we were together at 'Y' camp in the Adirondacks. Do you remember? The people in charge had set up a boxing night and I was chosen to fight another kid from Babylon. Despite a similarity in size, the other kid was much stronger and proceeded to knock me around the ring to the delight of all his friends in the front row. It was then that I heard a lonely voice from somewhere in the rear, 'Give it to him, Rafe. You can do it.' It was you, Jason. God, how that warmed my heart." He shakes his head. "But that's the only nice thing I remember."

Scanning the rocks for snow leopard, he leans forward, finds nothing moving . . . then continues his monologue. "I guess we were just too competitive. At least you were. You were always conscious of where we stood relative to each other, both with respect to grades in school and which one of us was the favorite at home. I don't think I ever felt that way, but it's possible that I've blocked it out. I'm not sure. I do remember, however, that when we were very young you gave us nicknames. You were Doc and I was Fat. It didn't bother me at the time but later on I began to see it in a different light. The name you gave yourself, 'Doc', had a ring of authority about it, suggesting a career ahead as a respected physician while the name I got stuck with was meaningless, particularly in the light of the fact that I was very thin. There are other things too. I see something similar in your habit of referring to me as 'Number Two Son' whenever we were together in a group. You, of course, always spoke of yourself as 'Number One Son,' implying some kind of superiority or at least something more than order of birth. At least that's the way it came across to me. I could be wrong.

"One thing is clear to me though . . . Mother contributed to the coolness between us by constantly comparing our performance in school. I remember the time . . . actually this happened several times . . . when I no sooner got in the door with my report card that she went to the lowboy in the dining room and pulled out your grades . . . which she had saved . . . for the year when you were my age. She then ran her fingers down the different subjects, Algebra, Chemistry, German and so on while I stood watching nervously. Each time she did this little comparison, your grades proved to be a bit better than mine . . . mid-90's instead of low-90's, thus confirming the generally accepted view that you were the brighter student. Along with both parents, I accepted the judgment that while we were both smart, you were significantly smarter. At the time, it all seemed O.K. with me. It was only later that I woke up to some different feelings."

The temperature is sinking now at a frightening rate . . . much faster than it used to back in Babylon or even in Cambridge. After some experimenting, he finds it helps to curl himself into a fetal ball, with face buried in his gloves, and knees as close to his stomach as possible. Up to this point, thinking about Jason and his parents has served as a distraction from the cold . . . but now the chill begins to assert itself. Considering that the night is still young and the temperature can drop much further, freezing to death suddenly becomes a real possibility. Movement is essential. He recalls that back home, birds, the ones like chickadees that don't migrate South in the Fall, manage to survive winter nights by sitting on protective branches and fluttering their wings for hours on end. They also conserve energy by lowering their heart rate, much the way that hibernating bears do. To Rafer who knows little about physiology, the former strategy seems reasonable while the latter smacks of voodoo, although he has read that, with years of practice, Tibetan monks can mentally control their body heat, allowing them to spend nights out in the snow covered with nothing more than a thin blanket.

With the chickadees in mind, he gets up now and begins dancing on the stone slab, adding random vocal sounds to his steps. Aware that he has a whole night to get through, he keeps his pace slow and alternates it with attempts at sleep. During one of his dancing episodes, while standing upright on the slab, he notices what could be a long, thick tail slipping behind one of the rocks below. The dancing stops immediately as he strains to see the rest of the animal's body. His heart goes into high gear when a leopard emerges from behind the rock, heading for higher ground. All at once an article about protecting yourself from bears and lions flashes through his mind. The advice was clear: with bears, especially grizzlies, you either back off slowly or get down on the ground and make yourself into a ball with your hands over your head. That way you present the least threat. With the cat family, a non-threatening posture won't work. If you back off, you risk activating the animals hunting instincts. If you curl yourself into a ball, you make yourself an even easier meal. What you do instead is to stand, make loud noises, and throw whatever you can in the cat's direction.

There is just enough light left to make out the leopard's white and gray form as it starts climbing toward the slab. When the beast is no more than 30 or 40 feet away, Rafer makes his move. Standing tall on the slab, he raises his arms to make himself look even bigger. When the leopard moves closer, he begins shouting and screaming at the top of his voice. The cat turns his head and snarls. It is at this point that Rafer reaches down and picks up a rock which he hurls at the cat's body. It glances off his haunches, provoking a second snarl, this time with mouth wide open and teeth bared. As Rafer looks frantically for a second rock, the beast begins to back away, slinking quickly into the dark. Still standing on the slab, Rafer follows his movements until the only trace of his visit is the lingering musk in the air. He rubs his nose to rid himself of the odor, breathes deeply, then sits back down on the tarp and resumes his fetal position. His heart is still racing; his hands and feet already numb. The night seems endless as he alternates between dozing, dancing and listening for signs of the leopard's return. What little sleep he gets is fitful and brief. He knows he will pay the price in the morning.

He is wide-awake before the sun casts its somber light on the snowfield before him. As he prepares to rise, the throbbing in his knees and shoulders, both raw from a night of rubbing against frigid stone, forces a moan from deep in his throat. He looks out onto the snowfield and sighs. This is his second day and still no sign of trees or anything to indicate an elevation low enough to support vegetation. The long ridge that up to now has protected him from the wind and offered snow-free walking is about to end. Beyond the ridge, everything appears white for the next three hundred yards until the snow suddenly drops off, leaving nothing in the distance but deep blue sky.

He pulls out the second of his four emergency C-type rations and breaks it in two, returning the second half to his backpack. Aware that this will have to last him the whole day, he chews slowly, savoring each life-giving bite. Still chewing, he stuffs the tarp back into his pack and grabs the ski pole. With a final sweep of his eyes across the area where the leopard was last seen, he starts down the ridge and onto the snow.

The snow is not as deep as he feared . . . two feet at the most, and powder light. Using the pole as a walking stick, he quickly gets into a rhythm as he heads for the drop-off. Since there is no other way to go, either to the left or to the right, he stops worrying about what lies ahead and focuses his attention on each step. As his mind clears, his thoughts wander back to the three people lying buried next to the plane. "If I ever get out of here," he wonders, "will I be able to come back for the bodies so I can at least give them a proper burial? Will I even be able to find the plane?" The questions are left unanswered as he lifts and drops his feet in rhythm to his breathing.

2

Trekking

As feet, pole and breath fall into a cadence, his thoughts return to Jason. It is the summer following his own freshman year at Harvard; along with four friends he is being paid to play clarinet and saxophone in a small dance band at the Tomahawk restaurant on Lake Ticonderoga. Evenings are spent playing soft rock and golden oldies while couples either listen from their tables or slither back and forth across the floor. Days, on the other hand, are reserved for reading all the famous novels he should have read before entering college but either never got around to or never even heard of . . . Tolstoy's War and Peace, Dostoevsky's Brothers Karamazov, Flaubert's Madame Bovary, Stendhal's The Red and Black and so on. It is now Sunday and a prior phone call has alerted him to a visit from his parents. When they arrive just before lunch, he is surprised to see that Jason has joined them. There is a polite shaking of hands but no hugging. The first order of business is the transfer of mail. Mother's fingers are noticeably twitching as she hands over several letters, the one on top featuring a formal-looking envelope from Harvard. From his position behind Mother, Jason announces that it is probably a report of Rafer's final grades for the freshman year. With nervousness obvious to all, Rafer tears open the envelope and scans the report. There are eight grades in all, one for each subject. He sees four A's and four B's, all minuses and pluses having been removed. Reading further, at the bottom of the document he comes to a Roman numeral indicating which of five Groups he has been assigned to. Rafer is aware that Group I is reserved for those students receiving all A's,

Group II for those getting half A's and half B's, Group III for all B's and so on down the line through C's, D's and F's. He is equally aware that Jason, who was named valedictorian in high school, consistently made Group III, that is, all B's, in both his freshman and sophomore years. As Rafe fumbles with the envelope, Mother grabs his arm and gasps, "Well?" "Group II," he replies, unable to conceal a wry smile. Jason is stunned. "They must have made a mistake," he whispers, his voice taut with anxiety. Mother asks to see the letter, lending weight to Jason's suspicions. "That's not too likely," interrupts Dad, "given that Rafe knew most of his grades in advance." "It's true," adds Rafe, "chemistry was the only one I wasn't sure of. The others, music history, gov, economics, English, German, psych, and fine arts are all right." "Good," says Dad, "I think this calls for a little celebration at lunch . . . everybody agree?" Mother, squeezing Rafe's arm, answers, "Of course." Jason says nothing.

Reliving the memory of that lunch now serves two functions, both positive: it distracts Rafe from the drudgery of plowing through a half a mile of deep snow while at the same time keeping his spirits from flagging. But it is the way the story ends a year later that brings the biggest smile to his chapped lips. When the grades for that year, his sophomore year, arrive in Babylon, placing him in Group II all over again, his father pulls him aside and offers a confession: "Rafe, I guess we've been wrong all along about you and your brother. Maybe he studied harder than you in high school and that's why he got better grades. Anyway, I'm sorry that we've been so slow in seeing the truth." That's all he says but it comes across like a judge's apology for years of wrongful imprisonment. To Rafe, the 'truth' referred to by his father, while never articulated directly, sings out loud and clear: "You are the smarter of the two. I'm sorry we haven't seen it before."

This story, repeated several times in all its narcissistic detail, carries him half way down the snowfield, still heading for the drop-off and whatever lies beyond. The wooden pole, made from a broken ski, proves to be essential in maintaining his balance in those areas where the snow reaches up to his knees. With the sun still rising and the temperature warming, he stops and clears a place to rest and eat . . . one bite on the C-ration and back into the pack it goes. With cap pulled tight against the scorching sun, he leans back and lets his mind wander again.

It's a phone call from Jason this time . . . a call that evokes both disbelief and anger. Both boys, now in their 20's, are on vacation from graduate school, Jason at home visiting their parents in Babylon, Rafer in Cambridge working on his dissertation. The words reverberate now like echoes from a distant mountain.

Jason: "Hey Rafe, it's Jase. How you doing?"

Rafer: "O.K. What's up?"

Jason: "Just wanted to let you know that my father is in the hospital."

Rafer (*stunned*): "What?"

Jason: "I said my father is in the hospital . . . something to do with his heart."

Rafer (*pausing*): "That's too bad . . . but where's mine?"

Jason: "What do you mean? I just told you he was in the hospital . . . actually he's in intensive care. I thought you might want to know."

Brushing snow from his knees now, he chuckles and shakes his head. "I'm sure I heard it right. *My* father is what he said, not *our* father . . . or just Dad. Can you believe that? Does he really think of our father as belonging to him alone? That's grotesque. Even when I responded, 'But where's mine,' he didn't get it. Was he even aware of what he said? I doubt it . . . Now, is this just an extreme case of sibling rivalry or is there something even weirder going on here." The next thought brings a roar from deep in his belly. "I wonder if when he prays, he says, "*My* father who art in Heaven, hallowed be Thy name."

The laughter fills his whole body with life-giving warmth as he sets off again into the snow. Still shaking his head, he continues talking to himself, "I guess it makes sense that he invited himself along on this trip even though I was never invited to join him on his post-graduation trip to Europe two years ago. As far as I can tell, neither Mother nor Dad ever suggested that he come along on this one. He simply wangled his way in. And what a price he has paid now for his aggressiveness. I suppose I should feel sorry for him but I can't help remembering how much I wanted to see Europe and how steadfastly he insisted that since the trip was meant as a reward for him alone, I would have to wait my turn, even though Mother and Dad made it clear they wanted me to come along."

As the sun begins its diurnal descent, he slows his pace, aware that he is gradually losing energy but hesitant to eat any more of his emergency bar. The drop-off is now only 25 yards away but still too far away to reveal what lies beyond. He makes a nest in the snow and sits down to rest. As he struggles to make himself comfortable, a new and disturbing thought enters his mind. With no one around to hear he finds it easier to think if he talks out loud as if he were speaking to a group of friends. "Mother's gone and that's going to make a big difference in my life, even though I'm not exactly sure how." In his mind he can almost hear her gasping "hello" as she picks up the phone. "No one else can make me so glad I called", he whispers, his voice already thick with emotion. His mind wanders back to the times when he called to report good news, like the day he learned that he had made a magna and was invited into Phi Beta Kappa, the honor society. "What's it going to be like when she is no longer at the other end of the phone? It just won't be the same talking to Dad who tends to be blasé about such things. Maybe I wouldn't even bother to call." He closes his eyes and leans back against the snow. "Do you realize what you're saying?" Involuntarily he shakes his head. "Can you see what this means . . . how weird it all sounds?" Disturbed by the direction his thoughts are taking, he quickly rises, grabs his pack and resumes walking.

A few yards down the slope the thoughts return, more insistent now in their demand to be heard. He stops in his tracks. "What does this say about my motivation? What does it say about all the effort I have poured into making good grades . . . years of study, years of worrying about exams, term papers and aptitude tests? Has it all been for me . . . or for her? If I really wanted success for myself, wouldn't I be contented whether or not I shared it with someone else?"

Just yards now from the drop-off, a final memory forces its way into consciousness. "I couldn't wait to tell her I had been voted into Phi Beta Kappa. Without thinking I immediately sent the key to her . . . for what? . . . safe-keeping? . . . or because I felt it really belonged to her. It must be in her drawer back in Babylon right now. Is that weird or isn't it . . . to actually give her the key instead of keeping it for myself? So . . . what does it say about our relationship?"

Still rooted to one spot, he allows his thinking to go deeper. "It's frightening to think that for years I've been shaping my life to fit her ambitions rather than my own. But perhaps mine really are the same as hers. Are they? That's something I've never really thought much about. I've always assumed that we wanted the same thing . . . prestige, maybe even fame, plenty of money, a family, some friends, respect in the community. Have I simply taken those things for granted out of a desire to please her, to win and hold her affection?" He leans on the walking stick to steady himself; his breathing accelerates. "If so, is there something different I really want but have never even considered?"

Standing at the edge of the drop-off now, his heart tightens as he surveys the scene before him. Directly in front is a steeply sloping bowl of pure white snow extending a half a mile in either direction . . . and below that, a glacier running perpendicular to the bowl. To the far left where the glacier ends, a hint of green can be detected, trees perhaps, he surmises, and the promise of easier climbing. The task, then, is to make his way down through the bowl to the glacier and then follow the glacier into the trees and lower elevation. The risk is obvious, even to one who has never hiked in the Himalayas before. The immediate danger is of an avalanche triggered by his own movements. "But what is the alternative?," he asks. "To circumvent the bowl means hiking an unknown distance to either the right or left in hopes of finding a gentler slope to navigate. That would require enormous energy and more food than he has; it is also a strategy based on chance, a chance, he concludes, that is not worth taking.

He breathes deeply, then steps down onto the slope, careful to move his feet slowly . . . and noiselessly. Using his pole for leverage, he starts zigzagging his way through the three-foot snow. "So far, so good," he murmurs, careful to keep his voice low. Little does he know as he inches his way down the slope that Mother Nature has an agenda of her own, one oblivious to the plans of even her most favored species. Suddenly, the snow in front of him gives way, separates, and starts heading for the glacier. Before he can change course, the ground behind him begins sliding downward, slowly at first, then picking up speed. In panic, he grabs his pole for balance, determined not to topple over and get buried. As the whole slope collapses toward the glacier, the air is filled with the screams of snow, ice, and rocks plummeting headlong to the bottom. Scarcely breathing, he crouches as if skiing, his only thought being to avoid being knocked over. The force on his back is overwhelming. It is as if he were being propelled from behind by a runaway truck that has lost its brakes. So rapid and relentless is the descent that by the time he reaches the bottom of the slope he is completely imprisoned in ice and snow.

When all outside movement stops and silence returns, he awakens to the peril of his situation. His body remains in a sitting position, tipped slightly to one side, with arms and legs imprisoned by several feet of densely-packed snow. Frantically, he pushes the crystals away with his head, searching for oxygen. There is none. "The pole, the pole," he murmurs. "I've got to make an opening overhead." His hands are still wrapped around the wooden shaft but he can't move his arms. Aware that he won't be able to hold his breath much longer, he thrusts his elbows outward . . . over and over . . . an inch at a time . . . gradually creating the space to move his arms upward. Gripping the pole as tightly as possible now, he draws on the last of his strength to push it up through the snow, closing his eyes and mouth against the suffocating powder that continues to slip down the shaft. With a final convulsive thrust, he breaks through the surface . . . then, still without breathing, jerks the pole up and down repeatedly to make a narrow column for the air. It appears to work. Using his nose alone, he draws the precious oxygen into his lungs, careful to keep his mouth closed against the encroaching crystals.

His strategy is now clear. Move the pole back and forth to widen the opening at the top until it is big enough to climb out. It is obvious that a small hole won't do the trick. It's got to be wide and deep enough to take the weight off his shoulders as he propels himself upward, using arms and feet. The task is both long and exhausting. When, an hour later, he finally crawls out of his tomb and into the light, he can do no more than sprawl spread-eagled on the surface and wait for a semblance of strength to return. Before closing his eyes, he looks down at the glacier, now no more than 50 yards away. From where he lies, it is impossible to tell how deep the snow is there. Whether it turns out to be a blessing or a test beyond his endurance remains to be seen. With that unnerving thought lurking at the edge of consciousness, he slips his pack under his head and falls asleep.

When he awakes, exhausted and ravenous, dusk has already settled in, bringing a chill to the air and early shadows from the ridge to the North. Sitting up, he reaches into his pack and tears open a C-ration, whimpering unselfconsciously like a wolf on the brink of starvation. One look at the darkening sky convinces him it's too late to continue hiking. The glacier will have to wait until morning. He turns around to see if there is something nearby he can use to protect himself from the wind while he rests. There is nothing to be seen . . . no rocks, no ledge, no trees . . . nothing but snow and ice as far as the eye can see.

The only alternative, he concludes, is to dig a shallow bed in the snow and place his pack just behind his head. As he digs with his hands, the graves of his mother, father and brother, lovingly dug just a few days ago, loom before him. "Of the four of us," he reflects, clutching that image, "I am the only one who will rise in the morning . . . the only one to see the sun and move on." He shakes his head in disbelief. "Is there some cosmic reason for this, some justification for my living and their dying . . . or is it just a matter of luck? He continues digging with his gloved hands until the bed is long and deep enough to fit his body. Still exhausted and no longer able to think clearly, he collapses and falls asleep.

Within five minutes he is awake again. Somewhere in the unlit alleys of his unconscious he recognizes that anything longer than a catnap risks a frozen death. As if on cue, whenever his body temperature sinks to a certain level, he opens his eyes, struggles to his feet, starts shaking his arms, dancing, shivering . . . anything to keep the cold at bay . . . anything to resist the lure of deep, uninterrupted sleep. When, hours later, the sun finally peeks over the ridge to the East, spreading its munificence over a lifeless world indifferent to its warming touch, he hikes down the remaining 50 yards and out onto the glacier. Nervously he paws at the surface with his boots. Moving out to the center, he is elated to find no more than six inches of powder on top of solid ice, a recipe for safe, sure-footed walking.

The glacier itself is perhaps 30 or 40 yards wide and narrows slightly as it winds down for over a mile before emptying into a basin surrounded by rocks and what appear to be trees. Trees, he reflects, suggest life, both animal and vegetable, perhaps even human habitation or at the very least signs of human presence. Buoyed by what he sees, he reaches into his pack and pulls out the last of his C-rations. "I'm almost there; another couple of miles and I'm bound to run into somebody . . . maybe a shepherd tending his sheep or a hunter pursuing ibex. Running water . . . that's what I want to see. Something besides snow to quench my thirst . . . perhaps an open brook . . . a chance to catch fish."

Slowly and deliberately he makes his way down the glacier. His spirits are high and would be even higher if it were not for the clouds overhead. Thus far he has been spared the burden of a fresh snowfall. There are a few flakes falling but hardly enough to impede his progress toward the basin. Through his parched lips he mutters a self-conscious prayer for clearing skies . . . a prayer addressed to a Deity he's not even sure exists. "No harm in asking," he reflects, "when the weather is beyond my control."

Before he can even congratulate himself on the power of his prayers, the flakes start to fall harder. Within minutes it becomes impossible to see more than a few yards in front of him. He stops and waits. Given the possibility of slipping into an unseen crevasse, he drops to the ice and curls himself into a ball, hoping to let the storm pass before moving on. It takes more than an hour for the sky to clear. He finally rises, brushing the snow from his jacket and cap. Where previously there was only six inches of light powder, there's now almost three feet of fresh snow.

Each step requires a monumental effort. After five minutes of lifting his legs as if he were climbing over a barbed-wire fence, he stops and reaches for an emergency bar, only to be reminded that he has already eaten the last one. His energy, already drained by his escape from the avalanche, is ebbing fast. He is aware that determination alone may not be enough. In hopes of reviving his spirits, he looks to see what lies beyond the glacier's edge. There are definitely trees in the basin; it is no illusion as he had feared. But does he have the strength to get there? For the first time since leaving the plane, he is beginning to have doubts. Uncertain, he trudges on.

Words heard time and again throughout childhood come back to him now. "Rafer," . . . the words spill from her lips like milk squeezed from swollen breasts . . . "you can achieve anything you want. Yes you can. Do it now. Do it!" His heart begins to race; his skin tingles with gooseflesh. He pictures her speaking from the grave, mouth open and eyes staring as she follows his every movement. He turns in the direction of the plane, nodding his assent. "Yes, you're right . . . I can do it . . . I can," he shouts, as his words fly toward the plane only to die unanswered in the frigid air.

The end of the glacier is close now . . . just yards away. Too exhausted to lift his legs, he forces his way through the remaining snow as if he were wading in deep water. Three more steps and the final barrier gives way. With eyes closed and Mother's incantation fresh in his mind, he steps off the glacier onto bare ground. Once free, he collapses, unable to go any further. He struggles to rise but there is no energy left . . . no reservoir of will . . . nothing but a voice whispering now from a distant grave. Around him the air is cooling as the sun recedes behind the ridge to the West. He wraps himself in the tarp and closes his eyes, fully aware that they might never open again. Under his eyelids, images of the plane return . . . then Mother and Dad . . . still alive, calling one last time. "Come with us," they seem to say. "It's quiet and peaceful here. You've done all you can . . . it's too late . . . you deserve to rest." Then Mother's voice alone, "Come Rafe, rejoin your family . . . this is where you belong. Come to us now, dear . . . come where you can find peace . . . where everything is gentle and luminous and we can all be together again." He smiles with a contentment unknown since childhood. And then the world goes dark.

3

The Monastery

Upon waking, he rubs his eyes, struggling to make sense of surroundings he has never seen before. Not a sound can be heard. From his straw bed he can see that he is in a small room with paintings of the Buddha on one wall and a full-length case filled with books wrapped in red and yellow cloth on the other. Sitting up, he strains to see what the books are about. All are written in a foreign script . . . Hindi or perhaps Tibetan.

Still confused, he turns his attention to his body which is stiff and tingling in its extremities. He wiggles his toes to get rid of the tingling, then reaches for his cheeks to find out why they are burning. Suddenly the image of a plane appears . . . then the crash. As his eyes close, he sees himself pulling bodies from the wreckage, then dragging them to holes he has prepared. The horror of their deaths returns, flooding his mind with pictures of bodies lying in the snow with their eyes closed, helpless to move or cry out as he stands over them with shovel in hand. He shakes his head, trying to banish the image.

It is at that point that a visitor appears. "Hello . . . I'm Tomo . . . how are you feeling?"

Rafer opens his eyes wide. "Ah, not sure . . . where am I?"

"This is Tibetan monastery . . . you are in lamp room of our temple . . . and I am trapa or what you Americans call student. You are American, aren't you?"

"Yes . . . are we in Tibet . . . I thought that . . . "

"No . . . in Sikkim . . . in northern India . . . a hundred miles south of Tibet border."

"How did I get here . . . the last thing I remember was lying in the snow at the foot of a glacier . . . too tired to go any further."

"Some of our monks found you when they went to the mountain to practice what we call tum-mo . . . where they sleep on snow covered only with thin rug. They stumbled on you up by glacier and carried you back here . . . (*pause*) . . . How did you end up lying in the snow may I ask . . . was your plane same as one we hear about on radio . . . the one missing for two weeks now?"

"Yes."

"You not alone, yes? What happened to others?"

"My parents and brother are still up there in the caldera . . . along with the pilot. I buried them all before leaving. I was the only one to survive."

(*Bowing*) "I'm so sorry. If you tell authorities where plane crashed, maybe they bring bodies back . . . (*silence*) . . . What is your name?"

"Rafer . . . Rafer Alexander. "Where did you learn to speak English so well?"

"I spent almost two years in the states . . . in Cambridge, studying at MIT. I thought I wanted to be an engineer . . . but change my mind and come back here to study Buddhism. My family is once from

Kalimpong in Tibet. My grandparents come down here to Sikkim when Chinese invade Tibet in 1950's . . . (*pause*) . . . You probably want to rest now . . . but when you are ready I show you around temple."

"Yes . . . later perhaps."

"By the way we worry about your feet . . . you know, frostbite . . . but your toes look O.K . . . all 11 of them. (*Laughing*) . . . that's the first time I ever see a person with six toes on one foot . . . better be careful if you travel in central India . . . the Hindus think person with six toes on one foot is a god who comes to save them. (*Chuckling*) We Tibetans don't believe that so we won't expect any miracles from you."

(*Smiling*) "Thank you . . . I feel relieved . . . but tell me, how do these monks you mentioned sleep in the snow covered with just a thin rug. It got to be below zero up there . . . I know from experience how painful that can be."

"It's just one of the siddhis you develop after years of meditation. I haven't reached that point yet but I hope to get there someday."

"Siddhis?"

"You know, special powers . . . what you Westerners call magical powers . . . like healing, visualization, levitation and walking on hot coals. These monks controlled their body temperature with their minds."

Rafer sits up. "So, what's the point of hiking all the way up there and maybe freezing to death? Are they trying to prove something?"

"In a way, yes. Controlling your body's temperature can help you . . . maybe if you plan to be for months meditating in freezing cave . . . which some will . . . but mainly it's like a test . . . you know, proving that their practice has reached very high point . . . (*pause*) . . . I will leave you now . . . and come back later. Is there anything you want . . . food, clothing, books?"

"No thanks . . . Tomo . . . did I get that right?"

"Yes."

"I think I'll just lie here for a while. But I want to thank the men who brought me back. If they hadn't found me, well . . . it's pretty clear what would have happened. I feel terribly lucky."

"Yes . . . or maybe you saved for important reason."

"Such as?"

"I don't know. Bye for now, Rafer."

"Friends call me Rafe."

"O.K., Rafe."

As he drops back against the pillow, still confused by this turn of events, the strangeness of his situation seizes him like a nightmare turned eerily prophetic. "Here I am in a comfortable bed, well fed and already making friends when only a few miles away Mother, Dad and Jason lie buried in tombs of ice and snow, shut off from the world, their eyes forever closed, their hearts no longer beating." He craves more sleep but the image of their frozen bodies refuses to go away, tugging at his sleeve now like a teary-eyed child who has not yet had his fill of attention. Yielding, he re-enters the scene, kneeling over each mound in turn, offering his last goodbyes. At his Mother's grave, he finally breaks down as apologies, confessions and farewells stumble over each other in a paroxysm of grief and guilt. Still shivering, he pulls the covers tight around his shoulders and waits for the scene to disappear. It is hours before sleep brings its numbing peace.

"Hi Rafe," comes the cheery greeting from the doorway. Rafe nods without smiling, eyes not yet fully open. "If you feel good enough, we can go to the village and arrange to have your parents brought back."

"And my brother . . . and the pilot," Rafe answers slowly.

"Yes . . . of course you have to go with them to show them where plane crashed. That means we must first take car trip to Gangtok where I think patrol headquarters are. But I'm not sure. I call them if you want me to."

"Yes . . . I would appreciate that. But I suppose we'll have to wait for good weather before it's safe to go back up there with a helicopter."

The news from Gangtok is not good. According to the police, the nearest rescue patrol capable of conducting such a search is located in Kathmandu. Before that item of bad news has a chance to sink in, Tomo adds that it might still be doable if it were not for the fact that all helicopters in Nepal have been temporarily co-opted by the defense ministry for its fight against the Maoist guerillas. Wincing at what he sees in the American's face, he finishes quickly, "And we not know when things get back to normal. I'm sorry, Rafe."

Without uttering a word, Rafer falls back onto his pillow and closes his eyes. Even this bit of closure is to be denied him. All his carefully thought-out plans of returning the bodies to Boston for a proper burial no longer make any sense. What is he to do . . . leave his family on the mountain in unmarked graves soon to be obscured by new-fallen snow, never to be seen again by those wanting to say goodbye?

He covers his face with his hands and shakes his head. As he sits slumped on his bed, struggling to come to terms with Tomo's news, incense from the adjacent meditation hall creeps into the room. He drops his hands and breathes deeply . . . and then . . . above the noise of children playing outside comes the soft, rhythmic sound of men chanting . . . OM MANI PADME HUM, OM MANI PADME HUM . . . over and over . . . like the gentle rumbling of far-off thunder. He has no idea what the words mean but is aware of their soothing effect. Slowly, he rises and heads for the door. Tomo, sensing his friend's struggle, offers to take him to where the men are chanting. Rafer nods silently. The entrance to the temple hall is lined with prayer wheels and bookstands along the walls. In the hall itself there are frescoes of both divine and demonic figures reaching all the way to the ceiling, with saints sitting cross-legged on lotus flowers sharing space with multi-appendaged bodies joined in sexual union. Up front, on a carpeted throne overlooking the assembled throng, sits a massive golden statue of another Buddha, one that Tomo calls the Buddha Maitreya. Once inside the hall, Rafer stops, tugs Tomo's arm . . . then sinks to an open mat on the floor. Looking around, he arranges his legs like the others . . . hypnotized now by the sound of a hundred men reciting the mantra in unison. Tomo tip-toes his way out of the hall; when he returns an hour later, Rafer is still sitting.

Later that day Rafer asks Tomo if they will let him stay for a while before heading back to the U.S. so that he can learn how to meditate. Tomo promises to ask the abbot, adding that "Maybe it is no coincidence that you end up in Tibetan monastery." In the meantime Rafer writes Kidder-Homans, explaining what happened with the plane and asking if it's O.K. if he postpones taking up his new duties until September 1st.

In the morning they re-enter the now empty temple. Tomo points out the statue of the 13th Dalai Lama as well as the throne where his namesake Tomo Geshe sits when giving a talk. "Geshe?," Rafer asks, staring at the ornate throne in front of the Maitreya statue.

"It's like a Doctor's degree . . . something he earned at university . . . but he's really a Lama, an enlightened man who spent 12 years alone in a cave just meditating. When he finally came out, they say he had superhuman powers . . . like power to heal. When they heard about him, monks from all over Tibet and India came here to join him. Together they built this monastery which is called the Monastery of the White Conch."

His curiosity raised, Rafe asks to meet some of the monks; he is curious about the enlightened state he's read about in Buddhist literature. Tomo answers that few of them are awakened or even interested in becoming so. Most of them, he explains, have moved to the compound from the country where, according to tradition, their older brothers have inherited the family farm. To them the monastery is primarily a source of food and shelter although they still have to go begging in the village each day to supplement their meals.

Once outside the temple and free to talk openly, Rafe asks his friend what enlightenment means. Tomo hesitates, then answers, "I guess you could say a state of deep peace . . . with no thoughts . . . seeing into the essence of things . . . beyond self, beyond words. It really can't be described, Rafe, only felt. But if you learn Tibetan, you can read what the great lamas of the past have said about it."

"Are you enlightened?," Rafer asks.

(*Chuckling*) "No, still working on it . . . maybe in next lifetime."

In the area just outside the temple Rafe first becomes aware of Tomo's physical appearance . . . maybe 5'10", slender, not quite as tall as Rafe, smooth bronze skin, straight black hair, large brown eyes, and a mischievous smile on the verge of erupting into a laugh . . . rather handsome in all. "Any girl friends," Rafe asks, hoping he's not intruding. "Not now," comes the answer. "I used to be friends with peasant girl who lives over there (*pointing*) . . . but abbot told me I need to give her up if I serious about spiritual practice. So I did . . . (*smiling*) . . . I can introduce her if you interested." Rafe shakes his head slowly as if to say "Nothing could be farther from my mind right now."

Tomo bites his lips. "Sorry . . . I shouldn't have said that . . . (*pause*) . . . Do you think you stay here longer . . . since you can't take your parents and brother back home?"

"Maybe . . . I really don't know what to do. I have a job waiting for me in Boston . . . a real good job . . . but it doesn't mean much anymore. Nothing does. I just feel empty inside . . . no stomach for anything."

(*Softly*) "Your family very important to you?"

"I guess more important than I thought, my Mother especially. Somehow . . . and I know this sounds strange . . . all my plans for the future, getting a PhD, moving up the corporate ladder, making a lot of money, having a big family, etc. were tied up with her. When I was still a kid, she and I even talked about my entering politics."

"You mean office like mayor . . . or big stuff like President of the United States."

(*Looking off into the distance*) "The latter. I even had a dream about it last night . . . (*pause*) . . . I was running for president and had to debate my opponent on national TV."

"I saw debate like that when I was at M.I.T. You really have to be on your toes. One mistake and you lose whole election."

"Exactly. I was scared stiff. Usually in tense situations like that I look around the audience for my Mother who raises her fist when we make eye contact . . . and I get this burst of adrenalin. But in the dream I couldn't find her. I got really desperate and began calling for her. When she didn't answer, I felt all the confidence being sucked out of me. I was helpless. On stage my opponent saw what was happening and raked me over the coals with one embarrassing question after another, ultimately ruining any chance I had for getting elected."

"That was all in dream?"

(*Looking down*) "Sick, I know."

In the days to come Tomo introduces Rafer to the abbot and several of the more serious monks. An older man by the name of Kioga proves to be especially helpful. To all outward appearance he doesn't seem to have any formal duties in the monastery, spending his days instead either cleaning the temple statues or playing with the children outside. White in beard, frail in stature and bent with years of bowing, he looks all of 70 if not 80. For some reason he takes a special interest in Rafer, bringing him butter tea in the morning and teaching him the chants used in the temple. By reciting the chants over and over in Tibetan Rafer gets to know the major ones by heart . . . and then asks Tomo to translate them into English. This soon becomes a central part of their daily discourse as their walks take them further and further from the monastery.

"It is so peaceful here," Rafer says one day as they wander out along a dirt road through the trees. "Kioga has me meditating every morning . . . all morning . . . and it's really changing my outlook on things."

"Like what happened up in caldera?"

"Yes. But more than that. I get the feeling that my goals are changing. Boston, the stock market, my job at Kidder-Homans, riches, fame, glory . . . they all seem more remote now, no longer my raison d'être. I might still go back there . . . but with a different attitude. What I've learned here at the monastery . . . well, it goes deeper. I know I still have to make a living and will probably get married someday . . . but I'm beginning to see that there are things a lot more important than worldly success."

(*With a sly smile*) "You mean sex, yes?"

(*Chuckling*) "Not exactly. You know what I'm talking about . . . you're seeking it yourself. It's what some of your texts refer to as 'seeing with the third eye' . . . seeing into the heart of things . . . beneath the surface . . . beyond form, color, or shape. And beyond feeling like a separate self in a world filled with craving, attachment and the fear of death . . . *(pause)* . . . I still don't know what I'm talking about, but something is sinking in and it's turning my life around."

"You're doing just fine. Stick around here long enough and you become lama."

"You sure you don't mean *llama*? My hair is already getting a bit long."

"I not notice tail yet."

"Why do you think I stay behind you?"

"Hmm."

The Sikkim countryside consists of sharply rolling hills, much steeper, Tomo explains, than the plains of the Tibetan plateau to the North. "This is the land where I grow up," he says wistfully, "but is not my true home which is several hundred miles from here. I hope I can go back there before I am too old to climb over pass to Shigatse."

"How high is the pass?"

"In feet . . . about 18,000. Many already die trying to escape Tibet into Sikkim . . . the weather changes just like that. My grandparents were in 40 years when they made it. They were very hardy."

Rafer nods. "Our plane crashed somewhere around 15,000 feet I think. I know how cold it gets there when the sun goes down. It's hard to imagine either old people or young children making that trek on foot."

In the weeks to come, Rafer finds himself growing closer to his new friend . . . leaning on him not only for information and advice but for reassurance that he is not alone in the world. On their walks into the countryside they discuss all sorts of things: religion, meditation, politics, sex, marriage . . . but mainly the cultural differences between East and West. Drawing on his two years at M.I.T., Tomo is quick to praise the United States for the freedom people have to express their opinions. "You can say anything you want," he exclaims, "and they don't put you in jail. You can make fun of president on a blog or say nasty things about religion. Is wonderful."

Rafer nods again. "The trouble is that if you live there, you tend to take those things for granted . . . and that can be dangerous."

(*Chuckling*) "Maybe American children should spend time in China where only freedom you have is to keep mouth shut."

(*Laughing*) "I'll keep that in mind if I ever have kids of my own."

Tomo smiles. "I also like flush toilets . . . not so smelly . . . and furnaces in basement that keep apartment warm in winter. It is not like that here in Sikkim. You notice . . . yes? And so many stores . . . in Cambridge you buy anything you want at big mall. For food . . . what you call supermarket . . . I never see so many things to eat in my whole life."

"So, what didn't you like about America?," Rafer asks, enjoying these reminders of life back home.

Several minutes pass in silence as they overtake a farmer leading a yak-drawn wagon filled with barley. "All the advertising," Tomo replies once they are alone again. "Everywhere you go . . . buy this, buy that. Everyone tries to sell you something. You see it on billboards, in newspapers, on TV . . . even in subway trains. Every day my mailbox filled with ads . . . people I never meet trying to make me buy something I do not want. Everybody wants to sell you something. You can't get away from it in America."

"True . . . but consider this," Rafer is quick to reply. "If it weren't for all those ads, the economy wouldn't work as well as it does. It's the buying and selling that keep our standard of living so high. Take away the consumer spending and we could easily slip back into a more archaic kind of economy . . . and that could mean a return to farmers' markets, freezing apartments and outdoor toilets. I don't think Americans would like that."

"Yes. I'm sure you are right Rafe. But it is all so . . . what should I say . . . is commercial right word? O.K., America is a country where buying and selling are more important than anything else. Everybody is trying so hard to get ahead, to make a buck . . . everybody want to be rich. Most important to you is having more things . . . more material things. It is not same here in Sikkim or Tibet. We might be poor compared to you but we have more important values."

"Like what?"

"Spiritual values for one thing. We don't make such a big thing about this life; is just a resting place on our way to higher state of being. When you see it as stepping stone to higher state, you don't make such big fuss about it. The wise person uses this life not to get rich but to improve self so he can reach Nirvana in next life."

"That could be, Tomo . . . but if you adopt that outlook, aren't you condemned to pay a stiff price in poverty, disease, illiteracy, limited lifespan . . . all the things people way back in the Middle Ages suffered from. Everybody was religious back then, like they are now in Tibet . . . but what American in his right mind would want to go back and live like that again?"

"Well, O.K . . . maybe our spiritual life not suitable for Americans . . . but making money is not only value, yes? What about education? I saw an article that said by time they leave high school, average American kid watches 10,000 hours of TV ads. Is crazy, yes? What if they spent that time reading books . . . or using TV to learn something important? Commercial society is bad for learning . . . it rots children's brains."

"(*Laughing*) "And brains of adults as well. We all watch too many ads. I thought we might see a change in viewing habits with the coming of digital video recorders . . . you know, the machines that allow you to record TV programs and play them back at your convenience. I figured that would be the end of TV advertising since DVR's allow you to skip over the ads when you play the programs back. But no, a study I read about said that the vast majority of Americans who own DVRs still watch all the ads even though they could easily fast-forward through them. At first I thought the results might be restricted to poorly educated viewers . . . but, to my surprise, they turned out to be equally valid for college-educated people. So, what can I say? We're hooked on advertising. We're so accustomed to watching it that even when we don't have to, we stop to watch. You're absolutely right; we have built ourselves a society based on the buying and selling of material goods. There are some good things about that . . . like a high standard of living . . . and some bad things . . . like the relative lack of interest in education, art and ideas."

"You think Americans are aware of different kinds of values?"

"Not really. I think we are so thoroughly committed to material values that very few of us pause long enough to consider that there might be alternatives. And that's unlikely change . . . at least for a while."

"I think you right Rafe. When I was in Cambridge, I like to go to baseball games . . . but I see ads everywhere . . . all around the stadium, even some on top of fence like Coke bottles at Fenway Park. Every time you look at scoreboard you see add for soda, beer or cars or insurance or something. When I watch baseball on TV, is even worse . . . ads before game, ads for line-ups, ads between innings, ads when new pitchers come in, ads for player of game, ads for scores of other games; I don't see how Americans can stand it. It spoiled game for me."

"So you like baseball. Interesting. How about football or basketball?"

"I went to see Patriots once. My friend explained the rules to me . . . and that made it more interesting. What seemed strange was how the players acted when they made good play. They pulled away from others so crowd could see them . . . then they made big fist or pounded their chest or did some kind of bragging. "See what I just did; aren't I a great player?" In Tibet they would be booed for showing so much ego. We prefer men to be humble, maybe to thank other players for helping them to make good play."

"True enough. We Americans seem to be ambivalent about ego. Like you Tibetans, we also praise people when they're humble. At the same time we tolerate bragging . . . even applaud it when somebody does something we like. Our sports heroes are expected to toot their horn after a success; if they don't, they might even be accused of lacking self-confidence."

"I laugh when I saw one player pointing to the sky when he made touchdown . . . like he was thanking God for helping him do it. What a strange kind of religion that is, Rafe. Does he think that God wants his team to beat other team? What kind of religion tells him God play favorites in sports? Or maybe he thinks there two gods, one rooting for each team . . . and when he points up to sky, he's thanking his god for beating other one."

(*Chuckling*) "I'm not sure about the two gods thing but believing that there's one God and that He wants your side to beat the other side is hardly new. Remember how in WWII the Germans rallied their troops with the slogan 'Gott Mit Uns.' Were the soldiers naïve enough to believe that God wanted Germany to win the war? Maybe. Of course, the English, French, Russians and Americans were probably convinced that God was rooting for them instead . . . (*pause*) . . . It all sounds pretty silly to me."

In the succeeding weeks, the two men spend many pleasant hours discussing cultural differences. Each conversation brings them closer as they experiment with seeing the world through the other's eyes. And thus it comes as a shock when Tomo announces one morning that he can't join Rafer on a walk because he has to see a specialist in Gangtok about a problem with his abdomen. "They want me to have tests," he explains, "to see what is causing pain. Nobody here know what goes on."

"You never told me about any pain," Rafer responds anxiously. "How bad is it?"

"In past not bad enough to say . . . but is worse lately. I hope is bug I kill with medicine."

To the shock of the entire monastery, the report from the Gangtok doctors states that he has cancer of the pancreas . . . and that the tumor is already too big to operate. The report concludes with the less-than-reassuring observation that it is the youngest case of pancreatic cancer ever seen in Sikkim. When the abbot is told in private that his favorite novice has two years at the most to live, he goes into seclusion, meditating night and day, refusing all food.

To Rafer, still struggling with the shock of losing his whole family, the news is devastating. He turns to his unofficial mentor, Kioga, for help. Driven by this added grief, his meditation goes deeper. When Tomo becomes confined to his bed, Rafer spends whole mornings at his side . . . they talk for a bit . . . then when Tomo falls asleep Rafer continues his meditation. Morning after morning they follow this routine. Gradually Rafer shifts from the mantra given him by the abbot to focusing on the cancer itself. He begins breathing into it . . . over and over. With each exhalation he aims his energy at the offending tumor . . . concentrating the way he would if he were using a magnifying glass to ignite a piece of paper. No one tells him to do this. He isn't following any theory or anything he has read. It's just instinct.

As his meditation deepens, Rafer notices a change in the way his mind is working. It is becoming easier and easier to block out the rest of the world . . . even thoughts surrounding his family. When he is alone now, he feels a deeper peace . . . a little breathing room from anxiety and fear. Kioga is aware of the change . . . nods his approval . . . and goes on bringing tea each morning. Some of the monks, the older ones in particular, can be seen whispering as he passes through the temple. Although he is not directly aware of it, the whole community has begun following his every move. Feeling renewed strength, Rafer extends the bedside regimen to afternoons . . . and then evenings as well. There are signs that the patient might be getting better. The abbot says nothing but bows silently whenever Rafer passes his door.

All of this is prelude to the night that changes his life forever. As he lies in his bed after a full day at Tomo's side, he sees an image of the Maine coast . . . rocks and water . . . an occasional bush along the shore. The image then shifts out to sea where he can see the waves very clearly. As he stares at the waves, he suddenly becomes aware of an unnamable presence behind the waves . . . or perhaps within the waves. And then it happens. The waves disappear, leaving an absolutely clear, empty, unbounded NOTHINGNESS. What remains is fathomless, infinite. It has no color, no lines, no border; nothing that can be used to describe it. It is truly empty . . . yet vividly so. He gasps, "Oh God." Before he can recover, the scene shifts from the sea to the sky. Now the same thing happens all over again. The clouds give way to a "presence" deep within. The same empty, unbounded space that he has seen embedded in the waves reveals itself again. It is as if this "Space" has been hidden behind the clouds all along. He is ecstatic, turned inside out . . . truly beside himself. His gasping and crying out comes not out of fear . . . but rather from feeling overwhelmed, carried away by a vision of THAT which lies hidden in the waves, in the clouds, and presumably everything that exists.

Days pass before he can even begin to make sense of what happened. Tomo insists that he has had an enlightenment experience in which the Buddha nature that resides in all things revealed itself in the waves and clouds. "I am envious, Rafe. I hope for an experience like that every since I return to Sikkim. So far, no luck. And I not alone. Many monks here who meditate for years still not see what you saw last week."

Rafer smiles at the compliment. "I'm still not sure what it all means . . . but I guess I should feel lucky."

"Blessed, Rafe, not lucky."

Despite signs of Tomo's improvement, Rafer continues meditating at his side day and night. On a morning mid-way through the second week of his vigil, Rafer is told that his friend must return to Gangtok for further testing. When Rafer asks is he really up to such a trip, Tomo smiles, gives a thumbs up, then slips into his street clothes. On his return that afternoon he reports that nothing short of a miracle has taken place . . . the doctors say the tumor is completely gone. The temple, known by all who meditate there for its undisturbed quiet, explodes with joyous celebration. Drums are banged, trumpets blare . . . as both hall and corridors fill with dancing monks. And all of this without alcohol.

When the noise has finally subsided, the abbot takes Rafer aside for a private talk. Tomo is asked to translate. "Do you know what siddhis are, Rafer?," the old man asks, leaning forward.

"He doesn't mean C-I-T-I-E-S," Tomo adds with a smirk.

"No, I don't," responds Rafer, disregarding Tomo's remark, "other than that they have something to do with magic."

"That's a common misconception," the abbot replies with a shake of his bald head. "It's got nothing to do with magic in the conventional sense. Siddhis, whether they involve levitation, healing, visualization or converting the physical body into spirit, are gifts. They typically come to chelas whose meditation has gone deep enough to access a kind of energy unknown to the ordinary person. It is that reservoir of pure energy that makes so-called miracles possible. So it is a bit of a mystery why you, who just began meditating weeks ago, should be given this ability. It has never happened this way before . . . (*pause*) . . . Mystery or not, we are extremely grateful."

"But maybe I had nothing to do with Tomo's recovery," Rafer protests through his translator. "He might have gotten better anyway . . . you know, through spontaneous remission. Things like that happen all the time. And when you consider that he was awfully young to have that kind of cancer in the first place, well . . . ."

(*Interrupting*) "I understand," the abbot says, leaning back in his chair, "it probably looks that way to you because of your training in the West. Here we see it differently. Such miraculous things do not happen by chance. To us it is clear evidence that you have been singled out for a special mission in life. You have the gift of healing . . . and there might be other equally extraordinary things to come your way in the future. (*Chuckling*) The extra toe on your right foot certainly points in that direction."

"I don't know what to say," Rafer responds. "Even if you're right, which is still hard for me to believe, why me? Of all the people in the world who aspire to such a role, why would the gift be given to someone who has never shown any interest in healing or any of the other siddhis you mentioned? I've never even heard of things like visualization and turning the body into spirit."

The abbot continues, "The Buddha spirit does not always work in predictable ways. The years of meditating, reading, and working with a guru that most of us have undergone may not have been necessary in your case. What happened, I would surmise, is that the death of your family caused you such despair that your normal sense of self broke down, allowing you to see what lies beneath the samsaric surface of things. That death, tragic as it was, brought you to a place that most aspirants never reach even after years of intensive meditation. In that sense, and in that sense alone of course, it was a good thing. You must continue on this path now, going even deeper into the mystery of life and helping others find what you have found."

Despite the abbot's kind words, Rafer remains unconvinced that he had anything to do with Tomo's recovery. If indeed the two are connected, he reasons, how does the connection work? How can one person's state of mind, however intense, produce a change in someone else's body? The abbot's theory of some kind of spiritual intervention, while appealing, seems too simple, too easy. In hopes of clearing up his confusion, he decides to write to Professor Pulaski back at Harvard, the psychologist whose course in Behavioral Economics he took several years ago. The professor, he recalls, is a hard-headed realist who, in both his course and in the books he has written, takes perverse pleasure in debunking the idea that consumers and investors are consistently rational in the economic decisions they make. "We are all more irrational than we care to admit," he says in the introduction to his latest book of experiments which he hopes will prove his case. Recalling that book now, Rafer becomes eager to learn what kind of sense the professor can make out of Tomo's mysterious recovery.

In his letter, he lays out all the facts of the case ... the original diagnosis, the gloomy prognosis, the miraculous recovery. To this he adds details of the plane crash, the death of his brother and parents, the days of grief to follow, his introduction to meditation, the days spent at Tomo's side, his brief "enlightenment" experience ... everything he can think of that might help the professor explain what happened.

A letter arrives three weeks later. It is not the hard-edged response Rafer expected. "I'm not ruling out the possibility that your meditation played a part in curing your friend," Prof. Pulaski writes. "It's important to remain open to all possibilities here, regardless of how strange they might sound to Western ears. This is especially true in light of the reading I've done lately on pancreatic cancer. The research findings indicate that spontaneous remission for this kind of tumor is very rare. That leaves the door open to alternative explanations for your friend's recovery." With that in mind, he goes on to suggest that Rafer's "enlightenment" experience might have activated a rare kind of energy that was then directed outward . . . either at the cancer directly or more generally at the friend's immune system. "In either case," he writes, "we simply have to assume that there exists a form of energy, rare and presently unmeasurable, that has the potential to cure disease when transmitted from one person to another . . . a rather big assumption, I know, in the absence of any empirical evidence but one that strikes me as eminently reasonable given that other variables (like the gene) were hypothesized long before they were actually discovered." He continues with the suggestion that any further speculation would be a waste of time until Rafer demonstrates an ability to cure other seriously ill patients as well. "Repetition is at the heart of the scientific method," he writes. "If you want, I can set up a controlled experiment here in the Boston area in which we take a random sample of terminal patients and have you meditate with half of them while the others gets nothing but their regular treatment. It would all have to be scientifically done and under the auspices of our local hospitals. Let me know if you're interested and, if so, when you plan to return."

Rafer is in no hurry to respond, partly because he is already putting roots down at the monastery and is loathe to leave so soon, partly because he is unsure of his ability to regain that experience of "borderless, empty space" that he found while meditating on Tomo. After all, he argues, Tomo is a good friend, someone whose recovery means a lot to me; these patients in Boston would be strangers about whom I know nothing other than that they are dying. So he writes Prof. Pulaski a non-committal letter in which he thanks him for his ideas and promises to give him an answer "when things have settled down a bit."

4

Uma

With Tomo now fully recovered and eager to spend time with the man he playfully calls his "savior," the two pass most of their days together, either meditating or exploring the countryside beyond the monastery walls. On a warm July day their walk takes them out along a dirt road past several farms where peasants can be seen cutting hay and pitching it into yak-drawn wagons. Their conversation is interrupted by a shrill call from a girl in one of the wagons. "It's Uma," Tomo whispers while waving. "She's the girl I tell you about, the one the abbot told me to stop seeing if I want to make spiritual progress." The two men stop to wait as Uma comes running from the field. When she reaches the fence, she calls them over. Turning to Tomo, Rafer rolls his eyes, exclaiming, "Wow, she's really pretty. I can see how it was hard to let her go."

Translating as he goes, Tomo reaches through the barbed wire to grasp her hand, then introduces his friend. At first Uma has eyes only for Tomo but finally turns to Rafer when she fails to find any sign of lingering desire in her former lover's eyes. Through his translator, Rafer asks about the yaks ("Are those horns dangerous?"), and her family ("Is your family originally from Tibet?"). Her smile is captivating . . . perhaps because it is so natural, uncorrupted as it is by any self-consciousness or desire to please. Rafer finds himself studying her eyes and lips, and the unblemished bronze skin of her face and neck. Her hair, jet black and wavier than Tomo's, falls almost to her shoulders where it rests attractively without any attention on her part. It is Tomo who moves away at last, taking Rafer by the arm as both men turn to answer her silent wave.

A few yards on, Tomo turns and says, "You like her, I see it."

"I don't know, Tomo. I'm not exactly in the mood for a girlfriend. Besides, my Tibetan is a bit primitive at this point."

"Who needs words when two people attracted to each other?"

Rafer reaches out for Tomo's shoulder. "I see . . . a man of the world. And just how much romantic experience have you actually had, sir?"

"I am involved when I study at M.I.T . . . but it not last. Her father was Chinese and turned her against me when he learned how I felt about independent Tibet."

"And that was it . . . in all these years? How old are you?"

"Twenty-five."

"Hmm. Not exactly a Casanova in the making."

(*Sheepishly*) "Well, I have some little flings along the way."

Rafer laughs. "Don't worry; my lips are sealed."

"You have more?"

"In high school, one fling. She actually wanted to get married after graduation. When I told her I wasn't in love with her, she said her parents weren't in love at first either, but they developed such feelings after the wedding. I wasn't buying it . . . I liked my freedom too much. In college I fell in love with this girl I met in a poetry class I was auditing . . . but she dropped out of school when it was determined that she was mentally ill."

"You never saw it . . . the illness?"

"She seemed pretty flaky, yes . . . pretended that the piles of snow outside the dorms were mountains we had to climb over, etc. but I chalked that up to her poetic nature. She had a pale, almost wan, lipstick-free face that I found captivating . . . more winsome than sexy but beautiful in its own way. Once she left school we never saw each other again."

"Do you try to see Uma again?"

"I might . . . if that's O.K. with you?"

"Absolutely. (*Chuckling*) Just don't blame me if your practice suffers . . . (*pause*) . . . She is not shy about getting physical. For me, thinking about a pretty woman fills mind with fantasy, making meditation hard . . . (*pause*) . . . but maybe you different."

"Hmm. We'll see."

In the weeks to come, Rafer makes almost daily trips to the meadow to see Uma. Typically, the moment she sees him coming, she goes to the wooden gate by the barn and places her hands on the railing. He does the same. After exchanging smiles, but with hands not yet touching, he pulls out his dictionary. As she watches, he scrawls "You are beautiful" in Hindi on a pad of paper. She leans over to read what he has written, then, instead of responding in words, simply points at him and nods several times as if to say, "You too." Neither says anything as they move closer, all four hands back on the railing. His eyes move from her lips to her hair, then down to her eyes, nose and back to her mouth. As he studies her face, she continues to smile, not at all concerned about what he might think.

As the tension builds, he slides his hand along the top of the gate until it touches one of hers. She doesn't move, but begins breathing more quickly. The change, however slight, adds to his excitement.

Silently he considers reaching over the gate and kissing her on the mouth. Her lingering smile suggests she might be receptive. Before he can act, however, they are interrupted by a loud, 'UMA!' It is the father calling from the barn. She quickly covers his hand with her own . . . then runs to the door where the yell came from.

Back at the monastery Rafer can think of nothing else. His daily meditation is flooded now with images of Uma's moist lips and fantasies of what almost happened at the gate. Each time he voices OM PADME MANI HUM the mantra is pushed aside by images of her face and the desire he saw written there. She clearly likes him, he concludes . . . perhaps is ready to fall in love with him. He stops trying to meditate and takes out his dictionary, hoping to memorize short Hindi phrases that he can use when they meet again.

Two days later he is walking down the dirt road when he sees her in the distance waving. As before, she's wearing a black full-length skirt bordered with white fur and an orange turtle neck top underneath a beige jacket also bordered with fur. She takes off her matching orange cap when she waves. At the gate they quickly touch hands. Nervous now, he pulls out his pad of paper and writes in Hindi, "I think of you." She takes the pad from his hand and scribbles, "I have you in my heart." His hand is shaking as he clutches her message. He leans forward now . . . not certain what to do next . . . his breathing heavy with desire. She smiles . . . then leans forward and brushes her lips against his. Without thinking he takes her by the shoulders and pulls her against the gate, pressing his lips hard against hers. She wiggles free and whispers in Hindi, "Come Friday, father in village." Slowly Rafer translates each word, stopping several times to ask her to repeat the message until he is sure what she is saying. "Next Friday," he writes on his pad, handing it over the gate . . . still not secure enough in his pronunciation to use his voice. She smiles her delicious smile and turns toward the barn. "Uma," he calls from the gate, blowing her a kiss when she looks back. She laughs, nodding her assent.

Friday is two days away . . . two torturous days for Rafer who can't think of anything but seeing her again. His whole body tingles with an electricity starting in his groin and radiating out to his arms and legs. He can't sleep; he can't meditate. When he tries sitting, Uma becomes his new mantra, her name reverberating throughout his psyche like a disembodied voice from outer space, beckoning him to come, promising him the world if he will but take her in his arms again.

He has never felt this way before, with neither Priscilla the girl he met in a college poetry class nor with Janice the statuesque blonde whose picture he compulsively masturbated over in high school. In his quieter moments, he is dimly aware that the loss of his family, his mother in particular, might have something to do with his sudden attachment to Uma. After all, he reasons, Uma is strong and motherly, receptive to his interest and seemingly eager to comfort him with her body. He pictures himself now in bed with her, snuggling against her ample breasts, the two of them locked in mutual embrace, her warm skin enveloping his own, her warm breath on his face. "But is it just comfort that I seek?," he asks with a shake of his head. "Don't I want to lose myself in her? Don't I want to forget who I am . . . even to forget who she is? Isn't it my deepest desire to enter a space where neither of us exists as a separate individual . . . where the only thing that exists is love itself. But is that even possible?" The question lingers on his lips as he goes about his daily rituals of eating, meditating, reading, walking. Perhaps he does yet realize that in his yearning to surrender his apartness and identity to the ecstasy of love, he could end up losing track of who *he* is, what *he* wants, what *his* values are. But that awakening, if and when it comes, will have to wait.

Friday arrives. As Rafer approaches the farm, Uma rushes to the gate and opens it, taking his hand as she leads him to the barn. No words are spoken. She looks up at him, smiling, as they enter the barn . . . the taut but radiant expression on her face giving evidence of her own torment in waiting for this day. Just beyond the barn door is a rack with saddles and reins hanging from hooks, She grabs a blanket . . .

then returns for a second . . . before climbing to the hayloft on a home-made ladder. He is right behind, his nose practically touching the hem of the long dress she is wearing. By the time she lays a blanket down on the hay his heart is pounding so hard that he is afraid he will forget all the poetic phrases he has so diligently rehearsed back in the monastery. Still fully dressed, she lies down on the one blanket, keeping the other next to her, her arms outstretched in unconcealed desire. Slowly he lowers himself to her waiting body and presses his cheeks to hers. She turns her face, offering her lips. When he fails to respond immediately, she begins licking his skin, then reaches over and moves his head until their lips meet. He sighs, then pries her mouth open with his tongue, her teeth parting slightly to allow him in. Within seconds, he feels her tongue touching his. The intimacy of the contact sends tremors of disbelief rippling through his frame. Can it be true that he is inside her mouth, that he can touch her tongue with his own, that he can actually play with it, taste it, and then draw it into his mouth where it becomes part of his very being?

With their bodies thus joined, they close their eyes and allow themselves to be overwhelmed by the sensations of the moment. Nothing exists beyond the smells and tastes of the other. For him, all the speculations of the past week, all the plans so carefully rehearsed, are now funneled into the pure sensation of lips on lips, tongues on tongues . . . a place where all thinking is sacrificed to that ecstasy which presents itself only when all else is forgotten.

Uma reaches down now to pull up her dress. Without looking, Rafer senses her move and rolls to the side to give her space. When the hem passes her knees and comes to rest on her muscular thighs, he grasps it and pushes it further until the soft, black bush surrounding her flower comes into view. He bends to kiss her there as she opens her legs in welcome. Rolling to his side again, he pushes his pants to his ankles then kicks them off onto the hay. At this point she reaches down and takes his hardened member in her warm hand and guides it to her sex. As he brushes his tip against her labia, moistening his shaft, she girds herself for the invasion of her flesh that is coming. After all, this is what she has dreamt of . . . to be taken, to be penetrated, yes assaulted . . . by the man she loves. She raises her hips slightly in anticipation of his thrust.

It is not to be. He enters cautiously, even timidly, as if he were not sure of his welcome. But no, it is more than that. He enters like one who is searching, probing, like a spermatozoon that has lost its way en route to a concealed egg. There is no breathless flurry of thrusting and pounding, no animal cries of victory as he plunges his manhood into her pink cavity. Yes, she can now feel his semen deep inside her but it comes not with the force of a volcano erupting but with the gentleness of a sloop entering harbor on a windless afternoon. Instead of bursting from his penis with a determination to possess, eager to fertilize another generation, it falls from his tip like the tears of a prodigal son who for years has longed for the comforts of home and is crying now at his joyful return.

She is aware of his recent loss and holds him tight against her chest. Slipping the straps of her dress down over her shoulders, she bares her breasts and offers him her nipples. It is in her nature to do so but it comes more from instinct than desire . . . after all, she wants to be loved not as a mother but as a woman. In the depths of her psyche, in that still quiet space remote from the demands of passion, she is aware that nurturing the grieving son cannot tame the hunger that lies buried in her loins. Holding him to her breast, she sighs deeply, slipping once again, willingly but without joy, into that state of protracted frustration expected of her gender. When he has drunk his fill of her kindness, he rises, puts on his pants and kisses her on the forehead. They kiss again at the gate; she forces a smile and runs her hands through his hair. With a final wave he heads down the road and back toward the monastery.

His gait is slow as he mulls over events in the barn. Somehow, although no words were ever spoken, he is aware of her disappointment, aware that he has let her down as a lover. Instead of joy or even relief, he finds himself wrestling with shame. Why did he cry when he came inside her? The truth is unsettling. These were not the tears of a grown man relieved of a great longing and delirious with pleasure but those of a baby who had been left out in the cold and was now back in the arms of its mother. No wonder she was disappointed; no wonder she never climaxed. The moment he pulled out of her, he could see it in her face . . . still smiling but with her mouth drawn tight and a look of disbelief in her eyes.

Half way back to the monastery he stops to consider what just happened. "Am I really that needy?," he asks. "Am I not man enough to bring a woman to orgasm?" He shuffles his boots in the dirt, leaving the questions unanswered. Instead a different memory arises and with it a new inquiry. "What happened to the power I felt when meditating at Tomo's bedside? My energy was so strong and my vision so clear I could have turned the world upside down . . . not that I wanted to . . . but it seemed like the potential was there. I felt potent, yes . . . but not in the usual sense of being able to overcome obstacles or impose my will on others. Nor did it come from an inner voice reminding me that I could achieve anything in the world once I set my mind to it. No, the power I felt at Tomo's bedside came from somewhere else, somewhere outside of me, from a source beyond personal will or intention . . . as if it were happening by itself . . . (pause) . . . Now they say I cured Tomo's cancer with my mind alone . . . (pause) . . . I'm still not sure of that . . . but whatever power I felt back then deserted me today with Uma. It's gone and it's not clear whether I can get it back again." With that thought nagging at his heels, he steps up his pace until he reaches the monastery, unprepared for the shock to come.

Before he has a chance to enter his room, Tomo comes running up and grabs him by the arm. "Kioga hurted himself playing with the children," he gasps, not pausing to get his verbs straight. "I think he fell and hit his head on concrete steps outside temple. I don't know for sure . . . but he is out of consciousness for last hour. They get ready to drive him to hospital in Gangtok."

Rafer (*eyes flaring*): "Jesus . . . poor guy. Are they really going to transport him in that open truck . . . over bumpy dirt roads all the way to Gangtok?"

"Yes . . . I think they want you go with him. The abbot told me he wants see you right away."

Rafer (*bewildered*): "What can I do . . . why is he asking for me?"

"He not forget what you did for me, Rafer. They think you can do something like that for Kioga. I go along as your translator."

Still troubled by his behavior in the barn, Rafer hesitates but finally agrees to help and spends the next two days by Kioga's side in the Gangtok hospital, trying desperately to regain the clarity of mind and power of concentration he had when meditating over Tomo. The task proves too difficult. His mind remains clouded with shame and self-doubt. Images of Uma, her disillusionment now carved indelibly into the face before him, compete with his mantra, undermining his ability to concentrate. On the third day Kioga develops pneumonia and the prognosis turns bleak. Despite a frantic effort on Rafer's part who stays with him morning, noon, and night, Kioga dies two days later, just after holding his hands out in gratitude to the man at his side.

When he returns to the monastery Rafer feels the eyes of the monastery on him, silently blaming him for Kioga's death. The following day he is called in by abbot who wants to know what happened. "You had strong feelings for him, didn't you?," he says, referring to the special friendship between the old man and his young novice. Rafer nods, then raises his eyebrows and turns both hands palm up in lieu of an answer. In the privacy of his thoughts, of course, he is quite aware of the answer but chooses not to talk about it. At that point, no one aside from Tomo is aware of his relationship with Uma and the role his feelings for her have played in the failure to save Kioga. It is his choice to keep it that way, at least until he can be with her and reassure himself that she still cares.

Much as he wants to, he can't go to her now, not with these guilty feelings weighing so heavily on his mind. But Uma has her own agenda. When a week goes by without signs of her lover, Uma comes into the monastery looking for him. Finding him asleep in bed, she sits down next to him and begins stroking his leg. Rafer wakes immediately. The slight twist to his mouth is sufficient to convey the message that he is not ready to be with her. She pulls her hand away, wincing at his coldness, her brows knitted, her eyes imploring. Sitting up, he grabs the dictionary from the night table, hoping to explain what happened with Kioga, thereby justifying why he hasn't gone to see her. The subject is too complex for his limited knowledge of Hindi. In frustration he throws the dictionary to the floor and pulls the covers to his chest. Neither one speaks. When Uma leans forward to look into his face, he turns away, eyes narrowed, aimed at the door. She waits until the silence is more than she can bear, then leaves.

The next few days are torture as he wrestles internally with a toxic mix of emotions . . . desire to see Uma and prove his manhood, shame over his previous performance, and guilt at failing to save his mentor and friend Kioga. Outwardly he is undisturbed, even as he is shunned by the very monks who, following Tomo's miraculous recovery, showered him with affection. Inwardly he feels trapped in a state of limbo, unsure of what to do next while fearing that he has outstayed his welcome. It is in that state that he receives a letter from Kidder-Homans, the brokerage firm in Boston, asking if he plans to return any time soon. The letter goes on to explain that the research position they previously offered needs to be filled. If he is no longer interested, the letter concludes, they will have to give the job to someone else. A week later Rafer decides to leave and informs Kidder-Homans that he is on his way. All that remains is to say goodbye to Uma.

He is not far up the road to her farm when he sees her on top one of the hay wagons. He whistles once, then again. She turns to look and waves, the smile on her handsome face evident even from the road. Rafer walks swiftly to the gate and waits for her to join him.

Moments later he hears a sound coming from inside the barn. It is a man's voice . . . loud and dominating, then the sound of a slap followed by a woman's cry. Before Rafer can run to her side, the irate father, clearly fearful of his daughter's debauching, appears at the barn door with pitchfork in hand. Rafer grips the gate tightly as the man strides quickly toward him, weapon at the ready. Just before reaching the gate, the father, with eyes blazing, raises his arm and points to the road. "Go," he yells in Hindi. For Rafer, just a few feet now from the pitchfork's glistening prongs, no dictionary is needed. He turns and heads back up the road. When he has gone a few yards, he stops to look back. The father is still there, watching, pitchfork at his side. Behind him, at the open door upstairs in the barn, Uma waves, then throws him a kiss. He smiles awkwardly, raises his hand in half-hearted farewell . . . then turns and heads back to the monastery.

At the tiny airport in Gangtok he and Tomo say their final goodbyes, interspersed with mutual promises to write and visit sometime in the future. Just as he is about to enter the plane, Rafer turns to his friend and says, "You were right when you said that sex and meditation don't mix. I didn't see it at the time . . . or maybe I did but I couldn't do anything about it. I'm just glad that it happened after you recovered and not before."

"Did you get a chance to say goodbye to Uma?," Tomo asks.

"Not the way I would like to . . . but I'll write to her when I get back to Boston. Can I send the letter to you and have you translate it for her?"

"Sure . . . but I curious about what happened with her."

(Smiling) "The father drove me off with a pitchfork. I wanted to . . . ."

(Interrupting) "Maybe I should have warned you. In Tibet fathers very protective of daughters."

(*Nodding*) "Well, it probably wouldn't have worked anyway. We're too different . . . in culture, background, goals and education, not to mention speech. Besides it's pretty clear that I have some emotional growing up to do."

(*Waving*) "Goodbye Rafer. I be thinking of you."

"Goodbye Tomo . . . I'll miss you old friend."

On the 20th of August he arrives in Boston, eager to find an apartment and take up his new job.

5

Kidder-Homans

B ack in the United States once more, Rafer Alexander begins looking
for a place to live. Compared to other cities, Boston is an obvious
choice since Kidder-Homans is located there although Cambridge
is also attractive, partly for its familiarity, partly for all the young
people who live there. A quick trip to Back Bay tips the scales in
favor of Boston. The first apartment he looks at is on Commonwealth
Ave, halfway between Fairfield and Gloucester and just a short walk
down the tree-lined path that bisects East and West traffic lanes to
the Gardens. From the swan boats, it's just a short hike across the
Commons to Tremont Street and down to Devonshire Street where
the brokerage office is located. He decides to take the apartment.
Since he's not expected at work until September 1st, he has more than
a week to tackle other duties.

Before spending a night in his new apartment, he rents a car and drives
to Babylon, New York to sort out his parent's belongings. As executor
he is required to make an inventory of all assets, including furniture,
clothing, appliances, automobiles, and bank accounts . . . and either
sell or give away whatever he doesn't need. The will, which he has
seen only once before, makes him and Jason equal beneficiaries . . .
with the proviso that in the event of either's death, both shares go to
the survivor. Rafer estimates the total sum, including bank deposits,
investments, and proceeds from the sale of the house, to be somewhere
between $300,000 and $350,000. Against the advice of a local mortician
he puts off plans for a funeral service until the bodies of his brother

and parents can be returned from Sikkim. Before submitting his inventory to the county probate court, he asks the coroner to write to Kathmandu to confirm that the plane is still missing and that all passengers are assumed dead. Five days later he heads to Connecticut to make a similar list of Jason's belongings. Before returning to Boston he rents a trailer and fills it with his brother's bed, desk, chairs and other pieces of furniture he can use in his own apartment.

Back in Boston he sits down to write to Tomo and find out the latest news regarding the Rescue Patrol. In his letter he admits not writing to Uma yet, a minor delinquency, he argues, that should be corrected once he clears up his confusion about their relationship. He then sends off a brief note to Prof. Pulaski informing him that he is back in town and suggesting lunch sometime in near future.

Once all the letters have been written and his duties as executor fulfilled, he pours himself a glass of wine, slumps into a chair, and lets his thoughts go where they will. They immediately turn inward where he immediately comes face to face with a question. Something important has changed in the way he sees himself and his relationship to the rest of the world . . . but what is it? Is it the freedom of movement that comes with living alone, the kind of freedom he knew before as a grad student in Cambridge? No, this is not the same. The freedom to do what he wants when he wants to do it is still there . . . but the context of that freedom has been altered. The force that up to now has given special meaning to his life, supporting and reinforcing its trajectory from the outside, is no longer there. There can be no question what that force is. What he feels now is freedom without a broader purpose, the kind of purpose he used to feel when he knew his parents were watching. Even now thoughts of calling home to tell them of his new apartment arise but quickly fade, leaving in their place a state of pointlessness . . . like sailing out of harbor without a rudder, without a destination. Before, everything happened in the context of a loving relationship with his family; that context gave his successes meaning and importance. Now his actions, however deserving of praise, stand naked . . . meaningful only in themselves, shorn of any role in some larger scheme of things. He shakes his head, at a loss for how to explain it all.

At 9:00 sharp on Monday morning he enters the Kidder-Homans building on Devonshire St. where he is met in the lobby by Graham Edwards, the research team leader. The handshake is warm and firm. "Right on time," Graham warbles in a deep but welcoming voice. His blonde hair lies flat on his head and is pulled straight back, affecting a hawk-like appearance, his thin, hooked nose and clear blue eyes adding to the raptorial impression. "Glad we had nice weather for your first day at Kidder-Homans."

"Yes, me too," Rafer responds, smiling. "I didn't realize you had so much pull with the meteorological folks. It was really pleasant walking here from my apartment . . . you know, down through the Gardens and across the Common. And it only takes 10 minutes . . . so if I'm ever late, don't let me blame it on the traffic."

"Glad you like your new setup, Rafe. It is Rafe, isn't it? I mean what you want people to call you."

(*Smiling*) "That's better than some of the things I've been called. And how about you . . . any particular handle you prefer?"

"It's hard to squeeze a nickname out of Graham . . . the guys here generally call me "Chief." That could be short for Chief pain-in-the-ass . . . or something worse for all I know . . . but Chief is fine."

"You say 'guys' . . . shall I take that to mean no gals?"

"Afraid so . . . at least for now. (*Chuckling*) Does that mean you want to quit?"

(*Laughing*) "I should probably check out my office first . . . it could make a difference."

(*Extending his arm*) "O.K. Right this way. We've got you installed on the fourteenth floor . . . nice open view of Boston Harbor . . . and five steps from the coffee machine."

Coming out of the elevator, they bump into two young men, one ruddy-faced, slightly plump and dressed in a natty gray business suit, the other thin and hunched, his lanky frame hanging precariously from unmuscled shoulders, his shirt both gray and crumpled, suggesting a do-it-yourself approach to laundering.

"Oh Rafe, let me introduce two of our team members. This is Wally (*pointing to the plump man*) whose specialty is natural resource stocks and precious metals. If it's gold, silver, oil or gas you're interested in, Wally's your man. (*Turning to the taller man*) And this is Morris, our local candidate for GQ man of the year. (*Laughing*) What he lacks in chic he more than makes up for in I.Q. I should warn you, though, he's a chronic pessimist who sees nothing but doom ahead."

Morris takes a deep breath and trains his large brown eyes on Graham. "Well, as long as you're sharing my resume, why don't you tell him how much money I saved our clients back in 2000 just before the tech bubble burst. You were glad you listened to me then, weren't you."

Wally puts his arm around Morris's shoulder. "Yeah, but that was then and now is now, my friend. If you keep cryin' wolf when the critter is long dead and gone, you're going to get left behind . . . 'cause this bull market we're in still has plenty of legs to run."

Rafer breaks into a big smile. "Looks like there's a little difference of opinion here. That's great . . . always helps to hear both sides of an issue . . . especially when there's no hard and fast way to prove who's right."

"At least until the future becomes the present," adds Graham. A year or two from now we should know whether the market is still flying high and everybody's getting rich or, as Morris predicts, we're all out on the street selling apples. But Rafe, c'mon; let me show you your office. We can meet the other guys later."

As they enter Rafer's new office, his enthusiasm is immediate. "Wow, this is gorgeous," he exclaims, going to the window and looking out over the harbor. "How am I going to get any work down with a view like this?"

Graham smiles. "Gladys will see to it that you don't lack things to do. She's in the next office (*pointing*) . . . where she'll be servicing both you and Morris."

(*With sly smirk*) "Servicing?"

"Hmmm. Maybe not the best choice of words . . . let's say she'll be handling your correspondence, word processing, reports . . . all the things that secretaries usually do." He stoops to pick up a sheaf of papers sitting on the desk. "This is an outline of your duties . . . or at least what we hope you can give us at this time. Since you're the first Ph.D. economist we've ever hired, this should be considered a first draft. But it's unlikely that our basic needs will change. What we don't have at the present is someone who can give us an ongoing assessment of the economy, including sector by sector analyses of strengths and weaknesses . . . the kind of stuff we can draw on as we prepare research reports for our brokers. The brokers, of course, are the lowlife downstairs who rely on that info when they recommend trades to their clients. It's all set out in this summary."

Rafer reaches out to take the summary. "I think I already know what's in here from the talks I had with you and others at my interview last spring. It's all pretty clear . . . and I look forward to getting into it."

"You told me last spring what your dissertation was on but I'm afraid I've forgotten."

"It was all about the stock market crash of 1987 . . . what led up to it . . . and things we could have done to prevent it."

"Oh yes, I remember. A little historical analysis will come in real handy now that economists are busy squabbling with each other. As you know, some are predicting that a bubble in stocks is forming and could burst later this year or next."

"Personally, I don't think we have to worry," says Rafer. "From what I've seen, the present bull market in stocks and real estate is being fed primarily by the Fed's low-interest rate policy and Congress's push to make it easier for low-income families to buy their own homes. And neither of those forces is likely to be withdrawn any time soon. So I really don't see a bubble that's in danger of bursting; in my opinion it's a healthy bull market based on real fundamentals . . . one that has a long way to go before running out of gas."

"Hmm. That's reassuring Rafe. You're going to make a lot of friends here if you keep talking that way. Now let me introduce you to Gladys . . . you'll be seeing a lot of her."

"You mean . . . ?"

Graham doubles over, laughing. "Well, not that way . . . but she *is* a real looker, if that's any interest to you. At any rate, the two of you will be working closely together."

"Understood."

Later at lunch he is introduced to two other members of the team, Nelson, a young, black man who specializes in emerging markets and is the sole representative of his race at Kidder-Homans . . . and Peter, a transplanted Englishman who covers both the U.K. and the Eurozone. There are questions about Harvard along with some prickly but gentle kidding.

"I thought you might be from Harvard when I saw you at the interview last spring," offers Peter, smiling. "You know, smart and confident without being too overbearing."

"*Too* overbearing?," chimes in Wally who has just joined them. "You mean a little is O.K.?"

"Well, he does have a Ph.D.," adds Nelson whose sensitivity to questions of status is well-known and respected, "so maybe he's entitled to a little swagger . . . especially when associating with us business school types."

With introductions out of the way, team members return to eating, their discomfort over where such talk might be heading evident in the lack of conversation. Breaking the silence, Graham stands and waves a newcomer over, introducing him as Jeffrey from the derivatives team and describing him as a member of a "secret cabal of mathematicians who hang out like bats in unlit caves up on the top floor." "They've recently created a new brand of financial products," he adds, "called Collateralized Debt Obligations or CDO's. I'd be happy to explain it to you but I would be risking the status I now enjoy as someone of close to average intelligence. But Jeffry can tell you everything . . . at least everything he's allowed to share publicly."

Rafer reaches out to shake hands. "I've heard of CDO's at school, Jeffrey, but don't know any of the details . . . except that they're the brainchild of a bunch of mathematicians . . . (*pause*) . . . So, you're the guys who actually created these monstrosities . . . (*grinning*) . . . and all this happened right here at Kidder-Homans. When I first heard about them I thought they were so powerful they might be declared illegal by the Securities Exchange Commission."

"Not at all," Jeffrey replies, sitting down. "They're perfectly legal, just a little new. We got the idea when the big pension funds told us they needed to purchase more AAA rated securities. You know, by law these funds can invest only in top-rated securities and over the years they've gotten so popular, the supply of new issues was running out. So we math types were given the assignment of creating a new kind of security that would receive an AAA rating from Standard and Poor's and thus be available to pension funds, insurance companies and the like. We did it by combining lots of different loans like mortgage loans, credit card loans, and automobile loans, none of which deserved a top rating, into a new package that we then divided into separate risk levels or tranches, making sure that the top few levels were solid enough to get an AAA rating."

Rafer leans forward. "But what about the other levels? If the top few tranches were stuffed with all the good loans, who would want to buy the rest?"

"Good question," Jeffrey responds. "The lowest tranches are the riskiest and get the lowest ratings because the loan default rate is so high, but they also offer the highest rate of return . . . you know, as a reward for taking on all that risk. They're the loans that are least likely to be paid back, so they need to offer an attractive yield. The whole point is to separate the high risk tranches from the low risk tranches so that those levels that are safest can get an AAA rating and thus be legal for pension funds and insurance companies to buy."

At this point Morris turns to Rafer, shaking his head. "What Jeffrey is not saying is *who* pays the rating agencies to decide which tranches, if any, deserve a triple A rating." He looks around, taking in the glares of his colleagues, then continues looking at Rafer. "I'll give you one guess . . . it's Kidder-Homans who pays them. The agencies know damn well what Kidder-Homans wants . . . we want the maximum number of AAA-rated CDO's because we can make a lot of money by selling those securities to pension funds that by law are allowed to buy only blue ribbon stuff. So we're basically paying the rating agencies to give our CDO's as many AAA ratings as possible. Given the way the system works, what are people like Standard and Poor's and Moody's going to do? Let's face it . . . they know where their bread is buttered. They're going to give us what we want . . . even if it means artificially jacking up the ratings on a bunch of junk loans that are never going to be repaid. And that's why I think that this whole thing is going to come apart . . . maybe not right away but eventually."

Graham forces a smile. "As I said, Rafe, Morris has his own special way of looking at things. We don't always agree, but we still like him . . . sort of."

Morris (*lips trembling*): "Maybe you'll like me a lot more when this whole house of cards comes tumbling down . . . or maybe you'll really hate me for being right."

Wally: "Or maybe we'll hate you whichever way it goes, Morris. The world doesn't like pessimists . . . and for good reason. You've had a frown on your kisser every since you got here . . . and my guess is that it was there when your mother took her first look at you. I'm no psychologist but something is clearly wrong. Maybe you're spending too much time alone. Go out and get yourself a wife or at least get laid. This world-is-about-to-end look of yours is getting on my nerves."

Nelson: "Maybe he should join the Jehovah's Witnesses. He'd be right at home there . . . you know, with their predictions about the Apocalypse and the like."

Wally (*giggling*): "I don't know . . . they might find him too gloomy."

Graham (*rising*): "I think it's time to get back to work. Let's go . . . we've got money to make."

Each day the mood at Kidder-Homans grows increasingly euphoric as the Dow-Jones Index continues its meteoric rise. Everybody on the team, with one notable exception, is bullish. Just look at the facts, they say. Real estate has been rising steadily since 2003; experts are saying that house prices could go up forever. Over at the Federal Reserve Alan Greenspan is stoking the fires by keeping interest rates extremely low. The tech bust of 2000-2001 is now a distant memory; the economy is growing nicely; the government is pressuring banks to make mortgage loans easier for the poor. Anyone can see that these are the perfect ingredients for a long-run bull market.

One day when lunching alone, Rafer is joined by Morris who pulls up a seat next to him, eager to talk. "Chief told me about your dissertation on asset bubbles, Rafe . . . but I don't get it." His nose is wrinkled, his eyes squinting as he lays down his knife and fork. "Doesn't all your research tell you that this bubble is about to burst . . . like it did over and over in the 1980's and 1990's. There's a pattern here . . . when bubbles burst, they tend to fall back to where they began. You should know that as well as anybody. Look at the Nasdaq . . . starts at 1500 in 1999 . . . then it's up to 5200 by 2000 . . . only to fall back to 1500 in 2001. The same is true for real estate. Isn't it bound to happen again? It's a pattern . . . there's no way of getting around it."

"You're right about the past, Morris . . . but I think this is different. Times have changed. Bubbles do burst as you say but I don't see that we're in one at the present. We're all optimistic to be sure but there are good reasons for being that way . . . new government policies, a budget surplus, a shrinking trade deficit, and new financial products like the CDO's Jeffrey was talking about. So, although I am very aware of market history, I don't see that it is relevant here. The circumstances are simply too different."

Morris (*leaning forward*): "They're different alright . . . but not for the better. At least that's my opinion. You mention Jeffrey's CDO's. They strike me as a ticking time bomb . . . just waiting to explode in our faces. The mathematicians think they can manufacture securities out of what amounts to thin air . . . then pay the rating agencies to bless them as safe. The whole thing stinks. And I think we're going to end up regretting it."

Rafer (*smiling*): "I take it you don't have any skin in the game."

Morris: "Not a penny. How about you?"

Rafer: "I'm all the way in. I see it as the chance of a lifetime to make a small fortune and I don't want to be left out."

Morris (*eyebrows raised*): "Maybe they're right when they say you can always tell a Harvard man but you can't tell him much . . . (*rising from the table*) . . . Well, at least I tried."

At home in evening Rafer tries meditating again but can't settle down; there are simply too many interesting ideas swirling inside his head. The serenity he felt back in Sikkim is so remote now as to be irretrievable but the loss, however regretful, is more than made up for by the excitement he experiences at work, particularly the chance to use his hard-won knowledge to make a killing in the stock market.

At lunch with Prof Pulaski Rafer makes apologies for not following up on the experiment which the professor had proposed earlier. He explains that his power of concentration vanished soon after Tomo's recovery and became public knowledge when he failed to save Kioga from pneumonia. Pulaski nods his understanding but adds that he has given the Tomo "cure" lots of thought, to the point of developing a theory of what might have happened. "In ordinary consciousness," he starts, "there are three steps we go through in orienting ourselves to our environment. Incoming stimuli are first sorted into sensations like sounds, smells and images; these sensations are then combined to form a perceptual field, a tableau made up of objects like cars, streets, sidewalks, pedestrians and so forth. At the final level, and this is something that only humans can do, those objects are named and evaluated. For example, we give an object the name "car"; we might add that it is beautiful, in the wrong lane or going too fast. In this way we orient ourselves to our environment by constructing a reality out of incoming information. All organisms are hard-wired to carry out at least the first two levels of orientation, that is, the sensation and perception levels. They could not survive otherwise;

without identifying sensations and organizing them into perceptual fields, predators could not catch their prey and prey animals could not escape. The same is true of humans; when crossing the street, we first sort stimuli into lines, colors, shapes and sounds, then organize those sensations into recognizable forms (like cars and people). As part of the perceptual process, we automatically locate each object in time and space (how far away is that oncoming car, how fast is it coming toward me?) and then make judgments about how to act (do I have time to cross?). These three levels or orientation (sensation, perception and cognition) require huge amounts of psychic energy, even though it's all happening unconsciously."

"I'm following you."

"Now here's the point, Rafe. When a person's meditation reaches an advanced level, a level like the one you reached in Sikkim, all these orienting mechanisms get turned off . . . no more colors, shapes or sounds, no more objects like cars or people, no more orienting yourself in time and space and no more thinking about anything . . . so where does that leave you? . . . (*pause*) . . . If you are no longer orienting yourself to the objects in your environment, what is it that you experience?"

Rafer, who has been listening attentively, raises his hand as if he were back in the classroom: "Sounds pretty familiar, professor. You'd be confronted with a Void . . . an all-consuming, empty space which can't be described since there's nothing in it. Right?"

"That's my guess too."

Rafer nods. "From the reading I did in Sikkim I'm pretty sure this is what the Buddhists refer to as sunyata . . . the very heart of enlightenment."

"It's what you experienced at the monastery, isn't it? . . . or so I gather from the letter you sent."

"Yes . . . but your explanation of how it happens and what it all means is very different from the way the Buddhists see it. From their literature it is clear they view the sunyata experience as something spiritual . . . as a glimpse into another world, a world beyond the everyday world of cars, trees and people. You obviously prefer to view the experience in psychological rather than spiritual terms . . . and that has some interesting implications. For example, the way to become enlightened, you seem to be saying, is to turn off the orienting mechanisms that help us get around in our environments."

The professor nods his agreement. "Yes. That's pretty much it. But let's be straight about this: the Buddhists may be right in holding enlightenment aloft as an ideal worth devoting one's life to. I have no quarrel with that. My objection is with the meaning they attach to the experience itself."

"O.K.," says Rafer, "but it's still not clear how all this enables one person to cure another person's disease through meditation alone. Are you going to argue that once an individual has become enlightened, the energy that used to go into orienting can somehow be used for healing?"

Pulaski breaks into a broad smile. "Ah . . . now we're getting there. My guess is that as soon as all three orienting mechanisms have been shut down, temporarily at least, all the psychic energy that went into the orienting becomes available for other uses . . . for example, healing. I'm still not sure how it happens, but I suspect that the saved energy, when aimed properly, is transmitted through space to another person . . . like your friend Tomo . . . where it stimulates the immune system into curing the disease."

Rafer struggles to contain his excitement. "So you're saying that when a person enters the enlightenment state, a huge amount of energy is released and can then be directed at other people . . . or I suppose at animals as well. If so, there should be some way of detecting this energy, of measuring it, even storing or otherwise manipulating it.

We already know how to measure brain waves . . . alpha, beta and theta . . . so how come we can't measure this psychic energy you're talking about. Maybe it's not physical."

"It's got to be physical. To me there's no such thing as a spiritual reality that is distinct from our physical world and yet interacts with it. Everything I know is physical . . . and that includes the psychic energy we're talking about. The energy is there . . . I'm sure of it . . . it just hasn't been detected with any of our instruments so far."

At the mention of a new, hidden kind of energy, Rafer's thoughts drift back to Sikkim. "Do you think this is the same kind of energy that Tibetan monks draw on when they perform miraculous things like levitation and visualization?"

"Of course. Only I wouldn't call them miracles. If my theory is right, these are things that anybody should be able to do. You just have to enter the kind of trance-like state that you got into when your friend was dying. How do you get there? You enter that state by suspending the orientation processes that we normally use to negotiate our way around the world. I think it's that simple Rafe."

"But wait a minute, Stefan . . . if you're no longer orienting yourself . . . if you now see the world as an infinite, empty space no longer filled with objects like cars coming toward you or trees about to fall on you, how are you going to survive? Don't you have to keep these orientation processes working in order to avoid getting hurt? It sounds to me like getting into that deep meditation place makes you extremely vulnerable. Unless you're orienting, you won't know what's going on around you . . . you won't know how to protect yourself from danger."

"I haven't figured that out yet . . . (*pause*) . . . The solution probably lies in cultivating the ability to see both the empty space and specific objects at the same time . . . perhaps by varying how much of each you see . . . but I need to do some more reading."

They part with mutual promises to stay in touch. The professor reiterates his offer to set up a clinical trial to test Rafer's healing powers. "Just let me know when you're ready." Rafer answers: "I'm a long way from ready right now. I don't know if I can ever get back to where I was in Sikkim."

6

Dow-Jones

Later in the month Rafer receives the inheritance from his parents' estate and immediately invests it in the stock market. He picks his stocks carefully, relying heavily on the research of his fellow team members. Stocks tied to real estate, namely home construction companies and the regional banks that lend to such companies are among his favorite picks. He also buys stock in the large banks and brokerages that hold millions of dollars of mortgage-backed securities, the kind of CDO's that Jeffery and his group upstairs had a hand in inventing. With so many real estate and bank stocks in his portfolio, every time house prices rise, he makes a killing At their weekly group meeting Wally reports that in northern New England house prices are rising almost five percent a month, an unbelievable rate given that historically house prices typically rise about the same as the rate of inflation. Everywhere in the country people are buying homes they really can't afford on the assumption that their investment will gain value as prices continue to soar. In hopes of attracting new business, bankers begin to relax their mortgage requirements to the extent that down payments are waived altogether and buyers are given the option of paying interest only (no principal) for the next ten years. Not to be outdone, one bank starts offering what it calls "option Adjustable Rate Mortgages" in which the customer can opt to pay minimal interest (no principal again) and have the unpaid interest postponed to a later date. The idea catches on immediately. Soon hundreds of thousands of home buyers are signing up for option ARM mortgages. As a result, housing and bank stocks go through the roof. Within a few months, Rafer's portfolio has doubled in value; by Christmas it has tripled. The Dow-Jones index is now over 14,000; a new book predicts that it will soon hit 36,000. The party is on.

It is not long before Rafer is flooded with calls from friends, landladies, and distant cousins asking for advice on how to play the market. Everyone wants in. At first he is reluctant. It's stressful enough to gamble with one's own money, he argues; taking on responsibility for somebody else just makes things worse. In time, however, he gives in and begins sharing ideas. Go with stocks related to real estate, he suggests; echoing the judgments of his research team, he adds that "the stars are aligned for a multi-year bull market that should see a doubling in both residential and commercial property values." As the Dow continues to rise, his phone rings night and day with advisees calling to offer their congratulations. Everyone is euphoric. Each evening, he hurries home to watch the business news on TV, even though he's been following the market all day at work. Sitting back in his leather chair, a glass of white wine on one side, the phone on the other, he luxuriates in the knowledge that countless people are making a fortune because of his advice. Could life be any sweeter? Well yes, it could be, he muses, if he could pick up the phone right now and call home. With that thought dancing in his head, he turns down the TV and drifts into fantasy. He pictures himself telling his parents how much money he has made and how many phone calls he has received from people calling for advice. Mother's gasp is almost audible as she exclaims, "That's wonderful Rafe; you're making so many people happy. I knew things would turn out well for you. As I've said a thousand times, you can do anything you put your mind to." Sleep comes easily that night.

On the following day the world turns upside down. By late morning it is clear that the stock market is tanking. By noon the Dow is down 350 points; investors are running for the exits. At the lunch table everyone is crowding around Morris, looking for answers. "The bubble has burst," he says calmly, addressing his fellow team members. "It had to happen," he adds, "all you have to do is look at history." In the ensuing silence everyone waits for the inevitable 'I told you so.' It never comes. Instead he reaches for the oil and vinegar and meticulously dresses his salad, covering first the lettuce, then the tomatoes, broccoli, cauliflower, and carrots in turn. He bites into the cauliflower with relish, utters an approving "mmmm" . . . then looks up, his eyebrows lifted, clearly surprised to see that no one else is eating. Around the table, burgers, soup, wraps, and pasta all sit unattended. "Did the waiter bring the wrong things?," he asks innocently. The whole team is watching but no words are spoken. With no more than the hint of a smirk, he loosens his necktie, then unbuttons his collar. "I don't see why we have to be so formal around here." When no response is forthcoming, he casts a final look at the untouched plates around him . . . then hunches down over the remains of his salad. Heedless of propriety now, he lowers his face to within inches of the plate, then shovels cucumbers, broccoli and tomatoes into a mouth already overflowing with flora. Still chewing noisily, he wipes his lips on his sleeve and signals his satisfaction with a porcine grunt followed by a loud fart. Looking at no one in particular, he whispers, "This is the best damn salad I've ever had."

By closing time at 4:00 the Dow has dropped 700 points. As he heads for home Rafer is mentally preparing for the phone calls he knows are coming. Above all, he must remain upbeat. "Be calm, be reassuring," he mutters; "don't let them hear the fear clawing at my heart." The phone is already ringing as he fumbles with his door key. He waits for it to stop, then rushes in and throws his coat onto the couch. Peace is what he craves. There will be no TV news tonight . . . no rehashing of the day's grim events . . . just a glass of wine, maybe two or three. He sits and waits, afraid to breathe lest he break the silence. No sooner has he poured the first glass of wine than the phone begins ringing again. He drags himself to the end table where the odious sound is originating. "Hello," he whispers, already regretting having answered.

"Hi, Rafer, it's George. What the hell happened today? Tell me."

"Well, it's probably just a correction George. When the market goes up as much as it has lately, it has to take a breather. It's normal . . . even healthy."

"Healthy? You've got to be kidding. We lost $12,000 today . . . that's $12,000 in a single day!. Edna is already beating on me for taking your advice. But you say this is just a temporary setback . . . something we should expect every now and then?"

"Yes. The market may even drop another 5-10% before resuming its upward movement. Just hang on and you'll be O.K."

"I hope you're right old friend. There'll be hell to pay here if you're not."

Even as he reassures his friend, Rafer is aware of the doubts festering in his own psyche. What if he's wrong? What if he's allowed his enthusiasm to get the better of him? That's not supposed to happen. He's got a Ph.D. from Harvard . . . he's supposed to have good judgment about these things. After all, that's what Kidder-Homans hired him for, isn't it . . . to exercise good judgment at a time when everybody else is getting swept up in their emotions?

The phone rings again. "Hi Rafe, it's Tony. How you doin?"

"Hi Tony. It's not one of my better days. You've heard no doubt . . .

Tony interrupts. "Yeah, it's got me concerned . . . you know, the Dow falling and everything. But the news I just got about house prices falling has me really scared. I told you I just bought this cottage in New Hampshire, more as a speculation than a vacation residence, on the assumption that I could unload it in a few years time after prices go up. Remember, you told me at the time you thought it was a smart move. (*Quietly*) I'm not so sure now . . . (*pause*) . . . What do you think?"

"Well, you can't be certain about these things Tony, but I think it's safe to say that all the pieces remain in place for still higher house prices ahead. I'm talking about low interest rates, mortgages with low teaser rates . . . even continuing increases in population. These are the things that have driven up prices so far and there's no reason why they should stop. That's the way I see it. Now, I could be wrong . . . but everything I've read or heard about points in that direction."

"O.K . . . so you're saying I should hold onto the property . . . not try to sell it now."

"That's what I would do."

The phone continues to ring throughout the evening until Rafer can't stand it any longer and yanks the plug from the wall. As he heads for the bedroom, the voices he has just heard reverberate inside his head. What if he's wrong? What if the Dow drops even further tomorrow? What will he tell people then? Unable to think straight, he stumbles into bed without undressing. It is the middle of the night before he falls asleep.

Panic hits Wall St. the next day when the Dow falls another 550 points. Newspaper headlines scream "Housing Bubble Bursts" and "Blood in the Streets." The office is in turmoil as angry clients call to sell stocks before things get any worse. Graham orders an emergency meeting to discuss strategy. At the table all eyes are on the expert whose job it is to keep everybody informed about broader movements in the economy.

"Well, Harv. Where were you on this one?," Wally asks, making no attempt to conceal his disdain for anything smacking of Ivy League.

"If it's just a temporary correction," Rafer answers, "then we don't have anything to worry about. Of course, if it's something more than that, we could all be in trouble."

"Well, which is it?," replies Wally, scowling. "What does that Ph.D. of yours tell you is coming?"

"That's what you're here for, isn't it?," adds Jeffrey, sensing safety in numbers. "I mean, you're supposed to know about these things, aren't you?"

"Well," says Rafer, "if I had to guess I would say . . . ."

Graham (*interrupting*): "I think we need something more than a guess, Rafe. We need a solid prediction . . . one based on careful analysis of market data, past, present and future."

Rafer (*reddening*) "O.K. If it's a prediction you want, I'll go out on a limb and say that the bull market is still intact and should, after a brief pullback, continue to rise for many months to come."

Cheers erupt from Peter, Jeffrey and Graham. Morris buries his face in his hands. Wally is the only one to speak, "We're going to hold you to it, Harv. You better be right." All get up to leave save Rafer who lingers at the table, waiting for his breathing to subside.

In the ensuing weeks, Rafer proves to be wrong, dead wrong, as the Dow continues to plummet, first to 8500 then all the way down to 6600. The evening phone calls from friends and relatives continue unabated for a month, then taper off as anger and disbelief turn to resignation. For weeks he avoids looking at his personal account. When he finally steals a glance, he is sickened to find that he has lost most of his $300,000 inheritance. He can only assume that those who took his advice have lost most of their investment as well. Overwhelmed with guilt for losing his parents' money as well as his role in the losses of friends and relatives, he sinks into a deep depression. Over Graham's advice, he asks for and gets an unpaid leave of absence from Kidder-Homans. For the next few months he spends his days brooding at home, refusing to answer either the door or the phone.

7

The Pencil

To get away from the pain, Rafer starts meditating again. His most urgent need is to forget the outside world . . . to stop thinking . . . to stop condemning himself for his poor judgment. Memories of Sikkim return and with them hope of rediscovering that unshakeable silence he stumbled onto at Tomo's bedside. Days go by with no formal meals, just nibbling here and there. He stops reading, turns his TV off, and unplugs the phone. All alone, without a job and with just enough money to pay for rent and food, he is free to devote his days to meditation. His goal: to escape guilt and shame, to lose himself in a nameless void free of worry and self-blame.

Gradually he grows still. His mind stops racing, slows down, then stops altogether as thoughts about his failings give way to the silence of OM. For days on end he sits patiently on his meditation pillow, eyes closed, his breathing scarcely audible. As his concentration deepens, a new kind of energy builds in his head, more diffuse than an ache yet threatening to explode if he doesn't stop. In his mind's eye he sees Kioga pointing to his solar plexus. Push it down, he seems to say; exhale into your abdomen; keep the energy there. The pressure subsides as he breathes into his gut where a powerful, warm glow soon forms, radiating out to his extremities.

One day while relaxing in his leather swivel chair, an image from childhood flashes before him. The sun is bright; he is in the backyard trying to ignite a piece of paper with a magnifying glass. Magically the paper starts to turn brown at the edges, then suddenly bursts into flame as he pulls his fingers back. The memory of that day returns now as he pulls his chair forward, training his eyes on a pencil in the middle of his otherwise clear and shiny desk. Out of nowhere he feels an urge to eliminate the pencil but hesitates to get up for fear of disturbing his concentration. Instead he begins concentrating on the pencil as if it were a new mantra. Without realizing what he is doing, he begins to will the pencil off the desk. In the process his mind clears, grows stronger and comes to a single point . . . until nothing but the pencil remains. Suddenly, embedded in the pencil and somehow emerging from it, he sees the same empty, borderless, fathomless space he saw back in Tomo's bedroom. His eyes grow large; his breathing stops. Now nothing exists but this empty space, no desk, no pencil, not even a self. His whole frame is flooded with joy. In a flash, all guilt and shame, all self-loathing, self-doubt, fear, and disgust, are brushed from his mind like cobwebs swept from an attic window, leaving nothing but a cloudless sky.

Seconds later he is shaken from his meditation by the sound of the pencil hitting the floor. Astounded at this turn of events, he gets up and places the pencil back on the desk. Returning to his chair, he concentrates again on the pencil before him. This time, he tries to move it in the opposite direction. Just as before, the pencil opens up to reveal a clear, empty space, a space with absolutely nothing in it. And once again it falls off the desk.

Still shaking at his discovery, he reaches for a nearby book and places it on the desk in the same position where the pencil used to be. He sits back, closes his eyes, and brings his mind to focus on the book to the exclusion of everything else. He wills it to the left; nothing happens. He tries again, this time to the right. Again the book remains unmoved.

Opening his eyes wide now, he lets thoughts re-enter his mind. It may have something to do with the weight of the book, he murmurs. With that hypothesis in mind, he tries again with the pencil and is relieved to see that he can still roll it off the desk in either direction. He tries with other objects, heavier than the pencil but lighter than the book. Nothing works but the pencil. Still giddy with his discovery, he goes looking for something round but lighter than the pencil. In the basement he spies a ping-pong ball, brings it back upstairs and places it on the desk. Returning to his chair, he slips into a trance and projects his will onto the ball. The ping-pong ball rolls off the desk so fast he breaks into a huge laugh. "So it really is a matter of weight; we're still in the world of physics," he exclaims to the empty room.

Sitting back again, he searches his memory for the right word for what has happened . . . psychokinesis . . . yes, that's it. He opens his computer and Googles the term. He reads the definition: "the act of moving a physical object with the mind alone . . . also known as telekinesis." There are many articles there . . . some personal and anecdotal, others scientific in nature, still others offering advice on how to develop the ability to move pendulums and the like. He comes away with a new awareness that psychokinesis, or at least a belief in it, is not all that uncommon. Being of a practical bent, he goes looking for reports of people who have put their psychokinetic ability to positive use. He is disappointed when his search turns up nothing. Mostly, he reads, it has been used as a parlor trick . . . a form of entertainment designed to titillate audiences.

In the days to follow, he returns to the pencil, relieved to find that he can still roll it off the desk. In the spirit of research, he tries lifting it straight up rather than rolling it off the desk. This fails . . . presumably, he reasons, because to do so requires more psychic energy than he can muster . . . more evidence, he concludes, that the process is purely physical. "So, where do I go from here?," he asks. "Such an exciting discovery . . . but what can I do with it? Anything at all?"

Weeks go by without an answer. In the meantime he spends most of his days meditating . . . drinking his fill of the deep peace his awakening has brought. That peace is broken one day by a rap on his apartment door. It's Graham. "Couldn't reach you by phone," he says, "so thought I'd pop over and see how you're doing. The guys have been asking about you. We're all in the dog house, of course . . . clients calling to ask how we screwed up so badly . . . even a few law suits started. But you appear to have been more affected than the rest of us." They talk about the disaster . . . the financial meltdown . . . prospects for a recovery. Graham ends by asking when Rafer plans to return. "Don't know," he says with a shrug, "haven't really given it much thought."

When Graham leaves, Rafer returns to the question he was asked but never answered. "Should I go back to Kidder-Homans and pick up the pieces? Or is there something else I would rather do?" Occasionally his thoughts turn to Mother and what she would say if she were here now. It's pretty clear. 'Go back Rafe . . . don't give up . . . this is just a temporary setback. There's nothing in the world you can't do if you want it badly enough . . . just put your mind to it.'

As the days pass, her words continue to rattle around in the recesses of his consciousness, kindling questions and doubts each time he tries to meditate. It is a week before he realizes what is happening. Those same words, so forceful and compelling in the past, so inspiring through the years as he fought his way to the very pinnacle of the educational world, now appear stale and unconvincing. They ring hollow, as if they were addressed not to him personally but to some larger, unseen audience. In his mind he speaks to her as if she were present. "You say I should go back and pick up the pieces . . . work hard and make a name for myself at the brokerage . . . build a fortune along the way and eventually enter politics. That's what you've always wanted, isn't it? And I've always agreed with you. I never really questioned your ideas. But maybe I should have. Maybe I should have spent less time listening to what you wanted for me and more time figuring out what I wanted for myself. Now I'm not sure what to do. The only thing that seems certain is that your plans for me, the plans we both harbored for years, no longer seem to fit. They don't fit because something inside me is changing. I'm beginning to see there may be something else in life more important than pursuing fame and glory or making a lot of money. Meditation has opened my eyes to that possibility. The idea is a new one for me and I'm not sure where it's all heading . . . but I don't think it has anything to do with what you always meant by success."

In the weeks to follow, his conviction that it would be wrong to return to Kidder-Homans grows stronger. He still has a little over $50,000 left in his bank account, enough he figures to support him in a down-sized lifestyle for another year or two. In May he writes to Graham to tell him of his decision. Then, still curious about the meaning of the pencil episode, he decides to write Prof. Pulaski and get his opinion.

Pulaski writes back:

Dear Rafer,

Such strange things are happening to you! But perhaps they are not so strange after all. On the surface this latest episode with the pencil sounds quite different from what happened between you and your friend in Sikkim . . . but the difference may be only superficial. Both events, the psychokinesis and the healing, point to something akin to what I suggested in my earlier, primitive attempt at a theory. Back then, you will remember, I suggested that entering a deep trance-like state where the world presents itself as an unlimited, empty space tends to unleash all the psychic energy we normally expend in orienting to our environment. Now, what can one do with that energy? Given what happened in Sikkim, it appears that you can direct it at another person or animal where it can be used to strengthen the other's immune system. But it is beginning to look like other things are possible as well. Your latest experiments with the pencil suggest that the same psychic energy can be used in a different way . . . to move physical objects around, particularly small, lightweight objects. While both possibilities are significant, the healing route strikes me as the more important of the two . . . one that I think you have a personal responsibility to develop further. Who knows how far you can go with it? I would suggest that the first step is to bring the healing process into the laboratory where we can test it scientifically. Proving that it is possible to cure another person's disease without medication or surgery or even speaking to the patient could turn the scientific community on its head . . . and in the process launch a program to teach other people how to do what you've done.

Regarding the second option . . . psychokinesis, I am a bit short on ideas (at the present). What kind of small, rounded object, other than a pencil or ping-pong ball, can you move with your mind alone? Other kinds of balls perhaps . . . but to what end? I've been toying with this question for days now without an answer. Last night when I got obsessing over it at the dinner table, my wife insisted on knowing what I was so preoccupied about. When I told her, her answer was simple and immediate. "Tell him to go to Las Vegas and use psychokinesis to manipulate the roulette wheel." Not a bad idea, I thought. It might work . . . since the ball is a small one and is free to roll around. To release enough psychic energy to make it move, you would have to first enter the empty, objectless space we've talked about . . . but then back out just far enough so that you were oriented enough to see the ball and make it move. That sounds rather tricky to me. If you back up too far, of course, you will lose the energy that comes from suspending the orienting process. But if you don't orient to your surroundings at least a little, you won't even know where you are and certainly won't be able to make the ball land where you want it to.

I don't know enough about roulette to make any predictions. But if you are suffering because of the stock market advice you gave your friends, perhaps you can rectify things with some winnings at the casinos out there. It might be worth a try.

I'm sorry I can't come up with anything more interesting . . . but I'll continue to work on it.

Fondly,

Stefan Pulaski

The idea strikes Rafer with the force of a thousand stadium lights switched on in the middle of the night. "My God, yes, a casino . . . the perfect place to put this gift to use." He quickly reviews what he knows about the game. There's the roulette table with its wheel, its small ball, and all the different ways to place your bet. You can play red, black, odd, even, columns and rows, even parts of columns and rows . . . but it's the individual numbers with their 35 to 1 odds that make it possible to win a lot of money in a hurry . . . *(pause)* . . . "But can it be done?," he asks. "Can I learn to slow down or speed up the ball with my mind alone? Can I make it land where I want it to? Is such a thing even possible?" His heart begins racing with the possibilities. If it works, he could make enough money to pay back the people who lost their shirts following his advice. It could add something to his own bank account as well. The idea tears at his brain, shaking his skull like a dog worrying a caught rat. He goes to bed, twisting, turning, unable to sleep, delirious with renewed hope, overflowing with thoughts of how to make it all happen.

8

As the Wheel Turns

A week later a package arrives bearing the return address Foster's Casino Equipment, Chicago, Illinois. Inside is a beautifully made mahogany roulette wheel complete with ball and cloth betting layout. He places both the wheel and the layout on his dining room table and stands back to admire his purchase. "My own little Harrah's . . . but without all the glitter," he chuckles as he smoothes out the wrinkles in the cloth. A few spins of the wheel are sufficient to convince him that the mechanism is perfectly balanced and should respond to small amounts of psychokinetic pressure.

Before playing, he spends several hours in meditation. There is no hurry now. Sitting cross-legged on his cushion, concentrating on OM, he slips into that wordless space that the philosopher Korzybski playfully calls the 'unspeakable.' He stays in that space long enough to erase all hints of the world of form. For centuries the Buddhists have described it as a state of consciousness without any thing in it . . . not even a self. The description fits.

Once he has reached the level of "empty space," he deliberately pulls back until he can once again orient himself to the table, the wheel and the ball. Standing right next to the wheel, he picks number 14 and gives the wheel a spin. He is aware that there is no point in trying to control ball near the beginning of the spin where it is moving quickly. He waits until it slows down, then leans over the wheel and tries to force the ball to settle into slot 14. To his dismay the ball shoots past

14 and lands six slots on the other side. He takes a deep breath then tries again; there is some improvement but he still can't get any closer than two or three slots to either side of number 14. It's obvious from the results that he's exerting some degree of control but not enough to produce a winner.

After repeated attempts, the idea occurs to him that instead of betting everything on a single number, he could increase his chances of winning by placing his bets on a block of adjacent numbers . . . a target number plus several of its immediate neighbors. He picks 22 and two numbers counterclockwise on the wheel from 22 (5 & 17) plus two numbers clockwise from 22 (34 & 15). He slips into his trance, then explodes with joy when 15 comes up. Quickly he tries again, this time with number 9 as his target along with its neighbors of 30, 26, 28 & 0. The winner is 11 . . . just one slot beyond 30 and thus a loser. Again he makes his bet, spins the wheel and goes into a trance . . . this time hitting the target right on the head. Elated, he sits back and reviews what has happened. The results are even better than what he had hoped for. There's no doubt now that he can use psychokinesis to control the movement of the ball; just three tries and he's already ahead of what he could expect from betting randomly. But one thing is clear; it is essential that he memorize the position of numbers on the wheel since they don't go in order from 0 to 36 like they do on the table where you place your bets.

Still giddy from his brief success, he sits back to calculate his odds of winning with this 'target plus neighbors' strategy. The instruction booklet that came with the equipment states that most American casinos pay odds of 35:1 for a single number . . . even though there are 38 numbers on the table when you count 0 and 00. With odds of 35 to 1 for any individual number, it is clear that if he bets on the target plus its four closest neighbors, he should win, by chance alone, about once out of every seven spins of the wheel. To make money, all he has to do is win more than once out of seven tries. To make things easier to calculate, he pictures himself betting $100 on the target number as well as $100 on each of its four neighbors. "O.K.," he says, finding it easier to talk out loud, "if the ball lands on any one of those five numbers, I'll win 35 times my bet or $3,500. But then I have to subtract $100 for each of the four neighboring numbers the ball did not land on . . . leaving me a profit of $3100 for each spin of the wheel. But there are going to be times when the ball lands outside my five-number series . . . despite my best efforts to control it. Each time it does, of course, I'll lose the $100 I bet on the target plus the $100 for each of its neighbors . . . or a total of $500. So let's be conservative. Let's assume that if I play ten times, I can get the ball to fall on one of the numbers in my series (target plus four neighbors) five times . . . but can't do it the other five. How much would I make? On the winning spins, I would collect $3,100 each time or a total of 5 x $3,100 or $15,500. On each of the five losing spins, I would lose $500 . . . or $2,500 in all. My overall profit for the ten spins would then be $15,500 minus $2,500 or $13,000."

His heart races at the prospects. But there are questions still unanswered. For example, how many times do they spin the wheel on an average day? If it takes a couple of minutes for people to lay down their bets, another one minute or so for the croupier to spin the wheel, and a final two minutes to pay off the winners, there should be somewhere around twelve spins of the wheel every hour. But there's another question. How long are the casinos open? In one day . . . say afternoons plus evenings (he figures they're probably closed in the morning) . . . they should be open around twelve hours. If that's true, he concludes, it should be possible to bet about 140 times a day. So . . . if he's around for 100 of those spins and doesn't get tired or otherwise lose his concentration (a big if), he should make somewhere in the vicinity of 10 x $13,000 or $130,000 per day. Grasping the calculator, he punches in the final numbers. The results are staggering. If he keeps this up for a whole week, making the rounds of all the big casinos in town (spending no more than one night in each so the people in charge don't think something fishy is going on) he should pocket close to $900,000."

"Is that possible," he exclaims, flopping down on the couch. "If so, why hasn't anyone else tried it . . . or maybe they have and I just haven't heard about it? Google turned up a number of articles on different systems used over the years . . . like the Martingale system where every time you lose you just double up on your next bet . . . which should allow you to recoup any losses along the way as long as you don't lose too many times in a row and run out of money. But what about the system that I want to try? If anyone has ever succeeded in using psychokinesis to control the movement of the ball, they have either chosen to keep that fact to themselves or haven't lived to tell about it. It may even be illegal although I doubt that there are any laws around to that effect . . . not to mention the fact that it would be pretty hard to prove to a jury that someone was using his mind to manipulate the wheel. Most people would scoff at the notion that it was possible to do so. I know I would have a few short weeks ago, but here I am . . . on the verge of staking my last few bucks on an idea that sounds so crazy I'm afraid to mention it to my best friends. But what if it turns out to be right? What if I can really do it? Making that kind of money in a short time would allow me to pay back all the people who trusted my advice . . . and that would take a huge load off my shoulders. But it says a lot more than that, doesn't it? The money is one thing . . . I don't want to minimize its importance . . . but proving that it's possible to control a roulette ball with your mind says something pretty serious about human nature and the power of individual consciousness. I mean, just how powerful is this thing called consciousness? Are there other things we can do with it? Healing is certainly one of those. Maybe there are others. Could it be that everybody . . . or at least every healthy human being, has the power, potentially anyway, to enter this empty space that I've gotten into and gain access to the kind of energy that allows you to do these 'miraculous' things?"

In the days to come, he spends most of his mornings meditating and then practices with the roulette wheel in the afternoon. To facilitate matters he leaves the cloth layout on his dining room table and eats his meals in the kitchen. While his confidence continues to grow, certain doubts remain. He speculates, for example, that it will be harder to maintain his concentration in a crowd with people talking and pushing to get to the table. With this in mind, he decides on a little experiment. He asks his closest neighbors, Ralph and Edith, to join him for dinner and a game of roulette. The purpose behind this uncharacteristic outburst of sociability is to see if he can still enter a trance state and maintain his concentration with others standing next to him. On the phone he keeps the seriousness of his purpose to himself and presents the idea as nothing more than a novel form of entertainment. This way, he muses, if he wins consistently, they will simply interpret it as a matter of luck.

At the dinner table Rafer dishes out a hastily prepared meal of pasta and chicken. To his guest's unspoken but obvious discomfort, the white wine he bought for the occasion is tepid, having failed to make it as far as the refrigerator. As to the entrée itself, the chicken is reasonably tasty although he is aware that the linguine is overcooked. His two neighbors, both amateur cooks themselves, eye their plates disdainfully but remain stoically silent. The conversation is polite but rarely gets beyond a rehashing of the day's news. In his rush to get on with the evening's business, Rafer forgets the cream puffs and chocolate syrup he had planned for dessert. With apologies for a skimpy meal he abruptly whisks away the plates, glasses and silverware and sets the roulette wheel down on the cloth layout.

After explaining the rules, he passes out poker chips and invites them to place their bets. All three are to play against the house although no real money is to be involved. After asking his guests not to speak to him, Rafer spins the wheel and goes into a trance. Using his target-plus-neighbors strategy, he wins three times in the first five spins. Ralph, who plays the colors with little success, expresses amazement while Edith who is more open to paranormal possibilities, begins to suspect something is up. Rafer notices the questioning look on her face and deliberately loses several times in a row. When they leave later in the evening, that look is still there. At the door, Rafer looks at her closely and holds his finger to his lips. She nods knowingly; no words are spoken. The next morning, satisfied that he can win consistently even with others around, he goes online to order a plane ticket to Las Vegas.

In the two weeks leading up to his departure, he works on perfecting his strategy. Most of all he wants to improve his ability to maintain a balance between the experience of 'empty space' (where the maximum psychic energy lies) and the demands of orientation (where some of that energy is used to locate and control the ball). Meanwhile, all the meditating he's been doing is producing changes on the inside. Never in his 26 years has he felt peace of this sort. While worries about paying people back continue to intrude, they arise less often now and are less bothersome when they do arise. Even the pain of losing his family shows sign of retreating into the background. His Mother's voice, once critical to his self-confidence, can still be heard on occasion but it is more remote now, less demanding and more easily lost in the quiet joy of meditating. Thoughts about what to do with his life seem to be undergoing their own metamorphosis as well. The question of what career to pursue, a question central to his thinking just weeks ago, has receded to the vanishing point. It doesn't seem to matter anymore. What matters most is developing this new ability he has stumbled upon. Yes, he wants to use it to compensate his friends and put their anger to rest but it is the question of *meaning* that interests him the most. Just what is this ability . . . where does it come from . . . what makes it work? Is Prof. Pulaski right when he says that it is related to healing . . . that moving objects with your mind draws on the same kind of energy that is used in curing disease through meditation? If so, are there still other uses this energy can be put to?

For the time being, that question goes unanswered . . . only to be replaced by a new inquiry even more mysterious. "Why is this happening to me," he asks over and over. "There's nothing special about my skills or personality, no history of weird, paranormal experiences. O.K., maybe losing my family in the Himalayas has something to do with it . . . or maybe all the meditation I got into at the monastery. But still, why me? Tomo has been meditating for several years and hasn't developed any special abilities . . . and he's committed his whole life to finding enlightenment. Even the abbot said my 'gift' was unusual. Apparently he didn't have it either. What really makes this whole experience strange is that I never asked for the ability to heal or the ability to move objects with my mind. I never even knew such things existed. So, why me?"

The question remains unanswered in the weeks to come as he continues to meditate and hone his psychokinetic abilities. It is still there on the day of his flight.

9

Las Vegas

W hen the phone rings in the small, dimly-lit foyer just inside the door, Rafer leaps up from bed where he is meditating, curious to see who might be calling so soon after he has arrived. It's the boarding house landlady asking if he would like to join the other guests for dinner at 6:30. He politely declines and returns to his practice, aware that he must maintain absolute clarity of mind if his strategy at the roulette tables is to work. Despite a growling stomach, he keeps meditating throughout the evening, foregoing wine, dinner and TV. Rising early in the morning, he nibbles on a sweet roll, drinks some tea, then heads for the Strip . . . a two mile walk he is told . . . which gives him a chance to acquaint himself with the area before the casinos open.

Walking along Las Vegas Ave., he is struck by how many famous icons of other cities have been incorporated into the local scenery . . . the Statue of Liberty from New York, a down-sized version of the Eiffel Tower from Paris, palaces and gondolas from Venice, government buildings from Rome . . . all in all a contrived hodgepodge of borrowed architecture. To his dismay there is nothing here that captures the beauty of the Nevada deserts . . . no sand, no cacti, no native grasses . . . just glass, concrete, bright lights, swimming pools, high-rise apartments, doormen dressed like monkeys, wedding parlors, shiny trams and Elvis look-a-likes . . . glittering testimony, he concludes, to the elevation of surface over substance. What in the world would Tomo think if he were here now? What would Uma say if she were to ride by, standing knee-deep in hay as she stares at it all from atop her yak-drawn wagon?

Quickly, he reminds himself that he is not here to judge but to make money. Above all, that means not getting caught up in personal opinions about what he does and does not approve of. His top priority is to remain clear-headed, focused, and free of all thinking other than that absolutely required for his project. Newly dedicated to his mission, he turns at the corner and heads for the nearest casino . . . the Mirage. Unexpectedly, it is already open.

Upon entering, he is confronted with a cavernous room lined with slot-machines, card tables, felt-lined boxes for shooting craps and a half dozen roulette tables. Not surprisingly for this early in the day, the room is not yet crammed with patrons. He picks one of the roulette tables at random and edges close enough to watch the action. When an older man with a cane pulls away, gripping his white beard and sighing visibly, Rafer takes his place and calls out to the croupier to sell him $3,000 worth of chips. For the first few minutes he watches while bets are placed and the croupier spins the wheel. After just two spins it is clear that he's standing too far away to follow the movement of the ball with the kind of precision he requires. He picks up his chips and moves around to that part of the table adjacent to the wheel. There are two young women in his way as he attempts to squeeze in. "Oops, I'm sorry," he says to the short, squat woman on his left. Her companion, a tall, slender, blonde woman in her late 20's, is quick to reply, "There's plenty of room over there (*pointing across the table*). "Oh no, that's O.K.," counters the first, turning to face the newcomer. Her voice is as flat as the shapeless, floral dress she is wearing but her smile is infectious. Rafer returns her smile with one of his own, whispering a thank you.

Squeezing in next to her, he takes out his chips and places them on the table. He now has a chance to study the wheel from a few feet away. As he stands watching, he lets his breathing go deeper. His eyes close half-way as he waits for the "empty space" to emerge from the objects around him. Suddenly there is a tug on his arm. "Aren't you going to bet?," the short woman asks, looking up at him.

"Well, yes," Rafer replies slowly, "I just wanted to get the feel of things first."

"I understand," she answers. "I felt the same way my first time too. This is your first time, isn't it?"

"Yes, it is," he nods.

"My friend and I have been here three days now . . . so I guess you could consider us old-timers," she quips. At this point Rafer looks down at the tiny stack of chips in front of her. She follows his eyes. "True, we're not exactly breaking the bank. In fact, this is all we have left from the $3,000 we came with."

At this point, her companion tugs on her arm and shakes her head, a clear signal that she disapproves of being this open with a stranger. The short woman answers by turning her palms up as if to say "What's the harm?" She then turns back to Rafer and says, "By the way my name is Molly and my friend here is Elaine. What shall we call you?"

"Oh, I'm Rafer . . . or Rafe for short. Nice to meet you. You from the Midwest?"

"Shows in my voice, eh? That's O.K . . . other people have said the same thing. Yes, we're from Wisconsin . . . Madison. And you?"

"Boston. But there may be a trace of Tibetan in my accent (*smiling*)."

"Tibetan? Why Tibetan? You don't look Tibetan . . . not that I know what Tibetans look like."

As he gives a quick summary of his time in the Himalayas, he can't help noticing the scowl on Elaine's face. He cuts his story short and closes his eyes half-way again, readying himself for his first bet. He exhales slowly as the wheel, the table, and the people around it begin to slip into nothingness. The voices next to him are just barely audible.

"If we're going to catch the bus to the airport, we better leave in the next ten minutes," Elaine whispers to her friend.

"Well, not until we give it one final try," Molly answers. "I don't think I can face Mother without the money."

Elaine persists. "But you're never going to make it to $14,000 . . . not with the few hundred that we have left now. It is $14,000 that you need, isn't it?"

(*Sighing*) "Yes. That's what the hospital said. I asked them to check it twice . . . and they did. It's $14,000 if the surgery goes alright. If there are any complications, it could be more . . . a lot more."

As Rafer stares at the wheel, his eyes still half-closed, he can't help listening to the conversation next to him. Without turning his head, he follows every word. As he does so, an idea takes shape in his mind. Slowly, he drops to his knees and pretends to be fishing around for something. As the two women watch, he rises and hands a $500 chip to Molly. "You must have dropped this," he says. "It certainly isn't mine."

"Oh no," she replies as she prepares to hand it back. "I don't think we ever had any chips that large . . . have we, Elaine?"

"I don't remember," comes the laconic answer.

"Well, maybe the croupier dropped it . . . or possibly someone who played earlier and has since left," Rafer replies. "Anyway, it's yours." With that, he presses the chip into her hand and turns back to the wheel to make his first bet.

He starts by choosing a number at random . . . 18 . . . and places $100 on it and each of its four neighbors, two to the counterclockwise side (31 and 19), and two to the clockwise side (6 and 21). Breathing deeply, he turns his attention to the ball as it makes its way around the spinning wheel. As it slows down, approaching the five slots he has bet on, he intensifies his concentration. The energy begins filling his head until it hurts; he pushes it down to his solar plexus, then leaning forward, pours it out onto the ball, willing it to stop somewhere near 18.

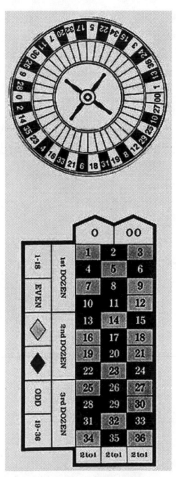

[*Illustration from Roulette, Wikipedia*]

"Number 21," barks the croupier as he rakes in the losers and prepares to pay off the winners. Rafer again feels a tug on his sleeve as the $3,500 from his bet on 18's nearby neighbor is pushed in front of him.

"Wow, Rafe. You did alright," Molly exclaims, releasing his sleeve. "You lost on four numbers but won big-time on the fifth. Where'd you ever come up that strategy? I read a lot about roulette before coming here but I never came across that one."

Rafer struggles to hold his excitement in check. "It's nothing new, except maybe the way I play it. The odds are clear. If you bet on five adjacent numbers, one of them should come up every seven spins of the wheel, just by chance. So if I win more than one time in seven, I'll be ahead. How about you? Do you have any particular strategy . . . or do you just go by instinct?"

"I don't know what I'm doing. I just huddle with Elaine here and we make a bet. We did alright on colors yesterday but lost it all last night when we got greedy and switched to individual numbers . . . (*pause*) . . . Maybe we should try your system."

"I think we should go back to colors," interjects Elaine. "I've noticed that red has come up the last three spins. So maybe it's time for black. It's worth a try . . . (*pause*) . . . If that doesn't work, let's get out of here before we miss our flight."

"I don't know," Molly replies. "What do you think Rafe? We only have a few hundred left . . . plus the $500 chip you found. Do you think we ought to stick with colors . . . or go all out like you just did and bet on the numbers?"

They continue talking while the croupier spins the wheel for another round of betting. "Well, if you need to leave here with $14,000, you're not going to make it playing conservatively . . . you know, by betting small amounts on either red or black. The only way you're going to go home with $14,000 is to play the numbers like I just did . . . (*pause*) . . .

Let me try my system a few more times . . . then if it works, I can let you play along."

"But how do you know which numbers to pick?," Elaine demands.

"We'll just have to take our chances," he replies. "Now, let me see what I can do first. While I'm experimenting, why don't you play a color or odd or even . . . just don't bet too much."

Unseen by her friend, Molly leans slightly to her right until she can feel Rafer's arm, then leaves it there hoping he won't withdraw. There's nothing romantic in her move . . . it just makes her feel safe, although if asked, she might find it hard to define the exact feeling. She watches him closely now as he places his bets on another cluster of five numbers. She is about to speak when she notices that his eyes are half-closed and he is staring intently at the wheel.

"What is he in a trance or something?," Elaine whispers as she too watches.

The croupier gives the wheel another spin. For the first few seconds it revolves too fast to identify the numbers. As it begins to slow down, however, a rough guess as to the area where it will land becomes possible. Standing as close as he is, Rafer can see that at its present speed the ball is probably going to stop short of the five slots he has chosen. There is no time to wait. Breathing all the energy he can muster into the ball, he forces it to speed up ever so slightly . . . until it lands just short of his target number but safely onto a neighbor, bringing cheers from a few of the other players who have been watching.

"You did it again," Molly shouts, quickly covering her mouth when she sees Rafer's frown. "You've made over $6,000 in the few minutes you've been here. I'm impressed. Can you tell us how you do it?"

"I'm still new at all this," he answers. "Give me a little more time." With that he prepares another set of five bets and closes his eyes halfway.

As the croupier shouts no more bets, he feels Molly's arm pressing against his own. He enjoys the warmth and begins wondering just what she is up to. His mind begins to wander. By the time he regains his concentration, the ball has already dropped into a slot. "Double Zero," cries the croupier as he rakes in everyone's bet.

"Oh," whispers Molly, "bummer."

"Yes," responds Rafer. "It's clear the system doesn't work every time . . . (*pause*) . . . but it might help if you didn't lean against me when the wheel is spinning. It interferes with my concentration."

"What's your concentration got to do with where the ball lands?," snaps Elaine.

Rafer smiles to cover his nervousness. "It's just an illusion I guess. Believing that I can control the ball helps me to stay motivated. It's like fans at a football game leaning to one side as a player races toward the goal line. They know it doesn't help but they do it anyway."

"You mean like trying to put English on something?," Molly asks.

"Yes. That's all it is. It's quite silly I know . . . but I still do it."

Far from prying eyes and ears, Rafer reprimands himself for even hinting at the truth behind his strategy. If even one person finds out, he reasons, the word will circle the table in a matter of minutes. Once the owners see what is happening, he'll be barred from playing not only here but at every other casino in Las Vegas. As he prepares for the next spin, he silently reaffirms his commitment to go it alone.

He asks Molly to give him one more chance to see if his "target-plus-neighbors" strategy is working. When he wins again, adding another $3,100 to his pile, he announces that he is ready.

"Shall I just put my bets on top of yours?," Molly asks.

"Not a good idea," Rafer explains, "since it's bound to attract attention. Other people might start doing the same thing which will really put the croupier on edge. It's better if I let you bet on the numbers while I stick to something simple like colors. O.K . . . before this next spin, I want you to put $100 each on 29, 8, 12, 25 and 10. I'll play black. Go ahead now. But please . . . don't talk to me or nudge against me while the wheel is spinning."

"I'm sorry. I won't do it again, I promise." Then, turning to her friend, she asks, "What do you think?"

Elaine hunches her shoulders. "Hey, it's found money, isn't it. What've we got to lose?"

Molly does as instructed and holds her breath as the croupier gives the wheel a spin. Rafer's trance-like stare goes unnoticed in the excitement of the moment. As the ball slows to a wobble, hanging precariously between 10 (a winner) and 27 (a loser), he gives a final grunt to force it into 10. The sound is quickly muffled by a shriek of joy from the woman next to him.

"We did it . . . we did it," she cries, tugging on his sleeve. "Oops . . . I didn't mean to do that . . . but we just made $3,100."

"That's O.K . . . tugs between spins are allowed. You need $14,000, right? So, we need four more wins like this one . . . that'll leave you a little for food and taxis on the way home."

"What makes you think you can win four more times?," Elaine asks, not bothering to conceal her peevishness. "I mean, isn't that kind of presumptuous? Or maybe you're a magician. I don't know. I just don't want to be part of something fishy that's going to get us in trouble."

"I don't expect to win four more times in a row, Elaine, but maybe we can spread it out over the afternoon."

"Spreading it out doesn't change anything," she answers. "There's still the question of what you're doing to get the ball to land on the right numbers. Nobody else here seems to be able to do it . . . so what are you doing that's different? That's what bothers . . . ."

Molly (*interrupting*): "Elaine, for crying out loud. What do you want? Rafer is being nice to us . . . he found us some money and is helping us to win more. Who cares how he does it?"

Over the next hour, Rafer mixes his own bets with an occasional bet from Molly. Both players do well, so well in fact that other patrons around the table begin to imitate them. Rafer senses trouble and turns to Molly, "How much do you have now?"

Molly quickly counts her chips and whispers, "About $11,500."

"O.K. Let's go for one more . . . and then call it quits before the alarms go off and they kick us out of here."

On the ensuing spin, Rafer tells her to place $100 each on 0, 9, 28, 2, and 14. By now his skill has improved to the point where he is hitting the target more often than the four neighbors. When the croupier announces 0 as the winner, a gasp goes up around the table as the last of the skeptics caves in and vows to follow Rafer's lead. Sensing the change, Rafer wisely gathers up his chips and prepares to leave. Molly and Elaine are right behind as he heads for the cashier's window.

"You have enough now . . . you know, for your mother's operation?," he asks, turning to Molly.

"More than enough, thanks to you," she beams. "I intend to tell Mother all about you. She'll probably want to write you a letter . . . she's good at that."

"You better get his address, then," adds Elaine.

"Oh sure," responds Rafer, reaching for a pen in his breast pocket. "Do either of you have a pad of paper?"

Molly hands him a small notepad where he can write down his address. With that bit of business finished and time to say goodbye, Molly turns to him with arms outstretched. "A little hug?"

"Why only a little one?," he answers, holding her tight. "Goodbye to you too, Elaine."

Once his own chips are cashed, Rafer waves a final farewell, crosses the floor and vanishes into the street. "Thirty two thousand in one afternoon," he muses, patting the check in his suit coat pocket. "And that's with no more than 30 or 40 spins of the wheel, some of which I let Molly play for me. If I'm willing to stand there all afternoon and evening and play strictly for myself, I can probably make five or ten times that much. That's assuming that nobody catches onto my method. But how could they? There's no way to know that I'm controlling the speed of the ball with my mind. At best they may notice that I'm watching the wheel carefully . . . but most players do that anyway. And if I bend one way or the other as the ball comes to a stop, they'll just see that I'm trying to put some English on it. (*Smiling*) Of course, that's what I'm doing . . . isn't it?"

Back in his room, he stretches out on the bed. Within minutes a feeling of deep peace returns and with it memories of Molly and her friend. Eyes closed now, the image of the two women gradually gives way to thoughts of dinner and a glass of wine, hardly too much to ask, he muses, after an afternoon of strenuous mental activity. The craving is momentary. Within seconds all thoughts of wine and dinner are pushed aside by the reminder that success here depends on maintaining an absolutely crisp, clear state of mind. If he is to succeed in this venture, it is essential to avoid things like wine, sex, or talking to people back home . . . anything that might undermine his power of concentration. With that reminder ringing in his ears, he returns to meditating and is soon lost in the selfless, wordless world of unbounded, empty space.

In the morning he walks up and down the Strip for two hours before deciding which casino to play. He stops to ask a passerby for information and is told that Bally's is only a block beyond Mirage where he spent yesterday afternoon. As he heads for Bally's, he suddenly gets the urge to peek in at Mirage again just to see if they are open this early and, if so, to find out if anyone is playing roulette. Once inside, he is astonished to see Molly and Elaine at one of the roulette tables. "I thought you were on your way to Chicago," he exclaims.

"Well," replies Molly, her face reddening, "our new flight isn't until 3:10 this afternoon so we decided to play a little more since we did so well yesterday."

"So, how are you doing?," Rafer asks.

Elaine shakes her head but remains silent. "We keep trying your system," Molly reports, "but we keep losing . . . five times in a row now."

"So, how much do you have left?," Rafer asks, struggling to contain his frustration.

Molly (*opening her purse and counting*): "Hmm . . . after paying our hotel bill and losing some this morning, we're down to a little over $12,000."

Rafer tinkers with a scolding reply, then settles for an understanding nod of his head.

"Will you stay?," Molly asks softly. "You seem to bring us good luck."

Rafer agrees on condition that if they can their holdings back up to $14,000, they will leave immediately, go get their luggage and take a taxi to the airport. Before they can reply to his offer, he adds that to make sure they leave this time, he will accompany them to the terminal and see them off. Elaine snaps back, "We're not children, you know." Rafer looks to Molly for a definitive answer; hearing none, he turns to leave. Casting a scowl at her friend, Molly grabs him by the sleeve and pulls him back. "We agree. Unconditionally. Just help us. Please, Rafe."

Over the next several hours they manage to get the total back to slightly over $14,000 at which point Rafer says it's time to go. Reluctantly the women leave the casino and head upstairs to their hotel room to get their bags. He accompanies them all the way to the airport, waiting until the plane is in the air before returning to the city. It is now 4:45 in the afternoon and time once again to head for Bally's. Once inside the casino, he stops to survey the surrounding glitter: blinking lights just inside the door, white lights overhead everywhere, arrow-shaped lights long the floor, blue, green and pink lights adorning the walls, neon lights flashing from the slot machines . . . in all, an array of glitz trumpeting the casino's commitment to "excitement." Rafer whispers an epithet to himself, then walks over to the nearest roulette table. Wedging his way into the throng and taking a place next to the croupier, he quickly slips into a meditative trance. Finally he is alone, a stranger to everyone around him. He has one last thought before the table, wheel and players all begin to dissolve into emptiness: it's time to get serious.

10

Eva

This time he plays non-stop until 11:30 P.M. By the time he is ready to leave, a cursory glance at his pile of chips tells him he has won somewhere between $70,000 and $80,000. While he is tempted to stay for another half hour and accumulate another $10,000, his fear of attracting too much attention cautions otherwise. Throughout the evening he has watched the croupier carefully, alert to any sign that he might becoming suspicious. Even though his skill at controlling the ball has improved to the point where he is able to win almost every other time, he deliberately loses on every third or fourth spin of the wheel. To lose he simply picks a random target number and places bets on it plus four adjacent numbers . . . and then lets the wheel spin without any attempt to control the movement of the ball. To further disguise his strategy, he stands exactly the same way whether he is trying to win or lose . . . that is, with eyes half-closed and looking down at the wheel. To an outsider, there's no observable difference between the times he wins and the times he loses. The fact that he wins more often than he loses appears to be a matter of luck and nothing more. Or so he hopes.

By 11:30 he is tired. Concentrating so hard for the better part of the evening requires lots of energy, especially when much of that energy is spent controlling the movement of something several feet away. With this in mind, he gathers up his chips, leaves a tip for the croupier and cashes out at the teller's window. He opts to have a check for the full amount ($74,320) deposited directly into his brokerage account back in Boston. Pleased with the way things are going so far, he heads for the restaurant upstairs and a much deserved glass of wine. By the time the waiter comes to take his order, however, certain doubts are arising. Most worrisome is the possibility that even a small amount of alcohol will undermine his concentration and interfere with his ability to control the speed of the ball. Unwilling to take a chance, he goes for iced tea and the day's special . . . pesto pasta with chicken.

Totally absorbed in the aromas and tastes of his late-night dinner, he fails to see a woman approaching on the left. Her voice is soft and cultured as she whispers a non-intrusive, "Good evening." He turns to see a tall, statuesque woman whose blonde curls enclose a beautifully proportioned head tilted now in a questioning smile. Her eyebrows are long and dark; the yellow of her hair standing in carefully modulated contrast to the black of her evening dress.

Rafer puts his fork down and turns to face her. He is aware immediately that he has seen her before at the roulette table . . . too far away at the time and of too little importance to attract his attention. "Hello," he replies. "Do we know each other?"

"No we don't. I'm Eva, Eva Nourini. I was about to sit down and have something to eat when I noticed you here by yourself. Since we're the only people in the restaurant, I wondered if you would like some company. If you don't, I won't be hurt. I like my privacy sometimes too."

"Well, I'm not exactly lonely, but I don't see any harm in it. I'm Rafer Alexander. People call me Rafe."

As she sits and calls the waiter over, he has a chance to study her. Once he has come to terms with her graceful beauty, he moves quickly to the question of motivation. She must be aware that he made a lot of money at the table today. Is she hoping to share in the spoils? But how? The thought of his $74,320 check making its way to his brokerage account in Boston brings a relaxed smile to his lips. He is aware, however, that in his breast pocket he's still carrying ample cash from the previous day's play. He resolves to be cautious . . . friendly but not overly so . . . then head back to his boarding house for a good night's sleep before shifting to another casino tomorrow.

They begin with the usual things . . . where are you from, what do you do for a living, any family, how long to you intend to stay . . . all of which leaves him with a concrete picture of who she is. Thanks to a combination of his persistent questions and her unself-conscious openness, he knows her to be widowed ever since her husband of six years, a man called Raymond, met his grisly end in an auto accident last year just outside the casino. He also knows that the same man, now deceased, was a professional gambler who supported the two of them on his winnings at the roulette table. For most of their married years she accompanied him to the casino, standing by his side and cheering him on when he won and consoling him when he lost. Now that she is alone, she continues to come, not to play since she has no money of her own, but out of habit . . . and, by her own candid admission, not having anything better to do.

After he shares with her a sketchy outline of his tragedy in the Himalayas and his equally disastrous experience at Kidder-Homans, he braces himself for the questions to come.

"So, do you think you can make enough money out here to compensate your friends for their losses? From what you say, it sounds like they lost a lot of money."

"True enough. I've got an uphill battle if I hope to win it all back."

Eva persists, but cautiously. "From where I stood over on the other side of the table, it looks like you did alright today. In fact in all the years I have been coming here, I have never seen anyone make as much money in a single evening as you did. I'm curious."

Her words feel intrusive, even threatening. He returns to his pasta without answering. Is this what she's after, he muses. Is this why she followed me here and asked to join me for dinner?

She is aware of the impact her last question is having and moves quickly to repair the damage."

"So, what are you planning to do tomorrow . . . more roulette?"

"Perhaps . . . or I may walk around and see a little more of the town . . . at least in the morning."

"Well, if you need a guide," she replies softly. "I'm at your service. I've lived here for most of my life and know just about everything there is to know about the place. We could walk or take my car . . . whichever suits you best."

Her offer is intriguing. Without answering, he continues eating while letting the idea swirl around in his head. What nicer way to spend a morning than to walk around the city with a beautiful woman who happens to be a native of the area? But is this a trap? She knows that I made a lot of money today; it only makes sense that she's looking to get a chunk of it for herself. Or is she hoping that I'll reveal my strategy and help her to get back on her feet financially? There's certainly danger here. But what's worse is that I might become attracted to her and lose my ability to concentrate. If that happens, the jig is up . . . the whole trip will be wasted and I'll end up feeling guilty all over again.

As he eats, Eva watches him carefully, trying desperately to decode the drawn look on his face. After all, this could be her meal ticket . . . a good-looking man roughly her own age, a man with a non-aggressive personality yet a boldness when it comes to making money and, thus far anyway, no hint of another relationship. As they finish their meal and head for the door, she takes a deep breath and makes her move. "Well, what about tomorrow? I can meet you anywhere."

Rafer hesitates. "Ah, I guess a walk together around town won't hurt. That'll leave the afternoon and evening for roulette. Why don't you meet me here around 9:00."

As soon as she is inside the door, Eva takes off her shoes and tip-toes into the living room. Slumping into the recliner, she lets her thoughts return to Bally's and the events of the last few hours. Her reverie is broken when the bedroom door opens and her mother appears, pulling her bathrobe tight around her waist. "Well, you're home kinda late aren't ya. It's almost 1:00 in the mornin. I hope nothing bad happened at the casino. Did it?" Without looking down, she reaches for the cigarettes on the coffee table, pulls one out and lights up. "Tell me."

For Eva, her mother's appearance stands in sharp and unflattering contrast to the glitter of Bally's, serving to remind her of how modest her own upbringing has been. Partly it's the language, partly the robe and cigarettes. It doesn't help that her mother's face resembles an apple left too long on a tree, its skin loosening, its color fading, its flesh pocked by holes where birds have dug out its fermenting juices. More than anything, it's the false teeth and the way her mouth caves in when she tries talking without them, as is the case early in the morning and late at night. Looking at her now, Eva's eyes are drawn to the area between her upper lip and her nose where the flesh is drawn into tiny rivulets, leaving a washboard of gray wrinkles. Eva knows her to be in her late fifties but, if pressed, would be forced to admit she looks closer to 80 or even 90. The raspy voice, toughened by years of smoking, simply reinforces the impression of old age.

"Well," comes the voice again, forcing its way up through a filter of smoke. "Aren't you goin to tell me?"

"I met a man at the restaurant in Bally's," Eva begins slowly, "a very nice man. I noticed him earlier in the casino where he was making lots of money and . . . ."

"Hey, wait a minute. I want to hear this." Eva sighs as Jack, her step-father, emerges from the bedroom, rubbing his eyes and stretching a bathrobe to cover his toad-size paunch. "Aggie, give me one of those," he says, looking over at the cigarettes on the coffee table. Agnes pulls one from the pack, lights it, and hands it to her husband. Once it is safely in his mouth, he heads to the china cabinet in the corner and pours himself a glass of wine from the decanter. "Anybody else want a drink?," he asks. Silence. "So, Eva," he continues, "you met this guy at the casino and then what happened?"

"Well, not an awful lot. I followed him upstairs to the restaurant where he invited me to join him for dinner. Well, it was actually my suggestion. He just went along with it. So, I sat down and . . . ."

"You mean the guy waited for you to suggest it," cries Jack, taking a seat on the couch next to his wife. "I don't get it. Here he's got all this dough in his pocket and this beautiful babe comes along . . . and he . . . what . . . just sits there? What's wrong with him?"

Eva sighs. "I'm not sure there's anything wrong with him, Jack. He's just not the aggressive type. But we're going for a walk tomorrow morning . . . so I should learn more about him then."

"What about the money?," Jack persists. "You said he made a killing at the table. So, how'd he do it? Was he playin colors or odd vs. even . . . or just numbers?"

"Just numbers."

"Well, was he using some kind of system? I mean . . . was he writing things down on a notepad . . . you know., keeping track of the numbers that come up."

"I didn't notice any notepad," Eva replies, not bothering to conceal her boredom. "The only thing unusual about him was the way he stood looking at the wheel while it was spinning. His eyes seemed to be half-closed and he never moved or talked to anyone until the ball landed. I have no idea what was going on."

"You didn't ask him while you were having dinner together?," Jack asks, incredulous at this lost opportunity. "Maybe he's got some kind of system that he'd share with us. I know most of the old techniques but maybe he's got a new one."

Agnes (*rising*): "Jack, why don't you go back to bed, honey. I want to talk to Evie alone."

Jack makes his way slowly to the bedroom, turning several times to see what is happening. At the door he hears Agnes suggest to Eva that she "wear something interesting tomorrow, like one of your short skirts and that low-cut peasant top that shows off your bosom so well." "Yeah, he whispers from the doorway, "get the guy into bed if you can. And if you need a little warming up beforehand, just give me a ring. I'm available."

"Watch your tongue," retorts Agnes with a snap of her head. "She's your step-daughter for God's sake." Turning to Eva, "I'm sorry, honey. Don't mind him. It's just talk."

In the morning Eva puts on a long plaid skirt that opens seductively all the way to the thighs. To this she adds a beige cashmere top that, when pulled tight, reveals the outline of her ample, braless breasts. At the full-length mirror in the hallway she smoothes her skirt and runs her hands across her chest. Her nipples respond by hardening. Smiling, she turns sideways to see if they can be seen under the cashmere. They can. Comfortable in the knowledge that she is attractive, she opens the door and heads for the casino.

Rafer is already there waiting for her. "Hope I'm not late," she says, offering a delicious smile. "I don't think so," he replies. "I'm not wearing a watch so I really don't know the time." Eva holds up her wrist and announces that it's 9:12. "Did you get something to eat?," she adds. "If not, there's a favorite bakery of mine that has the best apple-cinnamon muffins on the planet . . . plus great espresso if you're into that kind of thing." "I'm basically a tea man," he answers apologetically. "But the muffins sound interesting. Maybe later after we've worked up a little appetite."

As they walk down one street and up the other, the questions flow back and forth like they would for any two people getting to know each other. But all is not well for Rafer. He quickly becomes aware that all this talking is taking its toll on his ability to concentrate. He knows that if he were alone, he could look at the surrounding houses and stores without burdening his mind with trivial inner chatter. Just as he did the previous morning, he could look at something, a building perhaps, then silently bore into it until he could see the empty space embedded within. "I can't do it with her here," he muses. "When I have to listen to someone else, my mind fills up with thoughts and I can no longer see the space inside . . . (pause) . . . It's also true that I enjoy being with her."

Eva senses his ambivalence and asks, "Would you rather be alone, Rafer? If you want, I can leave you here. We can always get together later in the day."

Rafer is stunned by her offer. This is exactly what he would like but to say yes to her proposal strikes him as impolite, even unkind. Although they hardly know each other, he reflects, she doesn't deserve to have her feelings hurt. "That's a possibility," he says, eager to avoid a direct answer.

Eva interprets his response as a yes and turns to go. "Are you going back to Bally's this afternoon?," she asks before leaving. "Probably not," he replies. "I like to keep moving. Maybe Excalibur today. They've never seen me before." Eva pauses, then fluffs her hair before responding, "Is it O.K. if I join you there?" "Of course," he replies with a conviction that belies his uncertainty. Before parting, he makes a move to shake hands . . . and then, sensing the absurdity of the act, withdraws his arm and turns to go. "Hasta luego," she calls out. "Ah, you know Spanish," he says. "Just a little" comes the reply. "Same here," he adds. With that, he is gone.

They meet again at the Excalibur, just after lunch. By the time Eva arrives, Rafer is already at the table with a stack of chips in front of him. They nod discreetly to each other as she wiggles in beside him. "How you doing?," she whispers as the croupier gets ready to spin the wheel. "O.K.," he answers, pointing to his chips. "But look, Eva," he quickly adds, "I have to concentrate on what I'm doing. If you want to stand here, that's O.K. but please don't talk to me or nudge against me. It interferes with where I'm aiming."

She nods an O.K. as the croupier gives the wheel a spin and the ball goes whirling around. In the ensuing silence his words come back to her. "Aiming, he said. What in the world does he mean by aiming?" With her curiosity aroused, she turns to watch his movements more closely, determined to find out what allows him to win so consistently. Spin after spin, she says nothing, just watching and waiting. She sees only what everybody else sees, a man staring at the wheel with his eyes half-closed, not moving until the ball lands in one of the slots. Like the others, she also sees his pile of chips growing so fast that he is forced to make multiple trips to the cashier's window where his winnings are converted to a series of credit slips. Despite audible whispering around the table, no one seems able to figure out what he is doing. As his chips pile up, some of the other players begin waiting for him to place his bets before putting their own on top of his. To avoid playing host to a swarm of imitators, Rafer deliberately loses four, five, even six times in a row . . . until the others get tired or losing and start placing their bets elsewhere.

At 6:30, Rafer turns to Eva and asks if she's ready for something to eat. "I thought you'd never ask," she sputters, anxious to sit down and have a little conversation. At dinner Rafer shows no interest in continuing the friendly back and forth of their walk in the morning. A huge salad of Boston lettuce, broccoli, cauliflower, tomatoes, carrots and bacon bits is the sole object of his attention. She orders a plate of cold cuts but finds the meats tasteless. After eating in nearly total silence, they return to the roulette table where Rafer continues his winning ways, unwilling to finish until he has run up a total of $94,000. It is close to midnight again when they finally leave the casino and head for their respective homes.

When Eva enters the house, her mother and Jack are on the couch waiting for her. The living room air is thick with cigarette smoke; Jack is nursing a glass of red wine while Mother sips a Coke. She has her teeth in, a sure sign she wants to talk.

Without waiting for a greeting, Jack asks, "So, how much do you think he made today?"

Waving the smoke from her nose, Eva answers, "I would guess almost $100,000."

Jack leaps up from the couch. "Jesus Christ, Eva. Nobody ever makes that much in one day. And he won yesterday too, didn't he?"

"And the day before that too. I think he hopes to make $1,000,000 before he goes home."

"My goodness," sighs Agnes. "He's starting to sound like Superman... or maybe he's the Antichrist that people talk about."

Eva squints. "The what?"

"The Antichrist," Jack interrupts. "You know the guy sent to earth by the Devil to destroy mankind so Jesus can return and start all over from scratch. She got the idea from her brother . . . yes Petey, your uncle back in Boston."

Agnes: "I was only kidding."

Jack: "Like hell you were."

Agnes: "All I meant was that he's got some of the same features . . . you say he's very good-looking, smart . . . ."

Eva (*interrupting*): "Smart enough to get a Ph.D. from Harvard."

Agnes nods. "So. Maybe I'm not so far off. Smart, educated, and able to perform miracles at the roulette table. He certainly doesn't sound like your run of the mill gambler."

"But that hardly makes him a Superman," Jack rejoins. "For Christ's sake, Aggie, use your head. This Antichrist guy Petey talks about is no mere human being; he's supposed to be related to the Devil . . . he may even be the Devil himself. And he's coming to blow us all to Kingdomcome. Does this sound like the guy Eva just met? C'mon. If he really is the Devil, why would he bother to come to Las Vegas of all places? And why is he coming now and not a thousand years from now? It doesn't make any sense."

Agnes: "Well, they say he's supposed to come when things get real bad . . . and that could be now."

Jack: "Who says?"

Agnes: "The Christians. It's all in the Bible they say. I've never read it myself but Petey says it's in both the new and old testaments."

Jack (*sitting back down*): "Pardon my French, ladies, but that's a bunch of horseshit. Come to your senses gal. There ain't no such thing as a devil and this kid Rafer is just a regular human being who happened to get real lucky. The rest is baloney. I'll bet you anything he loses everything tomorrow."

For Rafer, tomorrow turns out to be his best day so far. The setting is the posh Flamingo. With Eva once again at his side, he slips into a routine which by now has become second nature. The routine involves picking a target number, placing $100 bets on the target plus each of the four adjacent numbers, two on each side, then slipping into a trance and using psychic energy to control the movement of the ball. Hour after hour he plies his trade with such skill that the only danger lies in winning so often that he becomes suspected of chicanery and is asked to leave. Clearly aware of this possibility, he balances his winnings with enough losses to divert attention and leave the impression that it is all a matter of luck. When his stomach begins to rumble, signaling time for dinner, he quickly counts his chips before stuffing them into his pocket and heading for the cashier's window. Silently, Eva counts along with him . . . $73,000 minus the $10,000 he started with . . . or a profit of $63,000 . . . all in one afternoon.

As they head out of the casino, she asks, "Would you like some company at dinner or do you prefer to eat alone?" The soft, beseeching sound of her voice masks a fear that her presence may be once again unneeded. She is thus delighted when he responds, "Let's get something together. I think we both need a break." When she reaches to take his hand, he pulls back quickly and moves away. Struggling to hide her disappointment, she turns to him, smiling, "I know you like pasta . . . and there's a really good Italian restaurant just two blocks from here." "Sounds good to me," he answers. "Let's go."

During dinner Eva is careful not to get chatty, much as she would like to. Instead she waits for him to talk . . . which happens only sporadically. For the most part he is fully absorbed in eating, an occasional murmur constituting the sole evidence that the meal is to his liking. And yet, despite his reticence, she is aware of a growing warmth between them, a warmth that shows itself less in words than in the way he looks at her. If she were asked to describe the feeling, she might say it feels like she is being caressed. It is enough to stir her heart. Each time it happens, she returns his gaze with a caress of her own.

After dinner they return to the casino and resume betting. There's a difference now. For the first time, he hands her a bunch of $100 chips and suggests that she place some bets of her own, the only stipulation being that she should avoid imitating what he does. However, he goes so far as to tell her to look first each time to see what target number he has chosen for the centerpiece of his five-number spread. "Check the color," he says, "and then place a bet on red or black. Or you can play a column or row that includes that target number . . . just don't put a chip on top of mine." She does as she is told. Her very first bet is a winner . . . followed by two more. As the evening wears on, her modest pile begins to grow, as does his.

As Rafer prepares to make one of his deliberately losing bets, he turns to her and whispers, "I'm probably going to lose this time, so don't pay any attention to the target number. Place your bet anywhere you want to." She bets on black and loses, then turns to him, smiling, "I don't do very well on my own, do I." Whether deliberately or not, he refuses to answer and heads back into a trance. They remain playing for the next four hours until the croupier announces that it is time for the "last three bets." At that point Rafer turns to Eva and suggests that she double up on her wagers. Over the next three spins she places $200 on black, then red, and the last one on even. All three turn up winners. By the time they prepare to leave, she has a total of $1,900. "This is your money," she says, pushing the pile in his direction.

"Oh no," he protests, "you earned it."

"That's really kind of you Rafer. I can certainly use the money but let me at least pay you back the chips you gave me to begin with."

"Not on your life. Think of it as payment for your services as my guide these last few days. I've learned a lot about Las Vegas thanks to you."

"Thank you. So, how much did you make today . . . afternoon plus evening?"

"It's been my best day so far . . . I can't be sure until we cash out but I think it's somewhere around $120,000."

"Wow. You've already made enough to pay back the people who took your advice, haven't you?"

"Not quite . . . and I still have to replenish my own account. And then there's the matter of taxes. So, I still have a ways to go."

Out on the street, they gulp the fresh air and prepare to separate. Neither one makes a move to leave. "I'm not ready for sleep yet, are you?," she asks.

"Not exactly. It usually takes me a while to settle down after all that tension."

"I suppose we could get a drink somewhere," she says, being careful to mask the seriousness of her desire with a look of nonchalance.

As she waits for a yes or no, Rafer mulls over the idea, then, much to her surprise, replies, "I have a little refrigerator in my room at the boardinghouse. It's stocked with beer, wine and soda . . . if any of that sounds appealing to you."

"That's a lovely idea, Rafe. Sounds very relaxing . . . a perfect way to end an exciting day."

11

The Next Morning

The sun is already high in the sky and warm on her back as she stands outside the door, readying herself for the deluge of questions to come. Once inside she is greeted by her mother and Jack, both still in their bathrobes, Jack with wine glass in hand, Agnes smoking a cigarette. Agnes is the first to speak. "Why didn't you at least call? We stayed up half the night waiting for you."

Eva heads for the bathroom, turning at the last minute to say, "I'm sorry. I thought you'd be in bed by the time Rafer asked me to stay. I didn't want to wake you." With that she disappears inside. Agnes, still without her teeth, continues to pepper her with questions from outside the door. "But you didn't even have a change of clothes. Why didn't you come home first to get your nightie and other things?" From inside the bathroom Eva answers, "Because it was raining . . . raining real hard. Didn't you hear it on the roof?"

Once she has the water running, Eva can no longer hear her mother's questions. Outside in the living room, Jack begins to pace like a caged tiger. Agnes remains standing, her eyes focused on the door handle as she rehearses the questions that have kept her awake all night.

When Eva finally appears, Jack is the first to speak. "Did you sleep with him?"

"We slept in the same bed, yes."

"That's not what I meant," he fires back.

Eva (*raising her voice*): "What we did or did not do in bed is none of your business."

"But what did you wear," asks mother. "You didn't sleep in these clothes, did you?"

"Rafer was kind enough to give me one of his t-shirts. I slept in my panties."

"Were they the sexy, orange ones?," Jack inquires, not bothering to conceal the grin on his puffy face.

Agnes snaps, "And how do you know what color panties Eva wears?"

"For Christ's sake," he bellows. "When you live in the same house, you get to know all kinds of things. What's the big deal?"

Agnes (*turning to her daughter*): "Did he make a lot of money again, honey?"

Eva: "Over $100,000. He also gave me some chips to play with . . . and I made $1,900.

Jack: "Another $100,000 . . . my God! How the hell is he doing it? It's gotta be some kind of mental thing . . . like when he's in a trance he can see the number that's comin up next."

Eva: "But if he knows what number is coming up next, why would he close his eyes and stay so quiet while the ball is spinning? And why would he tell me not to talk to him or even touch him until the ball stops? If he's sure what number is going to win, you'd think he would just sit back and relax."

Jack: "But what else is it if it's not mental?"

Eva sits down in a chair opposite the couch. "I'm not sure if this is part of it but other players seemed to press in around us . . . to the point where they would sometimes try to touch Rafer."

"And he didn't like it, right?," Jack replies.

Eva nods. "True. I thought at first they pressed in because he was winning and they just wanted to be close . . . like people try to touch football players or basketball players after a game. But when I checked my own feelings, I realized that it was more than that. My guess is that they felt the same kind of peace I got from standing next to him. When you're right next to him, you can actually feel the vibrations coming from him . . . I don't know if that's the right word . . . but it's really peaceful . . . and . . . ."

Jack (*interrupting*): "Of course. I get the same kind of feeling after a second or third drink. You stop worrying about things . . . your mind slows down and you feel relaxed."

Eva (*shaking her head*): "Not really. I know what you're talking about but what I felt at the casino was different than that. A few glasses of wine gives you a relaxed, laid back kind of feeling where nothing really bothers you anymore, but I wouldn't describe this kind of peace as 'laid back.' When I was standing next to Rafer, I was wide awake, alert . . . while everything inside me was quiet, yet solid, so solid that nothing could knock me over, no matter how hard it tried. It was a strong kind of feeling, not mellow."

Agnes: "You mean confident, ready to take on the world?"

Eva pauses. "Not exactly, Mom. There didn't seem to be anything personal in it . . . just this feeling that no matter what happened I couldn't be toppled over. I was powerful . . . not in the sense that I could get my way no matter what . . . but unshakeable in a quiet kind of way. Sort of like a tree with deep roots. No matter how hard the wind blows, it can't be knocked over. It was that kind of peace . . .

(pause) . . . I can't be sure but maybe the players who pressed against Rafe felt the same thing."

Jack *(chuckling)*: Rafe? Is that what you call him now?"

Eva: *(scowling)*: "That's what he said his friends call him."

Agnes: "So you think he had something to do with how you felt, that somehow he made you feel that way?"

Eva: "Something like that. It was wonderful. Once that feeling started, I didn't mind standing there for hours."

Jack *(grinning)*: "Well, you probably didn't mind making $1,900 either . . . or am I wrong?"

It is at that point that Agnes goes into the bedroom to get her teeth. When she returns she tells Jack she wants to talk to her daughter alone. Jack frowns, goes to the cabinet for another glass of wine, then disappears into the bedroom.

Agnes pats the seat next to her on the couch. "Come over here and tell me what happened last night, honey. Was it good? I'm worried about you."

"There's really not much to tell, Mom. We each had a drink . . . he usually drinks tea . . . and then got into bed. Almost immediately he sat up, pulled a pillow under him, crossed his legs and began meditating."

"Didn't he say anything . . . like goodnight?"

"Well, yes. He did say that much."

"But no kiss?"

"No."

"Well, what did you do?"

"I just lay there for about an hour, waiting for him to stop meditating . . . but he never did. Or at least he didn't stop while I was awake. After an hour I got so tired I couldn't keep my eyes open. The next thing I knew it was morning and I could hear him taking a shower."

Jack, who was listening at the bedroom door, peeks out long enough to say, "Did you ever consider that he might be gay? Any guy who chooses to meditate while he's got a gorgeous blonde lying next to him has got to be queer. Think about it."

Agnes snuffs out her cigarette and puts her arms around Eva's shoulders. "He's right, honey. Don't go blaming yourself. He's probably a homosexual."

Eva (*fighting back the tears*): "I don't know, Mom. He's awfully nice. Maybe I'm just not his type."

As agreed, Eva and Rafer meet at the Tropicana Casino the next day at noon. He seems happy to see her although no mention is made of last night. The surprise comes when he announces that he has moved his belongings into the Marriott Hotel up the street. "The boardinghouse was a bit small," he adds, "and not as private as one might like." As she waits for him to finish, her stomach tightens. "There's room there for both of us, if that's something you would like. It's only for a few more days . . . I'll probably be leaving sometime next week."

The joy she feels at his invitation evaporates quickly at the mention of his leaving. "Next week? Why so soon," she asks, trying desperately to hide the trembling. Rafer pauses before replying, "Well, I can't say for sure, but at the rate I'm going now, I should have all the money I need by then. Anything can happen, of course, so I'm not ready to schedule a flight."

"And where would you go . . . back to Boston?"

"I'm really not sure. Technically I'm on a leave of absence from my job at Kidder-Homans, but I'm not sure I want to go back there. If I can keep making money here the rest of the week, I should have enough to do just about anything I want."

(*Softly*) "Do you have anything specific in mind?"

"Not really. All I'm sure of is that I want to do more in the future than advise people about the economy. Beyond that my mind is a blank."

"Did what happened on Wall St. change everything for you? It sounds like you were pretty excited about your job a few months ago."

They enter the Casino and begin looking around. Just inside the door, Eva stops and takes him by the arm, "I asked you a question," she says, her voice showing the first signs of frustration. Rafer puts his hand on top of hers, "The stock market was certainly part of it but there were probably other things . . . ."

"Like losing your family . . . that must have been hard to deal with."

"That too . . . although I think it's what came afterwards that forced me to re-examine my goals."

"You mean the meditation?"

"Yes."

When the conversation ends, they move over to the roulette table and begin placing bets. Rafer buys $10,000 worth of chips from the croupier, then pushes five $100 chips over to Eva. When she squeezes his hand in appreciation, he nods but says nothing. By mid-afternoon he is well on his way to his goal of making $100,000. She too is doing well, having tripled her original outlay by betting on whatever color matches his target number. It is around that time that a new player squeezes in next to them and begins betting. He is unusual not only for his white hair and bent figure, but for the palsy in his hands that starts whenever he places a chip on one of the numbers. After struggling with the first few bets, he settles for an alternative strategy in which he calls out a number to the croupier who then rakes a chip from his pile and places it accordingly. This works for several spins until his voice gives out and the croupier can no longer hear him. He gets particularly upset when he tries to call out a number but cannot be heard over the buzz of the crowd . . . and is then forced to watch as the ball falls into the very slot he named . . . thereby denying him the $350 he should have won on his $10 bet.

From his place next to the old man, Rafer watches as the scene unfolds. With the memory of Molly and her friend still fresh in his mind, he leans over and pretends to pick up a chip from the floor. Handing it to the old man, he says, "This must be yours. You should take better care of your chips." The man looks at the chip carefully and replies, "Thank ya but I never did have a $500 chip. That's too rich for my blood. Must belong to the lady on your right." With that he hands the chip back to Rafer and gets ready to make another bet.

As Rafer and the old man resume their betting, Eva announces that she's heading home to get some of her things for the night. "I should be back in an hour or so." Whispering, she adds, "Too bad about the old man. I've seen cases like that before at the hospital where I used to volunteer. They only get worse."

"Parkinsons?," he asks.

"Probably." And with that she is gone.

By the time she returns with her luggage it is after 5:00 and time to start thinking about dinner. In her absence Rafer's pile has grown to such an embarrassing extreme that he has begun placing chips in his pockets rather than leaving them on the table for everyone to see. The old man with palsy continues to bet but with little success. When he can no longer stand, he calls for a chair and pulls it as close to the table as possible. Rafer offers to place his bets for him but is told, "I ain't a goner yet, sonny. You jis pay heed to yir own bets and I'll do the same." His response brings a smile to Rafer's lips. "O.K . . . but if you change your mind, just let me know. I'll be glad to help."

With that conversation ended, Rafer turns to Eva and whispers something in her ear. Having received the response he wanted, he then turns back to the old man and offers a surprise suggestion, "How about joining the two of us for a little dinner? We're going to a restaurant that serves the best chicken cacciatore you've ever had. Would you like to come?"

He turns to face Rafer, his hand in the air shaking. "Well, why the hell not. That's nice of ya. Just let me make one more bet here . . . and I'll be right with ya. But I'm goin to pay for ma own meal . . . ya better get that straight."

"That's fine," replies Rafer, adding, "I'd go with number 2 if I were you. I think it's due."

The old man stares for a second or two, then turns to the croupier and holds up two fingers. With the bet successfully placed, he leans over to watch. On his right, Rafer closes his eyes half-way and slowly brings his mind into focus. His target . . . number 2.

"Number two," announces the croupier as the ball comes to a stop. "Nicely done," Rafer whispers from his side. "Let's cash out now and go get some food. I'm hungry." The old man smiles and holds out his hand for a shake . . . then, clenching his teeth, pulls it back and stuffs it into his coat pocket.

At the restaurant Rafer and Eva take seats on one side of the booth leaving the other for their guest who introduces himself as Donnie Lambert from Cattle Creek, Wyoming. They chat for a few minutes, mostly about the casino, until the waiter comes to take their orders. All three order the chicken cacciatore. Drinks are served, Eva and Donnie opting for wine while Rafer sticks with his usual tea. Up to this point there is nothing unusual about their guest whose hands remain for the most part out of sight on his lap. This changes dramatically the minute he goes to lift his wine glass. Eva instinctively reaches out to hold the glass for him while he sips. As she does so, he knocks her hand away, spilling most of the contents in the process. A quick call to the waiter brings a sponge and a new table cloth. "Shall I get you a refill," the waiter asks as he settles the glasses onto the new cloth. "I'm O.K., growls Donnie. "I drank most of it anyway."

Once the waiter has left and the three are alone again, Rafer asks, "How long have you had the problem with your hand?" Donnie scowls, debating whether or not to answer. Finally, "I don't know. Maybe ten years or more . . . why d'ya want to know?"

"There's an outside chance we could do something about it . . . right here."

"Are you crazy or what?," he scoffs, hastily returning his hands to his lap. "For years I took meds up the kazoo before I come on the truth. There ain't no cure for this goddamn thing. It's a waste of money, that's what it is. It's jis another way for drug companies to squeeze a buck outta suckers like me."

"I wasn't thinking of medication."

"Then what?"

Rafer modulates his voice so that the people in the next booth can't hear. "Trust me, please. Put your hands on the table with your thumbs hooked under the edge . . . (*pause*) . . . yes . . . like that." From where Eva sits, Donnie's four fingers on each hand are now visible, the thumbs underneath. Nothing is said. To her left Rafer closes his eyes half-way and slips into a trance, just like he does when placing a bet at the casino.

Donnie: "What the hell is he tryin . . . ."

"Shh," Eva whispers, holding her finger to her lip.

In ten minutes the waiter arrives with the entrees and places them where they belong. For the next half hour the food lies on the table, cooling and uneaten. The waiter, observing from a distance, comes over and is about ask what's wrong when Eva shakes her head and waves him away. He obeys but not without turning around at the kitchen door to take another look. The scene is weird, even alarming. As he explains to the chef inside, "There's a booth out there with one guy closing his eyes like he's at a séance or somethin while this old coot sittin opposite him is hangin onta the table with his fingers twitchin real funny. All the while this broad just sits there cool-like, watchin this guy's hands and sayin nothin. Nobody's eatin anything."

"They no likka the food?," the chef asks anxiously. "You betta check da order. Maybe you makka mistake."

"If I made a mistake, they woulda complained when I brought the food. No, something else is goin on. Somethin crazy."

Half way through the thirty minutes, Eva notices that Donnie's hands are growing still. Donnie seems aware of it too and is about to say something when Eva presses her finger to her lips. Neither speaks as Rafer continues his slow, rhythmic breathing, his face pointed directly at the hands across from him. It is only when the trembling stops altogether that Rafer opens his eyes and smiles. Without a word he places his own hands on top of Donnie's.

"My God . . . they ain't tremblin no more," Donnie shouts as he holds his hands up for inspection. "That's a goddamn miracle. How d'ya do it?"

"I meditated on your hands and directed some energy your way."

"Ya mean like a prayer . . . is that what ya did?"

"You could say that, yes."

"Well, Rafe. That's the nicest thing that anybody eva done for me. I wanna thank ya from the bottom of ma heart."

"I'm glad I could help. You should be O.K. now . . . but if the trembling comes back just let me know and we can try this again." At that point the two men rise and embrace each other across the table. Struggling to hold back her tears, Eva reaches out and clasps Donnie's hands between her own. From the kitchen door, the waiter shakes his head in disbelief, then rushes over to ask if they would like their food warmed up. The offer is accepted gladly, all three heads nodding in unison. "And some more wine," shouts Donnie . . . "at least fir me and the lady. What are you goin to have Rafe. It's on me ya know."

"Another cup of tea would be just fine. Thanks."

After dinner, Donnie heads for his hotel room while Rafer and Eva return to the Tropicana. "Another $50,000 and I think we can call it a night," he whispers as they approach the table. She says nothing and squeezes his hand. Within minutes they begin placing their bets. Spin after spin Rafer slips into a trance and uses his mind to guide the ball into the appropriate slot . . . or at least into one of its close neighbors. His efforts are rewarded as the pile of chips in front of him grows exponentially. Eva's pile, though much smaller, grows proportionately. Two exhausting hours later they leave to take a much needed break. Sitting in the lounge, Eva turns to him and says, "That was a beautiful thing you did at dinner tonight, Rafe. I had all I could do to keep from crying when I saw what was happening. You changed that poor man's life . . . (*pause*) . . . Do you think it will last?"

"I sure hope so and yes, that would be my guess but I can't be sure. The only thing I have to go on is what happened in Sikkim where they say I cured my friend's cancer meditating the same way I did tonight. As far as I know, the tumor never came back. But I haven't heard from him lately . . . so who knows? (*Rising*) Now, ready for a final spurt to the finish line?"

Again she takes his hand as they walk back to the table. Much to her relief, he no longer objects. Thoughts begin to swirl inside her head. "Am I falling in love with this guy? I enjoy being with him but is that love? And what is he feeling for me, if anything? I better not let myself care if he's not feeling something similar. And remember, he's going to leave in a few more days. He hasn't said anything about including me in his plans. So, watch it girl; you could get hurt real bad."

They remain at the table until the croupier calls for the "last three bets." By the time the last bet is placed and paid, Rafer has over $110,000 in his pile; Eva has her own stack of close to $20,000. "A nice little haul," he whispers as they head for the cashier's window. "Should get us over the weekend," she quips. "I like it when you're funny," he replies. "You should do it more often." With that, they head for the Marriott with Eva's bag in hand. She can't help shuddering a little as they enter the central lounge. The arched ceiling with its painted landscapes and flowing fountain lend an air of grandeur that matches the feelings bubbling up inside her. At the desk Rafer picks up the key and points to the elevator. No sooner is the door closed than he pulls her to him and kisses her on the mouth. As the lift rises, her mind is flooded with images of what lies in store once they are safely in their room. At the same time, she is careful not to get carried away; after all, she muses, he spent most of last night meditating when she was lying right there beside him.

To her dismay, the night starts out very much like the night before. After a brief rehashing of the day's events, he brushes his teeth and climbs into bed. When she follows soon thereafter, he reaches over and kisses her on the forehead and whispers a gentle goodnight, then adjusts the pillow beneath him so he can meditate. The question, "Aren't we going to make love?" makes its way to her lips but dies there when she sees him close his eyes. In her frustration, she recalls the kiss in the elevator. "He does care," she muses silently . . . "but for some reason doesn't want to go any further. But why not? Has he been hurt by someone else . . . or does he have some kind of sexual hang-up that he doesn't want to talk about? Or is he gay, as Jack thinks?"

Refusing to acknowledge the cry for closeness stirring in her groin, she curls up as near as possible to his legs and falls asleep. A partial answer to her question reveals itself in the middle of the night when she is awakened by an uncomfortable tightening in her pelvis. Guided by instinct alone, and only half awake herself, she extends her arm across his hip in search of his member. At the mercy of her need now, she is in no mood to consider the consequences. After a minute or two of gentle massage, his manhood hardens beneath his shorts. She rolls over and checks his eyes . . . still closed, his breathing regular like someone asleep. She pushes her panties down to her ankles and kicks them off under the covers. Already moist, she straddles his legs and pulls his penis from under his boxers. Moving noiselessly, she guides it to her tortured flesh and slides forward, sheathing it with her vulva. Slowly now, all sensation in her pelvis, she rocks up and down on his shaft, still staring into his face. Desperate for release, she leans forward until his tip is rubbing directly on her clit; the sensation is intoxicating. She moves faster now, riding his cock with the abandon of a she-wolf determined to secure her one and only mate. Her climax comes just as he raises his hips, his eyes still closed, moaning softly like an adolescent lost in the sweetness of a wet dream. His semen bursts past her vulva, flooding her womb with a warmth that testifies to his desire as clearly as any caress of the lips or whispered confession of love. She gasps as her long-held breath envelopes his face. Neither one moves. When she is convinced that he remains asleep, she rolls off his body and onto the sheets, still nursing the gift inside her.

In the morning she looks for signs that he is aware of what happened during the night. Convinced that he remembers nothing, she announces that she needs to check on her mother but will meet him at whatever casino he intends to visit next. After a quick breakfast in the restaurant downstairs, she leaves and heads for home, eager to get her mother's views on recent events.

"But I want you to have it," she says, pushing the envelope into her mother's hands. "Just don't show it to Jack."

"My goodness, Evie, that's so much money. $10,000 will carry us for months, as long as I can keep you-know-who from getting his hands on it."

The door opens and Jack walks in from the porch. "Oh, speak of the devil," Agnes shouts, tucking the envelope into her robe. "Where'd you go so early in the morning?"

"Just out for a morning constitutional," he answers with an unconvincing nonchalance.

Agnes (*pointing*): "Hmm . . . and that bag you're carryin, the one that says Herman's Liquor Store . . . how'd you come up with that?"

"Oh that? I happened to be walking past the store when I remembered that I was getting kinda low on supplies back home."

Agnes forces a cough. "Low? You've still got an unopened magnum in the kitchen and another gallon jug tucked away in the bedroom closet."

Jack shrugs his shoulders. "I consider that low. (*Looking up*) But hey, Evie, what happened yesterday with your boyfriend? Another killing?"

Eva: (*sighing*) "He did alright."

As Jack hangs up his coat and disappears into the kitchen, the two women continue their conversation, this time with muted voices. "It's hard to believe that he keeps winning day after day," Agnes says. "Most people who win a lot one day give it all back the next. Your friend is exceptional."

"Yes he is. And exceptionally nice," Eva adds. The $10,000 I just gave you is only half of what I made at the Tropicana. His own winnings, of course, were much larger. I can't be sure but I would guess that by now he must have made around $400,000 . . . all in five days. I've never seen anyone do that . . . not in all the years I stood by Raymond's side night after night while he played. But what's even more astounding is what happened last night at Russo's, you know, the Italian restaurant down on Bristle Cone Drive. I still can't believe what I saw. We met this elderly man at the casino in the afternoon where we were doing quite well. The man was extremely fragile and his hands were trembling something awful. Rafer ended up making his bets for him since he couldn't reach far enough to do it himself. I felt sorry for him and was glad to see Rafer lending him a hand."

Agnes shakes her head. "I wonder what he was doing there if he was all that fragile."

"I guess he really needed the money. Anyway, Rafe invited him to join us for dinner which he did. Right away he spilled a glass of wine because he couldn't keep his hands steady. It was right after the spill that Rafe asked him if he was open to a kind of experiment. After some hesitation the man agreed and put his hands on the table as Rafe suggested. Rafe then went into the kind of trance that he uses at the roulette table . . . this time staring with half-closed eyes at the man's hands. For about a half an hour he just stared. Nobody ate anything. The waiter thought we were really weird although he was nice about it and said nothing. At the end of the half hour, all the trembling had stopped. The man was jumping for joy; I even cried it was so beautiful. Rafe was quiet through the whole thing . . . never took any credit for it . . . you know, no bragging or anything like that."

"My God, Evie. Do you know what you're sayin? He performed a miracle right before your eyes. When you think how much money he's making and . . . ."

Jack enters the living room, fresh from a drink in the kitchen. "Miracle, you say? C'mon Aggie, be sensible. Lotsa people have done things like that. You tell somebody you can cure 'em and if they're real eager to get better and dumb enough to believe you, you can manipulate them into willing their symptoms away. What do they call it . . . psycho something . . . oh yeah, psychosomatic medicine. But it's not real; it doesn't last. As soon as the spell wears off, the symptoms return. It's a well-known fact; you can read about it in any magazine."

Agnes turns to Eva, "Jack does read a lot, honey, so maybe he's right."

"I don't know," Eva replies. "I always thought psychosomatic medicine was about the how your mind affects your own body . . . like when you're afraid of something and just thinking about it is enough to give you a headache. The best example I read about had to do with ulcers. They were saying that if you worry too much, it can cause damage to your stomach lining and if that goes on long enough it'll give you an ulcer. That's just one case of the mind causing damage to the body . . . (*pause*) . . . I suppose it could work the opposite way too . . . where the mind does good things to the body, like curing a disease. But in the things I read they were always talking about the mind and body from the same person. There was nothing in those articles about one person using his mind to do something to another person's body."

Jack smiles condescendingly. "You just haven't read the right stuff, Evie. Maybe I got the name wrong but the research is out there . . . and these guys know what they're talkin about. But look, I don't want to deny that this boyfriend of yours is something special. I mean, he's makin a ton of dough at the tables and now he works a number on this old guy with the shakes. He's obviously got somethin goin for him. What the hell it is, I don't know . . . but I'm dyin to find out."

"The whole thing has got me worried," adds Agnes, shaking her head. "When you consider what Petey said about this Antichrist person . . . ."

Jack rises, standing over her. "For Christ's sake, Aggie, get off that shit. Petey'll believe anything. He's into flying saucers, alien invasions, Nostradamus, Armageddon . . . you know, the kinda stuff that only the nuts in this world believe. He's a nice guy . . . I really like him . . . but he's got his head screwed on backwards." When his pronouncement goes unchallenged, Jack retires to the bedroom, leaving the two women to continue their conversation alone.

Agnes waits until the door is closed and then turns to her daughter. "What worries me most, honey, is what this man is doin to you. I can see that you're beginnin to care for him . . . maybe too much, given some of the strange things he's capable of."

"I'm worried too, Mother. I can't really tell how he feels toward me. He seems to like having me around. It's assumed that we'll get together every day now . . . even sleep together . . . but what this means I don't know. And now he said he's leaving in a few days but hasn't said boo about where I fit in . . . (*pause*) . . . What does it sound like to you?"

"I don't know. I confess that he scares me a little . . . maybe a lot. I mean . . . just who *is* he? He certainly doesn't sound like anybody I've ever met. That was already true when you told me how much money he was makin at the tables. Now you tell me he cured this man with the tremblin hands. Holy cow, Evie. Be careful. Don't let yourself get attached . . . at least until you find out more about him . . . and even then I'd be extra careful."

More nervous now than ever, Eva rises and heads for the door. "Goodbye Mom. Take care of yourself now."

"Bye honey . . . and thanks again for all the money. Maybe I'll buy some new furniture and fix up the place a little."

"I just wish you could quit smoking. It's really bad for your lungs."

"I know sweetheart. But I figure that if the Lord wanted me to quit, he'd give me the strength to do it. And since he hasn't, I reckon he doesn't want me to."

With that bit of unassailable logic ringing in her ears, Eva heads out the door and off to the casino. Within minutes, Agnes is on the phone and talking to her brother. "Petey, it's Aggie. How ya doin?"

"Hey Ag, nice to hear from ya. You caught me at a good time. I was laid off last week and I'm jus sittin here in the kitchen going through the want ads. So, tell me . . . what's up?"

"I need some advice. We got some pretty weird stuff goin on here in Vegas and your niece has gotten herself mixed up in it."

"Evie? She's not one to get mixed up in anything too far out . . . is she?"

"Well, I think she's fallin for this guy from out your way. From what she's told me, I gather that he is, or maybe was, a kind of stock broker or at least had something to do with stocks. He apparently lost a lot of his money as well as that of his friends when the market went south last year. Now he's out here tryin to get it all back at the roulette tables."

"Well, how's he doin? Did she tell you?"

"Yeah . . . and that's partly why I'm callin. You sittin down? O.K . . . get this: in the last five days he's made over $400,000 just bettin the numbers."

"What? You kiddin me? That's impossible unless . . . well . . . unless the wheel is rigged and he's in on it . . . but it's the owners who usually do the riggin, isn't it? From what I've read, there ain't no system around that can bring in that kinda money. I don't get it."

"Neither do I. But here's another little tidbit . . . and maybe not so little when I come to think of it. The other night Evie said that she, her friend Rafer and this old fellow with Parkinson's disease went out to eat at a restaurant. The old guy was shakin terribly . . . couldn't even hold a glass of wine. So Rafer, the same guy who's makin all this money at the casinos, tells the old man to put his hands on the table . . . and then goes into a trance for a half hour or so. At the end of it, the guy's trembling, which he's had for ten years, is completely gone. He walks outta the restaurant a new man. Evie, who we all know is pretty soft, weeps for joy . . . and then goes to Rafer's hotel and sleeps with him."

"I smell a rat, Ag. This is no fuckin good, no matter how nice it looks on the surface. She's in trouble big time and you gotta get her the hell outta there before she gets clobbered."

"What kinda trouble, Petey? I know she could get hurt if he dumps her. We've already talked about that . . . so I think she's prepared in case he walks."

"Well, that too. But I was thinking more about the big picture. I've been studyin this whole Antichrist thing for years now . . . I've told you about it . . . I jis didn't know where or when this bird would appear. This guy Rafer could be him . . . or at least one of his forerunners. You know how John the Baptist got us all ready for the coming of Jesus Christ. Well, the same kinda thing could happen with the Antichrist. Before the Devil comes himself to torch the earth, he could send a forerunner to prepare the ground. Like John the Baptist, this forerunner will preach the comin of the Big Guy and lull everybody into thinkin positive about him. Then, just when everybody's feeling worshipful and all, this 'Beast' (that's what the Bible calls him) will appear himself and begin his dirty work. And when he's finished, the whole goddamn earth is goin up in flames."

"But Petey, this man Rafer doesn't sound at all dangerous. According to Eva, he's very generous. He gives her money to play with at the tables . . . and we all know now what he did for that poor old man at the restaurant. He does sound kinda weird sexually . . . but that's another story. Tell me . . . what makes you think he might be tied up somehow with the Devil in all this?"

"He's behaving just like the Bible says he will . . . nice and kind, generous, helpin other folks . . . just so he can get people to trust him. And when he's got everybody eatin out of his hand, he lets loose with the fireworks. It's just a front . . . he's really the opposite of what he looks like. It's a game he's playin . . . a very dangerous game for anyone around him. What he's got in mind is nothing less than the destruction of the whole fuckin planet."

"What can he do? . . . I mean, that would hurt us . . . or especially Eva?"

"I don't know for sure. The Bible doesn't give us all the details. I doubt that this Antichrist is concerned about any one person. His aim, and the Good Book is very clear about this, is to challenge the Lord's power here on earth and defeat him in a final battle. That's the battle of Armageddon . . . a final war between good and evil where the winner takes all."

"Oh my God, Petey. You mean we're all in for it . . . not just Eva?"

"Yup. That's what's goin to happen eventually. So we have to be ready. Now this guy Rafer may not be the Antichrist or even one of his representatives, but he certainly looks like he could be. The thing to do is follow him around, check on everything he does. If he's the real deal, he'll give himself away sooner or later."

"How? How are we going to know if he's the man the Bible talks about?"

"That's pretty easy. The Antichrist, when he comes, is goin to use his special powers to gain control over people . . . mental power, financial power . . . even political power. If we're gonna catch him before he strikes, we have to be on the alert for someone who is especially smart, rich, and persuasive . . . persuasive enough, let's say, to wangle his way into high political office. Right now, it looks like this guy Rafer has the mental power he needs to make himself a fortune. If he's our man, he'll probly bide his time 'til he's got enough dough to run for some high office . . . like Senator or even President. Then, when he's got everybody fooled into thinkin he's a great savior, he'll unleash his thunderbolts and bring the earth to its knees."

Agnes grips the phone tightly. "And then . . . what?"

"And then the Lord will appear on earth and challenge him to a fight. The Lord will win the final battle but not before the earth as we know it is in ruins . . . fire, floods, hurricanes, war, disease, starvation . . . every goddamn catastrophe you can think of. As bad as it sounds, it's all necessary. As the Good Book puts it, it's only after all this destruction that we can start over and build the kind of world that God wants us to have. It's just something we have to go through."

By the time Agnes puts the phone down, she is quivering and in desperate need of a drink. As she goes to pour herself a glass of wine, Jack appears from the backyard and prepares to join her. "Who were you just talkin to?," he asks. "You look all upset." Before she can answer, he adds, "Musta been your brother. Nobody can get you wound up the way he can."

"Yes. It was Petey. I told him all about Eva and this guy Rafer. He's as upset as I am."

"About Eva?"

"No. It's more the big picture with Petey. He thinks the Antichrist is comin soon and we're all in for mass destruction. It's just a matter of time, he says, before all those Bible prophecies come true. When I think of things like global warming, nuclear war, AIDS, people getting laid off . . . stuff like that . . . I'm inclined to agree with him."

"And he thinks Eva's boyfriend Rafer might be this Antichrist?"

"He's not sure Jack. Rafer could be just a forerunner, you know, somebody who is here to prepare the way. Whatever, I'm scared to death that Eva might be caught in the middle of it all. But she's not listening to me. She doesn't realize it yet but she's in love with the guy."

(*Chuckling*) "In love with the Devil. Wow Ag. We could write a book about it. I can see the title now: 'I Slept with the Beast and Lived to Tell About It.'"

"That's not funny, Jack. If he turns nasty, she could be the first to suffer."

"I wouldn't lose any sleep over it Ag. The Bible is full of stories that don't make any sense. Think of all the jerks who believe the world is about to end. I read once that even Jesus warned his followers that their grandchildren would be the last to survive . . . and that was almost 2,000 years ago. As far as I can tell, we're still kickin . . . so I wouldn't get too worked about what the Bible says. And that goes for the so-called Prince of Darkness. Most likely, people invented the idea of a Devil to explain why there's so much evil in the world. After all, if God is good and merciful, they say, he can't be responsible for all the bad stuff that's goin on. So what do you do if you're a true believer . . . you shift the blame onto somebody else . . . you make up a character called the Devil and dump all the nasties in his lap. And then you go even further. You make up a story about a final battle between this Devil and God Himself . . . a battle which God wins. Once the Devil is gone, the story says, evil will be banished forever and humans can finally live in peace . . . (*pause*) . . . Pardon my French but this is pure horse dung. We're always goin to have evil. It's built into our nature and no amount of storytelling is goin to make it go away. So what do ya do? You live with it. You stop fantasizing about some phony world where evil don't exist. And you stop makin up a lot of Mickey Mouse about a Devil who's goin to con us into likin him so he can turn around and blow us all up. In other words, you get real . . . (*pause*) . . . Now, let's forget this crap and have another drink."

"Maybe you're right, Jack. I don't know. Petey seems pretty sure that there's trouble comin our way. I just don't want our family to get caught in the middle of it."

At the casino Rafer is once again successful, this time to the tune of $124,000, his best day yet. Eva does well too, adding another $17,000 to her winnings. Over a midnight snack, the talk is light-hearted but turns serious when Eva raises the subject of the future. Straining to sound natural, she whispers, "Do you know which day you're leaving? I remember you said something about next week . . . and that was several days ago."

"It really depends on how soon I can get my winnings up to $600,000 . . . that's my new target. With that amount tucked away in my account back home, I should have enough to write checks to all the people who put their faith in me and lost. It should also cover taxes and still leave me enough to live comfortably."

Eva forces a grin. "Very comfortably I would say."

"Well, regarding the future, I've been thinking about going somewhere where I can do something for folks who are barely getting by. At the barber shop this morning, I read an article in The Economist about poverty in Mexico. In the two worst states, Oaxaca and Chiapas, the majority of people live in corrugate iron roof shacks and are just barely scraping by. Both areas rely heavily on tourism and have suffered a lot with the downturn in the U.S. and European economies. While I was reading the article, the idea occurred to me to go down there and use some of my winnings to help out . . . you know, try to make things a little easier for some of the hardest hit people."

"Like a modern Robin Hood?"

Rafer (*laughing*): "Well, if you mean stealing from the rich casino owners and giving it to the poor Mexicanos, then I guess you're right. But what does it sound like to you?"

"It sounds wonderful. I think it's a great idea Rafe. I would love to be a part of it."

Rafer pauses to take in the remark. "Are you saying that you want to come with me?"

(*Nodding*) "If you want me."

"I would enjoy your company . . . and you might be able to help out . . . you know, in getting to know people, winning their trust."

Eva (*frowning*): "But how do you really feel toward me? I'm glad you enjoy my company but is that all you feel?"

"You mean . . . am I in love with you? No, I'm not. But I think I can honestly say I love you."

Eva can feel her heart pounding. She knows the topic to be dangerous but feels compelled to proceed further. "You say you love me but are not in love with me. In your mind, what's the difference?"

Rafer (*sighing*): "You ask difficult questions Eva. I haven't really spent much time thinking about all this . . . and that's probably a mistake. I guess what I mean by being in love is . . . well . . . sort of like being intoxicated with another person. If I were in love with you, I would feel driven to see you, to make love to you over and over, to reassure myself that my love was reciprocated."

"And you don't feel that?"

"No . . . and I really don't want to. I know from my experience in Sikkim what that kind of compulsion can do to one's mental stability. All the good things that have happened to me lately . . . like making all this money and fixing that man's hand at the restaurant . . . have come from my ability to stay focused. Even this idea of going to Mexico comes out of the same deep peace and caring. I never felt this way before . . . it's the happiest I've ever been. I'm not sure why it's happening now and to me in particular . . . but I don't want to lose it."

"I understand. It's is a beautiful thing to watch, Rafe. The last thing I want is to get in the way of something this important . . . not just to you but to everyone around you. So that leaves love. What exactly do you mean when you say you're not in love with me but still love me in some other way? . . . (*pause*) . . . Forgive me if I'm being nosy but I have to know. I can't come with you until I know what I mean to you."

Rafer purses his lips while playing with his spoon. "Saying I love you means that I want you to be happy and that I am willing to go out of my way to see that you are. It also means that . . . ."

"But you felt that way toward the man at the restaurant, didn't you?"

"Yes, but let me finish. I also enjoy being with you, looking at you, talking with you . . . even sleeping with you. I don't feel any of that for the man with the trembling hands."

Neither speaks for a minute or two. Eva takes a sip of wine and puts her glass back on the table. "I guess what I'm not hearing so far is that you need me . . . (*pause*) . . . Is it fair to say that you enjoy me but do not need me?"

"I probably couldn't have come up with that distinction myself but your question rings true. I love you but I do not need you. What that means is that I find being with you pleasurable but your company is not essential to my happiness . . . (*pause*) . . . I wish I could say it less brutally but I want to be clear. If you decide to come with me, I don't want you to end up feeling misled and hating me for it."

Eva (*shaking her head*): "I've never known anybody to talk this way before. To be honest, it's disappointing. Like most women I want to be desired, not tolerated. It's one thing to be . . ."

Rafer (*interrupting*): "I'm not talking about toleration. I find it pleasurable to be with you. It's just that I don't feel like I *have* to be with you. I can go on being happy even if I can't be with you even though my preference is for us to be together."

Eva bites her lips. "But would you miss me if we separated?"

"I can't say that for sure until it happens, but I do know that I would be very aware of your absence . . . and think about you often. I just wouldn't pine over you."

She lowers her head. "It's not the most secure feeling to know that I'm enjoyed but not needed."

"Does it help to remember what I said earlier . . . that your happiness means a lot to me and that I will go out of my way to make sure you do not suffer?"

"A little. It's not the same as being desired . . . but I am glad to hear you say it."

"So, will you come with me to Mexico?"

She forces a half smile. "I really don't have anything I else I want to do . . . (*pause*) . . . So I guess the answer is yes."

They finish their meal in silence, each absorbed in thoughts about what was just decided. "My God," she muses, "I have never known a man like this. Raymond was so different. Yes, he was selfish, even greedy, but he left no doubt that he wanted me. That's the way most couples are, isn't it? They need each other; they're dependent on each other. That's what keeps them together. That's true even of friends. But Rafer . . . well, I certainly trust him, but even when he says he loves me he seems so remote . . . like a kindly old man who cares *about* me but not *for* me. I don't hear any desire in his words . . . and it's mutual desire, isn't it, that makes people want to live together and maybe get married. Rafer talks like he has no desire . . . at least for me; I'm not an essential part of his life. He's concerned about my happiness but says he can get along very nicely without me. That doesn't sound right. Don't you need both in a close relationship? Don't you need to be thinking about your partner's happiness while at the same time trying to get your own needs fulfilled? They go together, don't they?"

Without making eye contact, Rafer pursues his own reflections from across the table. "I know that I hurt her feelings but I had to take that risk, didn't I? I don't want to get down to Oaxaca and have her accuse me of having misled her into thinking I was in love. I know what being love is like from my days with Uma and this time feels very different. But why? Am I afraid of being rejected? Is that why I just told Eva that I don't need her? Or is something else going on with me? With all this meditation I've been doing, I get the feeling I'm drifting apart from the rest of the world. When I look around me, I see people coming together out of desire . . . in some cases, sexual desire or the desire for companionship; in other cases it's the need for a partner in the battle against the world. I just don't feel any of that. Perhaps I'm deluding myself, but if that were the case wouldn't I be feeling unhappy, lonely or at least frustrated with my situation? I don't feel any of those things. In fact, I've never felt this peaceful in my whole life. So, what in God's name is happening to me? I just don't get it."

With the issue of Mexico resolved, they finish their meal and head for the hotel. The following morning, Rafer purchases two plane tickets to Oaxaca City for next Tuesday, leaving just enough time to reach his goal of $600,000. Eva rushes home to tell her mother about her new plans.

12

Rumors of the Beast

Things have not gone well for George Komerov lately. Long despised by his Harvard Medical School colleagues for his work with alien abductees, he has recently been forced to suffer the humiliation of a publicity trick aimed at exposing his gullibility. Just weeks ago a skeptical journalist from New York came to him on the pretext of having experienced such an abduction and then wrote about her deception in a popular magazine. In the article Komerov is presented as an uncritical listener who bought her fabricated story hook, line and sinker without the slightest attempt to verify the details of the fantasized abduction. The medical establishment was stunned to learn of his behavior; his colleagues at Harvard were particularly mortified. The only thing that kept him from being fired immediately was his tenured position and the freedom of belief guaranteed by that contract with the University. Nevertheless, a minority of academics argued that he should be expelled on the grounds that he failed to maintain an attitude of objectivity in his dealings with his patient. To appease that minority, the doctor was stripped of his committee chairmanships and forbidden to speak with the media. He was also asked to explain his actions before a special meeting of the Medical School faculty. It is that response that he is preparing as he sits now at his desk.

Secretary: "Doctor Komerov . . . there's a man here to see you . . . says he called the other day to make an appointment. That was my day off so I didn't take the call. His name is Peter White. Shall I send him in?"

(*Sighing*) "I'm right in the middle of my presentation for tomorrow's faculty meeting."

"He says it won't take long . . . and it's very important. I think it's got something to do with all the alien abduction publicity."

"Oh God . . . you better send him in." As the door opens he saves his file to a hard drive and closes the laptop.

A young man, broad-shouldered with blue eyes, sandy hair and dressed in working man's clothes bursts into the office. "Hi, I'm Pete White. Nice to meet ya. Friends call me Petey." Still standing, he waits for a response. "Should I call you Professor or Doctor?"

"Either one will do. Please take a seat."

"Well Doc . . . me and my friends have been following your case in the Globe and we don't like the hard time they've been givin ya. This bitch . . . oops . . . sorry . . . you know, the one that pretended she was abducted and then wrote it up in her magazine . . . she otta be lynched for lying to ya like that. Me and the boys are real mad and we jis want ya to know we're behind ya 110 percent."

(*Softly*) "It's all over now. There's no use stirring it up again. But thank you for your support . . . (*pause*) . . . Now I've got some important work to do, so if you will excuse me."

"Wait jis a minute Doc. There's something else happenin that's goin to interest you big time . . . (*pause*) . . . What d'ya know about the Antichrist?"

"The what?"

"The Antichrist, you know, the One sent by the Devil to blow us all to Kingdomcome. His coming is prophesied in both the Old and New Testaments."

"Ah yes, the so-called Prince of Darkness. I've heard of him although I haven't kept pace with the latest Biblical research. Isn't he supposed to challenge God in the final battle of Armageddon?"

"Yeah . . . accordin to the prophets, God and the Evil One are goin to duke it out while the rest of the earth is goin up in flames. God will eventually win and send his Son Jesus back here to clean up the mess but not before millions of us humans suffer horrible deaths."

Komerov shifts uneasily. "Of course, just because a prophecy appears in the Bible doesn't make it automatically true . . . although I'm inclined to think there may be something to this one. With global warming, nuclear proliferation, flu pandemics, polar shifts in the magnetic field and so on, there are certainly signs that the end may be near. But there's no way to be sure."

"I agree. Things already look bad and they're going to get a lot worse. Just look at . . . ."

(*Interrupting*) "What does the Bible say about the timing? Is this End of Days scenario supposed to happen anytime soon?"

"Well, that's kinda what I come here to tell you about, figurin you'd be receptive to the idea. I don't wanta go into it right now but I've got some solid evidence that this Antichrist bird might already be among us . . . out in Vegas."

Komerov leans forward. "What kind of evidence?"

"I'm goin to present it at our meetin next Tuesday night at my place. The other guys in the group haven't heard it yet . . . so I wanna wait until we're all together. That's why I'm invitin you to join us, Doc."

"What kind of group are you referring to?"

"Just a bunch of guys I've known for years . . . some of them from way back when we wuz still kids. We all live up on the North shore and go to the same Evangelical Church, so it's easy to get together. One way or 'nother, we're interested in what the Bible tells us is comin our way . . . you know, things like the Antichrist and Armageddon, ideas that educated folks dismiss as crazy. You must know what I'm talkin about from your work with them aliens. Some ideas are so frightening that people not only refuse to believe them; they go around harrassin anybody who takes 'em seriously. That's why I come to you. I figured if there's anybody who would take us serious-like, it would be you. So, Doc, will you come to our meetin on Tuesday. We'd love to have ya. I think a man with your education and psychiatric background can keep us from gettin too emotional about this Devil character and flippin out or doin somethin we'd regret."

"Well, I must say you've got me interested Peter. Why don't you write down your address just in case my wife doesn't have anything else planned for Tuesday."

(Writing) "O.K. Doc. I'll tell the boys there's a good chance you'll be joinin us. Come early enough, say 6:00, so we can share some soda and pizza."

(Rising) "I better get back to my report now. As you know, I'm in hot water at the Medical School and tomorrow I have to go up before the whole faculty. I want to present the best defense I can."

"What are you gonna say?"

"Just that we now have aliens in our midst, creatures from another world whose motives are not yet known. As medical professionals it is our responsibility to help anyone claiming to have been hurt or even contacted by such beings . . . (pause) . . . That's the gist of my argument."

(*At the door*) "Good luck, Doc. We'll be thinkin of ya."

At dinner that night Komerov is unusually quiet, prompting a question from his wife Greta. "You're not talking. Are you worried about your reception tomorrow at the faculty meeting?"

"Well yes, but I was actually thinking about something else . . . (*pause*) . . . Have you ever heard of the Antichrist . . . the Devil's representative who is someday coming to earth to challenge God's authority? A man came to my office today claiming to have evidence that such a person may be already afoot out in Nevada. I don't know . . . ."

Greta (*sighing*): "For God's sake, George, you're not going to stir up another mess, are you? We're still not out of the woods because of this alien abduction thing. You keep this foolishness up and you're going to get yourself fired. And then what are we going to do? We don't have that much in our savings account, thanks to all the money you wasted on that nuclear bomb shelter out back."

Withdrawing into the privacy of his thoughts, George ponders the excitement of exploring yet another idea sure to be dismissed by his peers as paranoid fantasy. He can almost see the twisted frowns on their disbelieving faces as he lectures them on the imminent arrival of the Prince of Darkness. His smile broadens into a malicious grin. But is it worth the risk of being treated like a pariah . . . again? Greta's tremulous voice breaks harmlessly against his ears as his thoughts go deeper. Why do I find such ideas so appealing, even thrilling, he asks? As part of his training as a psychiatrist, he was required to take part in both individual and group therapy. There were a few hints along the way that his need to rebel against a dominating, opinionated father had something to do with the attraction of "weird" ideas but nothing conclusive ever emerged. Nevertheless, the pattern is there . . . in fact it can be traced all the way back to college when, to the dismay of his roommates, he gave public credence to a psychic's prediction that part of Japan would fall into the sea by year's end. And then in graduate school he again defied both family and friends when he took seriously the prophecy, announced in a book that subsequently sold 15 million copies, that the world would end in 1986. Even when the author later revised his prophecy to make 2000 earth's final year, George remained a believer . . . at an incalculable cost to his reputation. Yet through it all, he remained strong, seemingly unshakeable. What kept him going, of course, was the hope that someday one of his "weird" ideas would prove accurate and then the real fun would begin. In his imagination he sees himself standing alone, spear in hand, a solitary defender of the absurd, sticking it unmercifully to the skeptics who have raked him across the coals. "Take that, you creeps . . . maybe you'll believe me next time."

With that image in his mind, he recalls what his guest at School said earlier about the Antichrist . . . a man posing as humanity's savior yet secretly intent on destroying us all, a man of pure evil, strong and clever enough to bring the world to its knees. Nobody in his right mind is going to believe that, he murmurs, playing with his fork, certainly no one here at the Harvard Medical School. Aside from Biblical prophecies, there's no support for a superman among us who has the power to bend nations to his will. It's a crazy idea, he reflects, his heart already racing at the thought . . . but who knows . . . it just might be true. It's certainly worth investigating.

Tuesday night in Lynn. As usual, there are five young men present, including Petey, the husky, broad-shouldered leader. Sitting next to him on his right is Zeke, the bespectacled, curly-haired intellectual of the group. Then comes Thomas, tall and lean with penetrating eyes that make you wonder if what you just said is really true. Revy, next in the circle, is by far the shortest in the group but makes up for his physical shortcomings with his ample computer skills. He gets the attention he craves by keeping everybody informed about what people are saying on his list of favorite blogs and websites. Hunter, usually unshaven and dressed in farmer's overalls, is the least communicative, preferring to let others do the talking while he sifts through their opinions. He is the only one of the five who has ever had a brush with the law; that was when he got into a fight at a local bar and ended up breaking a man's jaw. He hasn't had a drink since, at least as far as the group knows.

At the knock, Petey opens the door. "C'mon in Doc. Glad you could make it. We jis finished our prayers. How'd your faculty meeting go?"

Komerov: "Not too bad. I actually had a few supporters."

Petey: "Great. And you've got some more here tonight. Let me introduce you to the boys. (*pointing*) Over here we got Zeke . . . our Bible scholar. If you want to know chapter and verse about anything in the Good Book, Zeke is your man. He was hopin to become a Jesuit priest when he was young but got caught cheatin on the Latin exam. But he still knows lots of words from the old language. Say something for the Doc in Latin, Zeke . . . (*pause*) . . . Go ahead."

Zeke (*palms up*): "Quid facit agricola?"

Petey: (*quickly*) "Hey, watch your manners. The Doc isn't used to foul language."

Zeke protests. "All I said was . . ."

Petey (*interrupting*): "And over here is Thomas . . . as in Doubting Thomas. Shake hands with the Doc, Thomas. We call him that because he challenges everything anybody says. You tell him that 2 and 2 is 4 and he'll prove to you that it's really 5. He used to be a Catholic but switched to the Evangelicals when he moved to Lynn. He likes our music better but he misses some of their rituals."

Revy interjects (*grinning*): "I think what he misses most is goin to confession."

Petey: "So what? A lot of people like goin to confession."

Revy (*hooting*): "Yeah, but Thomas had his own special reason."

Petey: "Like what?"

Revy (*whispering*): "He told me that at confession he liked to make up stories about doing little kids and then wait for the heavy breathing to come from the other side of the curtain."

Thomas (*raised eyebrows*): "So, what's wrong with that. The padre got to jerk off and I got a good laugh. It was fun."

Petey (*sighing*): "Don't mind these guys, Doc. They're jus horsin around. The little guy who was jus talkin is Revy. We call him that cuz he's like Paul Revere, you know, good at warnin people when trouble is brewin. He's got the nose of a bloodhound. Jis by lookin at the day's news, he can tell if somethin don't smell quite right . . . can't ya Rev?"

Revy (*sniffing*): "Right now I think the pizza is burning. Somebody betta git it outta the oven before it turns to charcoal."

Petey rushes to the kitchen. "Hunter, I didn't forget ya, buddy. Introduce yourself to the Doc while I get the pizza."

Hunter (*scowling*): "I ain't got nothin to say."

Petey (*handing out paper plates*): "Well, O.K. Doc . . . it's your turn. Tell the boys a little about yourself, if you would."

Komerov: "Well, Peter . . . you know why I'm here. I want to . . ."

Thomas (*laughing*): "Nobody calls him Peter, Doc. He's just an ordinary jerk like the rest of us."

Komerov: "O.K. As I told Petey at my office last week, I agree that there might be something to this Antichrist idea. After all, you've got all these writers, the learned people who wrote the Old and New Testaments, saying pretty much the same thing . . . namely that the End of Days is getting closer and there may be someone in our midst who is going to bring about a final Armageddon. What really got my curiosity up was what Petey said about this man out in Nevada whom he believes may be the person we're looking for."

Hunter (*turning to Petey*): "What person you talkin about? You ain't never mentioned that to us."

Petey: "O.K. I planned to tell you all about it tonight . . . so I might as well begin right here. Last week my sister Agnes called from Vegas to say that there's a guy out there, a big-shot Ph.D. from Harvard (no offense Doc) who has already worked the roulette tables for $400,000 . . . all in a matter of five days."

Thomas: "That may be a bit unusual . . . but a string of good luck don't make him Satan's right hand man."

Petey: "Granted . . . but that's not all. My niece, Eva, who seems to be falling for this guy, says he cured an old man's palsy just by going into a trance at the dinner table. She was right there and saw the whole thing. Accordin to Eva, he doesn't pretend to be anything special . . . real humble-like even though he seems to possess magical powers. She also says he comes from a rich home but lost a lot of dough in the stock market. Some of the $400,000 he's made at roulette is goin to friends who took his advice and lost their shirts jis like he did. He also gives her a few thousand to play with every day so she's been able to pile up her own stash of $25,000 . . . sounds like a pretty generous dude."

Thomas: "Still, if he's our man, he otta be doin bigger things than beating the odds at roulette or curing some old guy's palsy. Doesn't the Bible say he's going to bring about one disaster after another . . . war, famine, floods, hurricanes, plagues, drought . . . you name it?"

Zeke: "Yeah, in fact, seven long years of suffering worse than anything we've ever experienced. But maybe that's already happening."

Komerov: "You're referring to the Tribulation . . . yes?"

Petey smiles. "Hey Doc, so you know about all this stuff?"

Komerov shrugs his shoulders and leans back. "I started reading a little after our talk in my office last week. But I really don't know much. That's the main reason I came here tonight . . . to learn more."

Zeke (*reading from his Bible*): "I can give it to you right from the horse's mouth, Doc. St. Paul . . . you know who he is . . . is telling the Thessalonians that the 'day of Christ is at hand.' But he adds, 'Let no man deceive you by any means: for that day shall not come except there come a falling away first, and that Man of Sin be revealed, the Son of Perdition' (Thessalonians 2:3). In other words, Christ ain't gonna come again until the Devil's finished with his dirty work and all the non-believers are punished."

Komerov: "What's especially interesting to me is that God, who we must assume to be all-powerful, is allowing the Devil to wreak seven years of havoc on Earth before He steps in and puts an end to the Tribulation. In a sense, God is using the Devil to punish us for our sins. Am I reading that right?"

Zeke: "Exactly Doc. But let's not forget that some folks, the born-again true believers among us, are goin to be saved. He's goin to whisk us into the sky so the Antichrist can't hurt us. The Bible calls that the Rapture."

Hunter: "But the jerks who are left behind are all goin to get creamed, right? I mean, they deserve to get hit for doubtin and disbelievin and goin against the Commandments."

Zeke (*smiling*): "They're goin to get wiped out . . . to make room for Christ's return to Earth and the start of the Millennium . . . you know, the thousand years of peace that'll come after God defeats the Devil at the battle of Armageddon."

Komerov: "But where does the Antichrist come in? I'm getting confused about the relationship between the Devil and the Antichrist."

Zeke (*drawing a deep breath*): "O.K. The Antichrist is the Son of the Devil just as Christ is the Son of God. Some people say there's even more symmetry here . . . like between the Holy Spirit on one side and the False Prophet on the other. The Devil seems to be imitatin God by creatin a trinity of his own. Does that make sense?"

Komerov: "It does. But I still don't understand how the Antichrist, this Son of the Devil, is going to bring about such devastation during the seven years of the Tribulation. That's a pretty tall order for one individual, wouldn't you say?"

Petey: "I think I can explain that one, Doc. For a superman to bring the whole world under his thumb, things have to be centralized . . . like politically and economically. We see some of that already with the United Nations, the European Union, the World Trade Organization and World Bank. The world is shrinkin. You know what I'm talking about. Everything is goin global these days . . . the internet, phones, cross-Atlantic cables, stock exchanges, G-20 meetins, digital this, digital that . . . it's all makin things easier for one person to take over."

Komerov: "But still, no ordinary individual could ever gain the power to . . . ."

Thomas (*interrupting*): "I'm with the Doc on this one. For one guy to build an army strong enough to force everybody else into submission . . . that just doesn't seem possible these days."

Petey: "Granted that no ordinary person could do it . . . but you keep forgettin what the Good Book says about the Antichrist. He's anything but ordinary. He's not only smarter than anybody else; he's a master at connin people into doin what he wants them to do. And he ain't goin to go marchin through Georgia on this one; he's goin to be sneaky. He's goin to play up to people, lull them into trustin him, worm his way into a position of leadership, do some nice things, maybe perform a few miracles . . . then when they're convinced he's the Messiah comin to save them, he's goin to throw off his cloak and reveal the monster he really is. That's when all hell's goin to break loose . . . wars, floods, fires, plagues . . . the whole fuckin works."

Thomas: "Maybe so. I still have doubts that any one person in today's world can acquire that much power. But if it's true, the real question is whether this guy out in Vegas is the Beast we're talking about or just a lucky dude who happens to have some healing powers."

Revy: "We clearly need more evidence. Maybe this Vegas guy is just getting started . . . you know, with the big stuff still to come."

Komerov turns to Revy. "So, what kinds of evidence would convince you he's the Antichrist?"

Revy: "I would look for his movin into politics, runnin for governor or something like that. But he won't do it honestly; he'll somehow trick people into votin him into office."

Zeke: "The Book of Daniel puts it clearly. I quote: 'And in this estate shall stand up a vile person to whom they shall not give the honor of their kingdom . . . but he shall come in peaceably and obtain the kingdom by flatteries . . . and after the league made with him he shall work deceitfully . . . and become strong with a small people' (Daniel 11:21). These days I guess 'obtaining the kingdom by flatteries' means buyin votes."

Komerov (*shaking his head*): "I think it's incredible that Daniel saw all of that thousands of years ago. And even more convincing to have the warning issued again by Paul after Christ's death. It certainly lends an aura of credibility to the whole prophecy."

Zeke (*reading*): "And get this, Doc. This here book by Arthur Pink . . . he's the expert on this stuff . . . says that once the Beast gets going, he's gonna, I quote, 'proclaim himself God, demanding that Divine honors be rendered to him. Such wonders will he perform, such prodigious marvels will he work, the very elect would be deceived by him did not God directly protect them. The Man of Sin will combine in himself all the varied genius of the human race, and what is more, he will be invested with all the wisdom and power of Satan. He will be a master of science, acquainted with all of nature's forces, compelling her to give up for him her long held secrets . . . In this [person] will be concentrated intellectual greatness, sovereign power and human glory, combined with every species of iniquity, pride, tyranny, willfulness, deceit, and blasphemy such as Antiochus Epiphanes, Mohammed, the whole line of popes, atheists, and deists of every age of the world have failed to unite in any individual person.'"

Petey: "Whew! I never heard of Antiochus Whats-His-Name . . . but you gotta admit this Antichrist bird ain't no ordinary Joe. Which means we gotta be ready for the worst."

Zeke: "One thing we should probably be on the outlook for is the ability to persuade people with his speech. Just as listeners were astonished by Christ's speaking ability (in Matthew 13:54 we read, 'From whence comes this man's wisdom?'), they're going to be hypnotized by the Antichrist who speaks with what Revelations calls 'the mouth of a lion.' All in all, this guy is goin to be one hell of an orator."

Petey (*nodding his assent*): "My sister didn't say nuthin about politics or speeches . . . but maybe it's still too early for him to make his move. All I now so far is that he's made a ton of money at roulette . . . and cured this old man's hand. Oh, and there's this one other thing . . . Eva says that each night people crowd around him at the roulette table cuz he gives off peaceful vibes. She says she can feel it herself. Of course, they could jis be squeezing in close so they can see how he's gonna bet . . . I don't know."

Revy: "I'll add the Las Vegas papers to the list of media outlets I'm followin. If this guy does anything newsworthy, they'll be a piece about it on at least one of the rags. They probably won't report on how much money he's makin since he can keep that to himself, but if your niece is there with him every day, he might share that info with her. That would help. Maybe you could ask Eva next time you talk to her."

Hunter, who has been quiet through much of the evening, pounds his fist on the table. "I don't think we should keep on waitin to go after this guy. Once he gets some power, he could be hard to stop. Or he might split with your niece Petey and take off somewhere we don't know nuthin about."

Petey (*alarmed*): "So, what are you suggestin?"

Hunter: "Jis that we should have a plan for how to take him down . . . somethin we can go with in a hurry if we have to."

Komerov (*sternly*): "I hope you're not recommending some sort of violence. If so, I don't want any part of it."

Petey (*smiling*): "That's just Hunter's way of talkin, Doc. He don't mean anything serious-like. He's just sayin we gotta stay on top of this thing so if somethin new breaks out, we're ready to step in and cut it off. That's our mission here. Jis like Paul Revere warned the rebels that the Brits were comin, our job is to let other people know as soon as the Antichrist arrives . . . and to warn 'em of the harm he intends to do. Then, folks will be in a position to do somethin about it.

Thomas: "Yeah, but at best we can only minimize the damage. It's God, through his Son Jesus, who is goin to do this guy in at the battle of Armageddon. In the meantime the way we can help is to put a finger on the guy when he appears and tell other Americans about him so they can get ready. It's up to God to do the rest."

Hunter opens his mouth to speak, then changes his mind and heads for the bathroom. The meeting ends with a promise to get together again in two weeks time.

On his way home, George ruminates on the evening's proceedings. He pictures each man in turn . . . Petey, the leader, good at keeping everyone focused; Zeke, a scholar in his own way but without the pretensions of a formal education; Thomas, whose critical intelligence is important for holding emotions in check, and Revy, the newshound with a sense of humor who keeps everyone tied to the outside world. The only one he has doubts about is Hunter whose anger, probably family-related, has the potential to erupt with minimal provocation if not checked by others. As a whole the group is enthusiastic, even dedicated but not irrational as he had feared. Yes, they are simple people, certainly not the kind one sees at the Medical School . . . but in their speech and lack of sophistication they offer a reminder of his own humble beginnings, the same beginnings that offer such a convenient target for his Medical School colleagues, all of whom come from privileged families. He shakes his head now, fully aware that if it weren't for his brilliance and hard work, he would never have been asked to join the faculty here 15 years ago. Instead of Harvard, he'd be teaching at some state school out in the Mid-West . . . or supervising medical school drop-outs at some asylum for the insane. He shudders as a string of fantasies, each insidious in its threat to all he has achieved, floats unsolicited into consciousness.

As he continues walking, his mind is drawn to the young man in Las Vegas who is thought by some in the group to be the Antichrist. From what Petey has learned from his niece, this man has had all the advantages of an upper-middle class upbringing . . . a secure home, support from family and teachers, the best education possible, all leading to a job with some financial organization in Boston. What Komerov resents most is the family support. In his own home, praise was as rare as a ticket to a Red Sox game. Both mother and father were too wrapped up in their own troubles to pay any attention to how George was doing in school. Homework? As far as he can remember, there was no encouragement to do well, never . . . and certainly no help with the assignments. They were actually disappointed when, at his teacher's request, he applied to college and got a scholarship. Like their blue-collar friends and neighbors, his parents expected George to enter one of the local factories where he could earn a good salary right off the bat, eventually buy a home and get married. This was the way to go. College was seen as a waste of time.

George picks up his pace as he nears home. For this guy they talked about at the meeting, everything was just the opposite. Petey says his parents took him on a trip to the Himalayas . . . as a reward for getting his Ph.D. They must have really wanted him to succeed . . . (*he pauses, shaking his head*) . . . What a difference that could have made in my life. Mother didn't even know what a Ph.D. was . . . and if you told her, she'd say that it wasn't worth the effort. If you protested that it really was, she'd probably say O.K . . . but you're not good enough to get one. As far as support was concerned, she was a zero . . . no praise, no congratulations, not a whiff of encouragement. With all her negativity she really made things harder. Not too many people would understand, but everything I've achieved, I've achieved in spite of what my parents said and did.

Just outside his house, he stops to finish his thoughts. This man out in Vegas, he reflects, sounds like the very opposite. He's had the best of everything . . . a tightly-knit family, loving parents, financial support, and above all, backing for his ambitions. Now he's figured out how to make an obscene amount of money at the casinos. Then there's this business about curing an old man's palsy, not to mention Petey's niece falling in love with him. He seems to have it all . . . without all that much effort on his part. Whether the Antichrist or not, he's already gotten more than his share of the good things in life.

For a smart kid from the three-deckers of Somerville who has had to fight his way inch by inch for every little success in life, the thought of someone else's having it this easy is more than just irritating; it's infuriating. It also gets his larger than normal brain spinning with ideas. Maybe it's time for our spoon-fed miracle worker to suffer a little adversity, he muses. Maybe Hunter is right; maybe it's time to bring the Golden Boy down, although there are probably some non-violent ways of doing it. With that thought dancing in his head, he opens the door to his Beacon Hill condo and walks in.

13

Buen Viaje

After an uneventful flight from Las Vegas to Oaxaca by way of Houston and Mexico City, Rafer and Eva settle into Las Golondrinas (*The Swallows*), a small hotel situated on a quiet street in the northern half of the city. Unpacking quickly, they pick up a tourist's guide at the in-house store and head out to see the town. Just two blocks away is one of Oaxaca's most treasured sights . . . the Centro Cultural de Santo Domingo, a mammoth cathedral with a next-door convent converted to a museum replete with ancient artifacts from the Monte Alban ruins. As they make their way along the adjoining cobble-stone streets, they stop to admire the two and three storied 18th Century buildings with their flat facades of varying colors, each with aligned windows ornamented with wrought-iron balustrades. Some are disfigured with peeling paint and twisted grill work while others have been restored to their original perfection. The overall effect is of a restrained beauty, classical in its understatement, similar in its appeal to a Mozart concerto or David painting. Aside from the peeling paint, it is difficult to see why Oaxaca is considered one of Mexico's poorest cities. The impression of well-being is reinforced when the couple enters what purports to be a tourist information center only to discover a flower-filled atrium surrounded by a ring of offices adorned with rich mahogany lintels and doors, all fashioned in exquisite taste. The agent in charge is quick to explain that the complex once served as a home for the invading conquistadors who ruled the city throughout the 16th, 17th and 18th centuries. With the democratization of wealth and power, these homes for the rich were later converted to business offices, restaurants and condominiums. As he listens, Rafer is reminded of Boston's Back Bay where the five-storied single-family dwellings along Commonwealth Avenue have been broken into small, separate apartments . . . evidence of a similar leveling of wealth.

With guide book in hand, they angle their way south toward the zocolo, the two-tiered plaza which serves as the city's social center. Together, the two sections are about the size of a football field. While the upper section boasts a huge cathedral, once made of adobe but rebuilt in stone after the earthquake of 1696, the lower tier is an arboreal delight with broad walkways interspersed among giant hardwoods, all outlined in vivid red with hundreds of poinsettias.

Hungry after an hour of walking, the two travelers take a seat in one of the six outdoor restaurants that border the lower plaza on three of its four sides. Most of the tables have umbrellas but nothing else to protect them from the weather which tends to be dry and warm this time of year. They choose the restaurant called Primavera, more for the vibrant colors in its tablecloths than anything else. The menu offers a variety of Oaxacan specialties, ranging from mole negro with frijoles and white cheese to the more conventional chiles rellenos and tamales. The moles, they are told, are spicy sauces made of chocolate, garlic and chili, and are served on chicken, turkey or beef. Eva opts for the chicken and waits for Rafer to make up his mind. Concerned that the mole dishes might be a bit spicy for his New England tastes, he chooses the less exotic bean burritos with salsa. As they wait for their orders to arrive, they sit back, sip their tea and soda, and watch the flood of pedestrians flow past.

Half way through their meal, Rafer and Eva notice a young girl, especially pretty despite her dirty face, passing before their table and eyeing the food still on their plates. When she returns to look a second time, walking very slowly, Eva turns to Rafer and says, "I think she's hungry. Shall we invite her to sit down?"

By this time Rafer is also aware of the child's interest and nods his assent. Eva turns to the girl and smiles, "Tienes hambre?" (*Are you hungry?*) When no answer is forthcoming, she adds, "Le gustaria algo comer or beber?" (*Would you like something to eat or drink?*) The girl looks around as if to see if anyone is watching, then comes up to the table. Rafer pulls out a seat and says, "Sentarse por favor." (*Please sit down*). Once their guest is settled into a chair, Eva hands her a menu and runs her fingers down the list of entrees available. "Tiene todos lo que quieras." (*Have anything you want*). The girl chooses the beef torta and chocolate milk, again looking around to see who might be watching.

Eva smiles and leans forward. "Como se llama? (*What is your name*). "Lena," the girl answers softly without looking up. In an equally subdued voice, Eva replies, "Mi nombre es Eva . . . y mi amigo es Rafer." (*My name is Eva and my friend is Rafer*). The girl's eyes brighten. "Mi tia es Eva," (*My aunt is Eva*), she responds, practically shouting. She then turns to Rafer, obviously frustrated, "Tu nombre es Ra . . . Rafo . . . Roffo? Como se dice tu nombre en Espanol?" (*How do you say your name in Spanish?*) Rafer tries again in English, pronouncing his name as distinctly as possible . . . Ray-fer. When it is obvious from Lena's expression that she's still having difficulty, he smiles and says, "Puedes me Roberto llamar" (*You can call me Roberto*). She responds enthusiastically, "Oh, Roberto, si." Her smile is enough to persuade him to use his new name with any other children they meet. "And why not adults as well?," Eva adds with a smile of her own. "Personally I like it."

Just as Lena's torta arrives, a new face appears at her side. "Mi hermana, Monica," (*My sister, Monica*) she announces, proceeding to break the torta into two parts. Monica, probably six, is equally dirty and hungry . . . and practically shoeless. The latter problem becomes obvious when Eva bends over to pick up a fallen napkin and notices that most of the cloth covering the girl's sneakers is in tatters and about to fall off. Eva turns to Rafer, shaking her head, and says, "The tops of her shoes are so worn I can see through to her bare feet."

"What about Lena," Rafer asks. "Are hers as bad?" Eva asks Lena to lift her feet so she can get a closer look. "Almost," she replies. "No holes yet but the soles are coming off. They both obviously need new shoes."

Rafer waits until the girls are halfway through their tortas, then asks, "Te gustan los zapatos nuevos?" (*Would you like new shoes?*). Within seconds they are climbing off their chairs and heading across the zocolo. Once the table stops shaking, Rafer calls them back and reassures them he will take them to the shoe store as soon as they finish their meal. As the two adults look on, unable to conceal their smiles, the torta vanishes from the plate like an antelope carcass torn to shreds by two ravenous lion cubs.

Once the bill is paid, they all head for Tres Hermanos (*Three Brothers*), a shoe store on the other side of the zocolo. On the walk over, Lena stops to tell some of her young friends of her good fortune. Before they are even half way there, the group of four has grown to nine, two adults and seven children . . . with all seven kids squeezed into a tight ball, tugging desperately on Roberto's arms and legs. Throughout the plaza, heads turn and smiles flash as the tiny troupe marches toward the store amidst cries of "zapatos, zapatos, Roberto, zapatos."

By the time they reach the store, there are ten children in tow, each crying to be included in the promised bonanza. The owner, a short, nervous man in his forties, is standing at the door when the group arrives, his concern evident from the suddenness with which he blocks the way. With arms outstretched, he stares at the dirty faces before him, then turns to Rafer and asks, "Cuantos?" (*How many*). Rafer quickly counts the children and reports "Diez." (*ten*). "No mas," (*no more*) the owner replies. "Esta bien," (*O.K.*) answers Rafer, as he ushers his flock into the store. To the unconcealed irritation of the patrons already in the store, the children race around from one display case to another, trumpeting their joy at everything they see . . . which is of little help to the clerks who are waiting to fill their requests. While other customers watch helplessly, the noise grows to factory levels as children shout their preferences, change their minds, then turn to fighting with each other as the clerks fly back and forth to the store room with new samples. Since none of the children are wearing socks, hygiene requires that their feet be covered with plastic bags before being inserted into the new shoes. The procedure elicits a mild protest from Nadia who claims to have washed her feet that very morning. One by one, the children get their feet measured, choose what they want, then watch as their gifts get placed in a box and added to the pile on the counter where the cashier waits with Rafer's credit card in hand. The owner's sigh of relief can be heard throughout the store when the bill is finally paid and the group has departed.

As the children file out of the store with shoe boxes tucked protectively under their arms, they are immediately assaulted with stares from their frustrated friends who have been waiting at the door in hopes of getting inside. Through their somber brown eyes, they simultaneously accuse and plead. The only way Rafer can assuage their disappointment is to promise another buying spree tomorrow . . . at the same store, same time. He memorizes everyone's name so they can be assured of inclusion when the group meets tomorrow in front of the store.

As Rafer (now Roberto to all) and Eva make their way back to the Primavera for a drink, they are quickly overtaken by Lena and Monica. With one hand holding her new shoes and the other interlocked with Eva's, Lena lets on that her grandmother, who is here in the plaza selling scarves, never gets enough to eat. "Ella es muy delgada"(*She is very thin*), she says. The hint is taken and with a nod from Roberto, both girls rush off to find their grandmother. When the old lady appears at the Primavera several minutes later, she is invited to sit down and have something to drink. She chooses coffee . . . but declines to shake hands with either of her two hosts. Lena says her name is Maya. Chocolate milk (Lena), tea (Rafer), and orange juice (Eva) are added to the order.

Maya is tiny, small even by Mexican standards, gray-haired, very brown and very wrinkled. When she smiles, which is seldom, her mouth reveals a total of two rotting teeth, each broken off and deeply discolored. After speaking, she typically covers her mouth with the back of her hand, presumably to conceal the ugliness within. As the conversation begins, with Lena frequently speaking for her grandmother, Eva notices that Maya has something white stuck in her left ear. Upon closer inspection it turns out to be part of a napkin. When questioned, Maya shrugs her shoulders and presses her hand to the ear, wincing as she does so. Lena explains that her grandmother is too afraid of doctors to get help for her earache, relying instead on remedies she knows best, like the napkin. They are interrupted at this point when the waitress brings the drinks and sets them on the table.

The scene that follows strikes the two Americans as both bizarre and pathetic. Instead of lifting the coffee cup with her fingers, Maya leaves her hands in her lap and waits for Lena to transfer a straw from her chocolate milk to the coffee. While Lena holds the straw upright, the grandmother leans forward and begins sipping her coffee . . . the way one might with a soda or glass of milk. The strange practice goes without explanation until Maya reaches to adjust the napkin in her ear. Even from across the table it is clear that her knuckles are severely swollen and her fingers coiled inward like a bird's claw, making it impossible to lift the cup to her lips. Eva turns away and looks at Rafer. The silence that follows goes unbroken until Rafer looks at Maya and utters a single word, "Reumatismo?" Maya nods and puts her hands back in her lap.

Rafer and Eva are of a single mind as memories of the old man with trembling hands in Vegas return. Rafer looks at Eva, using a combination of movements to ask whether he should focus on Maya's ear or her hands. Eva answers by pointing to her own ear, the implication being that arthritic hands pose a more difficult challenge. Rafer nods his agreement and waits for Eva to gain the old lady's consent. In her pidgin Spanish, Eva tells Maya that Rafer has cured people before, just by meditating. After several unsuccessful attempts to make herself clear, she changes the wording from meditation to prayer and waits to see if it makes a difference. It does. Maya, a highly religious woman from childhood, manages an awkward smile and nods to Rafer. When Lena asks what's going on, Eva puts her finger to her lips and leans back in her chair. No one speaks as Rafer closes his eyes half way and slips into a trance.

Once he has found his way into the realm of "unbounded, empty space," he comes back far enough to re-orient himself to his surroundings. Maya is less distinct now but still stands out against a haze of shapes and colors teetering on the brink of nothingness. As if he were fitting an arrow to his bow, he aims his third eye in her direction and shoots a sustained burst of energy across the table into her ear. Eva's eyes never wander from Maya's face. By the time Rafer comes out of his trance, Maya is on her feet and getting ready to leave. A light nod of her wizened head is her only goodbye as she shuffles her way out into the zocolo and disappears behind a string of pedestrians. Back at the table Rafer and Eva exchange questioning glances but say nothing. When Maya is seen coming back ten minutes later, the napkin is gone. Tired from carrying the scarves on her shoulder, she sits down on the raised surface separating the trees from the walkway. In this position she is only 25 feet from the Primavera where Rafer and Eva sit . . . and directly in their line of sight.

"The napkin is gone," whispers Eva, "but look at her hands. Do they still seem curled up to you?"

"Yes . . . like she's gripping an invisible tennis ball," says Rafer, shaking his head.

Eva: "Do you think . . . ?

Rafer (interrupting): "From here?"

Eva: "Is it possible?"

Rafer: "I don't know. I've never tried from this distance before."

Without further talking, Rafer turns his chair slightly to face Maya and again closes his eyes half way. Eva keeps her eyes trained on the arthritic hands. Maya herself appears to be relaxed and looking at nothing in particular, apparently unaware that she is the object of intense scrutiny from across the walkway. As tension builds for the experiment, pedestrians continue to walk back and forth in front of the Primavera, alternately blocking and unblocking Rafer's view. Helpless to see through the bodies in front of him, he is unable to mount the kind of sustained effort he needs. Just as he is about to give up, a large truck filled with potable water for the restaurant appears on the walkway and parks to the right of Rafer and Eva's table, effectively blocking pedestrian traffic in front of the restaurant. Rafer smiles, then quickly refocuses his attention on Maya and begins sending energy into her hands. She again seems not to notice. Ten minutes go by without any interference from pedestrians . . . until a tap on his arm alerts him that someone wishes to be acknowledged. It's Lena. Slowly, Rafer opens his eyes and greets her smile with one of his own.

"Mira! (*Look!*)," she shouts, pointing to her grandmother. At this moment the water truck begins creeping across the walkway, inadvertently obscuring the platform where Maya has been sitting. Rafer and Eva jump to their feet and walk around the truck to get a closer look. To their astonishment, Maya is holding her hands up in the air, wiggling her fingers, sobbing in disbelief as she opens and closes them at will. When Eva steps forward to greet her, Maya reaches out and caresses her cheeks, then whispers in a voice crackling with joy, "Gracias, querida Senora, gracias" (*Thank you, dear lady, thank you*). Turning to Rafer, she takes his hand in her own and bends to kiss his fingers. Uncomfortable with this display of sentiment, Rafer pulls his hand back. "Usted es de Dios?" (*Are you from God?*), she whispers, looking up into his eyes. Stunned to hear such words applied to him, Rafer shakes his head vigorously. "It's just the meditation . . . anybody can do it," he protests, forgetting to translate into Spanish. Maya smiles knowingly. "Entendio" (*I understand*), she says, then gets up to leave. After three or four steps, she turns and opens both hands, holding them high above her head. As Rafer and Eva look on, she waves them back and forth like windshield wipers, as if to say "See what I can do now." When Rafer responds with a flourish of his own, she waves again until her tears get so heavy she has to brush them from her cheek. With the farewell complete, Rafer and Eva turn back to the restaurant to finish their drinks. Before sitting, Eva stops, turns to face her partner and squeezes his hand. He smiles, then squeezes back. No words are exchanged as they take their seats. The silence is finally broken when Eva says, "You know, Rafe, we haven't seen the southern half of the city yet. Any interest?" "Definitely," he answers, with a certainty that belies his inner confusion. "I'll just finish up this iced tea and we can be on our way."

14

The Other Half

As they leave the zocolo and head south down Bustamante, the world suddenly changes from cool, urban elegance to noisy city slum, from the muted whispers of Apollo to the exuberant shouts of Dionysius. The streets are full of trucks, taxis and buses, each honking its unique cry of frustration as traffic creeps fitfully between rows of illegally parked cars. Part of the problem lies with the vendors who have set up temporary shop either directly in the street where cars slip by inches apart or on the sidewalk where pedestrians have to fight to get by. Many of those on foot stop to buy food from the vendors, content to eat their meals on the run as they hurry back and forth to work. The displays of fruit and vegetables are dazzling in both their color and array. Huge bowls of oranges, grapefruit, papaya, bananas and melons compete for attention with lettuce, radishes, chilis, tomatoes, zucchinis and avocados. Other vendors, seemingly oblivious to the danger, are cooking bacon, pork and beef on camping stoves in the street with traffic just a foot away.

"What are those grayish-brown things over there," Eva asks, pointing to two huge mounds of cooked delicacies sitting in a cart.

"I think they're chapulines . . . french-fried grasshoppers. Want to try one?"

"You go first," she giggles.

Rafer picks one from the pile and puts it in his mouth. "Wow. Too salty for me," he reports, turning his back to the owner who stands hoping for a sign of approval.

"That bad?," whispers Eva. "Maybe I'll wait."

As they walk up and down the crowded streets, they pass one small shop after another . . . some selling food, others radios, CD's, toasters, computers or appliances. Most of the meat sellers are congregated on a section of Las Casas, a street where eviscerated chickens and slabs of beef hang undecorously from ceiling hooks, without refrigeration and all too often covered with flies.

"I don't see any supermarkets or malls, do you?, asks Eva. "Maybe they're out in the suburbs. Here it's all small shops or vendors . . . which means that you have to go to one person for meat, another for fruit, and still another for vegetables. It must take a lot of time."

Rafer: "Yes. And don't forget the wine or beer . . . that's another stop. It's hard to get used to, but I guess we shouldn't be surprised; after all, this whole region of Mexico is agricultural. But it's certainly a different kind of economy here . . . with Mom and Pop operations doing most of the business."

Eva: "I was thinking the same thing. There are hardly any office buildings . . . just a few automobile sales rooms and banks. Everything else is really small . . . and a lot of it temporary. If you're a street vendor, think of the work involved. You have to bring in your fruit or vegetables or CD's each morning and set up shop all over again. And since there are lots of people doing the same thing, you probably have to fight for a good spot. It doesn't sound like an easy life."

As they round the corner of Bustamante and Las Cosas, Rafer almost stumbles over a man sitting in a chair as he plays the violin. He is blind and wearing more clothes than the warm weather calls for. His black woolen jacket with its white stripes has a number sewn into its front . . . 077 . . . perhaps an institutional I.D. In back of his portable chair is a duffle bag, presumably filled with his life belongings. In front, secured between his two sandaled feet, is a small blue cup. As Rafer and Eva stop to watch, it becomes clear that the man is not really playing anything. Rather, he is simply yanking the bow back and forth across the strings while using his other hand to hold the instrument down between his thighs. The effect is a relentless screeching that tears at the ear drums, driving pedestrians to the other side of the street.

"How can he stand that noise?," Eva murmurs.

"I don't know. Maybe he's deaf as well as blind," Rafer offers. "At any rate he's not going to make any money sawing away like that. He'd be better off just to sit there and do nothing."

"Can't we give him something?," Eva asks. Then, not waiting for an answer, she opens her purse, takes out a 100 peso note and puts it in the old man's cup.

"Nicely done," Rafer says as they continue arm in arm up the street back toward the zocolo.

For the next several minutes, neither speaks. Uncomfortable with the silence, Eva turns to her partner and asks, "Where are you Rafe? You seem awfully quiet."

"I don't know. Maybe I'm still confused about what happened earlier . . . you know, with Maya and her hands. I don't understand what's happening to me."

"Aren't you pleased?"

"Certainly . . . it made me feel good to help her . . . just like that old man back in Vegas . . . but it doesn't make any sense. Why is this happening to me? Why me of all people?"

"Perhaps God has sent you here on some kind of mission."

"That really doesn't explain anything. You still have to ask why God is doing it . . . and why He chose me."

"Well, what other explanation is there?"

"I'm not sure."

Eva lowers her head, then asks, "What would your Buddhist friends back in Sikkim say?"

"Probably that I prepared for this in my previous incarnation . . . that I'm reaping the rewards of a virtuous life."

(*Squinting*) "Do you believe that?"

"Not really . . . I feel more comfortable with an explanation closer to home . . . you know, something psychological rather than religious."

"Well, O.K. I would imagine that losing your family in the Himalayas has something to do with it. Or maybe losing money in the stock market along with the respect of your friends."

(*Nodding*) "Yes . . . they're both tragic events in their own way . . . but what do they have to with healing? What's the connection . . . if there is one?"

Eva sighs. "I don't know. I'll have to think about it. All I'm sure of is that I feel very peaceful when I'm with you. My guess is that other people do too." As they pass through the zocolo on the way to the hotel, she smiles and hooks her arm in his; he doesn't pull away. Together they chat freely about the two halves of Oaxaca and what they have just seen.

Just outside the hotel, Rafer brings the conversation back to the question of 'Why me?' "I still don't get it, Eva. I'm just not the kind of person who gets into weird stuff like this. Up to now my life has been pretty orderly . . . hard work at school, summer jobs, a few minor relationships, graduations . . . nothing unusual at all. But now this? What the heck is going on?"

Eva stops and turns to face him. "I've been thinking about it too, but probably not the way you are. I feel more comfortable with images and stories rather than scientific theories . . . so I'm not sure I can be of any help."

"I'm listening."

"O.K. As we were walking up from the zocolo, an image came to mind . . . I saw a young bird in a nest high up in the trees. The bird was cared for by loving parents. The nest was strong and big enough to be shared with his brothers and sisters. One day the mother was captured by a hawk and never returned; soon afterwards the father was killed in an accident . . . and then all the siblings got sick and died. As if that weren't enough, a huge wind came up and blew the nest away . . . leaving the young bird perched on a bare branch all by himself."

Rafer smiles. "Go on."

"You can imagine how frightened he would be. He's all alone now . . . his whole family gone, plus the only home he has ever known. But fate is not finished. Barely able to fly, he starts spending time with other young birds of his kind. One day while exploring a nearby meadow, he discovers a huge fruit tree . . . bearing luscious red berries of a kind he has never seen before. Unaware that the berries are poisonous, he eats a few himself then flies back to tell his friends about his discovery. When they gorge themselves on the berries they all get sick . . . some even die. He holds himself responsible for their deaths and sinks into a deep depression. And so . . . "

(*Smiling*) "Wow. There is a point to all this I assume . . . ."

(*Shrugging her shoulders*) "I think there's a moral here . . . but don't hold me to it. Just tell me if I'm completely off base."

"Just kidding . . . Go on, please."

"O.K . . . (*pause*) . . . Losing his family and then all his friends is going to have a pretty negative effect on his outlook on life, wouldn't you say?

"For sure."

"But I think it's also going to affect the way he sees himself (assuming he can think and feel like we do). He's no longer surrounded by birds who love him and who look after him. All alone now, he's neither loved nor respected by anyone. His whole world is shattered. Wouldn't you guess that his basic sense of who is, his identity as an individual, will be threatened? Now that he has no parents or friends to bolster his self-image (like the stuff he used to get: "You can be anything you want to be; you're the smartest little bird that ever lived"), maybe he's in a position, for the first time in his life, to discover something deeper than his regular, old self . . . (*pause*) . . . Not that I know what that is . . . I'm just thinking off the top of my head."

Silence.

Eva: "I think I got carried away. I'm sorry. Let's get back to the hotel."

Rafer turns to face her. "No, please. You may be onto something here. It does sound a bit strange . . . but I want to explore it. Let's say this bird of yours suffers these calamities and begins to have some doubts about who he is and where he's going in life. What happens next?"

"I'm not sure. But if his family is gone, his friends are gone, and even his home is gone, something could open up inside him . . . you know, something that's been there all along but has been hidden beneath all this concern with himself, where he's going in life, and how other birds see him."

"And you're saying that this something underneath is what . . . the ability to heal?"

"Well, perhaps, but I think it's more than that . . . like a special kind of spirit or energy that has nothing to do with the self, with being a success, being liked, or making parents proud of us . . . you know, all the stuff we lose so much asleep over. I don't feel that kind of energy myself so I'm really not the best person to talk about it. But I sense it in you, Rafe . . . I feel it whenever we're together. And it's beautiful . . . really beautiful."

Once they are inside their room, Eva flops down on the bed, saying, "That was a long walk Rafe. I don't know about you but I'm tired. Do you mind if I take a little nap?"

Rafer looks down at her, fully aware of her beseeching charm. "Not at all," he replies, struggling to tear his eyes away. "I may join you as soon as I get rid of these shoes. Do you want me to take yours off while I'm at it?"

Eva nods. "That would be nice. It means I can lie right here."

"By the way," he says, moving to the end of the bed, "thank you for your story of the little bird . . . you know, the one who lost his family, then his friends, and finally his self. As an explanation of what is happening to me, that comes as close as anything I can think of."

(Lifting her foot) "Maybe we can do better when these new abilities of yours have worked their way out. But whatever happens from now on, I feel lucky to be a small part of it."

After removing Eva's shoes, Rafer unties his own and places them under the bed. He reaches for his belt, then hesitates, deciding ultimately to join her with pants and shirt still on. She immediately picks up on his ambivalence and says, "I think we'd be a lot more comfortable with fewer clothes, don't you?" Before he can answer, she gets up and pulls her dress over her head, tossing it playfully onto the chair as he watches. "Well, yes, I guess . . . why not," comes the uncertain reply. With both stripped to their underwear, they climb into bed, Eva on one side, Rafer on the other. A full minute passes before a word is spoken. Eva is the first to speak, "A hug would be nice, Rafe." Sensing that he might consider a face-to-face hug too intimate, she curls herself into a fetal ball and rolls over, facing the wall. Seconds later her instincts are vindicated when she feels him pressing against her, the two bodies joined now like nested spoons. Hidden from his gaze, she smiles contentedly when he reaches across her side and lays his hand gently on her breast. Within minutes they are both asleep.

15

Lili

Later that evening, Lena and Monica come to the restaurant with some new friends. By now all have heard of the shopping spree at Tres Hermanos and are desperate to be included in the next outing. Some are among the dozen already promised a return trip tomorrow; others are new to the group. Under siege, Rafer promises to make as many trips as necessary to get new shoes "for anyone who needs them." With that last stipulation in mind, the children hastily pull off their shoes and hold them up for Rafer's inspection. "Mira, Roberto, Mira," (*Look, Roberto. Look*) they shout as they point to holes, rips, and frayed straps in an attempt to win his consent. Some go so far as to tug on the present holes and pull on the rips, anything to highlight the wretched condition of what they are presently wearing. Rafer is sufficiently moved by what he sees to reiterate his promise to take them all to the shoe store tomorrow.

In the meantime he introduces them to a guessing game, soon to be called "cha-cha-cha" after the sounds he makes when he is flipping coins from one hand to the other. This is the way the game goes: first he picks one of the children to do the guessing, usually starting at one end of what is now a semi-circle of bodies scrambling for room around the restaurant table. He then reaches into his pocket and pulls out a five or ten peso coin, shows it to the guesser and proceeds to flip it quickly from one hand to the other as he utters "cha-cha-cha." When his fists close, the guesser has to point to the hand where the coin ended up. A correct choice wins the coin; a wrong choice means you have to wait until your turn comes around again. The only problem with the game is that it generates continuous noise as the kids insist on shouting their guesses whether or not they're the ones doing the choosing. Rafer, who is totally wrapped up in the excitement, is slow to realize how offensive this noise can be to other diners. It takes a tug on his arm from Eva to alert him to the fact that the ladies at the next table, their annoyance clear from repeated looks of disgust, have already complained to the waitress. Once notified, Rafer gets up from his chair and goes over to apologize. The women are understanding but not totally mollified until the waitress informs them that Rafer has paid their bill. The games end when a burly policeman comes over to escort the children out of the restaurant.

With quiet restored, Rafer and Eva return to eating. Half-way through their meal, they notice a young woman staring at them. Her smooth bronze skin indicates she might be in her late twenties or early thirties. She walks by the table slowly, pauses, then turns around and walks back, stopping to stare each time. Curious to know what she wants, Rafer waves her over to the table and asks if she would like something to eat or drink. She declines but says something in Spanish that neither Rafer nor Eva understand. When she gets no response, she says, "Usted Roberto?" (*Are you Roberto?*).

"Si," Rafer replies. "Porque me lo preguntas?" (*Why do you ask?*)

The woman drops her head and begins to cry. "Mi hija Lili esta in el hospital. Los medico dicen que se esta muriendo." (*My daughter Lili is in the hospital. The doctors say she is dying*).

Rafer: "Lo siento mucho oir eso." (*I'm very sorry to hear that*). "Como puedo ayudar?" (*How can I help?*)

"La gente dice que puede hacer milagros." (*People say you can perform miracles*).

Rafer shakes his head. "Hago lo que puedo pero no siempre funciona." (*I do what I can but it doesn't always work*).

At this point the woman reaches out and takes Rafer by the hand. "Vendra manana al hospital por la manana?" (*Will you come to the hospital tomorrow morning?*).

"Por supesto!" (*Of course*). "Que hospital es?" (*Which hospital is it?*)

"Benito Juarez del Centro Medico . . . pabellon del ninjos." (*Benito Juarez Medical Center . . . children's ward.*) Se llama es Lili Mendoza." (*Her name is Lili Mendoza*).

"Estaremos alli. Son las nueve un buen momento?" (*We will be there. Is 9:00 a good time?*)

"Si. Gracias Senor Roberto. Gracias." (*Yes. Thank you Mr. Roberto. Thank you.*)

As the woman hurries off to join the rest of her family, Rafer turns to Eva, "Apparently the word is getting around. I hope she doesn't expect too much."

Eva replies. "She didn't say what the problem was. My guess is that it's leukemia . . . if so, she's probably on chemotherapy."

"But the mother says she's dying, so apparently it's not working. That seems a little strange, doesn't it, since she's so young."

"Yes, it does. I wonder if there might be other things going on with her . . . ."

"You mean like emotional issues . . . "

"Mmm . . . things like depression or fear of rejection . . . even hating herself for some reason. I don't know. You hate to see things like this in someone so young."

At about 8:30 the following morning, Rafer and Eva take a taxi to the Juarez Medical Center where they are told that the children's ward is located in an adjacent building with an entrance of its own. It takes several more inquiries before they find themselves alone in the elevator heading for the third floor. Eva can tell just from standing next to him that Rafer who has been meditating since 7:00 and foregone breakfast in order to keep his mind clear . . . is already moving in and out of what he calls "empty space." The deep peace she feels in her own psyche is a sign that something good is about to happen.

Inside the waiting room, they look around for Mrs. Mendoza but do not see her. There are, however, several visitors seated at opposite ends of the row of chairs along the wall. Rafer points to two seats in the middle. After 30 minutes, there is still no sign of the Mendozas but something else has changed. Each time one of the other visitors gets up to use the water fountain or get a magazine, he, or sometimes she, returns to a seat closer to where Rafer and Eva sit. By the time an hour has passed, all three of the other visitors are bunched up on Rafer's immediate left. No one says anything about it. Eva simply smiles.

The ward door finally opens and Mrs. Mendoza appears, accompanied by a shabbily-dressed man, presumably her husband, and a bald, goateed doctor in a white coat. Both the Mendoza's are in tears. The wife comes immediately to where Rafer is sitting and bends down to take his hand. She is trembling. He stands and grips her shoulders to keep her from falling, then reaches out to introduce himself to the husband. Eva offers her own hand and a brief "Buenos dias." (*Good day*). The doctor, a small, wiry man in his fifties, nods in Rafer's direction, unaware at this moment that the tall American standing before him is anything more than a friend of the family. Mrs. Mendoza says nothing, but heads for the inner door, beckoning Rafer and Eva to follow. Just inside her daughter's room she confirms their suspicions that Lili is suffering from a severe case of blood and bone marrow cancer . . . in a word, leukemia.

At the girl's bedside, they are greeted by a spectacle that makes them gasp. A child of perhaps eight or nine lies covered up to the chin in white sheets amidst a tangle of cords dropping from various monitors above her head. Her brown eyes, too big now for the gray, emaciated face that surrounds them, are the only hints of life in a body clearly exhausted by its struggle with death. The mother is the first to speak. "Querida, este es el senor Roberto. El esta aqui para ayudarle." (*Darling, this is Mr. Roberto. He is here to help you*).

Rafer comes closer to the bed and smiles. "Hola, Lili. Te gustaria mejorar?" (*Hello Lili, Would you like to get better?*).

Lili lifts her head, straining to respond, "Oh, si, pero nada parece funcionar." (*Oh, yes, but nothing seems to work.*)

Eva reaches down to touch Lili's hand, then gives it a gentle squeeze. Her voice is warm and soothing. "Roberto sabe hacer major. El ha hecho con otras personas" (*Roberto knows how to make you better. He has done it with other people.*)

Lili squints. "Si el medico me no puede ayudar, que puede hacer?" (*If the doctor can't help me, what can you do?*)

The mother, who has been standing quietly in the corner, approaches the bed and leans down to speak. In a voice barely audible she says, "El puede te curar. El ha curado a otras aqui en Oaxaca." (*He can cure you. He has cured others here in Oaxaca*).

Lili's eyes open wide. Turning to her mother, she whispers, "Es Dios?" (*Is he God?*).

"No," says the mother, "pero viene de Dios." (*No, but he comes from God*).

Lili closes her eyes as she struggles to digest this latest piece of information. When she finally opens them, she turns to Rafer and asks, "Habla con Dios?" (*Do you talk to God?*).

Rafer says nothing. In desperation, he looks over at Eva, eyes signaling a need for help. She nods . . . several times, leaving no doubt as to her response.

"Hablamos a menudo" (*We talk often*), he whispers, hoping no one else can hear.

Her eyes grow wider. "Que hablarais?" (*What do you talk about?*)

Rafer looks again at Eva, gritting his teeth. She nods but says nothing. He takes a deep breath, "Mas recientemente El me pidio que viniera a ayudarle." (*Most recently, He asked me to come and help you*).

She gasps. "El sabe mi nombre?" (*He knows my name?*).

Rafer nods. "No solo eso, El sabe que estas enfermo y quiere que te majores." (*Not only that, He knows you are sick and wants you to get better.*)

The words bring a glow to her face. Breathing faster now, she asks, "Que tengo que hacer?" (*What do I have to do?*).

Rafer shakes his head. "Nada, Lili. Voy a hacer todo." (*Nothing, Lili. I will do everything.*)

With no further need for talk, Rafer pulls up a chair and begins meditating. It is not long before the room dissolves into emptiness and an unnamed power, by now familiar from previous sessions, begins to fill his solar plexus. He trains his inner gaze on her shrunken frame, sweeping back and forth across her body, using his mind alone to penetrate the veins and arteries that hold her cancerous blood. When Lili sees him close his eyes, she does likewise. Meanwhile, the parents sit quietly, casting a glance at each other before turning back to watch their daughter's face. Thirty minutes pass, then an hour. The silence is finally broken when a nurse enters to ask if everything is alright. Eva assures that all is well, then waves her back into the waiting room.

The sound of the nurse's voice is sufficiently loud to bring Rafer out of his trance. He rubs his eyes and looks around, nodding first to Eva then to the parents. When he leans over to see how Lili is doing, her eyes are wide open and she is smiling.

"Como estas?" (*How do you feel?*), he asks softly.

Lili is slow in answering. "No se. Algo se siente diferente pero no estoy seguro que lo de es." (*I don't know. Something feels different but I'm not sure what it is.*) Rafer takes her hand, gives it a gentle squeeze, then steps aside to let the mother and father come closer. As the parents stoop to look, their faces first tighten, then erupt into a broad grin. What they see is the same gray pallor, the same huge eyes they have become accustomed to, but a face adorned now with a smile, the first such smile they have seen for months. Almost immediately, the mother turns to Rafer and takes his hands between her own, kissing them repeatedly until Rafer grows self-conscious and pulls them away. The father continues to hover over the bed, alternately whispering things that no one else can hear and running his fingers through Lili's black hair.

Rafer and Eva wait for a few more minutes, then turn to leave, but not before promising to come back tomorrow to see how the patient is doing. There are more hugs and gracias at the door, broken up only when the nurse strides in, teeth clenched and clipboard in hand.

Back at the Primavera, famished after an emotionally draining morning, Rafer and Eva prepare to tackle their enchiladas verde when they are spotted by the children they promised to take shopping. Rafer assures them he has not forgotten but asks them to wait until he and Eva have finished their meal. Reluctantly the children retire to the wall opposite the restaurant where they sit, watching his every mouthful.

The minute the bill is paid, the children flock to the table, crying "zapatos, zapatos" and tugging on either an arm (the 8-9 year olds) or a leg (the 5-6 year olds). At the entrance to Tres Hermanos they are met once again by the owner who insists on knowing how many there are before opening the door. Following a routine now familiar to Rafer and Eva, the children (now 13 in number) swarm into the store like a horde of locusts ready to consume everything in sight. Racing up and down the display aisles, they shout out their choices, then change their minds when a friend points out something different. Some of the older patrons inch their way toward the door as the noise reaches ear-splitting levels. For the owner, it is either a bonanza or a nightmare; he cannot be sure. Any misgivings Rafer might have are quickly dispelled when several customers smile their approval.

Once the shoes have been purchased and the group is back outside, Rafer is surprised to hear the tugging and begging start all over again. "Ropa, Roberto, ropa." (*Clothes, Roberto, clothes*). This time the target is Milano, a clothing store with a popular children's department. Rafer nods his consent but is unsure which way to turn. He doesn't need to know. Before either he or Eva can ask for directions, he is yanked and pulled two blocks down the street. On the way he resists only to the extent of maintaining his balance. Within minutes the group arrives at the store, thirteen strong (plus two adults) and flies past both shoppers and clerks to the children's department upstairs. "Un regalo por persona," (*One gift per person*), Rafer shouts as the scrambling begins. Pants, T-shirts, blouses, socks, hats and jackets are torn from their hangers and tried on for sizing and either taken to the checkout counter or dropped where they are. Rejected items soon clutter the floor where, to the dismay of the increasingly alarmed clerks, they are stepped on. When everyone has finally made a choice, the group gathers at the main counter downstairs to have their purchases paid for and bagged. Rafer stands by with his credit card in hand. From her vantage point next to the counter, Eva watches carefully to make sure no one tries to cheat. Two culprits are detected with T—shirts inside of blouses and are asked to return one of the items. When everything has been paid for, the group makes its exit out onto the zocolo. Some of the children are profuse in their appreciation; others smile but say nothing. One of the boys begins shouting "Pelota, Roberto, pelota."

(*Soccer ball, Roberto, soccer ball*). Rafer nods and promises a trip to the sports store sometime soon. When the begging continues, Rafer sighs, then takes Eva by the hand and walks swiftly back to the zocolo where they resume their seat at the restaurant. Safely ensconced, they watch as the children filter back out into the crowd, looking for their parents and friends.

At the Primavera next morning, Rafer and Eva are making plans for the day when Lena comes running to the table sputtering something about Lili Mendoza. "Roberto . . . Lili es mi amiga . . . su mama dice que usted debe ir al hospital de immediato. Ella regresa a casa. Su Mama dice que es todo lo mejor." (*Roberto . . . Lili's my friend . . . her mother says you should go to the hospital right away. She is coming home. Her Mama says she's all better*)."

Rafer and Eva leave their yogurt and toast and rush to the taxi stand near the Santa Domingo cathedral. They arrive at the hospital twenty minutes later and enter the waiting room along with several other visitors. Just inside the door, they hear voices. Upon further inspection it turns out to be a doctor talking to Mr. and Mrs. Mendoza. Coming closer but still hidden behind the other visitors, they can see that it is the same bald, goateed doctor who was attending Lili when they visited yesterday. He seems frustrated and is trying to explain something to Mrs. Mendoza.

"Si, ella es mejor pero no es un milagro. El medicamento simplemente toma tiempo para trabajar." (*Yes, she is better but it is not a miracle. The medication simply takes time to work*). He smiles as he awaits her acquiescence. But the mother is not convinced, as evidenced by the vigorous shaking of her head. "No es cierto" (*It is not true*), she cries. When she sees Rafer and Eva coming in, she lets out a wild shout and rushes to greet them. "Mira," she says as she drags Lili with her, "Puede caminar. Ella regresa a casa con nosotros." (*Look, she can walk. She is coming home with us*). The doctor's smile quickly twists into a sneer as mother and father take turns bestowing kisses of thanks on whatever part of Rafer's anatomy they can reach.

It is only when the jubilation has subsided that the doctor takes Rafer aside and introduces himself. "Nice to meet you. I'm Dr. Alvarez," he says in perfectly good English. "You mustn't take these people seriously," he adds. "They are very superstitious. They'll believe just about anything you tell them."

"Perhaps," Rafer replies, introducing himself, "but do you think they are naïve enough to believe that the medication suddenly kicked in after not working for weeks?"

Dr. Alvarez reddens at the unexpected rejoinder. "I would like them to believe it but I do not expect them to do so. They are ignorant people, mired in a primitive, animistic form of Catholicism . . . like most of the population here in Oaxaca. A man of your intelligence and education must see that . . . surely."

Rafer waits to answer. "I just wonder . . . is it possible that you doctors are mired in your own primitive belief that if a patient recovers, it can only be because of your intervention?"

Alvarez tugs on his goatee. "So you doubt that we had anything to do with the child's recovery? It sounds like you not only believe in miracles but are convinced that you just performed one yourself. Am I hearing you correctly? Are you really a miracle worker, Mr. Alexander?"

"I'm not convinced that I personally had anything to do with Lili's recovery. What I am sure about is that your own efforts failed to cure her, despite what you are saying. Where that leaves us, I do not know."

"Do you consider yourself a religious man?"

"No, I don't."

"But you are a Catholic . . . yes?"

"No. I don't belong to any religion. I have my own way of making sense of the world."

"An atheist, perhaps? And yet the nurse said she heard you telling Lili that you were sent here by God Himself. A pretty tall order for someone who doesn't even believe in a Supreme Being, wouldn't you say, Mr. Alexander?"

"I'm not aware that I've told you anything about my beliefs, other than that I'm not conventionally religious."

Alvarez's sneer returns. "Of course . . . but you must see how that makes your motives a bit mysterious. If you're not a religious man, what is it that inspires you to interrupt your vacation for the sake of a total stranger, a dark-skinned child from a foreign land at that? Is it possible that you got paid for your services? A healer for hire, so to speak?"

Rafer pauses to glance over at Eva who has been listening. He assumes a look of mock indifference, then answers, "Well certainly . . . and why not. A man has to make a living some way . . . yes? But I am not as greedy as you might think, Doctor. When I make out my bill, I use a sliding scale . . . so poor people like the Mendozas end up paying as little as 100 pesos . . . a real bargain, wouldn't you agree? Some of my clients back home, on the other hand, have paid as much as 10,000 U.S. dollars for my services . . . and were happy to do so."

The Doctor snickers. "Not funny, Mr. Alexander. This is a serious matter. As you go about pretending to cure patients without knowing the least thing about medicine, you are undermining the public's trust in the hospital and its staff. We all know that patients must have faith in their doctors if they are going to get better. So, what will people think if they read in the newspapers that even though we used the most effective, scientifically-proven drugs available, we failed to save a lovely young girl . . . while a non-medically trained tourist appeared out of nowhere and cured her cancer just by sitting at her side? Just what are they going to think, Mr. Alexander?"

"I'm not sure. Perhaps that you people here don't know as much as you think you do. Or that there is more to curing disease than pills or surgery or whatever else they teach you in medical school. I think you could learn a lot just by listening to the people you treat. They may know more than you realize."

Alvarez starts to go, unwilling to risk any further display of emotion, then changes his mind and turns at the door for a final remark. His voice is carefully modulated, his mouth stretched to a wry grin. "Well, what can I say . . . other than thank you for your kind advice. I promise to share it with my colleagues who I'm sure will treat it with the same respect as will I. Goodbye Mr. Alexander."

With their business in the hospital finished, Eva and Rafer leave the room and head down the stairs. "So, what do you make of his response?," she asks as they step out onto the street and look for a taxi. "He sounded awfully defensive to me."

"More defensive than I expected," answers Rafer. I just hope I didn't make matters worse by teasing him about the money."

"I think he had it coming, don't you?"

"Perhaps. At any rate, his reaction is a clear sign that we have to be careful in our dealings with the medical profession. But this shouldn't come as a surprise. People who have spent years learning their craft are not going to take kindly to having an untrained outsider like me competing for their patients' trust and affection."

"So, what do we do?"

"I don't know. Other than to be courteous and not blow our own horn, I'm not sure there is anything we can do."

In Eva's mind, Rafer's use of the pronoun 'we' says more than he could possibly imagine. Warmed with new hope, she hooks her arm around his and asks, "Do you think we'll have more chances to help?"

"I don't see why not. We've only been here a couple of days and look what we've gotten into already. My guess is that there's a lot more to come."

In the days ahead, Rafer has the opportunity to apply his new-found powers to a variety of cases . . . an alcoholic with liver disease, a middle-aged man diagnosed as paranoid-schizophrenic, a young woman with Type I diabetes and an elderly man dying of lung cancer. All return to complete health with the exception of the paranoid-schizophrenic whose distrust makes any intervention impossible. Contributing to the success of these efforts is the budding friendship Rafer establishes with Dr. Ruiz, a lead physician at the Juarez Medical Center. Unlike his colleague, Dr. Alvarez, Dr. Ruiz is willing to concede that Rafer possesses the ability to cure disease without the help of either medication or surgery. In time, he starts calling Rafer's hotel whenever it appears that conventional treatment is not working. Neither of the two men, however, is ready for the call that is about to come, the call that will alter the way people think about disease, not only in Oaxaca but around the world.

16

Mother of All Miracles

The call comes on a day when Rafer and Eva are preparing to visit the suburbs where most of the Oaxaca population lives. Together they hope to survey the poorest neighborhoods with the idea of finding out what kinds of things people really need . . . a new refrigerator, a washing machine, a TV, new windows, some new plumbing, a bed, a couch and chairs, etc. It is a project that Rafer has been thinking about ever since they left Las Vegas. With the help of the hotel staff, they have recruited a young Oaxacan woman who is bi-lingual and whose speech, dress and general manner can put a local face on the survey. The phone rings as they are about to leave the hotel room.

"Hello Roberto, it's Manuel Ruiz over at the hospital. I hope I didn't catch you at a bad time."

"Hi Manuel . . . no, it's O.K. Nice to hear your voice. We were just about to leave but it's nothing that can't wait. What can I do for you?"

(Sighing) "We've got a real mess here. Last night the police brought in a teenager who survived a car crash in which his two friends were killed. I say 'survived' . . . but just barely. We've been working on him for 12 hours now . . . replacing lost blood, stitching up his face and arms, setting broken bones . . . plus stabilizing his pulse and blood pressure with medication. So far we've kept him alive . . . but just barely. I'm afraid his heart could give out at any time . . . I'm not sure. At any rate, can you get over here and try your meditation technique on him? He may be too far gone to benefit but there's no harm in trying. If you decide to come, you better come right away . . . he's not going to last much longer."

Rafer waves Eva back from the door. "I'll be there as soon as I can get a taxi, Manuel . . . shouldn't be more than 15 to 20 minutes, depending on traffic."

Ruiz sighs. "Right now, he's in and out of consciousness. If I can get through to him, I'll let him know you're coming. But hurry!"

Rafer grabs Eva by the hand and pulls her out onto the street, explaining the situation as they run for the nearest taxi. It is three blocks before they spot a vacant cab just north of the zocolo. "Juarez Centro Medico," Rafer yells as they jump in. "Rapido," he adds breathlessly. The driver is about to explain that he always drives rapidly, then decides to communicate through actions rather than words. As they go careening past trucks, cars and pedestrians onto the main artery, Eva grabs Rafer's arm and holds on. "My God," she whispers, "he's going to get us all killed."

Before they are even half way to the hospital, traffic unexpectedly slows down. As Rafer cranes his head to see what is holding things up, all cars come to a complete stop. Up ahead is a major intersection where cruiser lights can be seen blinking as the police attempt to make room for a tow truck. Even from 20 cars back Rafer can see that there's been an accident, both cars having been dragged to the side of the highway, still locked in fatal embrace. Horns are blaring as drivers voice their frustration; some get out and look around before resigning themselves to passivity. In the back seat Rafer grips the armrest as images of the dying teenager begin swirling inside his head. He turns to Eva, "I told Manuel we'd be there in 15 to 20 minutes. We'll never make it now."

"Is there some way we can let the hospital know we're stuck in traffic?"

Rafer leans over the front seat to see if the driver has a cell phone . . . then turns to Eva, shaking his head. When no way out seems possible, Rafer slumps back into the seat and closes his eyes. He starts by breathing slowly, then lets a picture of the hospital come to mind. Using the little information given to him earlier by Manuel, he imagines the boy lying on a gurney, surrounded by nurses, head wrapped in bandages as they pour blood into his body. Because the image is fuzzy and lacking in detail, he finds it difficult to direct energy to it in any meaningful way. The energy is there . . . but it remains locked up inside his nervous system, unable to zero in on its target.

It is close to an hour before they get to the hospital and meet Dr. Ruiz. When Rafer begins to apologize, Manuel indicates that he is already aware of the accident, adding that the two drivers involved have already been admitted to the emergency room downstairs. Before Rafer has a chance to ask how the boy is doing, the doctor's sluggish movements hint at the answer to come. "He died about an hour ago. The trauma was too much for his heart; it simply gave out . . . (*pause*) . . . His parents are inconsolable, especially his mother. I didn't realize until this morning that the boy was their only child. Apparently there were complications with the birth that ruled out any further conceptions."

Eva winces at the news. "Are the parents still here? Perhaps we could help by talking to them."

"Yes. They're in the waiting room, the same one where you met Lili's folks. I'm sure they would be glad to see you."

Rafer: "What about the boy's body? Where is it right now?"

Ruiz: "Do you really want to see it? It's pretty messed up."

Rafer: "Yes."

Dr. Ruiz shakes his head. "Come with me, then. I'll take you there."

As Ruiz leads the way, Eva takes Rafer by the arm, "Why don't I go and spend some time with the parents. I'll see you in the waiting room when you're finished."

The boy's body lies on a gurney in a small room adjoining the operating theater where it awaits the coroner. It is fully covered with a green sheet. Ruiz looks at Rafer, waits for his nod, then pulls the sheet back, fully expecting to see his guest gasp in horror. Rafer instead draws closer, staring deeply at the boy's once-handsome face, now ghostly pale and disfigured with bruises and stitches. "What's his name," he whispers.

"Javier . . . (*pause*) . . . Javier Lorenzo. Shall I leave you,?" asks Ruiz.

"Yes, please."

Left alone with the lifeless body, Rafer lapses into a state of deep quiet. He has no agenda, nothing he feels compelled to do. He is not even aware of why he asked to see the body, other than to give vent to his grief at not being able to help. "I'm sorry," he mumbles, looking down at the boy's face, "I wanted to be with you at the end. Together we might have made a difference." With the door shut and no one to observe, he feels free to say it again . . . out loud. Then, content to yield to whatever happens, he closes his eyes and begins to meditate. When his legs grow tired, he pulls up a chair next to the gurney. Five minutes pass without any movement, then ten. When 15 minutes have gone by, Dr. Ruiz grows alarmed and opens the door. When he sees Rafer meditating at the boy's side, he smiles, closes the door and returns to the waiting room where the parents sit clinging to each other, unwilling to leave while their son still lies so close.

Shut off from the outside world, Rafer sinks gradually into a universe where all material objects have been transformed into pure energy. Perhaps it is his own brush with death in the Himalayas that sends him so deep; perhaps it is the simple tragedy before him . . . a mere boy, the only son of devoted parents, killed in a senseless accident, cut down before he has had a chance to prove himself in the world. As he meditates, he is conscious only that he is entering a domain consisting of nothing but pure energy . . . energy so limitless that it fills the universe . . . energy so powerful that it defies any attempt to harness it. There is no separate self here, no Rafer, no Eva, no dead body, nothing that presents itself as a known object to a perceiving subject. Without forms like self and other, I and you, observer and observed to guide him, he initially feels lost. His hands grow clammy; his breathing accelerates. Conscious only of a mysterious force bubbling up inside, he squeezes his eyes shut and yields to the inevitable. Withdrawing slightly from the Void, he struggles to make sense of what is happening. It is then that he makes his discovery. If all objects are nothing more than temporary expressions of the pure energy that pervades the universe, he too must *be* that energy. He is not something apart; he and the energy must be one and the same.

He re-enters the trance state now with a new resolve. Looking down at Javier, he opens his eyes, then closes them half way. Sweeping back and forth across the prone body before him, he pours his very being into the boy's heart and lungs; he penetrates his organs, his muscles and bones, his eyes and ears. No part of that inert frame is left untouched as he seeks to stirs its dormant tissues back to life.

In all of this Rafer is no longer a vessel through which energy is flowing; he is the energy itself, the world's energy, the very life blood of the universe. No longer a separate self, dependent for its well-being on individual will, he enters the boy's lifeless body with the power of a thousand suns. Unlike heat or light, this energy is pure . . . slipping through skin, enclosing organs and tissues, calling quiescent cells from their sleep. There is no stopping to rest now, no pausing to see what is happening. Time itself no longer exists. Heedless of any personal discomfort, he directs every fiber of his being toward the body before him, flooding it with the searing, healing power of pure energy.

Minutes pass in silence before an unidentifiable sound stirs him to open his eyes. He looks first to the door but sees nothing, then behind him to the table where a book or chart may have toppled over. Everything is still in place. His heart begins to race as he lowers his eyes to the body in front of him. Now he sees what before he could only hear. There is a shuffling of legs under the sheet. He rises in his chair, shuddering at what he sees. The shuffling continues. His breathing comes so quickly now he can hear himself gulping air. He shudders again, afraid to look any further. A minute passes as muffled voices can be heard in the waiting room. Slowly . . . cautiously . . . he shifts his gaze from the boy's legs to his stomach and then to his chest. Nothing is moving under the sheet. He pauses and takes a deep breath as he readies himself for what is still to come. With a final thrust of will he turns his head just far enough to see the boy's face. A cry of horror reverberates throughout the room. Javier is smiling back at him.

Dr. Ruiz rushes to the door and flings it open. He looks first to Rafer's face, sees the terror in his eyes . . . then to Javier who is sitting up. As he screams for help, two orderlies come bursting into the room. They stop at the foot of the gurney, stunned into silence as the corpse of two hours ago greets them with a smile. From out in the waiting room, the parents can hear the doctor's cry but can only see the backs of the orderlies. Still looking, the mother reaches for her husband's arm and gasps, "Que esta mal?" (*What is wrong?*). "No se," (*I don't know*), he replies. Neither one moves. When the orderlies part, revealing an upright Javier, his smile evident as he brushes back his hair, the mother screams, then falls to the floor, clutching her husband's legs. Gently he lifts her to her feet and guides her into the room. She inches her way to the side of the bed where Javier sits with his arms extended in welcome. "Mama," he whispers. She raises her own arms for a hug, then pauses in mid-air. Still staring at his pallid cheeks, she begins shaking her head violently. "No, no, no," she screams as she turns her palms outward as if warding off an evil spirit. As her trembling mounts, the husband grasps her from behind and escorts her back into the waiting room.

Within the hour the waiting room is flooded with reporters demanding to know what happened. Rafer refuses to be interviewed, which leaves it up to either Javier or the staff to do the explaining. When Javier is questioned about his recovery, he replies simply that he slept through it all and remembers nothing. Dr. Ruiz is more forthcoming and does not hesitate to call it a miracle. The boy was dead for almost two hours, he reports, and somehow returned to life with all his vital signs still working. There is simply no way medical science can explain this. As the reporters take notes, he concludes, "One must turn to God for answers."

Dr. Alvarez is also interviewed but offers a very different perspective on the day's events. "I am convinced," he argues, "that the boy was never really dead. Our monitors said he was but they were wrong. Like humans, machines sometimes make mistakes. A reading of zero pulse and near-zero blood pressure needn't mean that the patient is no longer living; it can also mean that the machine is no longer working. And that is the case today. What went wrong we do not know . . . but we're already looking into it. Fortunately nothing was done to harm the boy while the machine was down."

Through it all, Rafer maintains a low profile, avoiding the cameras by mingling with staff and visitors. He even avoids the parents who remain huddled in the corner while their son gets dressed. "What can I possibly say to them," he asks himself. "I am as shaken as they are. For all I know, they may not even be glad to have their son back. I think the mother is afraid to touch him or even get close to him. And to be honest, I feel the same way. What if he wants to hug me . . . to thank me for saving him? Should I let him? What if he wants us all to go out to lunch together? Could I eat anything while looking across the table at someone who was dead just a few hours ago?"

Later in the day the news appears on the front page of every newspaper in Mexico: "Miracle in Oaxaca;" "Tourist Brings Dead Boy Back to Life;" "Resurrection Miracle." Some of the stories focus on the boy and the details of his death and recovery; others highlight the conflicting interviews given by Drs. Ruiz and Alvarez. Still other articles, especially those on the internet, direct most of their attention to the mysterious tourist and his role in the "resurrection." Their task is made difficult by Rafer's decision to avoid all publicity. Still struggling to digest the enormity of what has happened, Rafer refuses all interviews. The only photos of him are grainy and show the back of his head. It is only when he is alone with Eva that he begins to talk.

Eva: "You're still shaking. Are you alright?"

Rafer: "Not really. As long as I don't think about it, I'm O.K. But as soon as the thinking starts, I get nauseous. I don't know what to believe, Was Javier really dead? If so, did I bring him back to life?"

Eva takes his hand. "From what I could see, I'd say he really was dead and you brought him back to life. You probably don't like to hear me say it but you just performed a miracle. You made it possible for a dead boy to live again. It really was a miracle, Rafe."

Rafer places his hand on top of Eva's. "Do you think I've gone too far? I mean . . . am I interfering with the natural order of things? Am I trying to play God?"

"I don't see it that way, Rafe. You didn't have any intention of bringing him back, did you? Isn't it something that just happened?"

"Well . . . I suppose you could say that . . . but I did sit down next to him and begin to meditate. At the time I wasn't at all clear what I hoped to accomplish . . . but maybe some part of me wanted to perform a miracle. Maybe I really did want to play God? I don't know."

Eva: "Did the parents say anything to you? I was watching them for a while . . . when we left they were still clinging to each other over in the corner. I don't think they knew what to make of it all."

Rafer shakes his head. "I don't blame them. Javier has changed now. He's no longer the sweet young kid who's all smiles because he just got his driver's license. He's someone who left this world of cars, girls, school and home for a domain where none of us has ever been. To enter that world he had to stop breathing, let his heart stop beating, and allow his body to grow cool. He had to become what people on this side of the divide would call a ghost. And then, against his will perhaps, he was called back and forced to re-inhabit a body that lay lifeless under the sheets. It is this body, still cool and pale, that his parents saw when they first entered the room. I don't blame them for being confused."

Eva nods. "Perhaps more than just confused . . . probably frightened or even disgusted. You're right . . . he's no longer their little boy. He's tainted in some way . . . someone it might be dangerous to touch. It makes sense too that they don't want to talk to you. You and Javier are both tainted now . . . no longer completely human."

Rafer forces a wry smile. "A couple of untouchables? Is that what we've become? . . . (*chuckling*) . . . Well, you're free to sleep out in the living room, if that's what you want."

Eva grabs his hand and squeezes. "Not on your life. If anything, what happened today makes me want to be even closer . . . (*pause*) . . . I'm ready to go, are you?"

Rafer nods. "Yes. I'm exhausted."

17

Komerov

Komerov is the last one to arrive. Petey, Thomas, Zeke and Hunter have been anxious to get started ever since Revy hinted that he had some unusual news to report. As soon as Zeke finishes his prayer, Petey declares the meeting open. Revy begins reading from one of his favorite websites . . . the one called WeirdStuff.com. "Get this guys. Our Antichrist may not be the guy Petey told us about . . . you know, the one out in Vegas who's been raking in big bucks and curing old men's palsy . . . but he could be an American tourist vacationing in southern Mexico. According to this reporter, a white-skinned dude visiting Oaxaca brought a dead kid back to life, just by sitting at his side and meditating. Don't laugh; I'm serious. Several people witnessed it . . . a couple of docs and their orderlies, plus the parents. The boy was in a car accident and got beat up real bad. According to the article, the docs worked on him for hours . . . new blood, new tubing in his gut, stitches on his face and back, anti-biotics, the works. But they couldn't keep his heart going. He went into a coma and died somewhere around 10:00 in the morning. But that's when the story becomes interesting. Apparently this tourist, the same guy who recently saved a leukemia patient the docs had given up on, dropped by a couple of hours after the kid was declared dead . . . and . . . you ready for this? . . . sat down next to the body and began meditating. A little wacky, right, since the boy already had a sheet pulled over his head. But guess what happened next . . . the whole fucking hospital erupted . . . I'm paraphrasing here . . . when the kid who had supposedly been dead for two hours, sat up in bed and smiled. The mother was so distraught she refused to touch him. Everybody else went berserk . . . (*pause*) . . . Here's a photo of the kid . . . taken as soon as the photographers got to the hospital. He still looks a little seedy if you ask me."

Thomas: "Yeah. I agree. But what about the tourist who brought him back from the dead? Any shots of him?"

Revy: "Just this grainy one . . . all you can see is his back. He's standing over there on the right, next to this gorgeous blonde. The article says he's kind of shy, doesn't like publicity."

Petey comes over to look at the laptop monitor. "That's the tourist, there? (*pointing*)."

Revy: "Yeah. I wish to hell he'd turn around so we could see his face."

Petey starts to breathe faster. "Wait a minute. For Christ sake, look who's standing next to him."

Thomas: "Yeah, she's a real knockout, isn't she?"

Petey shouts: "No, no. That's my niece. That's Eva."

Revy: "What? This is Mexico, Petey, not Vegas."

Petey. "Don't be stupid. I know what my niece looks like. That's her. And that guy next to her, the mysterious tourist who won't show his face . . . that's gotta be her new boyfriend . . . the one she met in Vegas . . . the one who made all that money at the roulette table."

Hunter: "You sayin it's the same guy?"

Petey: "I am. I'm sure of it."

Revy: "You mean we don't have two suspects like I thought. You're sayin that the guy who milked the casinos for all that dough is the same guy who brought this Mexican kid back to life."

Zeke: "And the article you just read says he also cured a girl with leukemia . . . just by meditating."

Thomas: "Yeah . . . and don't forget the old geezer with Parkinsons. He cured him too, didn't he?"

Komerov takes a deep breath. "The evidence is certainly mounting that this man has at least some of the attributes of the so-called Prince of Darkness. Whether he's the real thing is still questionable though. From the passages in the Bible that Zeke read to us, he should also be a convincing orator . . . and a person of political stature. I don't see any sign of that so far."

Petey: "That could still be comin, Doc."

Zeke: "Yeah. He could jis be getting started."

Revy: "This certainly calls for more research. I'll check out some more newspapers and web sites. If he actually did what they say he did, reporters are goin to be all over him . . . and you know how persistent they can be. They'll be checkin out his family, his education and religious background . . . not to mention girl friends, business associates, criminal record, army record . . . all the usual stuff. It'll all come out sooner or later . . . we can be sure of that."

Greta closes the novel she's been reading and lays it on the coffee table. She shakes her head and looks at her wrist watch. "My God," she sighs, "a whole day reading this trash and nothing to show for it. Why do I keep doing it? Such a waste of time. If father knew, he would be appalled. No, he would be ashamed . . . ashamed to think that a daughter intelligent enough to get a master's degree in philosophy and win a job as editor for an academic journal was spending her days watching soaps and reading beach novels. I'm as disgusted as he is . . . probably more so since I'm the one who keeps choosing to do this."

Still struggling with her thoughts, she gets up and heads for the bathroom. Once inside, she looks at herself in the mirror. The sight is depressing. Before her is a face overrun with freckles and dominated by thick black eyebrows that stand guard above pale-blue eyes and a large, thin nose . . . all topped off by a hank of straight black hair falling headlong to her ears. The face, unprepossessing in its own right, is in turn set on a short, cubed frame devoid of any gender-confirming curves. She sighs. "What have I done to deserve these looks? Yes, I'm intelligent and educated, but what good is to be smart if you're this plain?"

She fluffs her hair, waving it attractively with her fingers, only to see it fall straight back down. Disgusted, she turns from the mirror and heads into the bedroom. Sitting on the edge of the bed, her thoughts drift back to the day of her wedding. "There's no question that George was eager to marry me . . . but for what reason? Certainly not for my looks. How else would you explain that we haven't made love now for several years? No, it's obvious why he pursued me. He saw me as a way to escape the blue-collar world of Somerville . . . or what he likes to calls Slummerville. From what he told me, his parents were content to scratch out a living with their hands and saw education as a waste of time. He wanted more than that so he began hanging around libraries and bookstores where he could meet interesting people . . . (*pause*) . . . Oh why am I going back over all this?"

She shakes her head and leaves the bedroom.

Back in the living room, the memories return, too strong now to be kept at bay. She slumps into the chair, her eyes closed as she lets the past unfold before her. "So, finally, the working class boy from

Slummerville gets his wish. In a Harvard Square book store he bumps into the daughter of a university professor. They stop to introduce themselves. Never mind that she's plain and unsexy . . . never mind that she's neither good at small talk nor clever with repartee. He's hooked, calls her, and is quick to initiate weekly dates that revolve around visits to her home and long conversations with her father. The eager but graceless daughter is miffed at the lack of personal attention but keeps reminding herself that she is lucky to be dating at all. They eventually marry and settle down near the Medical School where George is still a student. When, in the years to come, he fails to show any interest in love-making, she becomes depressed and, at one point, even suicidal. She loses interest in the world, stops calling on friends, gives up her job as editor at the Journal of Consciousness Studies, and begins filling her days with television and romantic novels. Sensing her withdrawal, George responds by drawing her into his own world. He makes her his confidant and primary supporter. He asks for her opinion on everything; he reminds her how much he needs her, how important she is to his self-confidence. Without intending it, her life begins to revolve around his wishes, his goals, his energy . . . she becomes a planet in orbit around his sun.

Sitting back in the chair, she sees it all clearly now . . . more clearly than she could when it was actually happening. She was too young then perhaps, too needy to catch herself before it was too late. Perhaps it is still too late, she muses; there's no way to know . . . no way to be sure. Tired now and eager to escape the burden of memory, she slips into fantasy.

Still sitting, she tilts her head back and yields to whatever comes. An image appears quickly, vague at first but clearing as it unfolds. Drawing on a child-like love for the things of nature, she pictures herself as a leaf blown into a small brook. Innocent of what is about to happen, she begins circling the water, content to be carried along on the surface. Gradually she is drawn into a small eddy that spins around an unseen vortex. As the water speeds up, she senses danger and begins to fight her way to the bank. It is too late; the eddy is moving too fast. With her energy ebbing, she can only watch as she is slowly sucked into the whirlpool and pulled below the surface. Completely soaked now, her leafy veins crumpled into a swirling ball, she closes her eyes and surrenders to her fate. She is unable to breathe . . . ."

The front door slams shut. George walks in and tosses his coat onto a chair. "Gret . . . where are you? I've got some exciting news." He rushes to the bedroom, then to the dining room . . . lastly to the living room where he finds his wife slumped in a chair, her eyes barely open. Still standing, George relates the news of the day . . . how a mysterious man down in Oaxaca, Mexico brought a young boy back to life after he had been declared dead by the staff. "From what Petey says, he's probably the same person who cured an old man's palsy in Las Vegas and who made more than a hundred thousand dollars playing roulette." When there is no response, he shouts, "For Christ's sake, Greta, wake up. This is important. For all we know, this guy could be the Antichrist who's coming to destroy the world."

Greta strains to listen, torn between the loathing that stirs deep inside and a need to give him the attention he craves. The tension claws at her throat, making it hard to breathe. "Can I possibly refuse him now when I've always been there, always standing by his side . . . even when the rest of the world takes him for a fool." Without intending it, she gives her head a shake. "This has all happened so many times . . . a play with the same two hapless characters, the quixotic rebel and his loyal sidekick . . . engaged in an endless variety of plots, all preposterous, all doomed." She sighs, biting her lip. "And here is the rebel once again, eager to defy convention but, as usual, afraid to stand alone . . . once again demanding that his sidekick go along with his latest crusade." She lowers her head, trying hard to conceal her disgust. "Now he wants my reassurance that he's right, that he alone sees something horrible coming, something to which the rest of the world remains blind. He wants me to certify that he is some kind of visionary, a modern-day prophet . . . (*pause*) . . . But this is no different from the alien-abductees. Although I went along with him at the time, I never believed those women and their stories of abduction. It was all fantasy and delusion like so many of his ideas. Remember the prophecy that the world would end in 1986 . . . and then in 2000. To the horror of everybody we knew, he embraced them both. And now it's the healer in Mexico who might be the Antichrist getting ready to destroy us all." She sighs. "Is there any limit to his foolishness? How can I bring myself to support him in this latest scheme when, like all the others, it is certain to fail?"

He edges closer, his eyes at once pleading and reproaching, his hands open and begging for validation. Shifting his feet, he continues: "It's still early to tell but he may be the most dangerous person on the planet." When she fails to respond, he raises his voice, "Didn't you hear me? I said he could be the most dangerous man on the planet."

She tries opening her eyes but gives up when they prove too heavy. Somewhere in the depth of her psyche, a cry of defiance takes form, rises quivering to her lips, then stops, not ready to give birth. "I don't want to be alone," she murmurs inaudibly. "There's nothing for me to go back to . . . it's too late now." She pauses, then lifts her head, whispering, "He does sound dangerous, George, Please be careful."

"Is that all you can say?" he shouts, looking down at her.

"I'm sorry. I'm feeling rather tired. Maybe I'll take a little nap right here. Don't worry about dinner. I'll be up in plenty of time to prepare something nice."

George, not even looking at her now and oblivious to her ambivalence, continues with his story. "I'd say dangerous is an understatement. With the kind of mental power he has, he could force the rest of us to do whatever he wanted. In time he could make himself a dictator . . . which is exactly what the Bible says the Antichrist will do."

Greta sighs and sinks back into the chair, her teeth clenched against the poison gathering within. "But it seems like he's doing a lot of good," she replies, no longer able to control herself. "From what you've told me, he sounds like a nice man. He doesn't seem all that interested in cultivating a worshipful audience."

George scoffs. "That's just a game he's playing . . . pretending to be shy and retiring. If he's the Antichrist, he's probably just the opposite . . . a schemer thirsty for absolute power."

Greta (*sitting up, biting her lower lip*): "Perhaps you are seeing what you want to see . . . or . . . ."

George (*scowling*): "What do you mean?"

Greta takes a deep breath, her heart pounding against her chest. In a voice barely audible, she whispers: "We all know how much you want admiration, George. You expect to be praised for every little thing you do. So maybe you're just projecting your desires onto this man in Mexico."

George comes closer until he is standing over her. Looking down, he booms: "Well, maybe you'd feel that way if you had been brought up the way I was. I got no praise for anything. Everything I achieved in school was taken for granted . . . or treated with indifference. Everything I've achieved in my whole life I've achieved on my own . . . without support . . . without praise from my family. So yes . . . maybe I am hungry for approval . . . but so are most men in our society. And this healer person . . . whoever he really is; he must want it too."

Greta can now taste the poison in her mouth. She can hold it in no longer. "Have you ever considered the possibility that unlike you, he may have gotten lots of approval from his family . . . and doesn't really need it from other people now. He may feel confident enough in himself that he doesn't have to insist that other people tell him how good he is." (*Rising from the chair, voice louder*) "You are like a whirlpool, George . . . you suck in praise and energy from everyone you touch. You can't live without it. What you don't realize is what that does to the people around you. You drain their energy, their love . . . the way a spider sucks life from a fly."

George steps back, stunned by her outburst. He considers leaving, turns his back to go . . . but turns again when he feels his stomach tightening. The words come slow and controlled. "But doesn't everybody need approval? We have studies showing that babies die when they're deprived of it. You think I'm the exception but I'm not. If anyone is weird here, it's you. You never ask for approval, you never brag . . . and it's clear why you don't. It's not because you're some kind of saint . . . it's because you don't have anything to brag about. You used to be smart, interested in things . . . then you gave up your job at the journal and stayed home. I tried to include you in my work . . . you know, giving you a chance to express yourself through me. And you seemed to thrive on it for a while . . . then you started pulling away. Now I can't even count on you for the simplest support. It's like when I was a kid all over again . . . everything I accomplish I have to do on my own."

Silence.

(*Softly*) "It's lonely Gret . . . (*pause*) . . . I miss the days when we were real partners. We were close then, weren't we?" When she greets him with silence, he kneels and places a hand on her knee. "It's not too late to get back on track. I'm a forgiving man; you should know that by now."

He searches her lips for an answer. Finding nothing there, he continues, "You want to know what Petey said at the meeting? He's convinced that the woman in the photo is his niece, Eva . . . and . . . ."

Greta shudders, then closes her eyes, slipping silently back into fantasy. Once again she is the leaf. The water is swirling faster now . . . moving in ever smaller circles . . . pulling her down . . . stealing her breath . . . sapping her will. Is it my fate, she asks, to be torn from my tether and delivered into the water's chilling embrace? Is it my destiny to be swept into the sea by a force that knows nothing of my own desires? What is the point of resisting? Why protest when I can lose myself in painless oblivion?"

"Well?," he asks, inching forward.

(*Wiping the tears from her cheek*) "I'm sorry George. It seems like I've let everyone down . . . you, my father, the people at work . . . and myself as well. I don't think I'm much good for anything anymore."

George says nothing. Instead he rises and heads for the door. Before leaving, he looks back to see if she is watching. Her body is still hunched into the chair, her eyes closed. As he watches, his lips curl into a wry smile. He shakes his head in silent disgust, then hisses through his teeth. When there is no response, he heads for his study to jot down notes about the Lynn meeting. In his rush to record what was said there, Greta is soon forgotten. Her talk about his being a visionary, however, has set his finely-tuned mind spinning with ideas. "If I were to expose this Beast, take him down . . . what then?," he asks himself. In his imagination he sees his colleagues at school, once his most vehement detractors, showering him with apologies. [We didn't know, George . . . can you ever forgive us?] He sees Greta on her knees, begging to resume her role as supporter and confidant. [I always knew God had some special mission for you George. I just didn't know what it was.] On the evening news he watches as world leaders deluge him with praise. Just who *is* this man, people ask. Who *is* this man who brought the Devil's own henchman to his knees? Out in the streets newspaper headlines blare the news: "Komerov Exposes Antichrist: Much Maligned Professor Foils Devil's Plot to Destroy World." He slams his fist against the desk in triumph.

The noise can be heard out in the living room where Greta remains slumped in her chair but still awake. "He sounds angry," she murmurs. "Maybe I've given him something to think about. I just wish I had done it years ago." Feeling a new peace, she rises and heads for the bedroom.

18

The Interview

In the days that follow the "resurrection," Rafer is besieged with requests for an interview. He refuses them all, preferring to stay clear of the news if he possibly can. It is only when a young Oaxacan man, the first of his family to graduate from college, comes by that he agrees to talk. The man, Pablo Espinoza, explains that he has just taken a job with the local newspaper and been given the assignment of interviewing the reticent "miracle worker from America." They meet at the Hotel Marques de Valle, introduce themselves and order a drink. When Pablo's English, although less than perfect, proves superior to Rafer's Spanish, they continue in Rafer's native language.

Pablo: "People here say only a religious man does what you do at the hospital. Are you religious?"

Rafer: "Probably not . . . but it depends on what you mean by religious. If you're asking if I belong to some traditional faith, the answer would be no. I'm neither Catholic nor Protestant . . . although I do have some affinity for Buddhist philosophy. If, on the other hand, you're asking whether I spend time pondering questions regarding the ultimate meaning and purpose of existence, then the answer is yes."

Pablo: "If you not religious, how do you explain that you bring dead man back to life? If you not see this as God's work, how you explain it?"

Rafer: "I agree. There's no easy answer. The best I can do is put it in psychological terms. There's a certain kind of energy . . . I would call it psychic energy . . . that lies hidden in every one of us. If you can gain access to this energy, for example through meditation, you can do marvelous things with it . . . things you couldn't possibly do otherwise."

Pablo: "So you say that we all have this energy inside us somewhere?"

Rafer: "That's my guess."

Pablo: "In other words, we all can do what you did at the hospital?"

Rafer: "Sounds far out, I'll admit . . . but I think it's true. I don't think God has anything to do with it. It's really not a miracle at all. Any healthy human being could have done it."

Pablo: "But why nobody ever do it? Just you . . . and Christ."

Rafer: "We don't know that for sure, Pablo. It may have happened many times in the past but never been reported."

Pablo (*writing furiously*): This is very weird . . . yes? You bring a man back from dead . . . then you say it nothing special?"

Rafer: "No. The act itself is certainly special. I'm just saying there's nothing special about me. Anyone can do it. All you have to do is enter that place in your mind where this psychic energy is stored up."

Pablo: "And how you do that?

Rafer: "As I said earlier, by meditating. You calm the mind, stop thinking, stop orienting yourself to your surroundings . . . then the energy presents itself. You don't have to make it appear."

Pablo: "But why nobody else do it? Many people meditate . . . yes? Also many good healers in world. But you only one make dead man walk again."

Rafer: "It has probably happened many times . . . in Tibet for example where people take their meditation very seriously. If it hasn't happened here, it's probably because healers haven't gone far enough with their practice. To access the kind of energy I'm talking about, you have to go all the way; you have to keep sharpening your mind until you enter the realm of unbounded, empty space. It's what the Buddhists call the state of enlightenment."

Pablo: "So you are enlightened?"

Rafer: "That's really hard to answer since in the enlightened state there is no self left . . . thus, no one to *be* enlightened or not enlightened. If you are still conscious of being a separate self, you are not enlightened. And if you are enlightened, that is, if you have gone beyond the world of subject and object, there is no self left that can claim that as an achievement."

Pablo (*chuckling*): "Is hard for me to understand. But I think you special, Rafer. Shall we have another drink . . . or must you go?"

Rafer: "I should go, Pablo. I need to back to my room and write a letter to my old professor. He wants to set up an experiment where this healing ability of mine gets put to a scientific test. I've postponed doing it up 'til now because I wasn't sure what was happening, But after the outcome with Javier, I think I'm ready."

Back in his hotel room, Rafer opens his laptop and begins his e-mail. In it he explains what happened in Las Vegas . . . the $600,000 earned in five days as well as his success in curing the old man's palsy. To this he adds what happened with Maya's arthritis, Lili's recovery from leukemia and most recently Javier's startling return from the dead. He summarizes by saying that as long as he continues to meditate every day, he should be able to go on healing indefinitely. The only thing that might get in the way, he adds, is if he were to lose his concentration in the pursuing some desire, like the desire for a woman, public approval or occupational success. So far, so good, he says in conclusion, choosing to omit that he currently has a traveling companion, a beautiful blonde who just happens to be sitting across the room.

Prof. Pulaski writes back almost immediately.

> Great news, Rafe. Sounds like you're putting your gift to good use down there in Oaxaca. It also appears that you've learned how to cultivate that gift . . . that is, how to access it and then keep it going once you feel it. What you said about avoiding strong desires comports with everything I've read in Eastern literature. And that makes sense. Once you start to crave something, whether it's a person, power, approval, or money, your mind fills with distracting thoughts . . . making it impossible to concentrate. So you're definitely learning.

> I must confess, however, that I was stunned to hear about the Javier Lorenzo case. Bringing a dead boy back to life is a far cry from curing someone's palsy or arthritis. Or maybe it isn't. Maybe I need to expand my concept of what is possible. I really don't know what to think. All I'm sure of is that you are stretching our traditional notions of human consciousness. We've all heard people say that we typically use no more than a fraction of the brain's power. Your work reinforces that notion. It's exciting to think about what may be possible if we can harness all the power that resides within us.

> The important thing now is to test this ability of yours in a scientific setting. It's all well and good to save a few

individuals from disease or even premature death . . . but your real contribution lies in proving to the scientific community that a non-medical intervention like meditation can produce positive results. While we have hundreds if not thousands of anecdotal 'miracle cures', we have no objective evidence of the kind that scientists demand before confirming the results. So let's give them that evidence . . . in the form of a clinical trial in which we compare outcomes for two different groups of seriously ill patients, those who get to spend time with you versus those who get nothing more than their usual treatment. Once you say O.K., I can start to make the necessary contacts. My guess is that we'll need a couple of hundred patients, half in each group . . . which means that all three of Boston's major hospitals . . . Mass General, Beth Israel Deaconess and Brigham and Women's . . . will have to get involved.

Of course, they're not going to sign on to the experiment until they are convinced that there is at least a possibility that meditation works. There's too much expense at risk to proceed without some preliminary indication that you can deliver positive results. That means you will need to work your magic on a few patients . . . let's say five . . . before we can get started. Once the hospitals see that you 'appear' to possess some rare kind of ability, they should agree to go ahead with the formal experiment.

Let me know when you plan to get back and I'll make the necessary arrangements.

Fondly,

Stefan

19

The Experiment

"So, tell me about Mexico," Pulaski says between sips of wine. "The newspapers and TV were full of stories about you and the boy you brought back to life, but I'd like to hear about it from the horse's mouth."

Rafer: "Neighhhhh."

Pulaski (*chuckling*): "Is that Spanish for 'I don't want to talk about it?'"

Rafer: "Sort of. Maybe later. Let's talk about the experiment first."

Pulaski: "O.K. Here's my plan. We draw a sample of 200 seriously ill patients from the three major hospitals in Boston . . . Mass. General, Beth Israel Deaconess and Brigham and Women's. All 200 should have negative prognoses . . . something on the order of six months or less to live. Then we divide the 200 into two groups, one that gets ongoing treatment only and a second that gets ongoing treatment plus your meditation."

Rafer: "So how do we decide who goes into which group?"

Pulaski: "We could match pairs . . . you know . . . if we put a 65 year old woman with kidney failure in one group, then we have to find another woman of the same age and with the same problem to put in the second group."

"Rafer: "Sounds difficult. I mean, you're not always going to find a perfect match, are you?"

Pulaski: "No. And so I think it's better to use a randomizing procedure where we go down the list of 200 and let a flip of a coin determine which group they get put into. That way we can be pretty sure of getting two groups with the same average age, the same number of women, the same number of kidney cases, etc."

Rafer: "And if the two groups don't come out equal, what do we do?"

Pulaski: "There are statistical procedures we can perform to account for any differences . . . (*pause*) . . . It's done all the time. You just have to have enough patients to begin with . . . and I think 200 should be enough."

Rafer: "O.K. What then? We have 100 patients in each group . . . all of them very sick people who don't have long to live. That makes sense, but does that mean that most of them are going to be old . . . like in their 70's or 80's? If so, chances are they're not going to live very long anyway, even if the meditation is a success. That will limit the significance of any findings we come up with, won't it? I should think it would be better if we could include some younger people in the sample, you know, some children or young adults."

Pulaski: "I agree. There are two ways of bringing in more young patients . . . one is to include Children's Hospital in the original sample, the other is to exclude patients over 70. It might take a little longer to find 200 individuals who qualify but it can be done."

Rafer: "Sounds good. So let's talk about the 100 patients I will be dealing with. What do you want me to do?"

Pulaski: "Let me ask you this first. Do you need to know what the patient's problem is when you begin . . . you know, whether it's a heart problem, kidney, cancer, etc.?

Rafer: "I'm not sure. Usually I just send energy to the body as a whole . . . and let the patient (probably unconsciously) direct that energy to the immune system."

Pulaski: "So, for example, you don't attack the cancer directly. You don't have to know whether it's in the pancreas or the lungs or the stomach."

Rafer: "I guess it would help if I knew where the problem was . . . but I don't think it's critical. What I see myself doing, at least so far, is boosting the patient's energy level . . . and then letting the patient direct that new energy to the organ or tissue that's not functioning properly."

Pulaski: "O.K. Let me ask another question. Does the patient have to know that you're trying to help? Can this transfer of energy you're talking about take place even if the patient has no knowledge of it?"

Rafer: "You mean, if the patient is asleep?"

Pulaski: "Yes. Or simply not informed that you're trying to send energy through meditation."

Rafer: "I'm not sure. Most of the people I've helped so far have been awake and within a few feet of me when I meditated. They were informed right at the beginning that I was there to help."

Pulaski: "But that wasn't the case with Javier Lorenzo, right? He was not only unconscious when you sat down with him; he was presumed dead. And yet you brought him back to life. To me, that suggests that your technique works whether the patient is aware of it or not."

Rafer: "You're probably right, I hadn't really thought about it in those terms . . . (pause) . . . So how does that affect the experiment . . . or maybe it doesn't."

Pulaski: "No, it really does. Let me show you how. Imagine for a moment that the experiment is over and everybody's reading the results. The numbers, let's say, show that patients who received your meditation treatment lived significantly longer than those who got only the regular treatment. Very impressive, yes?"

Rafer (*laughing*): "Well, so far . . . but I smell a rat coming."

Pulaski: "Good nose. Let me be the rat in question. I read the results and dispute the conclusion that this proves the effectiveness of meditation."

Rafer: "How could it not? The patients I spent time with lived longer than those in the control group. In your example, the statistics prove it, don't they?"

Pulaski: "Continuing in my role as the rat, I argue that it wasn't your meditation that did the trick; it was your personality or perhaps the little pep talk you gave each patient before meditating. We all know that patients who hope to get better live longer than those who are resigned to dying. So maybe you gave them new hope and that's why they lived longer."

Rafer: "Well, that's still an important finding, isn't it? Does it really matter what interpretation we give it? The important thing is that we helped people to get healthy and live longer."

Pulaski: "Hold on. Isn't the point of the experiment to show that meditation by itself can have a healing effect? We already know that lifting patients' spirits helps them to get better. Doctors, priests, rabbis etc. do it all the time. Family and friends chip in as well. There's nothing new there. What we're trying to design is an experiment that will prove once and for all that meditation by itself . . . without pep talks or hand holding, without either surgery or medication . . . has the power to cure disease. A finding like that will revolutionize our understanding of not only medicine and psychology but philosophy as well. It will turn the scientific community on its head. Isn't this what you want?"

Rafer: "Hmm. I guess I want several things. I want to do what I can to relieve people's pain and cure illness . . . and in the process I'd like to prove that meditation can work even when all else has failed. But what I want most of all is to convince people that the ability to heal is part and parcel of being human. We all have it. To me, that seems like the most important thing of all . . . to show others that the potential to cure disease with your mind alone is there in every healthy human being."

Pulaski: "Well, Rafe, that last goal is certainly an admirable one but it's not something we can demonstrate in the experiment we're talking about. You'd need a large sample of people like yourself to pull off a study like that. What we can do with our present experiment, however, is to prove to a skeptical audience that it is possible for one person, simply by meditating, to arrest disease in someone else. That would be a huge contribution, wouldn't you agree?"

Rafer: "Yes, but if we're going to convince the skeptics, wouldn't we have to show how the process works . . . you know, how energy gets transferred from me to the patient and how the patient then uses it to bolster the immune system?"

Pulaski: "That would be ideal . . . but it is not necessary at this point. We don't have any way of measuring the kind of energy that you're presumably sending to the patient. No one has demonstrated that such energy even exists. But that's going to happen in the near future. In the meantime, our task is to show that, by itself, meditation is capable of curing disease. Researchers who come after us can figure out how and why the process works."

Rafer: "So, first things first."

Pulaski: "Yes. A clinical trial of the sort we're talking about is the right place to begin. But we have to design the study in such a way that our critics can't attribute the results to something other than meditation."

Rafer (*smiling*): "I have the feeling that you're about to enlighten me."

Pulaski: "I have given the matter some thought, yes. This is going to seem strange to you, but hold on; it will eventually make sense. The only way to eliminate the possibility that any positive results can be attributed to something other than meditating, like your personal presence or your bedside manner, is to have you do your meditating in an adjacent room where the patient can't see you."

Rafer: "Wow. That does seem a bit weird. But the patient would at least be told that I'm next door trying to help, yes?"

Pulaski: "No . . . the skeptics could then say the results were caused not by meditation but by the lift patients got from being told that someone was in the next room trying to help them. If we want to prove that meditation by itself has the power to heal, we have to eliminate all other factors that can be used to explain the results. That means the patient can't be told that you are trying to help."

Rafer: "My God, Stefan. These skeptics sound impossible to please."

Pulaski: "No. They can still be convinced but the evidence has to be solid. We need an airtight design . . . using experimental and control groups . . . and then someone has to come along and replicate our experiment and show that they get similar results. Then and only then will people acknowledge that maybe, just maybe, it is possible to cure another person's disease using one's mind alone."

Rafer: "O.K. I'm with you. But I still think that the best way to bring about a cure is to introduce myself to the patient, give a little inspirational talk . . . and then sit down to meditate. Maybe for the experiment I have to be in a separate room . . . but in the real world I want to be there in person."

Pulaski: "I understand. And we can incorporate that concern into the design itself. We have 100 patients who are going to receive your treatment . . . plus 100 in the control group who will get nothing but their ongoing treatment. Let's divide the 100 who are getting your treatment into two groups of 50 each. With one group you meditate from an adjacent room . . . no personal contact; nobody informs the patient that you are even there. This is the meditation only group. If this group does better than the controls (the patients who received nothing more that their regular treatment), we will have proved that meditation alone can cure disease. That's huge. The other group of 50 under your care will get both meditation and the personal touch. You go into the patient's room, introduce yourself, give your pep talk . . . and then sit down to meditate. Unlike the meditation only group, this group gets the best of both worlds . . . meditation plus a chance to meet you. At the end of the experiment we compare longevity rates in the two sub-samples. If your hunch is right, the second group of 50, the ones who got both the meditation and the personal contact, should do better than the ones who got the meditation but no personal contact. Both groups, however, should do better than the controls who received no meditation at all."

Rafer: "I like it. I know from experience that both things are important. Meditation works . . . even by itself . . . but you get the best results when you combine it with personal contact. It certainly worked with Lili, the eight year old Oaxacan girl who was dying from leukemia. Remember, I went so far as to tell her that God had sent me to help her. She believed me; I could see it in her eyes. I got her hope up just by being there and talking. That personal contact set the stage for the meditation to follow. My guess is that the meditation wouldn't have been nearly as effective if I hadn't talked to her directly."

Pulaski: "You've got me convinced, Rafe. We just have to go out now and prove it to a broader audience. The first order of business is to try you out on a few cases where the physicians have done all they can and the prognosis is bleak. The hospitals won't be willing to participate in a formal experiment until you can show good results with a handful of patients first. That first little study doesn't have to be a formal clinical trial with proper controls, etc . . . it's purpose is to give the hospital administrators confidence that you're not talking through your hat. So, if it's O.K. with you, let me set up a mini-study in which you get to do your thing with a few seriously ill patients. If they seem to get better following your meditation, then we can go ahead and set up the formal experiment."

Rafer: "Sounds like a little work on your part, Stefan. I hope the results justify your faith in what we're doing."

Pulaski: "Don't worry about me Rafe. There will be articles, maybe even books, to write. There's plenty in this for me, some notoriety, maybe a pay raise . . . but nothing comes close to the excitement of proving what 99% of the scientific community refuses to believe. It could be the finding of a lifetime."

Rafer (*smiling*): "If it works."

Pulaski: "Don't worry; it'll work."

20

Golfing

When patients in the preliminary study show dramatic improvement within days after spending time with Rafer, Pulaski goes into action. All hospitals (four now that Children's Hospital has been added) are placed on a strict schedule calling for Rafer to spend one hour with each of the 100 patients in the experimental sample. At Rafer's request, meditation sessions will be limited to two in the morning (9:00 and 11:00) and another two in the afternoon (1:30 and 3:30), with Saturday and Sunday off. Special rooms are provided at each site for Rafer to do his meditating remotely in cases where the experimental protocol dictates that he be hidden from the patient. Given the possibility of unintentional biasing, none of the nurses are told which patients are in the experimental group and which are in the control group. If all goes as planned, the treatment phase of the experiment should be completed in about a month. Once treatment has ended, patients will be checked for health status (vital signs, tumor size, energy level, etc.) every month for one year and every six months for two years after that.

To cut down on travel time, Rafer and Eva take an apartment near Mass. General, the biggest of the four hospitals. During the day while Rafer is with patients, Eva explores Boston, including a trip up to Lynn to see her uncle Petey. On a tour of the town she learns that Lynn hosts a variety of immigrant neighborhoods and is awash with drug addicts. To even a casual observer, the city's financial troubles are reflected in the ubiquitous presence of low-rent public housing projects. As she and Petey walk the main streets, Eva cannot help feeling conspicuous in her new, gold-sequined dress from Bonwit Tellers. They chat about Las Vegas and the weather. At lunch the discussion turns serious.

Petey fires the first salvo. "Well, what's it like hangin out with a guy who brings dead people back to life? I mean, just how weird is he anyhow?"

"Aside from all the meditating he does, he seems pretty normal to me. He's very easy to be with."

"Well, what kind of relationship do you have exactly? Tell me if I'm snoopin, but are you lovers? Do you sleep together?"

(*Chuckling*) "You're snooping."

"Sorry. It's jis that I'm worried about you Evie. This guy ain't normal . . . however you define it. Anybody who can bring dead people back to life has got to be weird, wouldn't you agree?"

"Different, yes . . . and certainly special, but I wouldn't consider him weird. In his own way, he comes across as very loving and caring."

"Hmm. What do you mean 'in his own way'?"

(*Smiling*) "Well, he's not exactly a Casanova. I'm pretty sure he's not in love with me, at least he's not all over me."

"Do you wish he was?"

"Of course."

"Then how come you stay with him?"

"I'm not sure. He's awfully nice to me . . . and there's no one else I'm attracted to. I really don't have anywhere else to go."

"You could always go back to Vegas and live with your mother."

"And do what? Hang out at the casinos in hope of landing a rich husband? That might have appealed to me a while ago . . . but no longer."

"You sayin you've changed?"

"Probably."

"Because of this guy Alexander?"

"I think so. He's got something I never dreamed possible."

"You mean lots of money and a secret way of making tons more?"

"No, I meant that he's at peace most of the time. I've never seen him get angry, even when people go out of their way to annoy him. I think it's got something to do with all the meditation he does. Or maybe it's just his personality. I don't know. He's been this way ever since I met him."

"Did you ever consider that he might be puttin on an act . . . you know, as a way of coverin up something he doesn't want the rest of us to see?"

(*Squinting*) "What could he be trying to cover up? I don't see it."

"We've talked about this Antichrist thing before. You don't seem to take it very serious . . . (*pause*) . . . I do . . . and you should. I'm not sayin it's a sure thing . . . but your Mr. Peaceful could be gettin ready to unload some real fireworks. And I'd hate to think you was right in the middle of it all. So be careful honey . . . that's all I'm sayin."

"I appreciate your concern Petey . . . but I think you're barking up the wrong tree. From everything I've seen so far, Rafe is unusual, yes . . . but in a good way. He may not be much of a lover but he genuinely cares about other people. And he has a special gift for helping them when they're sick. If he really is . . . "

(*Interrupting*) "But don't you see? This is just his way of gettin people to trust him so that he can lower the boom on 'em later. It's all in the Bible. For Christ's sake, Evie, read the Good Book, especially Daniel and Revelations. It's all in there. Read it before it's too late."

"O.K. There's a copy at the apartment. I'll get it out tonight."

On Saturday Rafer heads for the golf course in suburban Newton where this year's Player's Championship is being held. Only those players who made the cut after Thursday and Friday's rounds are eligible to play on the weekend. With five straight days at the hospital behind him, he is ready for a little relaxation. What makes this years' tournament special is the comeback attempt of Charlie Haffner, a former star who fell by the wayside when his wife of seven years left him for another man. In the run-up to the contest, The Boston Globe has featured several stories about his recent failures in the Masters and British Open. In the latter match, he did so poorly that he didn't even make the weekend cut, attributing his downfall to a combination of wayward drives and poor putting. Having played golf in college where he had his own ups and downs, Rafer is eager to see if Haffner can recapture his former greatness. According to a recent press release, the prognosis is not good. In a story headlined, "Can Haffner Get His Confidence Back?," people who know him well agree that he is still suffering from a case of nerves . . . and that it shows up most dramatically in his putting. The article concludes by questioning whether he has the personal strength to pull himself together in time for the tournament. For Rafer who has followed Charlie's career for years, the prospect of another failure is disheartening. But he wants to be there to see for himself. As he drives to the course, the thought enters his mind that in some unknown way he may even be able to help. "Who knows," he asks, "stranger things have happened. Just think of the casinos."

He arrives early at the Newton Country Club, hoping to watch some of the players go through their practice routines before the Saturday round opens at 9:00 A.M. There are other observers already there, most of them gathered around either Evan Jones or Darryl Perkins, the two favorites. Jones, the black golfer from California, has apparently picked up where Haffner left off, winning both the Masters and the U.S. Open. Perkins, a British transplant, has come in second on each occasion despite his boasts that this was his year to "win it all." Haffner is down at the end of the practice tee, hitting driver and fairway metal shots. Rafer immediately identifies him from his pictures in the paper . . . tall and lean, sandy-haired with an expression of perpetual astonishment. He is all alone as Rafer approaches. It is only when Haffner finishes a bucket of balls that Rafer steps forward to introduce himself. "You must be Charlie Haffner . . . I'm Rafer Alexander, a fan of yours ever since I saw you on television eight years ago."

Haffner (*looking up*): "Ah. Hi."

Rafer: "I don't want to get in your way . . . just wanted to say hello and to let you know that you've got at least one fan here who wants you to win this thing."

The words, common enough in the past but the exception now, have a soothing effect. Charlie tosses his driver onto the ground and holds out his hand for a shake. "Nice to know there's at least one of you left. Which asylum are you from?"

(*Chuckling*) "Well, I guess you could call the New York Stock Exchange an asylum . . . but I no longer work for the big boys."

"Escaped, eh? Are they still after you?"

"They seem to have given up on me . . . don't even want me back now."

"So, you're a free man. Why then are you wasting time following an over-the-hill slob like me when you could be hovering around those young Turks over there *(pointing)*?"

Silence.

Rafer gathers his thoughts before answering. "I'm not sure . . . maybe because I don't think you're over the hill. Could be that you still have some gas left in the tank."

"Nice thought. I appreciate it. But my tank seems to have developed a serious leak. And, frankly, I don't know how to fix it."

"Maybe I can help. I've helped other people in the past."

"Who?"

"Sick people mainly."

Charlie's eyebrows go up. "You think I'm sick?"

"Not in the conventional sense," says Rafer. But maybe emotionally . . . in the negative feelings you're carrying around . . . you know, in the way you see yourself."

"You a psychiatrist?"

"Nope . . . but I've had some success in restoring people's self-confidence. That could be the only thing keeping you from being a winner again."

(Smiling) "So where's the catch? How much do you charge?"

"No charge. No bill. Just the pleasure of seeing you get back to being the person you used to be."

"Forgive my paranoia, but just how do you propose to go about helping me? Are we supposed to have a therapy session before each round . . . or are you going to hit me with an electric shock each time I get ready to putt?"

(*Laughing*) "Interesting ideas . . . but not exactly what I had in mind. I just meditate . . . you don't have to do anything."

"And just how's that supposed to help? It would make more sense if I was the one to do the meditating . . . wouldn't it?"

Rafer nods. "That might help, but it could take years for you to get to the place where I am right now. So let me do the meditating for you."

"And what's supposed to happen to me when you meditate? What should I expect?"

"If it's O.K. with you Charlie, I'd rather not answer that question right now. Maybe later. Too much talk can get in the way of the process."

"Alright. What did you say your name was . . . Richard?"

"Rafer . . . rhymes with wafer. But most people call me Rafe."

Charlie stoops to pick up his club. "I have to get back to my practicing now . . . still having trouble straightening these drives out. And then there's the putting . . . whew! I still don't what's wrong there. That's what's really killing my score."

"I'll leave you now, Charlie. A pleasure meeting you. If it's O.K. with you, I'll follow you around the course once you tee off."

"No harm in that I guess. I should be teeing off in about 45 minutes . . .
(*tipping his cap*) And thanks for dropping by."

When Charlie's name is announced at the first tee, there is a smattering
of applause . . . polite at best, with one enthusiastic exception. Charlie
turns to acknowledge Rafer's presence, then tees his ball up. After
three practice swings, he lets fly with a powerful drive that starts
down the middle of the fairway and then hooks ominously into the
left rough. His shoulders sag as he watches it land behind a small
grove of pine trees. Jim Reeves, a local favorite, hits next and sends
his drive almost 300 yards down the middle of the fairway. The
small gallery of fans erupts into loud applause as Jim tips his hat
in response. When the players leave the tee and head for their balls,
Rafer follows at a distance, along with three other fans, obvious from
their conversation to be friends of Reeves.

Once Charlie finds his ball, it is clear that he has no direct shot at
the green from behind the trees. The only alternative is to lay up to
the apron with an iron. This he does with considerable skill, but still
leaves his ball 100 yards short of the flag. As he prepares to hit his
third shot, he is aware that given the sorry state of his putting, he will
need to chip the ball within five feet to be assured of a par. His nerves
make this impossible. The chip instead travels well beyond the hole
to the far edge of the green, leaving a putt of 25 feet. In his mind he
can already see the bogey five on his score card. "A terrible way to
begin the tournament," he mutters as if it were already true.

As Charlie lines up the putt, Rafer takes a position on the other side
of the green where he can follow the ball as it comes toward him. He
closes his eyes and slips into a trance, confident that his sun glasses
will obscure what he is about to try. Reeves putts out and starts up the
path to the second hole, taking his tiny troupe of followers with him.
Charlie and Rafer are now alone. Twice Charlie rubs his hands on his
pants, hoping to remove the sweat from his palms. It doesn't work.
When he takes the putter in his hands, it slips and falls to his knees
before he can grab it. Rafer comes out of his trance just far enough to

see it happen. Abandoning the world of pure, empty space, he allows the objects in front of him to come back into focus . . . first Charlie, then the ball and finally the hole.

Charlie takes two tiny practice swings, then putts the ball. Within seconds he realizes that it is too far to the right and has no chance of hitting the hole. His shoulders sag. From the opposite side of the green Rafer sees the ball coming toward him; it is moving too fast and at least a foot offline. He can feel the psychic energy surging in his brain. With eyes still half-closed, he aims it at the ball. Still concentrating, he steers the ball toward the hole while simultaneously slowing it down. As Charlie watches, the ball begins to veer toward the cup. At the last second it touches the right side of the opening and drops in. From the path where he has been watching, Reeves yells, "Nice putt." Charlie waves to Reeves and then stares across the green at Rafer. "What the hell,?" he mutters, careful to keep his voice down.

Up on the next tee, Reeves turns to Charlie and asks, "How the hell did you know there was a ridge between you and the hole? I couldn't see it from where I stood."

Charlie shrugs his shoulders. "I don't know. I just let the ball fly. Actually I was surprised to see it curve that much. I was lucky to get out of there with a par."

Charlie's drive is straighter this time and avoids the deep rough. On his second shot, he is thrilled to see the ball land within five feet of the cup . . . a definite birdie opportunity. As delighted as he is with the outcome, he is fully aware that this is a putt you have to make if you want to score well. For the last two years, putts of four and five feet have been his nemesis, costing him countless strokes and any chance of a victory. He stands there now, staring at the ball, then the hole. It is a straight putt; all he has to do is aim for the center of the cup. Before taking his usual two practice swings, he looks to see where Rafer is. Just as on the first hole, Rafer is standing on the opposite side of the green, his arms folded, his eyes zeroed in on the ball. Still breathing fast, Charlie sets his feet and grips the handle of the putter. It is clear from the whiteness of his knuckles that he is gripping the handle too tight but he is too anxious to notice and make the adjustment. He glances at the hole one last time, looks down and swings. Because of the tension in his hand, the blade of the putter is tilted by the time it meets the ball. Charlie lets out a groan as he watches the ball slip off to the left. The pace is right but the direction is wrong. He's about to turn away in disgust when half-way to the hole, the ball changes path, veering back to the right. It is now exactly where it should be. When the ball rolls directly into the hole, he rubs his eyes in disbelief. Bewildered, he looks across the green for answers. There is no one there; Rafer is already on his way to the next tee.

Over the next few holes, Haffner's play seems to improve. As he makes his way down the fairway, his gait seems more brisk, his face more relaxed. The change in demeanor is starting to show up in his score which by the seventh hole stands at two below par for the tournament, just five strokes off the lead. The short eighth hole, however, proves to be his undoing as his tee shot falls short of the greenside bunker and rolls back into the water, costing him a stroke. By the time he makes the turn at the ninth, he is again seven shots back of Darryl Perkins, the Brit who predicted a month ago that he would win the tournament.

As he gets ready to drive on the 10th tee, Charlie looks over at the crowd to his right . . . a crowd which has doubled in size with news of his good play. He breaks into a smile when he sees Rafer waving back, with hands raised and thumbs up. Reassured, he looks down the fairway, imagines where he wants the ball to land, and sends it flying 300 yards down the middle. As he stoops to pick up his tee, he glances back at Rafer and nods. His chest is fuller now, his eyes brighter. Although he might find it hard to articulate, he is aware of something new in his gut, a visceral feeling that he just might be strong enough, good enough, to win the whole thing. "Seven strokes back is not that much," he muses as he hurries down the fairway. "I've got this back nine plus all 18 holes tomorrow. It's doable."

Events would seem to justify his optimism. By the end of the round, he is in fourth place, only five strokes behind Perkins. After finishing up at the 18th hole, he turns to look for Rafer who has been watching from behind the ropes. "I hope you can make it again tomorrow," he gasps, as he reaches out his hand. "You've become my lucky charm. I don't know how else to explain why things went so well for me today."

Rafer smiles. "I think you were due for a good round. The talent has always been there. Personal matters apparently distracted you from your game."

"Well, maybe, but I can't help thinking that you've got something to do with it. Like some of those putts . . . especially those on the first few holes. I still don't know how the hell they went in. You saw them; didn't they seem kinda weird to you?"

Rafer looks off into the distance. "Yes, I saw them. I just chalked it up to your ability to read greens. You apparently saw things the rest of us couldn't see. It's a real gift . . . one that could make the critical difference in this championship."

"I want to think you're right . . . but I can't help getting the feeling you were somehow steering the ball into the hole . . . (*pause*) . . . Were you?"

Rafer pauses to consider his reply. "Like anybody who's rooting for you, I tend to lean one way or the other, you know, trying to put 'English' on the putt . . . but I doubt it has any effect . . . (*pause*) . . . Maybe you don't realize just how good a putter you are."

(*Chuckling*) "Or maybe you don't know how much of a magician *you* are. Whatever is going on, I'm grateful. I don't think I'd be doing this well if you weren't here. So thank you, Rafe."

"I'll see you here tomorrow morning, Charlie. Get yourself a good night's sleep."

21

The Final Day

On Sunday morning, Darryl Perkins and Evan Jones, the top two scorers, wait to be introduced at the first tee. They are the last pair to start this fourth and final round of the championship. Already half way down the fairway are Jim Reeves who is in third place and Charlie who is currently five strokes back and fourth from the top. To the gathering throng of onlookers, Charlie, with his barrel chest and brisk stride, exudes the confidence of one who is at the top of his game. He smiles at the growing crowd, occasionally doffing his cap when someone yells his name. As he prepares to hit his second shot, he briefly scans his audience, finds Rafer, and nods a secret greeting. The shot, a five iron, finds its way to the center of the green, no more than three feet from the hole. The crowd erupts with applause. Turning to his caddy, he exchanges his club for a putter and heads for the green where he taps in for a birdie before Rafer even has a chance to position himself.

Once the ball is safely in the cup, Charlie places a three on his scorecard and draws a driver from the bag. As the crowd parts, he races up to the next tee where he quickly tees up his ball, only to be told to wait for Reeves who, disappointed with his bogey five, is slow to arrive. Dispensing with his usual practice swings, Charlie lines up the ball and lets fly with the full force of his muscular body. When it soars some 325 yards down the middle of the fairway, the crowd claps wildly. Rafer, easily distinguished by his Free Tibet shirt and Red Sox cap, raises his fist in brotherly salute.

By the fourth hole, the leader board at the green shows that both Perkins and Jones have collapsed; Reggie Nesbitt, the Aussie just ahead, has forged into the lead and now stands only three strokes ahead of Charlie who is one under for the round so far. Three holes later the gap has been narrowed to a single stroke as Nesbitt begins to wilt under the pressure. As Charlie approaches the eighth tee, he is aware that a good shot on this tough par three could even the match. He is ready . . . in fact, more ready than at any time in the tournament. His caddy hands him a seven iron, the same club that fell short and cost him two strokes last time around. Charlie is torn between a desire to prove he can make it with a seven and an inner voice cautioning prudence. He decides on the latter and replaces the seven with a six. He tees his ball up and takes a single practice swing. His mind is clear, uncluttered and focused on his goal which is to land the shot within ten feet of the pin. It seems that nothing can distract him . . . nothing in the world . . . until out of the corner of his eye he recognizes a woman standing in the front row next to a man of Middle Eastern descent. She is wearing a sleeveless summer blouse, a beige mini-skirt and sandals; the man has his arm around her waist. It is his ex-wife Sophie and her new boyfriend.

Only his caddy is close enough to hear him mutter, "For Christ's sake, what is she doing here?" His heart begins to race; his hands grow sweaty. He leans on the club to stabilize himself, then takes two more practice swings. Fighting a desire to look at her again, he grits his teeth and looks down at the ball. To his surprise, it appears to have shrunk and is now balanced precariously on a tee seemingly no thicker than a nail. The thought that he could miss it completely creeps into his psyche, elbowing aside all reason. "Absurd," he mutters as he looks at the ball through fevered eyes. "I haven't whiffed a shot since high school." He takes a final deep breath, then swings. To the horror of the crowd, the ball flies wildly to the right, sailing over both spectators and tree tops, landing on the fairway of the adjacent hole. Onlookers are shocked into silence. Then, above the rumble of muted whispers, he hears a giggle. Rafer hears it too and turns angrily to identify its source. With all eyes on her, Sophie lowers her head and purses her lips, feigning apology. Her true feelings refuse to stay put. Within seconds, as others glower in reprimand, she bursts into a raucous laugh, coming to a stop only when her boyfriend puts a finger to her lips. Heads shake in disbelief as spectators drift away, unwilling to countenance such an egregious breach of common decency.

From the adjacent fairway Charlie powers a pitching wedge up over the trees and into a bunker just short of the green. The crowd is again quiet as he contemplates a difficult shot from deep in the sand, his hands fidgeting for the right grip, feet planted precariously on a downhill slope. He is aware that Sophie and her boyfriend have moved off to the left, separated from everyone else but still watching. With the sun in his eyes it is hard to see her face; all he can be sure of is that the boyfriend's hands are now massaging her neck as she rotates her head in apparent bliss.

Rafer squeezes his way to the front of the crowd, hoping to provide reassurance by his mere presence. It doesn't work. Unable to keep his hand from trembling, Charlie skies the ball, sending it directly over the hole but fifteen feet beyond the pin. Because the ball has some spin on it, it begins backtracking toward the hole as soon as it hits the green. As it rolls, it gradually slows and appears to be stopping ten or twelve feet short of the cup. A single putt from here would give him a bogey and drop him two strokes behind Nesbitt. To everyone's amazement the ball keeps rolling, actually picking up speed, until it drops into the center of the cup. The applause is deafening as Charlie lifts his club in triumph. Unnoticed in the celebration, Sophie and her boyfriend head back toward the clubhouse, apparently done for the day. On the path up to the next tee, Charlie brushes against Rafer who is leaning against the ropes. When Rafer winks, Charlie responds by giving him a gentle poke in the stomach. Nothing is said but their eyes tell it all. The pact is now explicit; Rafer will not let him lose. Up ahead, the leader board shows Haffner still one stroke behind Nesbitt. As he strides onto the tee, Charlie tips his hat to the cheering throng and pulls his driver from the bag. With a subtle nod to Rafer, he tees up the ball and sends it thundering down the middle of the fairway.

Halfway to his ball, Jack, his caddy, turns and whispers, "Charlie, I just saw on the leader board that Nesbitt screwed up the hole in front of us . . . so right now we're dead even. A birdie could put us in the lead." Charlie smiles, then breaks into a semi-trot. Over on the side of the fairway, Rafer elbows his way past the other spectators, eager to keep up with his silent partner.

By midway through the back nine, Nesbitt and Charlie are both playing brilliantly and have pulled away from the flock. It's a two-man race from here on in with each player posting birdie after birdie. Charlie breaks the deadlock at the par five 17th with a sensational eagle three. Nesbitt, at the 18th, responds with a final birdie, leaving Charlie just one stroke ahead as he walks up to the last tee. "A par here will do it," Jack whispers. "That's all we need . . . a simple little four. No need to get fancy . . . just get us a four." Charlie looks over at Rafer who is standing by the ropes, then turns back to Jack. "Count on it," he whispers. "It's in the bag."

There is no sign of nervousness as he drives down the middle of the fairway. So far so good. A long five iron to the green leaves him a putt of about 20 feet; all he needs now is two putts for his four and the championship. The crowd is on its feet as he walks back and forth between his ball and the hole, trying to gauge both pace and direction. "Just lag it up there close," whispers Jack. "You don't have to make this putt. It's the next one that counts." Charlie nods his assent and moves to address the ball. As usual, he takes two small practice swings before initiating contact. And that's as far as he gets.

The screams from the club house send everyone scurrying from the green. Before running to help, an official steps forward, signaling a temporary halt in play; all players are told to mark their balls and stay where they are. Along with several other men, Rafer rushes to the area where the screams are originating. The scene is chaotic. A large tent, traditionally reserved for members of the club, has fallen, pinning two women under its heavy steel pipes. Both are bleeding profusely and appear to be unconscious. Rafer, who is one of the first to arrive, kneels next to a cross piece and places his hands underneath. When it refuses to budge, he waits for several other men to position themselves at intervals down the line. At his signal they all lift together while the two women are pulled out from under. Within minutes an older, corpulent man comes running from the club house and kneels between the two bodies to administer first aid. When Rafer slides in next to him, inadvertently brushing his shoulder, the man shouts, "I'm a doctor. Get out of my way." Rafer pulls back to a safe distance and watches while the doctor staunches the bleeding and searches for points of trauma. "Cracked ribs here," he mumbles, examining the younger of the two women. "Possibly a broken neck over here," he adds, turning to the middle-aged woman who remains unconscious. "Don't anybody touch them," he barks as he stands to address the club manager who has just arrived on the scene. "How long before we can get an ambulance here?," he asks. "They're on their way", replies the cowering manager. "Five minutes at the most."

Later, as the two women are being lifted into the ambulance, Rafer steps forward and introduces himself. "I'm a relative. I think I can be of help when they regain consciousness." His statement, carefully rehearsed, is said with such conviction that no one objects. Once inside the ambulance, he takes a seat opposite the two prone bodies, closes his eyes half way and quickly falls into a trance.

Back at the course, play is resumed as soon as the ambulance leaves. Charlie, who is slated to putt next, scans the crowd for Rafer's reassuring face but finds no one. His heart, quiet up to this point, begins to beat faster as he considers the significance of his next shot. "Just lag it up there close," Jack reminds him. "That's all we need." To Charlie, that which seemed a mere formality thirty minutes ago, now looms as a task of gargantuan proportions. He looks again to see if Rafer has returned. Failing to find the familiar face, he begins to tremble. The crowd, sensing his fear, grows deathly silent. Deep in his psyche the sound of Sophie's voice echoes, giggling, taunting. In defense he invokes the image of Rafer with fist raised and thumbs up. It is not enough. The putter slips from his hands, falling to the ground. A young woman in the crowd gasps. Still shaking, he picks it up and stands over the ball with head down, unmoving. When a minute passes without any action on Charlie's part, an official moves onto the green, heading in his direction. Charlie looks up, nods his assent, and takes the first of two practice swings. He stops for a final deep breath, then hits the ball. To his relief, the ball heads straight toward the hole some 20 feet away . . . but stops short of the cup, leaving a clinching putt of six or seven feet. It is a straight uphill putt . . . no curves or ridges to worry about; his only concern is the pace. But he hasn't missed a putt this short all day . . . so why should it be any different now? And yet it feels different. "If only Rafer was here," he mutters, dropping his head. "I never seem to miss when he's around. Even if I start a putt off line, somehow it makes its way to the hole. Buy why? Is that his doing . . . or mine? I'd hate to think I owe it all to him. What good is it if I can only win if he's around?"

The crowd is on its feet now, ready to explode with applause when the putt goes in. They remember how good Charlie used to be and how hard he has tried to come back. They want him to win but they know how sensitive he is, how easily he loses faith in himself. Who could forget Sophie's cruel laugh when he shanked his drive earlier? She had no right to come here with her boyfriend and upset him like that. He deserves better. Make this putt Charlie, they seem to be saying. Make it and win the championship.

Charlie can feel their tension. Added to his own, it threatens to send his body spinning out of control. He tightens his grip on the club to keep it from slipping. In the enveloping silence a crow high in the trees flaps it wings and utters a lonely "aawk!" Charlie scans the crowd one last time, looking for Rafer. With a final shake of his head, he takes a deep breath, addresses the ball and swings his club. To the collective groan of almost everyone there, the ball slides past the cup on the left and lands two inches beyond. Resigned to his fate, Charlie taps in for a bogey and a tie with Nesbitt. Within seconds, the clubhouse official announces that an 18-hole playoff for the championship will commence at 9:00 tomorrow morning. "All tickets for today will be honored tomorrow as well."

Later in the afternoon, as Charlie slumps against a tree overlooking the 18th green, sipping his third wine cooler, he is startled when someone grasps his arm. It's Rafer. "I got back as soon as I could," he whispers. "Guess I didn't make it in time."

Charlie gives his hand a squeeze. "Are the women O.K.? (*Rafer nods*) I sure could have used you on the last putt. I pretty much fell apart."

Rafer smiles. "You'll do just fine tomorrow."

"You're going to be here, aren't you?," Charlie responds with unconcealed agitation.

Rafer pauses, searching for the right words. "I have to be at the hospital all day tomorrow, Charlie," he says softly. "It's part of an experiment we're doing. There's no way I can get out of it."

Charlie sags. "There goes the championship. I can't make it without your help, Rafer. Didn't I just prove it with that last putt?"

"I'm sorry . . . ."

Charlie's eyes begin to moisten. "Couldn't you call in sick or something? Just this one time . . . (*pause*) . . . I'll even split the pot with you if I win."

Rafer steps back to consider his options. "Charlie, you have all the skills necessary to win this match tomorrow, with or without my help. You seem to think my presence is important but I'm not convinced you really need me. The critical thing is that you believe in yourself."

Charlie bows his head. "I guess I've come to believe more in you, Rafe, than in myself. Not a good way to look at things, I know."

Rafer smiles as a solution presents itself. "You know what I *can* do Charlie. There's a TV in the room where I'll be working and I can follow the match play by play on the screen."

"Yeah, but can you do your usual thing from that far away? You know what I mean . . . your magical stuff."

(*Chuckling*) "You mean my special brand of English? I don't see why not. I'll just make sure the TV is on throughout the match. I may have to fight off the head nurse who prefers the soaps, but I think I can handle her."

"O.K. I feel better already . . . (*pause*) . . . Jeez, I wish I wasn't such a wimp in all this Rafe. Maybe if I can get a couple of wins under my belt, I'll feel better."

"I'm sure you will, Charlie. And tomorrow is a good place to start. By afternoon you're going to be holding the trophy, the first of many to come."

"I wish you could guarantee that, Rafe."

Rafer smiles. "I'm counting on it. You should too."

Charlie reaches out to shake hands. "Can we get together tomorrow night . . . after the match is over? Whether I win or not, I've got some questions I want to ask you."

"I'd like that. How about dinner at Durgin Park?"

"You mean the one down in Faneuil Hall?"

"Yes. The one famous for its Indian pudding. Ever had it?"

"Nope . . . but I'd like to try . . . (*pause*) . . . They do have a bar, don't they? I'm going to need something stronger than lemonade."

(*Turning to leave*) "They do. See you there at 6:30?"

"O.K. But don't forget to turn that TV on at 9:00."

"I'll be watching you on every hole."

On his way home Rafer ponders the ethics of lying. There is no doubt; he did lie. "There's no way I can watch TV while meditating with my patients. And even if I could, there's no reason to believe I could help Charlie from that far away. So why did I do it? I want him to win; it's that simple. But am I undermining his confidence in the process? Do I risk making him so dependent on me that he can no longer function on his own? And what about tomorrow? If he wins, it's not going to be with my help . . . I'm going to be busy doing my own thing. But if he *thinks* I'm helping, what's the difference? He's still dependent on me . . . and that's not good for his future confidence. So what do I do?"

Rafer is still pondering a solution as he enters Mass. General in the morning. In between patients, he sneaks down to the main waiting room where there is a TV. When it is clear that no one is watching, he switches the channel to the PGA match out in Newton. Charlie is smiling as he approaches the fifth hole where his ball lies ten feet from the cup. The leader board behind the green shows him in the lead by one stroke . . . with a chance to go up by two if he makes this putt. Rafer smiles and whispers a throaty "Go get 'em, Charlie." Without intending it, he closes his eyes and slips into a trance. Before he can reach a state of 'empty space', however, his concentration is broken by a voice behind him.

"Ah, there you are," says Ms. Kaufmann, the head nurse. "Dr. Howells wants to see you in his office. He says it's important." Rafer shakes his eyes open and heads for the door. As soon as he's gone, she turns the knob back to channel 4 where 'This Is Your Life' is playing and pulls up a seat in front of the set.

At lunch in the hospital cafeteria, Rafer hears the news he has been hoping for. Charlie has won the championship. According to the people at the next table, victory was assured when Nesbitt drove his ball into the water at the eighth hole. Apparently Charlie never let up, adding to his lead right up to the last hole which he birdied with an impossible 25 foot putt. The people at the adjacent table go on to say that at the trophy-awarding ceremony, Charlie paid tribute to his caddy, his former teachers and "to the prayers of a dear friend in the hospital." Rafer can tell from their comments that they assume the 'dear friend' to be a patient, perhaps someone right here at Mass. General. He smiles and shakes his head at the irony of it all. "So, now that he has won," he asks, "what can I say at dinner tonight? Should I tell him the truth . . . that I never got to watch the match . . . and run the risk of an emotional meltdown . . . or should I keep up the charade, thereby locking the two of us into a dependent relationship that could go on forever?"

By the time Charlie bursts through the door at Durgin Park that evening, Rafer has made up his mind. He will tell the truth whatever the consequences. His intention to do so, however, is thwarted by Charlie's rambunctious embrace. "I can't thank you enough, partner," he shouts, bringing caustic stares from the other diners. "We really did it, Rafe. I could feel you right there with me on every shot. I still don't know how you managed to help from so far away . . . and maybe I don't want to know . . . but I do know this. The trophy is as much yours as it is mine . . . and that goes as well for the prize money. I've already written a check to you for your half of the proceeds . . . $400,000 . . . and I'll put it in the mail as soon as I get your address. Now, how about a victory drink?"

Rafer waits for Charlie to sit down, then takes a deep breath. "That's great news about your victory. I heard about it at lunch. The guys at the next table were . . . ."

(*Interrupting*) "What? You didn't hear about it until lunch? Is this a joke Rafe? You were with me all morning for Christ's sake. That 25 foot putt on the 18th green . . . you don't think I did that on my own do you? And then at the award ceremony . . . didn't you hear me say something about a dear friend in the hospital? You must have known I was talking about you."

Silence.

"I didn't get to watch the match on television, Charlie. I was too busy."

"Hey, Rafe. This is too serious to joke about. I know goddamn well you were there. I could feel it . . . just like Saturday and Sunday when you followed me around the course. I knew you were there. I could feel your energy."

Rafer smiles. "That wasn't me you were feeling Charlie. That was you . . . the old you that won all those tournaments in the past, the you that's gone missing recently. But it's clear he's back now and that's who won the tournament today. I had nothing to do with it. So, please, tear up the check. If you don't, I will."

Charlie sits shaking his head. "You're telling me I did it all on my own today? That's a nice thought, Rafe, but if you really knew me, you'd know it couldn't have happened that way. Remember, I thought of you all day long. Before every shot, I pretended that I could see you in the crowd, with your fist raised and thumb up, willing me on. If I had known that you weren't even watching the match on TV, I would have . . . well, I don't know what I would have done . . . maybe collapsed . . . I don't know. But it wouldn't have been pretty."

Rafer nods. "So, what kept your spirits up was nothing I actually did, but simply the thought in your head that I was watching you. In other words, what inspired you to play so well was nothing more than a belief on your part . . . a belief that wasn't even true."

At this point the waitress arrives with their orders . . . roast beef, mashed potatoes and corn for Charlie and a seafood salad for Rafer. When they are alone again, Charlie is the first to speak. "Maybe so. But what am I supposed to take from that? You want me to pretend that you're there each time I play, even when I know you're not? C'mon Rafe. I may be a sucker for a pretty face but I don't think I'm that gullible."

Rafer puts his fork down and takes a sip of tea. "What it says is that believing in yourself is crucial to success."

(*Interjecting*) "Easier said than done."

"Well, look at the facts. You played brilliant golf today without a scintilla of help from me . . . in fact, without help from anyone else. The talent is obviously there . . . you just proved it; you just won a championship completely on your own. So, how can you not believe in yourself? Who else do you think did it?"

(*Smiling*) "You make it sound easy, sir. But I appreciate the effort."

Rafer leans closer. "Let me put it this way. If you can believe in me . . . a man you met barely days ago, someone whose ability to affect your game remains a total mystery to you even now . . . why can't you believe in *you* when it is *your* arms that swing the club, *your* hands that putt the ball, *your* desire to win that propels you forward?"

Charlie smiles. "You're a hard man to argue with Rafe. Let me think about it. I think there's some crap left over from childhood getting in the way here . . . you know, people telling me I'm no good, that I don't have what it takes . . . stuff like that. Maybe if I start hanging around with guys like you I can shake it. I don't know. But I'll try."

(*Nodding*) "Let's stay in touch Charlie. Maybe even play a round of golf together . . . if you can stand the competition."

(*Laughing*) "I don't know . . . that could be scary. What if you start doing your magic in reverse . . . making me miss all my putts?"

"I'm not sure it works the other way around but I'm eager to find out. Just in case, I can always turn my back when you putt."

Charlie tilts his head. "Hmm. That might not be enough. How about wearing a blindfold?"

"I'm game . . . but would you feel even better if I wore a hood?"

"Actually, I think a straight-jacket might be best."

The banter continues throughout the meal as they review Charlie's round hole by hole. By the time the Indian pudding arrives, Rafer knows as much about the match as if he had been there himself. The pudding is warm and comes in a large bowl with a scoop of vanilla ice cream on top. With spoon in hand Charlie leans forward as he prepares to attack this oft-heard-of but never-tried New England delicacy. As he goes to get some of the ice cream on his spoon, it slides down the pudding to the side of the bowl. He sighs, then spoons the ice cream back up the pudding. "I like it on top," he mutters to no one in particular. A second attempt to get ice cream and pudding on his spoon at the same time produces the same result . . . the ice cream slides down the pudding and ends up hanging over the side of the bowl. When it happens a third time, he sputters, "Goddamn it. Why won't it stay there?" When there is no response from his friend, he looks over at Rafer who remains silent; his eyes are half-closed as if he were in a trance.

Charlie reddens. "You devil," he shouts, his eyes twinkling. "Can't a man eat his dessert in peace around here?"

Rafer shakes his head and opens his eyes. (*Squinting*) "What in the world are you talking about, Charlie? Is there something wrong with the pudding? I was hoping you'd like it."

(*Sighing*) "You know, Rafe. You're a real menace. A guy has to be careful when you're around."

(*Eyebrows lifted*) "Really? I've always seen myself as pretty harmless... (*pause*) . . . By the way, there's a ping pong table over at the hospital. (*Smirking*) Would you like to have a go at it sometime?"

Charlie struggles to control his laugh. "Oh yeah . . . I can see it now. I think I'd have a better chance swatting flies with a toothpick."

The evening ends with a promise to stay in touch through e-mails and phone. As Rafer heads home, he is aware of a warm feeling in his gut. "A good day's work," he muses. "Eva will want to hear all about it."

22

Emotions

When the phone rings, Eva rushes to answer. "Oh, hello, Professor Pulaski . . . I'm just fine, thank you . . . Yes, he's here. Let me get him for you."

Rafer: "Hi Stefan. What's up?"

Pulaski: "Well, nothing too startling . . . but we've got a little information you might be interested in. The first preliminary results from the experiment are coming in and so far it looks pretty good."

Rafer: "But the experiment isn't even over yet. We've got another week or so to go, haven't we?"

Pulaski: "True enough . . . but several of the patients in the control group died this past week."

Rafer: "What about the people I've been seeing?"

Pulaski: "So far no one in your group has died. Now don't get excited. I know the sample is too small to generalize from but it does suggest that a difference is already emerging. If all goes well, the difference in mortality rates between treatment and controls should be a lot bigger a month from now and go on to reach statistical significance in six or twelve months. Our plan as you know is to follow all patients for at least two years and maybe even longer than that if the data look at all promising."

The phone call lifts Rafer's spirits. Turning to Eva, he shouts, "Honey, guess what. Stefan says . . . ."

(*Interrupting*) "You never called me honey before. What have I done to deserve that?"

(*Shaking his head*) "Oh. It just slipped out. Anyway, Stefan says he can already see a difference between the controls and the patients in my group. Several people in the other group died last week whereas all my patients are still kicking. It's still too early to conclude anything . . . but it's pointing in the right direction."

Eva comes over to the couch and sits down next to him. "That is really good news, Rafe. I just feel sorry for the people who got assigned to the other group; they may die early because you didn't get to meditate with them."

(*Putting his feet up on the hassock*) "We'll see. It's a little early to say anything definite."

Eva (*eyeing his feet*): "You wouldn't like a foot massage, would you? I'm pretty good at it."

"Why not?," comes the immediate response. I've been tramping around the hospital all day. A massage would feel nice . . . but only on the condition that you let me reciprocate."

"Of course. I would love it too. Now let's get your shoes and socks off."

As he settles back into the couch, she kneels by the hassock and begins undoing his shoe laces. Once the shoes are off, she takes off his socks one by one. As she places her hand on his bare skin, she cries out,

"Rafe, I never knew you had six toes on your right foot. Why didn't you tell me?"

(*Smiling*) "I didn't think it was essential to our relationship. Is it?"

"Well, no, but . . . ."

"But what?"

"Well, you must admit, it is rather unusual."

"Yes, I'm a freak. Is that what you mean?"

"I don't like that word. I would rather think of it as just another sign that you're a very special person."

With that, she begins kneading his foot, alternately pressing the heel of her hand into his flesh and pulling on his toes. When she sees him close his eyes, she slows her breathing and lets her mind drift. "What would Petey say if he knew about this?," she muses. "Should I even tell him? I don't want him to do anything crazy."

Rafer (*opening his eyes*): "You know what the Indians say, don't you?"

"Which Indians . . . our American Indians?"

"No . . . the Calcutta Indians."

"Tell me."

"They say that an avatar . . . possibly an incarnation of Vishnu . . . will someday come to save them. And that this person will have six toes on one foot."

Eva freezes.

(*Pulling his socks on*) "A crazy idea, wouldn't you say. Why six toes? I mean, don't you think you could recognize such a person from other features . . . like his personality or acts of charity?"

(*Softly*) "Or his ability to heal the sick."

"Well, I suppose that too . . . but the whole idea is based on a belief in reincarnation . . . a belief that strikes me as absurd. You have to be pretty gullible to believe that a soul can survive death, disappear into the unknown for hundreds of years, then reappear draped in a brand new body."

"I guess you better not go to India unless you want the attention . . . or at least don't go swimming in the Ganges."

(*Grinning*) "I'll try to keep that in mind in planning my next vacation . . . (*pause*) . . . Now . . . how about my turn to play masseur?"

In the days to come Rafer throws himself into his work. The more he meditates, the deeper the experience seems to go. In addition to the four hours a day he spends with patients at the hospital, he meditates before breakfast and then again at night before going to bed. In time it begins to have an effect on his behavior . . . and the relationship. Eva is the first to mention it.

"You seem to be meditating more lately. We hardly get to spend any time together . . . (*pause*) . . . Are you getting tired of me?"

"Not that I'm aware of. We still talk, don't we?"

"Well, yes . . . but something is different. I get the sense you're changing . . . in a way I don't understand."

"Really? Like how?"

"For one thing, you hardly ever talk about yourself anymore. You seem very alert, very focused on whatever you're doing . . . yet at the same time you seem . . . well . . . not exactly here."

"You mean absent-minded. Off somewhere?"

"No . . . not absent-minded . . . more . . . I guess you could call it remote. Maybe even aloof . . . (*pause*) . . . You don't act like other people."

"Really . . . in what way?"

"Well, when's the last time you got angry? Or defensive? Probably back in Vegas when I followed you into the restaurant and interrupted your dinner. Most people I know get irritated pretty often . . . and they're quick to defend themselves when they hear anything the least bit critical. I don't see you doing either."

(*Chuckling*) "Maybe I'm good at hiding it."

Eva takes his hand. "It's more than that, Rafe. You don't seem concerned about the way others see you. Most people I know want to be approved of . . . so they do things that will make others think highly of them. They talk about themselves; they brag; they love to tell us 'I told you so'. You never do any of that. When Charlie won the tournament in Newton, you could have gone into detail about how you helped him do it . . . but you said practically nothing. The same is true of your work at the hospital. It looks like your meditation is saving lives . . . but I don't hear you say much about it."

"It's a little early to celebrate. Who knows what might happen in the next few months."

"True . . . but that doesn't change what I see happening to you. You're becoming someone I don't understand, a beautiful person, yes, but a person who just doesn't have the instincts of a normal human being. And that makes it hard to be close to you."

Rafer puts his hand on top of hers.

Eva (*her eyes moistening*): I see myself as a pretty average person. I want to be liked. I want to be loved. I especially want to be loved by you . . . and I don't see it happening. You're kind to me . . . more generous than I have a right to expect. But you don't seem to need me. You don't let me take care of you, baby you, listen to your problems, or hug you when you wake up from a bad dream. Isn't that the way most couples behave? They're each other's best friend. They help each other weather the storms of the day. But we're not like that, Rafe. And it's finally becoming clear to me why we're not. You don't have any problems. You don't need my help . . . or anyone else's. You seem contented to stay in your own little world . . . far away from the pain and suffering that the rest of us go through."

Rafer turns to look at her. "But I want to use whatever gifts I have to help others. That doesn't come through?"

She pats his hand. "O.K. I shouldn't have said that. You obviously do care. In Mexico I saw the effect you have on others . . . buying shoes for the children, curing Maya's arthritis and Lili's leukemia, even bringing Javier back from the dead. You know how to make people feel peaceful just by sitting next to them; I get that all the time with you . . . (*pause*) . . . What I should have said is that you don't act like the rest of us. You go out of your way to relieve other people's suffering but you don't seem to suffer yourself. That's all I meant . . . (*pause*) . . . I didn't say it to be critical. It's really a beautiful thing. You shouldn't take it as a put-down."

Rafer puts his arm around her shoulder and pulls her close. "But it leaves you frustrated . . . and I'm not comfortable with that."

(*Sitting up*) "I don't see any way around it. That's just who you are and it's up to me to accept it. After all you warned me back in Vegas that you were like this. So, I don't feel deceived or anything like that."

"So, how do you feel?"

"Frustrated . . . a little lonely . . . but also curious. I often wonder what you are feeling. I mean, if you're not worrying about how other people see you . . . the way the rest of us do . . . just what *is* going on inside you? What kinds of things do you think about?"

Rafer pauses. "You probably won't like this but it's the truth. I don't do a lot of thinking. When I'm with Stefan and we're planning the experiment . . . sure . . . thinking is necessary. Most of the time, though, my mind is pretty clear. I just stay tuned to whatever is going on . . . you know, simple things like the sound of traffic, the smell of food cooking, the looks in people's faces . . . ordinary sensations."

"But what about feelings? Don't you have emotions of some sort?"

Rafer sighs, uncrossing his legs. "Well, I felt elated when Maya showed me she could open her hands again . . . and when I saw Lili come to greet me in the waiting room. And, of course, I was delighted when Charlie won the tournament up in Newton. Is that the kind of thing you mean?"

"Well yes . . . but you never seem to express anger or sadness. Don't you ever get upset about anything?"

"I'm upset that you're upset right now. Doesn't that show?"

Eva shakes her head. "I hate being so negative Rafe but no, not really. You don't strike me as upset right now . . . at least not the way most people would be."

"Do I come across as cold?"

Eva (*biting her lips*): "Cold may not be the right word . . . since I know you *are* concerned about me. It's just that you don't get worked up about it . . . about anything for that matter. You're very placid about everything. And that seems unnatural . . . at least it seems that way to me. Of course, it could be that I expect too much . . . that I'm just too needy, that I can't stand on my own two feet. I hate to admit it but I may not be the right person for you, Rafe."

(*Squeezing her hand*) "I disagree. It is clear that you need me, but what might not be so obvious is that I need you too. Maybe not in the conventional sense where I need you to tell me I'm O.K. or that I'm loved. It's more like we're partners . . . (*pause*) . . . That's what we are . . . partners. It should be obvious from the things we did together in Mexico that I respect your judgment and that I turn to you for advice on lots of things. My guess is that in the years to come we're going to grow even closer that way . . . assuming you're willing to hang in there with me."

Eva forces a smile. "I know you respect me, Rafe, and that pleases me. But it's not quite what I had in mind. What I miss most of all is . . . well . . . I think I've already said it. I need to be loved, but in a way that doesn't seem to register with you. I want you to desire me . . . to want me . . . to be unhappy when we're not together . . . (*pause*) . . . You're not going to change so there's no point in going over it again. It's up to me to accept things the way they are . . . or to leave. I've given it a lot of thought and my choice is to stay."

23

Anxiety in Lynn

P etey: "Help us O' Lord to do the right thing. Keep us on the path you've chosen for us. Make us strong when we have doubts; make us brave when we git scared. Don't forgit us. We ain't forgotten You. Thank you for your blessings."

Group: "Amen."

As soon as he is finished, Petey follows up with a report. "I don't know if this is important or not but I thought I'd pass it along jis in case. My niece Evie tells me that she just found out that Alexander has six toes on one foot. Maybe it's nothin but who knows, it could be a sign of some sort."

Zeke: "Hmmm. Revelations says the mark of the Beast will be a number . . . 666, but Daniel refers to him as 'The Little Horn' . . . signifying a king, but 'little' because he's still a minor figure until he ascends to absolute power over the other kings. I don't know . . . could this sixth toe be the 'Horn' Daniel is speaking of?"

Thomas: "Maybe . . . but it could also be something else entirely. I remember reading about a legend in India that says a six-toed man will come to save them. If this guy Alexander is the Antichrist, maybe he plans to go to India to launch his takeover of the world from there. Seein as how poor and uneducated they are over there, it might be a good starting place."

Revy: "Not to change the subject, but did any of you guys follow the golf match in Newton on TV last weekend. Our man Alexander was there following Charlie Haffner around the course. Several times I saw the two of them exchanging winks after he made a difficult putt. At the time it made me wonder if something funny was goin on. What really got me thinkin was the weird way some of Haffner's putts went in. At first they seemed like real bad putts, you know, way off line . . . but then they suddenly curved back toward the hole and went in. Each time it happened Alexander was right there followin the ball like he was steerin it into the cup."

Thomas: "Yeah . . . I saw that too, but there ain't no way the Beast could have made the ball go in. He was too far away."

Revy: "Well, consider this. Haffner could have won the tournament on the last hole if he made his last putt . . . but he collapsed and missed by a few inches. Strangely enough, it was just before the putt that Alexander left to help out with the fallen tent, you know, the one that fell on those two women. Maybe it's just a coincidence . . . I don't know . . . but it sure looks fishy to me. Maybe it's related to what Alexander did at the roulette tables in Vega."

Petey: "But Revy, Haffner played beautiful on Monday when Alexander wasn't there. He won the goddamn tournament, right? So . . . we really don't know what was goin on . . . maybe nothin."

Doc: "We obviously don't know enough about Alexander yet. What would help is if I could get to know him personally. I consider myself a pretty good judge of character . . . so if he's putting on an act . . . you know, pretending to be this shy healer when he's actually a threat to the human race, I think I'll be able to see through his mask. All it takes is . . . ."

Revy (*interrupting*): "But Doc, weren't you taken in by that woman from New York . . . the one who made up the story about being abducted by an alien? What makes you think that . . . ."

Petey (*alarmed*): "Revy, for Christ's sake, watch your manners. Doc's our guest. You shouldn't be insultin him like that."

Doc (*smiling*): "That's O.K. A lot of people think I was fooled by this woman. It's not true. She may have made up the facts of her abduction but I'm convinced that below the surface she had an unconscious wish to be abducted. And that's what I responded to. I tried to help her come to terms with her fear by confronting her with her unconscious wish to do the very thing she was so afraid of. I don't know if it worked or not but I was never fooled by what she told me."

Revy: "Sorry Doc. I had no idea what was really going on with you two."

Doc: "Nobody else did either, Revy . . . so I got raked over the coals needlessly. Now when it comes to this guy Alexander, I feel confident that if I can get him alone, I'll be able to find out if he's playing a game or not."

Petey: "How you goin to do that Doc? He's pretty slippery."

Doc: "I can always introduce myself at the hospital . . . tell him I'm interested in this experiment he's working on . . . the one that's supposed to be hush-hush but everybody knows about . . . and invite him to my house for dinner."

———————————

A week later.

Petey: "So Doc, tell us about your dinner with Alexander. What did you find out?"

Komerov: "I'm afraid nothing. I had an emergency at the hospital that night . . . one of my patients attempted suicide . . . and I didn't arrive home until Alexander had already left."

Petey: "You mean he stayed and had dinner with your wife?"

Komerov: "Yes he did . . . and it apparently worked out just fine. By the time I got home, Greta was bursting with enthusiasm . . . couldn't stop talking about him. This is a little hard to believe but ever since that night she's been a different person . . . less depressed . . . rejuvenated in a way. She's even taking interest again in how she dresses and wears her hair . . . which in itself is rather remarkable."

Zeke: "I wonder what did it."

Komerov: "Maybe nothing specific. Apparently he asked her about her master's thesis on Buddhist philosophy . . . then convinced her she should try to get it published. He went so far as to invite her to meet with him and a psychologist named Pulaski to discuss healing . . . to see if they can figure out how it's possible to cure disease with meditation alone . . . without surgical or pharmaceutical intervention . . . you know, the kind of thing they're experimenting with at the hospital. So she's all worked up about using her mind again. From what she says, I get the sense that she feels needed again . . . which is fine, I guess. But it comes with a price. Our evening talks used to revolve around my work at school and the work I was doing with the alien abductees. Now she hardly seems interested . . . instead keeps steering the conversation to Alexander and this theory of healing they're supposedly working on. Quite frankly, I haven't seen her this enthused for years."

Thomas: "Maybe she's falling in love with him."

Komerov: "Not likely. Most men don't find her very interesting. She's actually quite plain, if I must say so. We haven't been physically close since right after the wedding."

Thomas: "So why'd you marry her, Doc? She doesn't sound like much of a looker."

Petey: "Hey, Thomas . . . careful."

Komerov (*sighing*): "I suppose I married her because she was smart . . . and came from an educated family. I found her mother and father especially interesting; they were very different from my own family . . . interested in books and the arts. I loved going over to their house and discussing ideas."

Hunter: "Yeah, but even if she ain't spreadin her legs for 'im, she might be tellin 'im about us . . . you know, our meetins here in Lynn . . . and that we're keepin close tabs on 'im."

Thomas: "Hunter's right. If she tells him, he's goin to get cute and start coverin his tracks."

Komerov: "I'm not sure she's told him anything about our meetings . . . but in case she has, I can always tell her that we've stopped meeting . . . you know, that we've decided he's not anybody special."

Zeke: "But what are you gonna tell her when you leave home every Tuesday night to come up here? Maybe a faculty meeting at school?"

Komerov: "The faculty rarely meets at night. It'll have to be something else."

24

Return to Mexico

Rafer is in the kitchen when the phone rings.

"Hello."

"Ah. Is this Mister Alexander?"

"Yes."

"I am Raul Mendes, attorney for Senor Carlos Santana. You hear of him, yes?

"Of course. One of the world's wealthiest men . . . Mexican banks I think."

"Yes. He is very wealthy . . . but not so good now. He is very sick. Some time he has tumor in stomach . . . doctors say cannot operate . . . too big . . . so he is back home now . . . waiting for end."

"I'm sorry to hear that. How can I help?"

"We hear what you do in Oaxaca . . . with leukemia girl and boy killed in auto crash. Senor Santana wants you to come to Mexico and meditate for him. Maybe you can do more than doctors."

"I'm certainly willing to give it a try but right now I'm all tied up in an experiment and . . . ."

(*Interrupting*): "Senor Santana ready to pay you good for helping him."

"That's kind of him but I never charge for what I do. Anyway, I have to be here at the hospital for another week . . . that is, until the experiment is finished. But after that I'm free . . . if you still want me to come."

"Yes, please, we want you to come, Mister Alexander. Sr. Santana have house in Mexico City plus more house in Oaxaca and Cancun. Which one is good for you?"

"I know Oaxaca pretty well."

"Esta bien. We send private jet to get you . . . in seven days . . . Tuesday. Is noon good for you Mister Alexander? You come to Logan airport in Boston where we pick you up."

"Wow. This is all pretty sudden. Let me call you back after I've checked with the hospital. What's your number?"

"I am in Mexico City. Call 011-64-943-5217. Is O.K. if I tell Sr. Santana that you come to help him?"

"Yes. Tell him I want to come. Is it O.K. if I bring a woman friend? We live together."

"Cierto (*Certainly*). We have apartment for you both in Oaxaca. Is all ready."

"That's fine. I will call you tomorrow to let you know if everything is set."

"Gracias Mr. Alexander, Gracias. Will talk to you tomorrow."

"Yes. Bye for now Sr. Mendes. And thank you for calling."

When Rafer and Eva step out onto the tarmac at the Oaxaca International Airport, Mendes is there to greet them.

(*Grinning*): "Hola, Sr. Alexander. Was trip good?"

(*Shaking hands*): "Very good. Even the lunch was great. The plane was a little crowded, however."

(*Squinting*): "Crowded? I no understand."

(*Smiling*): "Just kidding. That's the first time I've ever had a whole plane to myself. Well, nearly to myself. (*pointing to Eva*) This is my good friend Eva Nourini. Eva, this is Raul Mendes, the man who invited us down here."

Eva (*shaking hands*): "Mucho gusto. It's a pleasure to be here."

Mendes: "Ah, you speak a little Spanish, yes?"

Eva: "Very little I'm afraid. But I want to learn more. Rafer and I love Oaxaca and want to spend more time here."

Mendes: "Bueno. People here already know your name. You do miraculous things last time you visit. Sr. Santana hope you can do it again."

Rafer nods. "Where is Sr. Santana?"

"We go there now. First we go to apartment we have reserved for you . . . and then we visit the Senor. He is excited to know you come."

Eva: "He doesn't live alone, does he . . . not in his condition?"

Mendes: "No. He has private nurse to stay there . . . and his daughter Rosita come on weekends. Usually he is in Mexico City and Rosita visits every day. She is very good daughter."

After leaving off their luggage at the apartment, Rafer and Eva accompany Mendes to Sr. Santana's home just outside the city. For Rafer, the house is not as pretentious as he had suspected, given the owner's unlimited resources. There is a uniformed guard at the gate, or course, and a short tree-lined driveway to the house itself . . . but the dimensions of the building are modest. At the front portico they are greeted by an old man whose skin is as wrinkled as his pants. He is introduced by Mendes as Fidel, a long-time man-servant who never strays far from the boss who rescued him from work in the silver mines years ago. The guests are ushered into a long hallway adorned with nondescript paintings of horses and railroads. To the right of the hallway is a door leading into the main sitting room where they find a man asleep in a reclining leather chair. With his finger to his lips, Mendes whispers, "This is Sr. Santana. Is good if we let him sleep. Fidel will get us something to drink while we wait. Should not be long."

As he sips his lemonade, Rafer scrutinizes his new patient carefully. Although he knows from a magazine article that Carlos Santana recently celebrated his 65th birthday in Mexico City, the man before him has the bloodless, wizened look of someone much older, someone exhausted and teetering on the edge of death. His facial skin has lost all color, whitening to a lifeless gray more typical of a centuries-old death mask. Even though he is covered with a sheet, the fetal-like swelling in his stomach is evident from across the room. He has no choice but to sleep on his back. As he lies stiffly, his breathing is labored and punctuated by soft, sporadic moans.

He opens his eyes. "Fidel, estas aqui? (*Are you here?*). "Si, Senor," comes the immediate answer, "quiere tomar algo?" (*Do you like something to drink?)*. "Agua, agua con hielo." (*Water, water with ice*). He looks around. "Raul, que son estas personas? (*Raul, who are these people?*)

"Ah Senor, (*pointing*) this is Mister Rafer Alexander . . . and his friend Senora Eva Nourini. They come to help you."

(*Sitting up*) "Oh, yes . . . do you wait long?"

Rafer: "Just a few minutes."

"Please forgive me . . . my English not too good . . . habla Espanol?"

"We're learning . . . but still beginners. I think it best if we stick to English."

"O.K . . . I try . . . you forgive . . . (*laughing*) . . . is right word?"

"Good word. Now, when do you want to me to come for a meditation session? Anytime is good for me."

"Si, maybe tomorrow morning. I am best in morning."

"What time?"

"After breakfast . . . 9:00 . . . O.K.?

"I'll be here at 9:00 in the morning. Now, is there anything we can do for you while we're right here?"

"No, thank you. I have Fidel and Raul. My daughter Rosita comes in evening. Mostly I sleep . . . and get ready for you tomorrow."

"Alright. We'll see you in the morning. I think we'll head back down to the zocolo to see if we can find some of the children we met last time we were here."

Mendes: "Can I give you a ride in the limousine?"

Rafer: "Yes, thank you . . . we should probably go to our apartment first to freshen up a little. From there we can walk to the zocolo."

Once safely back in their apartment, Rafer pours himself some bottled water and stretches out on the bed. Eva follows, snuggling up close. "Well, what do you think?," she asks. "Can you help him . . . or is he too far gone?"

"It really depends on his attitude. If he's desperate to recover, I can probably help him . . . but that's a big if. And who knows how he feels about the power of meditation? For all we know, he may be skeptical."

"But he wouldn't have flown us all the way down here unless he was open to the idea, would he?"

"Good point . . . (*pause*) . . . You want to come with me tomorrow? I'd feel better having you there."

"Of course. Now, what about the rest of today? What are you in the mood for?"

(*Smiling*) "That's not obvious?"

"I know. You want to go down to the zocolo and look for Lena, Monica, Javier, Vincente and the other kids we met last time . . . (*smiling*) . . . You're such a kid yourself . . . (*pause*) . . . Do you have coins for your cha-cha game?"

"A few. We can stop at the bank and get some more."

Eva leans over to kiss his cheek. "We could also make a trip to the shoe store. I doubt that we'll have trouble finding volunteers."

"Are you hinting that you could use a new pair yourself?"

"I don't know. My feet are pretty sore after all our walking today."

"Would a foot massage help?"

(*Smiling*) "Hmm . . . lovely thought . . . definitely cheaper than buying me a new pair of shoes."

"If it saves money, I'm all for it."

"You mean it's not pleasurable?"

"I don't know. Let me give it a try. It helps that you have such beautiful feet . . . although I've noticed that you're missing a toe on your right foot."

(*Laughing*) "If we ever have children, do you think they'll be born with eleven . . . or will they come with the usual ten?"

Rafer sits up and moves to the end of the bed. "Hard question . . . it's really up to our Maker. If he's feeling magnanimous, he could go for eleven. Then again, if he's in a foul mood or having a bad hair day, he could settle for ten."

(*Poking him in the chest with her foot*) "So, what did you do to deserve special treatment?"

"I was born that way, so I really didn't have time to do anything special. Maybe I had some other deficiency like an undersized pancreas or pea-sized brain and He felt a need to compensate me. I don't know."

(*Shaking her head vigorously*) "You are one silly man. It's a wonder I put up with you."

As he begins running the heel of his hand down into the arch on her foot, she sits up, smiling, "You know, it would feel even better if I took off my pantyhose. But I'll need a little help."

Startled at first, he smiles awkwardly, then runs his hands up her legs to the top of her pantyhose. When he reaches the elastic band, he stops and looks up at her. "I don't know . . . this may not be a good idea, Eva. I should really stay concentrated, you know, for tomorrow's session with Santana."

"Can't you concentrate on me for a change?," she replies with eyes fluttering. Before he can respond, she pushes her pantyhose down to her knees, exposing her light brown curly bush. "You haven't paid a visit for some time now, Rafe," she giggles. "Wouldn't you like to renew acquaintances?"

"I don't think I'm up for it right now. Perhaps after we've seen Santana tomorrow." Staring at the bulge in his crotch, she replies, "Your member seems to be saying otherwise. Am I wrong?"

He forces a grin. "There could be a breakdown in communication . . . maybe a problem with the internal wiring."

(*Opening her arms*), "Why don't you come inside me while we talk about it. I'm pretty good with communication problems." When he hesitates, she leans forward and unbuttons his pants. Still ambivalent, he allows her to help in shedding both pants and underwear. With her hand firmly on his penis, she guides him back on top of her and into her vulva. Her legs open slightly as she welcomes him into her chamber, now moist with the nectar of desire.

His mind begins to race. As id and superego battle for control, a light suddenly goes on in his head; why does sex have to be considered a distraction? Why can't I see it as just another kind of meditation? After all, the Tantrists in India have always viewed love-making as an integral part of their spiritual practice. According to their texts, you just have to remain mindful . . . focused completely on every sound, sight, smell, touch or taste. In other words, stay alert and don't let your mind drift off into *thinking* about what you are sensing. In principle it's no different from following one's breath or the sound of your feet as you walk, things I do all the time.

With his dilemma resolved, Rafer lowers his face to Eva's, free finally to explore the texture and taste of her lips. Just as he is about to kiss her, she sticks her tongue out and laughs. Hesitating only long enough to smile, he captures it with his lips and draws it into his mouth. They lay unmoving for minutes while she slides her tongue in and out of the pocket he has made for her. "My turn now?," he finally whispers. She nods and opens her mouth in readiness for his entry. Within seconds, an assault comes, but not where she expects. Groaning like an freshly awakened grizzly, he moistens his tip on her labia, pries opens her vulva and drives his member deep into her pink cave. As he penetrates her soft inner flesh with repeated thrusts, she muffles a scream, then cries into his ear, "Come to me, darling, come." When his breathing signals a climax is near, she tightens her legs around his thighs and lifts her hips to meet him. "Oh, love me, love me my sweet." That is all that he needs to hear. All restraint gives way as he explodes into her vagina, flooding her cavity with the life-giving cream of manhood. In response she flings her arms around his neck and bites his lips as her body answers with an ecstasy of its own.

"Oh, Rafe, you do love me, don't you."

When he fails to answer, she asks, "Where are you?"

He shakes his head, unable to speak. Several minutes pass before a thought intrudes. "I'm right here. Are you O.K.?"

(Softly) "Better than O.K. Come, let me hold you while we sleep. We can go down to the zocolo later." Without a word, he nestles down next to her and pulls her close. Gradually their breathing slows as passion gives way to contentment. Hours pass without any movement. They are still there, arms entwined, when a nearby church bell rings five times, waking them from their dreams.

That evening they return to the Primavera, one of seven restaurants bordering the huge two-tiered plaza known locally as the zocolo. Dinner "al fresco" is followed by round after round of "cha-cha-cha" with the shabbily-dressed chicos and chicas who flock to their table. The games end only when Rafer runs out of coins. As the children recede into the enveloping darkness, Eva places her hand on his. "They really seem to love you . . . and I don't think it's just because of the money."

"Maybe they like hanging around you. They've probably never seen anyone so beautiful; their mothers certainly aren't anything to rave about."

Eva shakes her head. "No . . . I think it's about you. They can tell you love them just by what they see in your face and hear in your voice. Kids are very perceptive that way . . . maybe more so than adults."

(*Chuckling*) "I don't know. I've always been better with kids and pets than with adults."

(*Stroking his arm*) "You do just fine with adults. This afternoon was especially nice, don't you think?"

"Yes. I enjoyed the little nap we took."

(*With mock alarm*) "Just the nap?"

(*Grinning*) "Oh, and that other stuff too."

"Other 'stuff'?"

"Just kidding. It was really nice. I was more attentive than ever to the way your body felt, especially to the smoothness and warmth of your skin. It was very much like a meditation."

(*Squinting*) "But did you like it?"

(*Pausing*) "To tell you the truth, I never stopped to analyze my feelings. I just . . . ."

(*Interrupting*) "I didn't ask for an analysis. I asked if you enjoyed making love to me."

"Looking back I can say yes, I enjoyed it . . . but at the time the only thing I was aware of was how you felt, smelled or tasted. So I can't really say whether or not I . . . ."

(*Scowling*) "Forget it. Let's get back to the apartment before it's too dark to see our way."

25

Carlos Santana

Within seconds of a knock, Sr. Mendes appears at the door and extends his hand in welcome. "Please come in Sr. Alexander and Senora Nourini. Sr. Santana is in his study waiting for you."

Rafer and Eva step into the foyer, "Thank you. How is he feeling?"

"He looks maybe better . . . hard to say."

"How would you describe his mood . . . you know, his attitude? Is he hopeful?"

"Not know. Maybe you ask him."

As they enter the study, Sr. Santana rises in his leather chair and extends his hand, his eyes still cloudy with sleep.

Rafer shakes his hand. "You look better today Sr. Santana. That's nice to see."

"Thank you . . . but please . . . call me Carlos. We no longer strangers."

"O.K. I'll call you Carlos if you call me Rafe. Is it alright if Eva sits in the corner while we work?"

"Yes, Rafe. You lucky man. She is very beautiful woman. My daughter Rosita, she is beautiful too. You will see."

"I look forward to meeting her. Now, let me ask you a few questions."

"Anything I tell you."

"Fine . . . (*pause*) . . . How badly do you want to recover? Not everyone in your condition feels the same about this."

"Oh . . . very bad. I am only 65 years old . . . still a young man. Life has been very good to me. I am, as you Americans say, at top of my game. They say I am richest man in whole world, but I am only starting. I have plans for spreading business to Asia and Middle East where there is shortage of big banks. There is so much to do. I don't want to die now Rafe, not for long time . . . (*pause*) . . . Is question answered?"

(*Nodding*) "Yes it is, thank you. Now . . . just one more question. Do you think is possible for one person, without any medical or surgical help, to cure another person's disease using his mind alone? A lot of people would say no . . . (*pause*) . . . I'm interested in what you have to say about it, Carlos."

(*Sighing*) "Before you bring Javier Lopez back to life, I say not possible. Medical science is better. But now . . . I am open to possibility. I think you special Rafe . . . maybe you can do it, but not others."

"That's fine. Having a positive attitude really helps. Now, I'm going to go into a meditative trance . . . there's nothing you have to do other than stay where you are and don't talk. As the meditation deepens, you're going to feel energy passing from me to you . . . but you don't have to do anything with it. Your body already knows how to use incoming energy to kill any cancerous cells in your body. Now . . . are you ready to begin?"

"Yes . . . but maybe we tell Fidel to lock front door and turn off phone."

"Good idea."

When all is silent, Rafer closes his eyes half-way and begins his meditation. Eva sits quietly as he slips into a trance. Although seated several feet away in the corner, it takes only minutes before she feels Rafe's energy filling her body. All thoughts are floated away as she is enveloped in a breathless, healing peace. A glance at Carlos tells her that she is not alone in her ecstasy. His face, while still shriveled from radiation and chemotherapy, has a new glow about it. His eyes are not as swollen, the lids less red. When he turns to meet her glance, there is even a tiny smile on his lips. She responds with a smile of her own.

An hour passes before a cough out in the hall breaks the silence. Rafer opens his eyes, raises his head, then looks around, first at Carlos then at Eva. Eva still has her head down, breathing slowly. Carlos meets Rafer's gaze with his own, then struggles to get up out of the chair. By the time Rafer gets there to help, he is on his feet and smiling. His hand slides down to his stomach. "Es milagroso (*It is a miracle*). The tumor, she is much smaller. Maybe tomorrow all gone away."

Rafer reaches out to embrace him. "It does look smaller. You can hardly see it now. How do you feel . . . any different?"

(*Raising both fists*) "More energy . . . not tired and weak like dying man."

Eva rushes over to see. "There's more color in your cheeks," she says, beaming. "I think you even look younger."

"Oh, gracias querida senora." (*Oh, thank you dear lady*). At this point, he sits down, buries his face in his hands and begins sobbing. "I sorry, I sorry. Too much feeling for old man . . . (*shaking*) . . . so afraid to die . . . so afraid . . . now maybe live for long time . . . see business grow, see grandchildren grow up."

Rafer waits for the sobbing to stop. "Regarding the tumor, Carlos, I think you're right. It may take a few more days for it to shrink completely. In the meantime we can always do another session if you think it would help."

Carlos walks briskly across the floor and opens the door. "Ven aqui, Fidel. Mira . . . puedo caminar." (*Come here, Fidel. Look . . . I can walk*). Fidel utters something inaudible, then takes Santana's hand and kisses it. Clearly moved by this display of affection, Eva sidles up to Rafer and squeezes his hand. In response, he puts his arms around her waist and pulls her to him.

Turning back to Rafer, Carlos says, "Another session, yes. Tomorrow maybe? I reward you big. What you ask, Rafe; I give you what you ask."

Rafer shakes his head in response. "There's no charge, Carlos. I told you that before. If you want, you can take us out to dinner; the money you just saved on a funeral should cover it."

(*Laughing*) "Oh yes. I invite whole world to come and celebrate."

(*Nodding*) "Well, let's wait until we get rid of the tumor altogether. It looks like another session should do it. Shall we come back the same time tomorrow?"

"Yes. Yes. I wait for you here in study. But be careful. Don't get overrun by automobile . . . (*approaching*) . . . Now, give me hug. You are my savior." As they hug, Carlos begins sobbing again . . . then steps back, wipes his eyes and turns to Eva. She puts her arms around him and whispers, "How many grandchildren do you have?"

"Eight, so far," he answers through his tears.

She pats his back. "You're a lucky man."

Just outside the door, Carlos can be heard talking to Raul and Fidel. Rafer turns to Eva, "What did he just say, something about the doctors at the hospital I think."

"Yes. He's going to call them and tell them what just happened. He sounds angry."

When Rafer and Eva arrive in the morning, they find Carlos in an exhilarated mood. Before they can inquire, he announces that he has just returned from the hospital where the doctors found no evidence of the tumor . . . not even a trace. "They were . . . what you say . . . dumb . . . ."

"Dumbfounded?," Eva offers.

"Si . . . dumbfounded . . . until I tell them Rafer's name. They know about you from last year. Dr. Ruiz, he say you a miracle man."

Rafer: "Dr. Ruiz is a fine doctor . . . and a good friend of mine. But there are other doctors there who don't share his opinion."

"I think you right. But no matter. You save my life, Rafe. Just tell me what you want and it is yours. What you say, I give you."

"Thank you . . . but there's nothing I need for myself. I've got enough to live on for some time."

Carlos lifts his hands. "What about give to others?"

"Well, I *have* thought about starting a fund . . . a children's fund, you know, for poor kids here in Oaxaca . . . especially kids who can't go to school because they are needed to work at home."

"Si . . . sounds like good idea. You want to help children here. So I help you help children (*laughing*) . . . yes? Remember, I am big moneybags."

"Yes, I read somewhere that you're worth over 30 billion."

"Si . . . that is 30 billion dollars, not pesos. Nobody in whole world has more than me. So tell me Rafe . . . how much you want for saving my life? I give you what you say."

Rafer looks over at Eva. His eyes slip from her face to her arms, then to her hands. Her thumb is up. He looks again, unsure, his eyes questioning. She nods, confirming the direction of her thumb.

Rafer takes a deep breath, then whispers, "A round number would be nice. We could help a lot of children with that."

Carlos breaks into a broad smile. "Of course. One million U.S. dollars . . . Is O.K . . . I write you a check tomorrow."

Rafer looks across at Eva. Her head is shaking. There is a frown on her face; her lips are tight; her thumb still up. He squints to make sure that he's not misreading her. When he opens his mouth in astonishment, she nods again, more vigorously this time.

"What is a million dollars?," Carlos asks, still waiting for an answer. "If I live 20 more years, I pay only $50,000 for each year you give me. Is big bargain . . . yes?"

"I meant a billion," Rafer says, barely able to believe his own words.

Carlos gulps. "You say a billion? Is crazy, Rafe. What for you need so much money?"

Rafer's mind races. "Well, there are all the children . . . I've already talked about them . . . and then there are thousands of adults who need help as well. As you know, Oaxaca is one of the poorest areas in Mexico."

"Yes, Rafe . . . but a billion dollars for people I not even know? Mi Dios. (*My God*) You think I rich enough to take care of whole world? What about my own family? They count on big inheritance . . . three children, eight grandchildren . . . they have need too."

Rafer nods. "That's O.K. Carlos, I understand. Let's drop the whole thing. As I said earlier, I already have plenty for both myself and Eva. Our mission in coming down here was to help you get better . . . and we've succeeded in doing that. So, let's forget the money and do something fun to celebrate your recovery. Remember, you promised to take us out to dinner."

Carlos struggles for words. "But, we no decide on how much. Is million O.K. with . . . ."

Eva (*interrupting*): "May I ask you a question, Carlos?"

(*Nervously*) "Of course senora."

Eva takes a deep breath and comes closer. "Think back to the time when the doctors told you there was no hope of recovery and that you could expect to die soon. You remember that day?"

(*Shuddering*) "No forget that day. Worst day of my life."

"O.K. Now, what if Rafer had come to you the next morning and said he could cure you but it would cost you a billion dollars. How would you have answered?"

Carlos bows his head, saying nothing.

Rafer takes Eva by the hand and heads for the door. "I think we'll be leaving now, Carlos. If you still want to go out for dinner, give us a call at the apartment."

"But we still no decide . . . I can't . . . ."

At the door, Eva nudges Rafer and whispers into his ear. He turns to address Carlos, "Oh, I forgot to mention something. If you have a relapse . . . you know, if the tumor comes back . . . you can always call me in Boston. I'd be happy to schedule a return trip."

Carlos opens his eyes wide. "A relapse? Is possible?"

Eva (*nodding*): "It's fairly common . . . especially with cancers of the abdominal area. And of course, a tumor could always reappear somewhere else as well. You never know."

Carlos stumbles toward the door. "Maybe we talk at dinner tonight . . . (*pause*) . . . Mendes calls you."

Rafer: "Great. You pick the restaurant. I'm in the mood for a real Oaxacan meal . . . I'll leave the specifics up to you . . . just order me something with a mole sauce, chilis and local vegetables."

Eva (*opening the door*) "That same for me too, but please, hold the grasshoppers."

Carlos forces a smile. "Si . . . no chapulines."

At the restaurant Carlos appears uncharacteristically quiet. When Eva asks him about local food customs, he offers one word answers. Finally after a half hour of just sitting there, he reaches into his jacket pocket and pulls out a check. It is a registered bank check with most of the information already filled in. He turns to Rafer and asks, "What you call your new fund?"

Rafer drops his fork to the table and wipes his mouth. His eyes shift quickly to Eva. "I'm not sure . . . maybe something simple, like The Oaxaca Fund."

(*Frowning*) "Not say much, Rafe. Name not tell where money come from. With all I give you, better name is The Carlos Santana Oaxaca Fund . . . yes?"

Rafer (*squinting*): "That's a mouthful Carlos . . . too many words. We need a name that's easy to say and remember. The Oaxaca Fund sounds better to me."

Carlos drops his head, not pretending to hide his disappointment. Neither speaks. As he fills in the missing check information, Eva who is looking over his shoulder, signals to Rafer by holding up a single finger and lipping a silent "B." He looks confused. Before she can try again, Carlos returns his pen to his breast pocket and pushes the signed check over to Rafer.

Rafer's hands tremble as he scans the check. "Wow, Carlos. That's really generous. Thank you. With this we can transform Oaxaca and . . . ."

Carlos: (*interrupting*) "Nada, nada. I want to help. But please, no deposit check until next month. To make cash I need to sell stocks but not good to sell all at once. If I flood market with sell orders, it drive price of stocks down."

"I understand. That's no problem since the Fund won't be up and running until the IRS approves our application for non-profit status. And that could take another month at least. So I'll just hang onto the check until then."

"Is good. If people ask who gave you all that money, don't be afraid to tell them . . . yes?"

"Of course."

Back in the apartment, Rafer and Eva pass the check back and forth as they take turns dreaming of all the things they can do with it.

Eva is especially excited. "We can start with the Children's Fund but even if we give scholarships to a thousand Oaxacan kids, that's not going to use up much of the billion."

"True, but it could take more than scholarships to get these kids off the streets and into school. We might have to pay the parents to let the kids go. What's stopping them now is not so much the cost of books and school uniforms; it's the labor lost at home. They simply can't afford to run the vegetable stand or the farm . . . or sell goods in the zocolo . . . without their kid's help. So, if we pay them a little something every week, they can go out and hire someone to do what the child used to do."

Looking again at the check, Eva says, "That makes sense . . . and with all this money we could support the family all the way through college, assuming the son or daughter wanted to go. By the way, how much interest can we get each year from the billion Carlos gave us?"

"Depends on what we invest it in. If we stick to conservative stocks and bonds, we should be able to count on seven or eight percent a year."

Eva closes her eyes. "So let's see, that's about seventy or eighty million a year . . . is my math right?"

"On the nose. Which means we can do a lot more than this school program we're talking about."

Eva nods excitedly. "You know what I'd really like to get into, Rafe . . . fixing up Oaxaca . . . you know . . . making it more beautiful so that more tourists would come and spend money."

"How would you do it? We certainly have enough money to do something."

"This is just off the top of my head, but how about giving grants to businesses to fix up their shops . . . especially the outsides that everybody sees. You know . . . new paint, new doors, refurbished grill work . . . things that would restore the building's original beauty and make tourists want to take pictures and spend money . . . (*pause*) . . . Am I getting ahead of myself here?"

Rafer breaks into a big smile. "Not at all. I like it. We could even ask the city to create a commission of architects, painters, and artists of different types who would decide which grant requests to honor."

"Yes. The whole idea would be to make Oaxaca more beautiful. Oh Rafe, remember that lovely restaurant on Cinco de Mayo, the one up near the cathedral where we had lunch last time we were here? That whole area is potentially gorgeous. Of course, you can't always tell now because of all the peeling paint and flaking stucco. But it wouldn't take much to make it beautiful again. And if attracted more tourists, wouldn't that create jobs? That's what they really need here, isn't it?"

"For sure. Right now, there are no new businesses opening up in Oaxaca. Most locals work on farms or as fruit and vegetable street vendors . . . plus of course, those who operate or work in small shops. Improving the city's looks should help but what the place really needs is some industry . . . preferably light industry, the kind that wouldn't detract from the tourist business."

(*Smiling*): "You sound like you might have something in mind . . . am I wrong?"

"Well, yes. I *have* given it some thought. A bunch of software businesses would be ideal . . . you know . . . information technology stuff . . . the kind of thing they've done over in India. Trouble is, you need a solid skill base for that . . . and that means lots of people who are good with computers."

Eva frowns. "I don't see much evidence of that in Oaxaca, do you?"

"No . . . but maybe we could do something to change that. If we started a school for software development here, we might be able to attract students not only from Oaxaca but from all over Mexico. A school like that would draw in lots of people, not only students and faculty but start-up entrepreneurs who need access to a technically-trained labor force. And then there are all the people who will service the industry . . . clerks, accountants, financial experts, hardware companies, even construction people to put up new buildings."

"Whew. You do think big, Rafe. Starting a new school sounds like a huge undertaking . . . (*pause*) . . . but I guess we do have enough money, don't we?"

(*Smiling*) "More than enough. There might even be enough left over to buy you a new dress. I've noticed you've been wearing the same old things for some time now."

(*Fluffing her hair*) "Hmm. It's nice that you notice what I wear. I wasn't sure."

"Well, I see other men looking at you all the time, so that makes me take a second look."

(*Sly smile*) "Does that mean you're getting jealous?"

"Nope. Just want to make sure I haven't missed anything."

26

Rosita

Back in Boston, Rafer and Eva spend most of their time going over plans for the Oaxaca Fund. The three basic projects remain central . . . the school program, the beautification program and the software school. Throughout it all, the memory of Carlos's generosity remains a constant in their thinking. The huge check has been deposited in a new account set up in the name of The Oaxaca Fund at Boston's First Federal Bank. A recent notice from the bank indicates that the check has cleared safely. It comes as a complete shock, then, to hear on the evening news that Santana was killed this morning in a plane crash while flying back to Mexico City from a vacation in Cancun.

A phone call from Rosita, Santana's daughter, comes the very next day. Using English polished in her work as attorney for Mexican companies doing business in the U.S., she quickly drops a bomb. "Mr. Alexander, this is Rosita Santana Gomez, Carlos Santana's daughter. How are you?"

"Fine thanks. It's nice to meet you finally. After hearing of your father's death on Monday, I've thought a great deal about you and your family. I'm so sorry . . . it's a terrible thing for him to go like that so soon after he had won a new lease on life. When I last saw him, he was . . . ."

(*Interrupting*) "I don't have a lot of time Mr. Alexander, so let me get right to the point. After consulting with other attorneys here in

Mexico City, I have come to the conclusion that the check my father wrote you is invalid since it was made out to a recipient (The Oaxaca Fund) that was not in existence at the time of the writing . . . (*pause*) . . . I realize this will be disappointing to you but if you agree to return the money, I will make out a new check for $1,000,000 . . . an amount that is more in keeping with my father's intentions. I think you will agree that a million dollars is more than enough to repay you for your services. Let us be civil about this and settle matters privately. If you do not return the money with five days, however, I will be forced to start proceedings against you . . . (*pause*) . . . Mr. Alexander, are you there?"

(*Softly*) "Yes, I'm here. I'm thinking of how to answer you. It sounds like your father never told you about a letter he appended to the check, a letter which, given the circumstances, I suggested that he write."

"What in the world are you talking about?"

"Your father was quick to see that the check could be challenged on the grounds that the payee was not yet a legally recognized entity . . . so . . . ."

(*Quickly*) "Of course . . . that's what I am saying."

" . . . so he agreed to write a letter acknowledging his awareness that the Fund was applying for status as a non-profit charity and making clear his desire to transfer the money anyway . . . on condition that the Fund receive its charter within the next 60 days . . . which we . . . ."

(*Interrupting*) "I don't believe this."

" . . . which we did two days ago, well within the 60 days allowed."

(*Sharply*) "Were there any witnesses to the signing? Under Mexican law, without at least two witnesses, it cannot be considered . . . ."

"Both Raul Mendes and Eva Nourini watched as your father wrote the letter . . . and signed their names at the bottom. I will send you a copy tomorrow; just give me the address."

"I don't want the copy. I want to see the original."

"I am willing to send a copy, Ms. Gomez. Given the unpredictability of mail delivery in Mexico, it is best if I keep the original here. If you want to contest the check in court, I will certainly make it available at the appropriate time."

(*Her voice wavering*) "You steal from my family, Mr. Alexander. One billion dollars for an hour of meditation is crazy. How can you live with that?"

"Your father was certainly pleased; he said that it saved his life."

(*Quietly*) "Perhaps, but he's dead now . . . so what good was it, really?"

(*Pausing*) "It gave him the chance to live a longer life. The tumor was killing him; if we hadn't . . . ."

(*Trembling*) "If you hadn't gotten rid of the tumor, he would never have gone on vacation to Cancun and . . . ."

(*Softly*) "I understand. I'm truly sorry Rosita . . . (*pause*) . . . He talked of you often. It was clear from what he said that he had great respect and affection for you. Given how close the two of you were, it must be very difficult to accept that he is gone. I just hope you will remember how much he loved you."

(*Crying*) "Yes. I know. We were so close. I miss him terribly . . . (*pause*) . . . I'm sorry Rafer, I shouldn't have spoken so harshly . . . (*pause*) . . . Let's forget about the check. I know you will do marvelous things with the money . . . Papa would want it that way . . . (*pause*) . . .

Sorry for all the tears; maybe I should hang up now before I break down completely."

"Of course. Thank you for your understanding, Rosita. I hope we can meet some day. Perhaps you will join us at the Fund . . . as a board member or trustee. We would certainly appreciate your input."

"Thank you for saying that. Goodbye Rafer."

"Goodbye."

27

The Results

With preliminary results of the experiment already featured in the Boston Globe and Herald, attendance at today's special meeting at the faculty club is brisk. By the time Prof. Pulaski gets up to speak, every one of the 150 seats is taken. The meeting has been arranged into two parts; first Pulaski is to present details of the experiment and take questions about the findings; second, Dr. Alexander will talk about his role as meditator and discuss theories of healing. Dr. Atkins from Internal Medicine will serve as chair of the meeting. Prof. Pulaski is introduced amid mild applause.

"Let me begin by reminding you that the results we have thus far should be considered preliminary. We won't know for sure how successful the experiment is until the six and twelve month data are in. As of today we have results for the first three months only . . . hence the findings should be considered tentative at best.

"The overall view looks very promising. Of the 100 patients in the treatment group (that is, those that received the meditation treatment), 98 are still alive today. Of the 100 who received ongoing treatment but no meditation (the control group), only 81 are still living. The difference is statistically significant at the .01 level, meaning you could expect to get a difference this big by chance alone only one out of a hundred times. Further analysis shows that results were equally good for males and females; the hospital where patients were treated (remember, there were four different hospitals in the study) also made no difference.

Dr. Williams, a psychiatrist, raises his hand to speak. "But what about the role of charisma in all this? Isn't it possible that Dr. Alexander's personality had a lot to do with patients' success . . . that it was his bedside manner rather than his meditation that helped them?"

Prof. Pulaski: "Good point. The results are quite interesting. When we break the meditation group into those who met Dr. Alexander face to face and spent the hour sitting with him versus those who were neither introduced to him nor told that he was in the adjoining room meditating on their behalf, we find significant differences. While both groups did better than the controls who received no meditation, patients who had face-to-face contact with Dr. Alexander did the best. The fact that physical contact helps should comes as no surprise. After all, we already have plenty of evidence indicating that patients respond well to emotional support. It will surprise many, however, that meditation still works, although not as powerfully, when it is given by someone remotely, that is, by someone not physically present."

Dr. Williams: "O.K. But don't the patients in this group know that someone is in the next room trying to help them? Even if they can't see that person, aren't they buoyed by the knowledge that he is in there, meditating for them?"

Prof. Pulaski: "They are never told. They are completely oblivious to the fact that someone is nearby meditating on their behalf . . . and still it works! This is one of the most important findings of the experiment. It means that meditation can be effective as a treatment even when the patient has no idea that it is happening. In other words, its efficacy doesn't depend on personal contact, trust, charisma or some inspirational talk on the part of the meditator. Of course, the data show that meditation is even more effective when the meditator is in the same room with the patient, introducing himself, explaining what he's going to do, instilling hope etc."

A hand goes up in the back of the room. "I'm no conspiracy theorist but is it possible that the nurses tipped off patients that Alexander was in the next room meditating for them? If so, the results could be due to emotional and cognitive factors like hope and faith rather than the meditation itself."

Pulaski smiles. "The regular staff nurses were not told about Dr. Alexander's role in the experiment. At each of the four hospitals, patients in the experimental group were ushered into a special room for monitoring. Dr. Alexander was given his own key to the adjoining room where he locked himself in while meditating. There is no way either the nurses or the patients could have known he was there."

From his seat at the head table, Dr. Atkins poses a question. "I haven't heard anything so far about patients' beliefs. Did those who accepted the possibility of healing through meditation do any better than those who pooh-poohed it?"

"Ah yes," replies the professor. "I wish we could have tested that one . . . but we just didn't have the time or resources. It is certainly something we want to explore that area next time around. Commonsense would suggest that patients who pooh-poohed the idea wouldn't benefit as much as individuals who were more open to it . . . but I'm not sure. The results I've already talked about show that meditation works even when patients are unaware that someone is trying to help them. That leads me to believe that having a positive attitude toward meditation may help but it's probably not critical for success."

Dr. Ramsey, who holds a joint appointment in medicine and psychology, stands to speak. His voice is clear and penetrating. "Let's go a little deeper into this question of cause and effect. You say that patients who received the meditation treatment, either face-to-face or remotely, did better than those in the control group. And you explain this as a result of some kind of energy getting transferred from Dr. Alexander to the patient. But if no instruments are available for measuring this form of energy, how do we know that any of it ever got transferred. In other words, how can we be sure that any 'treatment' ever happened?"

Prof. Pulaski: "Great question. Someday, soon I hope, we'll figure out how to measure this kind of psychic energy, but in the meantime we're forced to rely on indirect measures to show that a transfer took place. Here's what we did. At the end of each session, Dr. Alexander filled out a simple form indicating how deep his meditation was. He had made it clear in the beginning that some days were going to be better than others. With that in mind we had him rate the 'depth' of his meditation on a scale running from very strong to very weak with several points in between. We then correlated his responses with data on patient mortality and morbidity. The results indicate that patients who were on the receiving end of sessions rated strong by Alexander did better than those on the end of sessions that he rated weak. This suggests that something indeed was being transferred from the meditator to the patient. It is far from conclusive evidence, I'll admit, but until we learn how to measure psychic energy, it's the best we have."

Pulaski looks at his watch. "Time for one more question before I turn it over to Dr. Alexander."

From a woman in the front row, "If you were to do another experiment, what other variables would you like to test?"

Pulaski laughs. "There are many, probably too many to count. For one thing, we'd like to vary the number and length of meditation sessions. Are two sessions better than one, three better than two? Is a one hour session better than a half hour one, and so on. Geographic distance between sender and receiver is another variable that needs exploring. We already know that the meditator can be effective from behind a wall, but how close does he have to be . . . a few yards, a city block, a mile? We simply don't know. Another unknown factor that needs testing is the type of disease being treated. Are cancers, for example, easier to treat than heart problems or ulcers? What about mental illness and drug addiction? Then there are questions surrounding the patients themselves: how relevant are patients' beliefs about meditation; how important is the desire to recover; does the patient's mental state during treatment (for example, awake vs. sleeping) make a difference? I'm sure you will agree that there's enough work here to last a lifetime . . . maybe several. But I don't want to keep Dr. Alexander waiting any longer than necessary, so let me turn things over to him right now. Dr. Alexander . . . ."

28

A Call Home

"Hi Mom."

"Oh, Evie. How good o' ya to call. You still in Mexico?"

"No. We're back here in Boston. Got back a couple of weeks ago."

"Honey, wait 'til I get my teeth in . . . (*a minute later*) . . . O.K. I'm ready. So, tell me, are ya happy with your new boyfriend . . . the one with the funny name?"

"His name is Rafer, Mom . . . (*pause*) . . . Mostly I guess. Some things are better than others."

"You don't sound too worked up about him. You gonna stay together? You're welcome to come home any time you want to. You know that, don't you?"

"Yes Mom, but I don't have any plans to leave, not right now anyway.

"So, what's wrong honey?"

"It's the same old thing. He's just really different than any man I've ever known. With Raymond there was a lot of fighting . . . about small things . . . he always wanted to have his way and I had to give in or see him get mad. Rafer is not that way at all. We hardly ever fight and when we do he never even raises his voice."

"I wish Jack was more like that. We could use a little more quiet around here."

"Yes, it is nice in a way but I wish Rafer was a little more emotional."

"You mean about you?"

"Well yes . . . but really about everything. He's pretty quiet most of the time . . . except maybe when he's playing with kids like he did down in Oaxaca. He seems to come alive then."

"Does he tell you he loves you?"

"Not really . . . at least not in the way I think you mean. The only time he says he loves me is when I ask him if he does. And then what I get is that he cares for me and wants me to be happy and so on . . . the kind of thing a parent might say to a child. It's really not what I want to hear."

"Which is?"

"You know, that I'm desired, needed . . . that I'm the most important person in his life, that he can't live without me . . . the kind of things that most women want to hear. He never talks that way."

"Tell me if I'm intruding Evie . . . but what's he like in bed?"

(*Sighing*): "Hmm. That's a real disappointment. With Raymond, we'd make love maybe two or three times a week. With Rafer, it's more like once a month, if I'm lucky. And it's strange the way he goes at it. I mean, he stays cool through the whole thing, hardly ever says anything. When I asked him what he was feeling, he said it was like a meditation for him . . . a place where each touch of the skin reveals a cloudless, empty space where nothing, not me, not even himself, exists . . . (*pause*) . . . Those were his exact words."

(*Whistling*): "That does sound weird, honey. You sure this guy is on the up and up . . . you know, normal like?"

"He's definitely not your average Joe . . . and in many ways I love him for that. But it does get a bit lonely sometimes."

"You think he might be seeing someone else?"

"I doubt it. He doesn't show much interest in other women . . . even when they make themselves available."

"Well, what *is* he interested in? Does he ever talk about getting married or having kids?"

"Never. I mentioned kids once but he didn't even answer."

"Yes, but is there some place he's tryin to get to, some kind of goal he has in the back of his mind? We know that he likes money . . . is there anything else?"

"If you mean ambition, he doesn't seem to have any . . . at least for himself. From what he's told me, it sounds like he used to dream about being famous when he was younger. Losing his family in the plane accident over in India seemed to change everything."

"I remember you told me. That must have been horrible . . . losing both parents and his only brother. Was he real close to them all?"

"Mainly his mother I think. She was the ambitious one . . . but it was mainly for Rafer and his brother Jason, not for herself. He told me one night that she expected him to enter politics some day and become a world leader."

"Sounds like she was shootin pretty high. What about the brother . . . same thing for him?""

"I think Rafer was her favorite. Her whole life revolved mainly around Rafer . . . the grades he was getting in school, where he planned to go for college, what he wanted to do for a career . . . ."

"Poor guy . . . sounds like she was all over him."

"She was his biggest supporter . . . poured all her dreams into him . . . and backed him up all the way. He told me that her favorite saying was, "Rafe, you can do anything you set your mind to." She said it over and over until he came to believe it . . . at least until he had to bury her up there in the mountains."

"What a horrible way for her to die . . . and for him to see her like that. So, you say that after the crash he began to change?"

"That's the impression I get, Mom. Whenever he talks about it (which isn't very often), I get the sense that all of a sudden he realized that all the talk about entering politics and becoming famous was her idea, not his. Looking back now, he says that ever since he was a child, he bought into her ambitions, thinking that's what he wanted for himself. But it really wasn't. And it took her death to wake him up to the truth."

"Wow, I hope I haven't done anything like that to you, Evie . . . (*pause*) . . . Have I?"

"No Mom . . . you've been real nice about letting me find my own way. So far, I haven't done a very good job with it . . . but that's my fault, not yours."

"I like what you've become, honey . . . (*pause*) . . . So, you think maybe he's done a 180 . . . you know, gone overboard in the opposite direction?"

"What do you mean?"

"Well, you say that he doesn't want anything for himself now, that he has no goals, nothing he's aiming for."

"True . . . but he's still ambitious . . . it's just not for himself anymore. I wasn't going to tell you about this quite yet, but I might as well now. A man from Mexico who was dying of stomach cancer came to Rafer last month and asked him to meditate for him, the way he did with several patients in Oaxaca. Well, it worked . . . and after recovering the man was so grateful he made out a huge check to a charitable fund Rafe was starting. The only problem we have now is how to spend all the money. That's what we talk about every night . . . you know, what can we do to help the people of Oaxaca? We've already come up with several exciting ideas, beautifying the city, scholarships for the kids and so on. So you *could* say he has goals . . . and is ambitious in a way but . . . ."

(*Interrupting*): "You say a huge amount . . . you mean like $10,000?"

(*Smiling*): "More than that, Mom . . . much more."

"$100,000?"

"It's better if we don't talk about it, Mom. It'll just stir up trouble."

"What do you mean . . . trouble?"

"Well you know . . . Jack . . . he'd get all excited . . . and start poking around. You know."

"Well, yes . . . but can't you tell me? I don't have to share it with him."

"You promise to keep this to yourself?"

"Yes, of course. Now tell me. How much did this man give Rafer?"

(*Pausing*): "A billion dollars."

(*Screaming*) "What? A billion dollars? That's unbelievable . . . (*trying to catch her breath*) . . . Wait a minute; I have to sit down . . . (*pause*) . . . Now, did I get that right . . . one billion dollars? How rich is this guy anyway?"

"Plenty rich. He died recently in a plane crash but before he died he had over 30 billion dollars in stocks and bonds. That's why I told Rafe to ask for a billion instead of the one million he originally offered us."

"You told Rafe how much to ask for? You have that much influence over him?"

"He does respect my judgment in some things. And he's glad now that I spoke up because we have all this money to spend on projects in Oaxaca."

"How come Rafe didn't ask for the billion? Why did he wait for you to do it?"

"He just doesn't think that way. In fact, he kept reminding the man that there was no charge for his help. I think he was perfectly happy just to see the guy recover. But I stuck my big nose in there and now we have a billion dollars to play with."

"Good for you Evie. But whew . . . I had no idea you had come this far. It's more than I ever imagined . . . to think that my daughter is handling that kind of money . . . and hanging out with a man who performs miracles. I just never thought of you that way, honey."

"I understand. Just don't tell Jack. Remember, you promised."

(*Whispering*): "Speak of the devil, he just came in."

"Say hello for me."

"He wants to ask you something . . . (*muffled whispers*) . . . O.K . . . Evie, you still there? He wants to know if you found out how Rafer made all that money at the casino."

"Tell him it's still a mystery to me. The only thing I'm sure of is that he meditates the same way whether he's gambling or trying to help some sick person. I don't think he's reading the future or anything like that. It's more like he's sending out some kind of energy and the energy works magic . . . but I don't know that for sure. As I said, the whole thing is still a mystery to me. I figure that if he wants me to know, he'll tell me."

"Jack says you should ask him right away. It could be that he's uncovered some kind of secret that we could use here in Vegas. It wouldn't hurt him to share, would it . . . especially after getting that huge check."

(*Alarmed*): "Mom!"

"Oops . . . (*whispering*) . . . Sorry, that just popped out. But honey, we could use a little help . . . what with the recession and all . . . (*pause*) . . . What do you think?"

"I'd rather wait for him to tell me on his own, Mom."

"Of course. Do what you think is right, darling. We'll get by somehow."

"I've got to go now, Mom. Good talking to you. I'll call again soon."

"Sorry to see you go already Evie. But I'm sure you have more important things to do . . . So yes, goodbye for now. And call again whenever you can. Love ya."

"Love you too. Bye."

29

The Grilling

When Prof. Pulaski finishes his presentation, a few people get up to leave but most stay for what they figure to be the main attraction. A rustling in the crowd can be heard as Rafer makes his way to the podium. For many in the audience this is their first chance to meet the young man who, according to the newspapers, has defied the scientific community with cures that have all the earmarks of the miraculous. A bevy of photographers lines the back of the auditorium.

As expected, most of the questions are theoretical in nature. Prof. Adams, the first to speak, puts it bluntly: "Dr. Alexander, I ask you: How can one person cure another without resorting to any of the standard surgical or medical interventions? It doesn't make any sense given our usual assumptions about cause and effect."

Rafer (*grinning*): "I thought we might get a question or two about that."

From the back of the room: "Make that three or four."

Laughter.

Rafer: "O.K. Let's see if we can make some sense of what the experiment is telling us. There are two theories that could help; the first comes from Prof. Pulaski himself and centers on the role of psychic energy, a form of energy that has not yet been detected by any of our present instruments. According to the Professor, this energy is released in the brain when the perceptual mechanisms by which we orient ourselves to the world are temporarily shut down, as they tend to be during deep meditation. The saved energy is then directed to the patient where it gets used to strengthen the immune system."

Prof. Adams again: "I don't see the logic of it. How can you direct energy to the patient if you can't orient yourself to your surroundings? If your meditation is so deep that forms and shapes are no longer visible, how can you target that energy to any particular person or place?"

Rafer (*nodding*): "At the deepest level of meditation (the so-called enlightened state), objects no longer exist. All you're aware of is a vivid but empty Void. In other words, you are still conscious but no longer conscious of any *thing*. If you remain totally in that state, it would be foolhardy to do anything requiring a precise orientation to your environment, for example, crossing an intersection with traffic coming in both directions. What may not be obvious is that you can move back and forth between this objectless Void and the ordinary world of shapes, lines, and colors. As Prof. Pulaski explains it (and this is consistent with my own experience) it's like having a dial in your head . . . if you turn the dial all the way clockwise, you get the ordinary world of objects; if you turn it all the way in the other direction, you get the Void. Like a compass, all the points in between the two extremes are possible. To direct energy to a patient lying in bed a few feet away, all you have to do (once you've entered the enlightened state) is move the dial around from the Void to where you can just barely make out shapes and forms again."

Prof. Adams: "But wouldn't that imply giving up some or all of the energy that was released in meditation?"

Rafer: "You definitely have to give up some of it . . . but if you only move the 'dial' a little bit, you can preserve most of the energy. At that point, objects (including the patient) will appear recognizable but less substantial than they do in ordinary consciousness. It's a trade-off; to target your energy you have to use some of it to re-orient; that means your healing efforts will be somewhat less intense."

Prof. Baldini: "I find myself wondering about this psychic energy you keep talking about. You say it heals by strengthening the patient's immune system . . . but might it not have therapeutic value above and beyond any impact on the immune system? If so, aiming that energy directly at a tumor might be sufficient to kill it."

Rafer: "That could be. The immune system explanation is only a hypothesis. I don't know. As you suggest, psychic energy may very well possess the power to heal in and of itself. One clue that supports that view comes from my own experience. When new energy is released during deep meditation, it evokes feelings of deep peace, joy and love; I can only guess that something similar happens to the patient. And those feelings could be curative of disease whether or not the immune system gets activated."

Prof. Baldini: "That's interesting . . . but why do you think these feelings and not some others arise when you meditate? And to go a little further, what makes you think those feelings could have therapeutic value when transferred to someone else?"

Rafer: (*pausing*) "Big question. Let me take the three feelings I mentioned in turn. The first is peace. So, why should peace and not anxiety or fear arise when I enter the Void state? I think it's got something to do with the loss of self-awareness. For most of us the self is our major source of worry and frustration. It follows, then, that forgetting the self, even if temporarily, will make you feel more peaceful. To see that, just imagine what it would be like not to be concerned with accumulating possessions, achieving success, or safeguarding your reputation. With the self temporarily forgotten, the world becomes incomparably simpler. It leaves you feeling peaceful; the greater the forgetting, the deeper the peace. And if this is true for me when I meditate, my guess is that it is true for my patients as well."

Prof. Pulaski: "If I can butt in here, I would add that simply sitting next to Dr. Alexander when he's meditating produces a similar effect. I know that from personal experience. If I'm right, it means that to benefit from his energy, you don't have to be the target of a deliberate healing effort . . . although the effect is even stronger if you are."

Rafer: "Thanks Stefan. Let me go on to the second feeling I mentioned . . . joy. By joy I mean an all-encompassing, global feeling of elation, not the kind of happiness we feel when 'everything is going our way.' It's not just a matter of getting what we want . . . of fulfilling our desires. It's a kind of joy that is untied to any specific object, any concrete event. It's a feeling that has no particular reference and thus cannot be explained to others when they ask, "What makes you so happy?"

From a woman in the second row, "But what is the answer? Why should meditation make you so happy? There's got to be an explanation, doesn't there?"

Rafer (*smiling*): "Good question Ethel. I'm sure there is one but I don't happen to know what it is. Maybe joy, or at least the kind I spoke of, is a natural mental state for humans, a state that gets obscured by our concerns about who we think we are and how we want others to perceive us. If so, it follows that if meditation helps you to forget yourself, even temporarily, the joy will reveal itself."

Ethel (*shaking her head vigorously*): "That's a rather quaint idea, don't you think Dr. Alexander? I mean, where is the evidence for such a view?"

Rafer: "As far as I know, the idea has never been tested in a formal clinical trial . . . but let me ask you this. Considering the human life cycle as a whole, in what part of it do individuals seem to be the most carefree and happy?"

Ethel (*quickly*): "Early childhood, of course . . . those are the golden years in almost everyone's life."

Rafer: "Precisely. And isn't that related to their lack of concern with self-image, a concern that doesn't really kick in until they enter school? And doesn't that concern grow stronger with age, often reaching obsessive levels in adolescence and beyond?"

Ethel (*softly*): "Perhaps."

Rafer: "Doesn't it follow then that forgetting the self, even temporarily, will restore some of that peace we felt as children? . . . (*pause*) . . . Now, let's move on to the third feeling I mentioned . . . love. Why should love surface in meditation and be transferrable to patients? While it is certainly possible to love someone or something without becoming enlightened first, love without enlightenment usually takes the form of what the Greeks called Eros . . . the kind of love we have in mind when we say two people are in love with each other or when we say we love chocolate or we love to go swimming. Love in that sense means that we desire something, cherish it, long for it . . . that we gain some kind of satisfaction from obtaining it. What the Greeks called agape is something quite different . . . namely, love without thought of getting anything in return. The term is typically applied to those situations where we simply want the best for the other person . . . greater pleasure, more contentment, less pain. A more common name for it is altruism . . . the kind of love where our concern for another person's well-being overshadows any concern for our own. We see it sometimes in a parent's love for a child although more often than not the mother or father expects to get something in return . . . to be made proud, to be loved or wanted, to succeed through identification, to be given material comfort in old age, etc. It is my sense that altruistic love, like the joy I mentioned earlier, is a natural emotion that is built into our human nature; we don't see it very often because it is obscured by our obsession with self-satisfaction. When we become self-forgetting, as we do in enlightenment, that natural but hitherto hidden inclination to reach out emerges in the form of a desire to help others find joy or relief from suffering. The experience of self-forgetting also has the effect, as I said earlier, of liberating the psychic energy previously bound up in orienting to our environment. In the healing process the two get combined: our caring feelings get infused with the energy released when we turn off our orienting mechanisms. Those energy-boosted love feelings are then transferred to the patient where they work to eliminate or at least diminish the toxic barrage of fear, anxiety, and frustration that's been inviting disease into the body. The psychosomatic effect is that the patient gets better."

Dr. Hightower, a psychiatrist known throughout the School for a stoical response to his wife's recent death, stands to speak. "You talk a lot about the loss of concern for the self and the role it plays in releasing feelings of love but I think there could be a simpler explanation for where this love is coming from. If in the enlightenment experience you find a 'boundless, empty space' embedded in every person or object around you, including yourself, wouldn't that experience in itself bring you closer to everyone else? Wouldn't it help you see that we are all made of the same stuff . . . and thus evoke feelings of oneness and love?"

Rafer: "For sure. I think we're really talking about the same thing . . . from a slightly different angle. Self-forgetting and seeing the world as an undifferentiated One go together. You can't very well identify with everything around you until you've given up your identity as a separate, isolated individual. The two experiences not only go together; they happen at the same time during enlightenment. The result, whichever way you define it, is a powerful desire to help others . . . in a word, compassion."

Dr. Hightower sits, then gets back up again. "Just a minute. Are you saying that to become a compassionate person you have to reach enlightenment first? I'm asking because I know several people who love selflessly the way you're talking about but who are very impaired in other ways . . . that is they're compassionate but definitely not enlightened."

Rafer (*nodding*): "I know several people just like that. You're right . . . you don't need to be enlightened in order to be compassionate. On the other hand, when you become enlightened you automatically develop the capacity to love selflessly. Seeing into the Oneness of the universe implies transcending the limitations of self-separateness; as a result, forgetting the self invariably brings with it a capacity to love selflessly."

Prof. Adams: "Sometime ago, you mentioned that there were two theories that could explain how remote healing works. We've heard about the first, Prof. Pulaski's theory of how energy is saved when we stop orienting. What about the second?"

Rafer: "Good memory. In all this discussion of feelings, I almost forgot that second one myself. It's really not my theory at all . . . I heard it first from Dr. Komerov's wife, Greta, who likens enlightenment to splitting the atom; the two are similar she suggests in that they both release huge amounts of energy. What we're talking about here, however, may be more like cracking open a walnut than splitting an atom. It happens whenever a stimulus hits a sense organ (an eye, ear, skin etc.) while our orienting sensors are turned off. The effect is to strip the stimulus of its identifying characteristics (sight, sound, touch, etc.), thereby releasing the energy within. There may be a parallel here to Einstein's $E = MC^2$ where enormous amounts of energy are given off in the process of converting matter to energy. According to Mrs. Komerov's theory, it is this energy, heretofore buried in the stimulus but now released, that makes it possible to cure disease. It could probably be used for other purposes as well, although the theory doesn't specify what those uses might be."

Dr. Bacon, a visitor from the philosophy department, raises his hand. Faculty members who know him from previous meetings cringe in the expectation of an esoteric question that only a philosopher would understand. He doesn't disappoint them. "Does this atom-splitting or walnut-cracking theory of Mrs. Komerov imply that incoming stimuli are nothing but energy at their core, essences so to speak, and that attributes like color, line, texture, pitch etc. are only illusions, as the Buddhists have long argued?"

Although no philosopher himself, Rafer nods knowingly having considered the question many times. "I would not consider line, color and shape illusions. To me, both the embedded energy and its sensory markers are equally real. By temporarily suspending orientation to the environment, the brain screens out all external identifiers like color, line, pitch, smell, touch, etc., giving the impression that they were unreal to begin with. However, those identifiers still exist for the person next to you; they are simply no longer perceived by the individual undergoing the enlightenment experience. Thus, they should not be considered illusory. At any rate I would not call the energy that lies embedded within an object an 'essence' in the sense that there is a real but insubstantial entity lurking there. I don't believe in essences anymore than ghosts. Both strike me as fictions, tempting in their imperviousness to disproof and thus often used to explain mysterious events, but totally without substance."

Prof. Thompson: "Could we get back to healing? There was apparently some evidence in the experiment that healing works better with some people than others. Although you didn't test it directly, you seem convinced that it works best with patients who believe that non-medical healing is possible to begin with. Could you elaborate on that?"

Rafer nods. "Sure. My own thinking on the subject started with Lili, the nine-year old Mexican girl with leukemia whose religious beliefs seemed to play a big role in her recovery. When she asked if God knew that I was there to help her, I went along with the idea and told her that He had indeed sent me to cure her. When I . . . ."

Prof. Thompson (*interrupting*): "Despite the fact that you don't even believe in a personal God."

Rafer: "Yes. It was all an act . . . but it seemed to work. Since then I've become even more convinced that a patient's beliefs and expectations regarding recovery are crucial for success. Such beliefs vary across a wide spectrum, as might be illustrated with an analogy. Consider someone, for example, who is convinced that healing (at least of the sort I do) is nothing more than a pipedream. For such a skeptic, healing through meditation is close to impossible; it would be like trying to light a campfire with branches that have been lying in a nearby lake for years. It's not going to happen. Now take a patient who is open to the possibility but is basically non-religious. That person might be willing to at least listen to my own non-theistic theory of how psychic energy gets transferred from one person to another where it is used to stimulate the immune system. That might be like starting the campfire with branches that have been out in the rain for an hour or two . . . doable but not exactly easy. Move on now to someone who takes his or her religion very seriously . . . someone who prays every day to a father figure in heaven who is loving and eager to see her get better. Healing such a person would be much easier . . . akin perhaps to getting the fire started with completely dry grasses and wood. Finally, to complete the analogy, consider an individual who not only prays to God every day for recovery but is convinced that the person He has sent to make it happen is standing right in front of her. Picture now a bundle of dry wood and grasses doused in gasoline. All you have to do is toss a match in the right direction."

Laughter ripples through the audience.

"That analogy captures my own feeling that psychology has everything to do with disease and the capacity to recover from it. So, if I have to choose between arguing for my own scientific theory and going along with a patient's more pietistic beliefs, I will take the latter, even if means acting out something that is foreign to me."

Prof. Thompson: "But what if a patient accepts your scientific theory of energy transfer to begin with? Wouldn't that person respond as well as the patient who sees you as God's representative?"

Rafer: "I doubt it. Believing in a loving God who has sent someone to cure your disease has the power to catapult you into a state of mind where all incoming energy gets multiplied exponentially. It electrifies the whole mind-body and prepares you to use that energy in a way that a more rational, scientific explanation is incapable of doing, no matter how intellectually satisfying that explanation might be."

Prof. Thompson persists. "I tend to go along with your emphasis on psychology, but I'm wondering if you really need religion in all this. What if you tell a dying patient that he can cure his cancer by himself . . . that all it takes is a strong desire to get better. In the course of your conversation, you assure him that you have seen it happen countless times. You even go on and cite psychosomatic research that documents how powerfully the mind can affect the body. While you agree to play a supportive role, you leave no doubt that whether or not he lives is really up to him. He is convinced and gives it his best shot. Won't that patient do as well as the one who prays every day and is convinced that God has sent you to cure him?"

Rafer: "Probably not. Even though the psychological scenario fits my own beliefs better, it lacks the motivational power of a setting where some kind of helper is involved. It leaves too much up to the patient's own desire for recovery; everything depends on him. In contrast, the patient who believes either that God wants to save him or that a meditator is there to help is likely to feel strengthened by what he perceives to be an outside force. And I'm not talking about a loving spouse, parent or friend. I mean someone thought to possess unusual healing powers. For a terminally ill patient who believes he has such a helper on his side, getting better is no longer his sole responsibility; he's not alone. By contrast, the person who relies totally on his own will to live has a harder row to hoe. No matter how strong that desire, it's unlikely to match the fervor (and hence the receptivity to healing energy) of the individual who is convinced that someone else, someone with unusual healing powers, is there to help him. In our experiment, you will recall, patients who received the meditation treatment remotely, that is patients for whom I meditated secretly from behind a wall, did better than the controls but not nearly as well as those with whom I interacted face-to-face. That tells me that meditation helps even without the patient's awareness but *knowing* that you are being helped improves your chances of recovery significantly. Seeing your helper face-to-face increases the odds even further."

Dr. Almeida (*hesitantly*): "I don't want to change the subject . . . but . . . ."

Rafer (*smiling*): "But you do, yes?"

Laughter from the back of the room.

Dr. Almeida (*scowling as he turns to face the audience*): "Hey. I just wanted to ask about other things you can do with this psychic energy he's talking about. Maybe there's more to the story. Listen up and you could learn something."

Rafer: "Well, there are probably many uses other than healing but conflict resolution is the one that interests me the most. Although I've never tried to resolve an interpersonal conflict through meditation, I get the sense from what people say that it could be done. This is particularly true of the woman I live with who says she gets an enhanced feeling of peace whenever I go into a trance. Nothing is said about it; nothing planned. Without intending it, the energy I am experiencing somehow finds its way over to her and to anyone else sitting nearby. When I later ask those present what they were feeling, they typically report feelings very similar to the peace, joy and love that I experienced during meditation.

"There are other possibilities we could explore as well . . . including telepathy, psychokinesis and clairvoyance as well as more exotic phenomena like levitation and visualization. The only evidence we presently have of such phenomena is anecdotal and thus unreliable; what we need is a series of controlled experiments like the one we just finished on healing. Of course, if such experiments demonstrate the validity of paranormal events, we'll have to construct a theory to explain the results. This will necessitate a new, broader Weltanschauung . . . one that includes what science tells us but goes further."

Dr. Sullivan stands and waits for the room to grow silent. "Unlike most of my colleagues here, I consider myself a religious man. If we can assume that the results of your hospital experiment are valid . . . and of course we won't know for sure until they are replicated . . . we are left with the question of why you and you alone have the ability to do this. It's impossible for us on the outside to know what kind of power, divine or demonic, is working inside you. I for one would like to know if you feel any kind of 'celestial' presence when you meditate. I realize that you don't believe in a personal God but what about other spiritual influences? Do you sense that you have been chosen for this mission by forces from some other, non-human realm of existence?"

Rafer: "Quite the contrary. My sense is that any healthy human being is capable of doing what I have done . . . and probably a lot more. I see myself as a very ordinary man. Despite what I told Lili, the girl with leukemia, I have not been sent down to earth to help people. Like most of you, I've never even been to heaven. I was born and grew up in a small, blue-collar town in upstate New York and I can assure you it was anything but paradise."

Chuckles ripple through the auditorium.

Dr. Atkins is quick to pose the obvious question: "But if you're so human, Dr. Alexander, how come we don't see a lot of other people doing the same thing . . . namely healing patients just by meditating?"

Rafer: "Well, now and then we do hear about individuals who appear to have healing powers . . . but I agree that the number of such cases is small and the reports unreliable. The critical factor here is the healer's state of mind. To gain access to the energy that makes healing possible, you have to enter the mental space we call enlightenment . . . or at least something approaching that state. My guess is that most would-be healers, and even those who have achieved some success, never attain the clarity of mind needed to turn off all orienting mechanisms and release the psychic energy saved in the process. But any healthy human being has the potential to do exactly that. And that's why I say just about anyone can do what I have done so far . . . and probably more."

Dr. Atkins: "So you're saying that when you come right down to it, the only thing that makes you different is your enlightenment experiences."

Rafer: "Yes . . . and that's something available to anyone. The only people I would leave out would be the mentally ill or drug-addicted. The vast majority of humans are perfectly capable of attaining enlightenment and gaining access to the energy released by that experience. The reason it happened to me can probably be traced to the fact that I lost my whole family in a plane crash and in the aftermath had my sense of self shaken to its very foundations. But please bear with me; I'm not recommending that as a suitable strategy."

Soft laughter.

In the middle of the auditorium, George Komerov rises. "Dr. Alexander, I have a different kind of question . . . something a little more personal. I will understand if you prefer not to answer."

"As long as it's not about my secret bank account in the Caman Islands, fire away."

Laughter.

Komerov: "Thank you. Here it is. I'm just wondering, could those special powers of yours be used for less benign purposes? Suppose for example that someone does something to offend you . . . could you slip into a trance and send negative energy to hurt him . . . or at least make him stop?"

Rafer: "That's not likely to happen since the kind of psychic energy I'm talking about is accessible only in the state of enlightenment and you can't enter that state without a shrinking of the self. In most cases it is our attachment to the self that makes us vulnerable to being snubbed or criticized; more often than not that vulnerability provokes frustration and anger, leading to retaliation and acts of violence. Forget about the self . . . and those things no longer happen."

Komerov smiles. "Well, O.K., let's change the situation slightly. Say you are at home some night in your study when thugs break in and attack your wife who is watching TV in the living room. Would you come to her defense?"

Rafer: "Of course. I would do what any husband would do, but in your example there wouldn't be time to go into a trance. In reacting, my main concern would be to protect my wife, not to hurt the intruders . . . (*pause*) . . . I should add of course that I'm not married . . . so all of this is quite theoretical."

Komerov (*chuckling*): "I understand. Now, if you don't mind, let's make things even more personal. Let's say you have been taken hostage by a terrorist who assumes you have some important information he wants. He binds your arms to a chair and straps your hand to a butcher block. Holding a hatchet in his own hand, he threatens to cut off one of your fingers if you don't tell him what he wants to know. Assume further that you have had plenty of time to go into a trance. Now, would you try to use your special powers to stop him? For example, would you try to direct energy at his heart in hopes of incapacitating him . . . perhaps even killing him?"

Mumbling ripples through the audience. In the front row, Prof. Pulaski grimaces, then turns to the man next to him, "What the hell is George trying to get at?"

Rafer waits for the noise to die down. "If that were the only way to survive without losing my fingers, yes . . . I would do what I could to stop him."

Komerov: "So, you're saying that you probably *do* have the capacity to kill someone using your mind alone?"

Rafer (*hesitantly*): "That's just a guess. I certainly hope I never have to put it to test."

Komerov: "Well, yes, I think we all share that hope, Dr. Alexander. But wouldn't you agree that someone walking our streets with the ability to kill using his mind alone represents a danger to society? What if you were to develop a grudge against one of us, a grudge serious enough to incite violence? How could we possibly defend ourselves? You look normal enough, you carry no weapons, you wouldn't even have to make physical contact. Wouldn't we be at your mercy?"

When Rafer fails to answer immediately, Komerov draws his mouth into a wry smile, sits back and crosses his legs. The professor next to him reaches over and taps his knee, silently acknowledging the skill of his interrogation.

When minutes pass without a word from Alexander, Prof. Pulaski rises to offer a rebuttal. "We have just witnessed another example of Dr. Komerov's flair for fantasy, a flair embarrassingly evident this past year in his dealings with patients claiming to have been abducted by creatures from another planet. All of you here at the Medical School have suffered from guilt by association for this unconscionable lapse into the absurd. Now, we are presented with yet another example of his erratic thinking. I'm sure you will agree that it is ridiculous to think that Rafer Alexander . . . the man who just demonstrated in a controlled experiment that he has the ability to rescue patients from certain death . . . would use his unique gift to turn around and destroy lives. As Dr. Alexander said earlier, the capacity to heal through meditation is reserved for those who have risen beyond the petty concerns of the self . . . concerns like pride, jealousy, envy, and greed. Once you've put those concerns behind you, as I know Rafer Alexander has, there are no occasions left to inspire hate and the desire for retribution. I know him well and I can assure you that he doesn't have a malicious bone in his body."

Komerov (*softly*): "Unless, of course, he's about to have his fingers cut off."

30

Mark of the Beast

Lynn. Tuesday night.

After calling the meeting to order, Petey turns to his late-arriving guest: "Doc . . . did you get a chance to talk to Alexander like you said?"

Komerov: "Well . . . I never got to talk to him alone like I wanted but I did have a chance to ask him a few questions at our last faculty meeting. He was very evasive but I finally got him to admit something I consider extremely important; he admitted that he has the power to kill another human using his mind alone. Knowing what I do about him, it didn't surprise me that much but the people in audience, mainly physicians, were shocked. Of course, it doesn't prove anything but it's certainly consistent with his being the Antichrist. Who else would have that kind of power?"

Thomas: "Maybe he was bragging . . . just wanted to impress you guys. We don't know if he could really do it, do we?"

Komerov: "The fact that he was reluctant to admit it tells me he was not making it up. If anything, he was trying to hide it. Like the Bible says, he wants to project the image of a man who is here to do good . . . a virtuous man, a man who turns the other cheek instead of striking back . . . in other words, a saint. And he could have gotten away with it if I hadn't pressed him."

Petey: "Yeah . . . you're pretty good at that question stuff Doc. Now . . . I've got some new info straight from my sister in Vegas who talked to Evie last week. Evie, you know, is living with Alexander. The thing is, though, that this has gotta stay quiet . . . I mean real quiet. I promised Aggie that I wouldn't tell anyone . . . but seein as how this guy could bring the whole fuckin world down, I'm passin it on. But it stops right here . . . O.K.?"

Petey looks around; all heads are nodding in agreement.

Petey: "Alright. Now, Aggie says Alexander has just come into a huge sum of dough . . . believe it or not . . . a billion dollars. This rich Mexican, Carlos Santana, came to him for help with a tumor in his stomach; doctors had given him only a few months to live. When Alexander cured him, Santana was so grateful he gave him a billion bucks for his new charity . . . the Oaxaca Fund. Now that Alexander's got control of all this dough, he's going to rebuild the goddamn city . . . give it a new look, build new museums, a software industry, send poor kids to school . . . God knows what else. This is dangerous because he now has the money to do whatever he wants. For example, he could use the money to launch a political career which the Bible says is part of the Antichrist's plan to take over the world. You can't deny it; he's on a fuckin tear."

Zeke: "I agree with Petey. I've been doing some research on this guy, you know, like a background check. So far he looks pretty clean, except for the fact he was born in upstate New York . . . in a little town called Babylon. This could be the sign we've been waiting for. (*Waits for reaction*) You don't see any significance in that?"

Thomas: "Well, there's lots of towns up there named after ancient places . . . towns like Rome, Syracuse, and Utica. Babylon is just one of dozens."

Zeke: "Maybe so . . . but let me read you something from Arthur Pink's book on the Antichrist . . . then tell me if I'm going overboard.

(*Opening the book*) He quotes this guy Newton who's talking about where the Antichrist was born: 'Besides, no place can be pointed out more meet (that means perfect) for the nativity of Antichrist than Babylon, for it is the City of the Devil . . . always diametrically opposed to Jerusalem, which is deemed the City of God; the former city, that is Babylon, being the mother and disseminator of every kind of confusion, idolatry, impiety . . . a vast sink of every foul pollution, crime and iniquity . . . the first city in the world which cut itself off from the worship of the true God . . . The consummation, therefore, of impiety, which is to have its recapitulation in Antichrist, could not break forth from a more fitting place than Babylon'. End of quote. This is based on a reading of the Book of Daniel, verses 7 and 8 . . . so it could be the real deal. He's tellin us where the Antichrist was born."

Hunter: "Yeah . . . but the real Babylon is in Egypt, ain't it?"

Zeke: "Mesopotamia, in other words, Iraq. I'll admit that's a long way from upstate New York . . . but try adding this to the pot. The zip code for Babylon, NY is 12666 . . . and you all know what the mark of the Devil is, right?"

Silence.

Zeke: "Yeah, you got it . . . 666."

Thomas: "Jesus Christ! That's scary."

Zeke: "You're goddamn right it's scary. We gotta start thinking of ways to head this guy off . . . before it's too late."

Hunter: "I told you guys a long time ago we should take him down. If you want me . . . ."

Komerov (*interrupting*): "Look it, Hunter. If you're planning murder, I don't want any part of it. There's got to be other ways of stopping him."

Thomas: "Like what?"

Komerov: "I don't know . . . let me think about it. I'm still not sure who this guy is . . . other than the fact that he's powerful and up to no good."

Petey: "What more evidence do ya need, Doc? We already know that he can cure the sick, raise the dead, outsmart any casino he goes to and con the rich into givin him a billion bucks. Does that sound like any normal human bein to you?"

Komerov: "No it doesn't, Petey. Like I said, I'm convinced that he's a danger to the world . . . but I still don't know what he's up to. Is he the Antichrist mentioned in the Bible, the devil's disciple who's come to destroy the world, or is he just a freak of nature who takes delight in playing games with us ordinary folks?"

Petey: "Well, if he's jis playin games with us, that's not so bad, is it? I mean, it's not as bad as the kind of stuff the Good Book is talkin about . . . you know, bringin on fires and floods, startin wars, killin us off with disease."

Zeke: "I think Doc is saying that we need more evidence . . . and I agree. If this guy is really the Antichrist and not some weirdo freak playing games with us, he should start gettin serious about his plans to take over the world. Somewhere in the Bible (I think it's Daniel 11:21) it says that through "chicanery (whatever the hell that means) and intrigue" he's gonna rise to political power. And then he's gonna use that power base to start doing things militarily, like invading other countries. Isaiah says somewhere that he'll use his armies to 'shake kingdoms' and 'make the earth to tremble'. If that's what the Antichrist is gonna do, I don't see any signs yet that our man Alexander is moving in that direction."

Petey: "You're right Zeke . . . he ain't done anything political yet . . . but now that he's got that billion bucks, he could be gettin ready to make a move. We gotta be real careful. Somethin could be brewin in the next few weeks."

After further discussion, plans are made to meet again next Tuesday.

31

Getting Political

Once inside the door, Rafer slowly looks around, taking in the rich mahogany walls and crystal lighting that Locke-Obers is famous for. The aroma of ribs, scallops and lobster assails his nose, suggesting something much heavier than the modest lunch he has in mind. Actually he has come to meet Prof. Pulaski and his brother, Julian who works in the U.S. State Dept. According to Stefan, Julian has been dying to be introduced ever since he heard about the results of the meditation experiment.

Out of the corner of his eye, Rafer spots Stefan waving him to a booth next to the wall. "Rafer," he beams, standing, "this is my brother, Julian. Julian . . . my good friend and partner in crime, Rafer Alexander."

Early conversation centers around food and the décor.

Rafer (*looking around*): "From what I've heard this used to be *the* place in Boston to eat lunch a generation ago."

Stefan: "I've been told the same thing. That may be a little hard to believe when you consider what most diners ordered back then. A typical lunch apparently lasted two hours; it began with ox-tail soup and proceeded to ribs and lobster, accompanied by a baked potato, corn and gravy, all washed down with two or more martinis."

Julian (*grinning*): "No dessert?"

Stefan: "Forgot the dessert. Chocolate cake and ice cream was the favorite I think."

Rafer (*shaking his head*): "These guys must have fallen asleep at their desks when they got back to work."

Julian (*looking around*): "It's not exactly crowded today. Could be that people are starting to avoid the place. From what I see in the menu, it looks like they haven't changed their offerings all that much. But I'm still glad we came . . . there's lots of history here."

Rafer (*staring at the menu*): "Hmm. Lots of beef, lamb, pork, lobster and potatoes . . . I wonder if they know what a salad is."

Stefan: "You might have to draw a picture."

Rafer (*chuckling*): "How do you make a broccoli floret?"

Stefan: "A carrot might be easier."

When the waiter arrives to take their orders, all three immediately opt for the lobster bisque, a house specialty. "We can always get salads at home," Rafer explains softly, as the other two nod their silent approval.

Julian is the first to break the silence. "Rafe, Stefan has told me all about you and your work as a healer. The results of this hospital experiment are going to reverberate around the world. It's going to force people like me to reconsider our rational, scientific view of the world."

Rafer: "Actually, Julian, there's nothing in our work that challenges basic scientific principles; it merely pushes the envelope of investigation. There are things going on in the universe, important things like psychic energy, that we don't know how to measure yet. Once we learn to measure these phenomena, we can use the traditional concepts of physics, chemistry and biology to explain how they work. If we need some new concepts, we can add them to those we already have."

Julian rests his spoon in the bisque: "O.K. That's pretty clear. The whole field of medicine is going to be shaken up, for the good I assume. But actually, I'm more interested in something Stefan heard you say at your Medical School meeting last week . . . namely the possibility of using meditation to resolve conflicts. Correct me if I'm wrong, but you apparently said that when you meditate, it changes what other people nearby are feeling. Stefan mentioned peace in particular, although there could be other feelings as well."

Rafer: "That's true."

Julian leans forward, eyes sparkling. "Every since Stefan told me about it, I've been wrestling with the question of whether that finding could be used in a political setting . . . like the meeting we've got planned next month with the Israelis and the Palestinians."

Stefan: "Really? I hadn't heard. Where are you going to meet?"

Julian: "We're still negotiating the details; you have to be very careful about things like this . . . everything over there has symbolic meaning. But it looks like it'll be some neutral site in Jerusalem, if they can find one agreeable to everybody."

Stefan: "So where does Rafer fit into all this? I'm intrigued."

Julian: "In political negotiations everything depends on attitude. You can talk about borders, settlements, refugees and so on until you're blue in the face and never get any agreement because of the underlying hostility. When emotions are running high, nobody listens to anybody else. By now, after years of war and terror, positions have hardened, perhaps beyond repair. The P.L.O won't negotiate until Israel stops building new settlements and returns conquered territory; Hamas goes further, refusing to accept Israel's basic right to exist; for its part, Israel seems more interested in setting the two Palestinian delegations against each other than in furthering peace."

Rafer: "It sounds like nobody trusts anyone else."

Julian (*grinning*): "That's an understatement. Let's face it . . . they hate each other. And as long as they feel that way, we're not going to get anything done at this conference next month. To President Burrows, that's unacceptable. It's going to make him look bad if we come away empty-handed. Now that he's committed himself to going, we've got to come out of there with some positive results."

Rafer: "I'm listening."

Julian: "To our way of thinking at the State Department, the key lies in softening some of the underlying antagonism. Emotions are running so high they don't even consider the actual proposals. If we can get them to start listening to each other, they just might . . . ."

Stefan (*interrupting*): "But for Christ's sake, Jules, they won't even shake hands. How the hell are you going to get them to listen? And even if they listen to each other, how are you going to get them to agree on anything?"

Rafer: "I think I see where Julian is going with this. If we can get them to stop hating each other, even temporarily, we might get an agreement on some of the basic issues. All three parties certainly have a lot to gain from such an agreement."

Julian: "Exactly . . . and that could serve as a stepping stone to the ultimate two-state solution that everyone else wants to see."

Stefan: "O.K. So you want Rafe to go over there with you, do his trance thing and make everybody around the table feel kindly toward each other. Once you've banished the hate, you can start talking turkey."

Julian: "Well, that's a bit simplistic, but that's essentially what we have in mind . . . (*pause*) . . . I should probably say that's what *I* have in mind. So far, nobody else in the Department knows about the plan. In fact, I'm not even sure they have to know."

Stefan: "Assuming that Rafer agrees to the idea, how are you going to work him in without your boss's approval?"

Julian: "As you know, in my position as Assistant Secretary I have the authority to hire back-up staff . . . for example, people with expertise on finance, trade, military support, government protocol and so on. Without consulting with anyone else, I could appoint Rafer to an attaché position. We could present him as an expert on matters related to potential trade between Israel and a new Palestinian state. (*Turning to Rafer*) We've got tons of background material on the subject back in Washington, stuff I could get to you as soon as you give us the green light."

Rafer: "Wow. You do think big, Jules. I had no idea you had something like this in mind when we planned this get-together."

Julian (*chuckling*): "Would you have come if you had known?"

Rafer: "I'm not sure what I might have said back then. In fact, I'm still not sure now that you've told me about it. Some more details would help."

Julian: "O.K. I envision you sitting down around a table with the four heads of state and their foreign ministers. The top brass will include the prime ministers of Israel, Hamas, and the PLO as well as our own Pres. Burrows, plus the four foreign ministers. Like the other junior staff, you'll be seated in a second tier behind the leaders where you can whisper advice and so on. Back there you'll be out of sight so you can meditate without attracting undue attention."

Rafer: "So, how many people are going to be in the room? I ask because I've never tried going into a trance in front of a large group. It's always been with one or two people, usually a patient and a parent or friend. I don't know if I can generate any peaceful feelings if there are lots of people around."

Julian: "How about directing your energy to the three principals . . . that is, the three prime ministers? They're the ones that count the most. If we can cut through their hostility, the others should follow suit."

Stefan: "That sounds feasible from what Rafe has told me, but what good will it do if the voters back in Israel, the West Bank and Gaza cling to their hatred? They're not going to start trusting their enemy just because their leaders had a change of heart. And that makes it unlikely that the three parliaments will approve any decision made at the conference. Without that approval, of course, the whole conference could end up being a waste of time."

Julian: "I've thought about that and I think they're may be a way out. Just imagine what's going to happen when the four leaders sign an agreement covering all of the basic issues."

Stefan: "The media will go wild. It'll be all over TV, the press, the internet. People around the world will be jumping in the streets. Israel, the PLO and Hamas will be lauded in every corner of the globe for an historic breakthrough. And our own Pres. Burrows, of course, will come out smelling like a rose."

Julian: "Exactly. Now, wouldn't you agree that all that excitement is going to make it difficult for the people back home in Israel and Palestine to repudiate the decisions made at the conference? Failure to ratify those decisions will brand them as pariahs, robbing them of the support they once had and cutting them off from material help."

Rafer: "Whew! You've really thought this through, Jules. Your argument makes sense, but I'm no expert on foreign affairs. I wish you could share your views with your colleagues in the State Dept . . . and get their take on this whole scenario. They may see it differently."

Julian: "It just wouldn't work, Rafe. People who end up in the State Dept tend to be very rigid . . . and the higher you go in status, the more rigid they become. I can assure you that the people at the top would have me tossed to the wolves if they knew what I was thinking."

Rafer: "And their objection would be . . . what?"

Julian: "That it's not the proper way to do things. There's a protocol for major conferences like this and sneaking a healer in to secretly induce peaceful feelings is not on the menu. In the Department's book, asking four politically powerful men to sit down and meditate together would be seen as weird enough. Arranging for you to send psychic energy to them remotely would be considered downright bizarre. No, if we're going to do this, it'll have to be on the sly."

Rafer: "Do we have anything to lose by giving it a shot?"

Julian: "Not really. If we fail, no one else will know that we even tried."

Stefan: "When do you go?"

Julian: "The first meeting is scheduled for four weeks from tomorrow. If all goes well, we should be out of there in three days."

Rafer: "So, you're going to get me some background reports on the area?"

Julian nods. "You should get them in the mail by the end of the week."

Rafer: "How about clothing? As an attaché, is there anything special I should be wearing?"

Julian: "Do you have a dark suit . . . summer weight?"

Rafer: "It's old but I guess it'll do."

Julian: "I'll call you as soon as we have firm dates for the conference. Just come to Washington the day before we leave. You can stay at my apartment unless you'd rather have your own place. We'll pay for it if you do."

Rafer: "Your place sounds just fine."

Julian: "I'll give you all the details . . . street address, apartment number, phone number, etc . . . when I call."

Rafer (*grinning*): "No SSN?"

Julian (*laughing*): "Not until I know you better."

32

Jerusalem

At the Jerusalem airport, the Washington contingent is met by police and escorted to the old Armenian quarter, a site selected after days of intense wrangling among the three local parties. Meetings are to be held in a compound of giant tents erected on the Old Cow Pasture, one of the few areas in the Old City without historical ties to either Jews or Muslims. After a brief lunch in which introductions are exchanged with participating members, Rafer and his fellow staff members are ushered into a large meeting area featuring a large oval oak table at its center. President Burrows and his Israeli and Palestinian opposites are already seated. Rafer, now sporting an I.D. on his lapel, is guided to the circle of chairs located just behind the principles. He takes a seat no more than ten feet from where the P.L.O. prime minister is sitting. A brief scan of the room reveals that there are around 30 people present, perhaps 20 of them males. To his immediate left is an attractive Israeli woman who introduces herself as Rachel. She too is here as a consultant on economic affairs. Her English is perfect, first learned at a kibbutz outside Tel Aviv and honed at the London School of Economics. While they wait for the meeting to begin, the two trade details about where they live, courses they have taken, the areas they specialize in, etc. Her speech is subdued, almost lifeless, giving no clue of the agitation that is yet to come. President Burrows is the first to speak, reviewing the history of the peace process and setting the stage for the detailed proposals to follow. "The eyes of the world are on us," he intones with more vigor than usual. "If we can resolve our issues here, it will set a precedent for peaceful negotiations all over the globe."

Half-way through the speech, Rafer looks across the table where Julian is nodding repeatedly, a signal for him to begin meditating. Returning the nod, Rafer clears the area in front of him, returns his briefcase to the floor then closes his eyes. Meanwhile Rachel moves closer, about to ask a more personal question. When she sees his eyes close, she scowls, then leans back in her chair, perplexed by this obvious breach of etiquette.

Just as Rafer is bringing his mind to a single point, the Hamas prime minister rises for his introductory speech. There is no talk of peace, no warm words of welcome. Without hesitation he begins detailing the number of homes destroyed and individuals killed in the Israeli occupation. His arm is outstretched, his finger poised in accusation as he stares menacingly at his Israeli counterpart. No more than a minute into his trance Rafer feels a jab in his ribs as Rachel rises to answer. "But what about the rockets?," she shouts, intending her question for the prime minister but swinging her arms at the nearest target. "Do you know how many Israeli children you've killed or maimed with your rockets?," she cries hysterically, heedless now of any pretension of civility.

The moderator bangs his drinking glass on the table to restore calm. In the silence that ensues, Rachel reaches over and touches Rafer on the arm, "Sorry, I guess I got a little excited . . . but I couldn't let him get away with that." Rafer opens his eyes and nods politely. "I understand," he whispers. "It's got to be hard on everyone." Clearly frustrated with his non-committal response, she pulls back, her rapid breathing still audible to those nearby.

Once all four of the principals have given their opening remarks, the moderator declares the session over and invites everyone to a special lunch prepared by the staff. Eyeing members of the American contingent, he adds in fractured English, "Maybe you never have lamb and couscous . . . with hummus, olives and baklava. This is big treat. You try. Yes?"

Over lunch, Rafer and Julian fine-tune their strategy for the afternoon session. "It's a little hard to settle down when you're being poked in the ribs," Rafer explains. "And that voice of hers . . . I'm lucky I can still hear."

Julian smiles, "I noticed that. I was afraid you were about to poke her back. Make sure you take a different seat this afternoon . . . if you can. She may try to stay close. It's possible that she's interested in starting up something a little more intimate. It was hard to tell from across the table."

Rafer (*chuckling*): "I can always tell her I'm married and have seven kids back home in Boston."

Julian (*smiling*): "Or that you're gay. Or maybe that your father is a disaffected Muslim who emigrated to Iran so he could help work on their bomb."

Rafer (*laughing*): "You're wicked . . . you know that, don't you?"

Julian (*nonchalantly*): "I've heard rumors to that effect."

Back in the meeting room, Rafer finds a chair at the end of the row and sets his briefcase on the table. From ten feet away, Rachel watches carefully, gives a quick shake of her head and sits down. Her curled lip and flaring eyes leave no doubt she is aware of his evasiveness and is stung by his lack of interest. Silently she resolves to pay him back.

Despite Rafer's best efforts, the afternoon session is nearly as raucous as the morning one. Now it is the two Palestinian factions that are trading verbal blows while the Israelis sit smugly by. When the subject of terrorism is introduced, the noise reaches ear-splitting levels, leading Rafer to abandon his meditation altogether. At dinner that evening, he apologizes to Julian who in turn apologizes for the primitive display of tribal emotions. "This is the worst I've ever seen," he says, "and I've been to a number of these get-togethers. I wish I could promise it'll be better tomorrow . . . but there's no guarantee. At least, it can't get any worse."

Rafer (*grinning*): "They could start throwing chairs."

Julian: "Spit balls we could handle but . . . ."

Rafer (*interrupting*): "Maybe I should sit in the adjoining area . . . behind a wall where I wouldn't have to listen to all the noise. In our hospital study I meditated that way with some of the patients."

Julian: "How did it work?"

Rafer: "They did better than the controls, although not as well as patients I talked to face-to-face."

Julian: "Let's give it a try. I think I can arrange a place for you behind that partition over on the left. Right now they're using it for staff meetings."

Rafer: "Just make sure no one else is allowed in."

Julian: "O.K. I'll get you a key. One thing that might help tomorrow is that they're going to start the meeting off by having an iman and rabbi offer prayers. Who knows, it could quiet things down a bit."

Rafer: "Hmm. If they drag it out long enough, it could give me an opening. For meditation to have any kind of effect, especially with this many people in the room, everybody has to be quiet for at least a few minutes. Once the noise level rises and barbs start flying, I'll be as helpful as a Buddhist preaching compassion at a championship boxing match."

Julian: "Well put. Let's hope tomorrow is different."

The mood at the next morning's session is noticeably different. Perhaps it is the negative response from the international media in which conference participants are mercilessly lampooned. A cartoon in Der Spiegel is especially effective. It pictures the Israeli and Palestinian prime ministers in short pants throwing birthday cake at each other while Uncle Sam watches helplessly from the corner. A frustrated participant has scattered copies of the tabloid around the table prior to the start of the session. The effect is dramatic. Nothing is asked; nothing said. Even the usual morning greetings are eschewed as members withdraw to the privacy of their thoughts. By the time the iman and rabbi have finished their opening prayers, the silence is electric.

Rafer is aware of all this as he prepares to enter the adjoining room. The change in mood is exactly what he was hoping for. It's now a question of whether he can take that mood deeper before tempers erupt again. As he settles into a seat, he lets his mind run freely, then grows quiet as all thoughts and speculations give way to the rhythmic sound of breathing. Within minutes everything . . . the conference, the room, the chair . . . is swallowed up in a wordless Void. All lines, shapes and colors have vanished, leaving a universe of unblemished space where "there is nothing for the mind to take hold of." It is a familiar place. From past experience, he knows it as that realm from which psychic energy originates and flows out into the world. He breathes slowly, holding it in his solar plexus, then projects it outward into the conference room. Two hours pass without interruption.

The next thing he is aware of is a rustling at the partition door. He rises slowly and flips the lock. It's Julian. He's beaming. "Did you hear what happened?"

Rafer shakes his head.

Julian: "Sorry . . . there's no way you could have known. Anyway, it was a complete turnaround from yesterday. People were falling all over each other with milk and honey. Lots of apologies, talk about brotherhood."

Rafer: "So the meeting is over?"

Julian: "Yes."

Rafer: "Did they decide on anything, I mean anything important, like what to do with the settlements, the refugees or Jerusalem?"

Julian: "No, but I think the ground has been prepared for some decision-making tomorrow. They're in a mood to compromise . . . believe it or not. From what I heard today, the next session could produce the first major agreement in ten years. The mood has changed 180 degrees . . . and my guess is that you had a lot to do with it." Julian reaches out and grabs Rafer by the arm. "Can you do the same thing tomorrow? It's hard to believe but I think it's working."

Rafer smiles and squeezes Julian's hand. "Sure . . . but I'm a bit surprised that the meditation had an effect on a whole room of people. In the past it's always been one patient at a time . . . or maybe a patient and her parents . . . Of course, we can't be sure that I played any role at all."

Julian: "There's no other way to explain it Rafe. The German cartoon might have embarrassed people into behaving a bit better . . . but it certainly couldn't account for the warm feelings everybody was giving off this morning. No, that was clearly your doing. There's no doubt of that in my mind. So, c'mon. Let's get some lunch before they run out of food."

Rafer: "Hmm. Sounds good. I'm hungry."

33

Rachel

In the dining hall, Julian and Rafer take seats at a long table more suitable for communal gatherings than for the private meeting they have in mind. Before the waiter has a chance to take their orders, Julian is called away by his superior at the State Dept., leaving Rafer at the table by himself. Within minutes, he feels a hand on his shoulder . . . it's Rachel, asking if she can sit down. Rafer nods an O.K. and moves over to make room.

Rachel: "You missed a great meeting this morning. Where were you?"

Rafer: "Uh . . . a little stomach problem . . . nothing serious."

Rachel: "So you'll be with us this afternoon?"

Rafer: "I don't know. I don't want to take any chances. There are a lot of bugs going around."

Rachel: "Really? That's the first I've heard of it."

When the waiter asks for their orders, Rafer instinctively points to one of his favorite entrées: palak paneer, a popular Indian dish designed to project the international flavor of the conference and appeal to its Eastern observers. The item comes with an order of Naan and a side of hummus . . . all in all a very full offering for mid-day. Before formalizing the order, he stops, sensing that Rachel is watching, and at the last minute switches to a small cucumber salad. His stomach groans at the apostasy.

Rachel: "Sorry about the stomach. Hope you're better by tomorrow."

Rafer: "Thanks. So, tell me about this morning's session. Julian says it went real well. Everybody seemed in a much better mood."

Rachel: "Someone from the P.L.O. delegation made an astounding suggestion . . . I couldn't believe it at first. He started by saying something we could all agree on, you know, that the settlement issue and the refugee issue were interlinked and that one can't be resolved without the other. And then came the bombshell. He proposed that we resolve both at once by having the Israelis turn over all settlements to the Palestinian refugees in return for their giving up the right of return. He later amended it by saying some exceptions could be made for settlements near the proposed 1967 border . . . but essentially it was a trade-off, settlements for refugee rights."

Rafer: "Wow. That is revolutionary. But how would it work? I mean, could your government ever persuade those settlers to leave their homes voluntarily? They're pretty fanatic aren't they?"

Rachel: "It could happen if we offered them similar housing somewhere else in Israel. They won't go peaceably for sure . . . but with the right inducements, they could be persuaded."

By now Rafer is aware that Rachel has unbuttoned the top button on her blouse. Every time she leans forward to speak, she reveals the area on her chest where her smoothly tanned breasts divide before going their separate ways. She smiles knowingly when Rafer pretends to look the other way.

Rafer: "It . . . it sounds too good . . . you know . . . well . . . to be true," he murmurs, aware that he is stumbling over his words. "How did your boss, the prime minister, respond?"

Rachel: "Like everyone else in our delegation, I was surprised when he said he would think it over. Just yesterday, that would have been unthinkable. (*Shaking her head*) So much has happened in one day."

After lunch, Rafer returns to his little room on the other side of the canvas partition, still hungry but encouraged by what he has learned. The afternoon session begins with some spirited talk about Jerusalem but quickly descends into name-calling when a Hamas representative refers to the Israelis as "invaders." As the clock winds down toward evening, it is clear that little progress is going to be made. Old animosities are creeping back into the dialogue; a consensus seems to be forming that perhaps they went too far in the morning. In private discussions, many drive home the point that there are the citizens back home to think of. An Israeli delegate puts it concisely, "Can we really expect the public to endorse proposals as radical as the one we discussed this morning?" Over in the Palestinian delegation a similar voice can be heard, "You think the people down in Gaza, the ones who just lost their children and homes to the Israeli occupation, are going to go along with this stuff?"

By the time the session concludes, the conference appears headed back to square one. There is but one day left to turn things around. The Americans are on the verge of panic. With all the media hype preceding the conference, there is a lot of face waiting to be lost should nothing be accomplished. According to Julian, President Burrows is already preparing a press release that will absolve him of all responsibility for the failure. In the release, blame will be laid instead at the feet of "irrational, tribal mentalities that defy resolution despite the auspices of concerned outsiders."

That evening Rachel seeks out Rafer again in the hotel dining room. "Feeling any better?," she chirps, fluffing her black, wavy hair. "Stomach wise, yes, thanks," he answers, "but not so sanguine about the conference. Sounds like we're heading back to zero . . . and that's a shame given the way things were going this morning."

Rachel (*sitting down*): "I've thought about nothing else . . . except you. Do you have any interest in taking a walk around Jerusalem after dinner? I know the area well."

Rafer is surprised by the invitation, especially after the fierce look he got at yesterday's session. For some unknown reason, it appears that she's come around and wants to be friends. His response is friendly but not enthusiastic.

Rafer: "A short walk might be nice . . . and then I should get back to my hotel room to go over some notes for tomorrow. It could be an interesting session. I just hope my stomach holds up. But let's have dinner here first. They have a stuffed grape leaf appetizer I want to try."

Rachel (*picking up the menu*): "People here rave about the chicken kabob with basmati rice too . . . (*pause*) . . . "I'm glad you want to go for a walk later. I've thought about it all day."

Rafer shifts uneasily in his chair as warning bells begin sounding inside his gut. He draws back in his seat and pretends to peruse the menu. "I should tell her right now that I'm not interested," he muses. "Be up front about it," he adds. "Don't lead her on. It'll just make things harder down the road."

Rachel puts her elbows on the table and leans forward, eyes fluttering. "Did I lose you Rafe? Come back to me, please."

Rafer (*thinking quickly*): "I'm still here. I just remembered that I promised to call Eva, the woman I live with back in Boston. She'll be waiting by the phone about the time we finish dinner."

Rachel sits back and takes a deep breath. "Are you married?"

Rafer: "No. Just friends . . . good friends."

Rachel pauses for a moment then takes the plunge. "Do you sleep with her?"

Rafer: "If you mean, do we have sex, yes . . . now and then."

Rachel (*sitting back up*): "It doesn't sound terribly romantic. Are you in love with her?"

Rafer (*putting the menu down*): "I wouldn't use that term exactly."

Rachel: "What term would you use?"

Rafer: "Well, I do love her . . . but not in the usual way. We're more like friends I think . . . ."

Rachel (*wry smile*): " . . . who just happen to make love now and then . . . (*pause*) . . . I wonder how she feels about the arrangement."

Rafer: "She seems happy enough, although she probably would like something more conventional."

Rachel looks around to find the waiter, then turns to Rafer: "You can make your call as soon as we finish dinner. I'll wait in the lobby for you. And then we can go for our walk . . . assuming you still want to."

Rafer: "Yes, if you do . . . (*pause*) . . . I hope I haven't offended you. Perhaps I should have mentioned Eva earlier."

Rachel (*forcing a smile*): "That's alright. Life is full of surprises; some of them good, some bad. I've had my share of each."

Once dinner is over and the call to Boston completed, the two meet in the lobby, as planned. Just outside they are greeted with a cool breeze lightly perfumed with the scent of purple bougainvillea. "It's a beautiful night for a walk," she says, taking his arm. He says nothing but makes no attempt to move away. As they walk the streets of Jerusalem, down to the Muslim quarter and back along the Wailing Wall, the talk turns back to the conference and tomorrow's critical session.

Rachel squeezes Rafer's arm. "If we can just get back to the way people were feeling yesterday morning, we might come to an agreement . . . even on issues like settlements and refugees. I think it's possible. Do you?"

Rafer: "I'm new to this whole peace process so my opinion probably isn't worth much. But I'm certainly hopeful."

Rachel: "I am too but it's hard to be optimistic when you consider that the parliaments back home have to ratify any agreements we make here. I can easily imagine everything becoming unglued once the public gets involved."

Rafer: "Yes. Things could degenerate very quickly once the conference is over. But all is not lost. I don't know if I mentioned it but we . . . by which I mean the Americans . . . have a plan for dealing with the reaction you're alluding to."

Rachel: "What exactly is that?"

Rafer: "The idea is to flood the media with kudos for the work achieved here, assuming of course that we actually do something to warrant approval. Pour it on heavy . . . with articles, TV shows, and speeches, all celebrating the agreements reached at the conference. Get everybody involved . . . the U.N., the IMF, WTO, Jews, Shias, Sunnis . . . leaders from every continent. Pour on so much approval that it will be impossible for people on either the right or left to vote the agreements down . . . (*grinning*) . . . You could call it a form of psychological warfare."

Rachel: "Wow. I like the plan. Who thought it up?"

Rafer: "I don't know. My friend in the State Department told me about it."

They walk further, still arm in arm. As they cross a side street, the sound of children playing soccer can be heard. "I guess they don't need much light," Rafer says, glancing up at the darkening sky.

Rachel: "They look pretty happy. They probably have no idea what's going on inside our conference room . . . even though their lives could be affected dramatically."

Rafer smiles. "A silly thought just occurred to me. I wonder what would happen if those children were allowed to attend the conference . . . or even run it. Could they do any worse than we're doing now?"

Rachel: "Well, you're right. They're probably not old enough to feel the poison that consumes their parents . . . so, they might do better. Should I suggest it at tomorrow's session?"

Rafer (*chuckling*): "Not unless you want to be thrown out on your ear."

They pass the next block in silence. Rachel is the first to speak. "I keep coming back to the children. Isn't there some way to involve them in all this? They are so innocent, not at all burdened with questions of religion or ethnicity . . . (*smiling*) . . . like me."

Rafer reaches over and puts his arm around her shoulder, tugging playfully. "You can get worked up, that's for sure . . . but you seem pretty open too. I admire that."

As they approach a small bistro on the left, Rachel points to the lights inside and says, "I've been in there. It's rather quaint. Are you in the mood for a drink or a little dessert?"

"Why not," Rafer replies. "A little baklava would taste awfully good right now."

Rachel turns and smiles. "Your stomach seems to be improving. Am I wrong?"

"Maybe it's the company," he replies.

Inside they find a corner table and sit down. Rachel orders a peach parfait, Rafer settles for chai tea and baklava. Before the food arrives, Rafer offers a suggestion. "You know, what I said earlier about letting the kids run the conference was meant to be funny, but there may be another way we could get them involved."

Rachel: "Hmm. I'm listening."

Rafer: "This plan actually occurred to me some time ago but I haven't worked out the details yet. And it all depends on getting an agreement tomorrow on the basic issues. The idea is to swap kids. The Israelis would send 50 of their adolescent children to live with a P.L.O family for one year . . . and another 50 to Gaza. In return the P.L.O and Hamas each would each send 50 of their kids to spend a year with an Israeli family. The children would be expected to learn the host's language and go to the same school as the boys and girls they're living with. Now, here's the point. With all those kids living across the border, nobody's going to fire rockets or spray towns with artillery. After all, your own kids might be living there. Besides the obvious peace benefit, each kid would learn a lot about the host culture . . . its values, rituals, history, etc . . . and share that knowledge when they return home. It can't help promoting a little mutual understanding . . . which they're a bit short on now . . . (*pause*) . . . What do you think?"

Rachel: "Holy Cow! (*chuckling*) That *is* an American expression isn't it? Rafer . . . you're taking my breath away. Is that your idea?"

Rafer: "I think it's been tried elsewhere. I don't remember where."

Rachel: "I think it's absolutely brilliant. You've got to present it at the morning session."

Rafer pauses, groping for an answer. "I don't know Rachel. I think it would be more effective if it came from one of the local participants, either an Israeli or Palestinian . . . especially if it's a woman who has kids of her own. If it comes from an American who has nothing to lose in such an exchange, the idea won't be taken as seriously."

Rachel: "I don't have any kids, but you're probably right that it would be better for me to do it, even if means taking my life in my hands."

Rafer: "What do you mean?"

Rachel: "You know, some fanatic is going to tell parents that I'm willing to get their kids killed . . . all for the sake of a piece of paper that the Americans conned us into signing. That could get people pretty worked up, don't you think?""

Rafer: "Yes, but as long as enrolling kids in the plan is optional, it shouldn't stir things up too much. Nobody is suggesting that parents be forced to do it."

Rachel: "That's true."

Rafer: "Are we agreed then? You'll offer it at the morning session?"

Rachel: "Alright. I'll have to O.K. it with the delegation head first . . . but I think he'll go along."

Before they can finish their dessert, Rachel excuses herself and heads for the ladies room. When she returns minutes later she has an impish smile on her face. Rafer is puzzled but says nothing. After a bite of her parfait, she leans across the table and whispers, "I have a present for you." When Rafer looks at her hands, she adds, "No silly . . . under the table." With that, she reaches under the table and stretches her hand toward his. Their hands never meet. What Rafer feels instead is something soft and silky, warm and smooth to the touch. It is only when he withdraws it to his lap that he recognizes it as a pair of panties.

"Yours?," he asks, still incredulous at his discovery.

"Of course," she answers with a devilish smile. "Are they still warm?"

Rafer runs his fingers across the satiny material, then looks up, "Yes . . . especially here in the front."

"Rub them on your cheek," she whispers. "See how smooth they are."

Rafer looks around the café. When assured everyone is busy, he drops his head and touches the warm panties to his cheek. A soft, barely audible moan escapes his lips.

With eyes sparkling, Rachel adds, "I tried a new coconut body rinse this morning. Can you tell?"

Rafer looks around again then buries his nose in the panties. "Hmm. Yes, it could be coconut . . . or perhaps something a little spicier."

Rachel laughs, drawing disapproving stares from the next table. "I hope it doesn't spoil your baklava."

"On the contrary," he replies, swallowing the last chunk of pastry. "It's never tasted this good."

Outside the café Rachel takes a deep breath, then turns suddenly and throws her arms around Rafer. "Thank you for your beautiful suggestion about the children," she gasps, her lips only inches from his. "This could change the world." Not waiting for a response, she adds, "I am so happy. Will you make love to me tonight?"

When Rafer hesitates, she presses her lips to his ear, "I can be very discreet about such things. You have nothing to worry about."

He has always found her attractive, even when she was railing against the Hamas leader. Looking at her now, in the fading glow of a summer evening, he is dazzled by her beauty. Her face is oval, her skin taut and browned, her hair pulled back into a ponytail. Her lips are more pink than red, moist now and slightly parted as if in anticipation of a kiss. But it is her long, black eyebrows that stir him the most. He steps closer. In his imagination he begins tracing each in turn with his fingertip . . . starting just above the nose and moving slowly in a half-circle around each eye, pressing just firmly enough to feel the bone underneath, stopping only when he has reached her temple. Through it all she remains unmoving . . . as if she were posing for a portrait. Now, back in the real world, he touches a finger to her cheek and lets it slide to her lips. When their eyes meet again, his knees begin to buckle.

"Well?," she asks, eyes ravished with longing. "Do you want me?"

"Aargh," he cries as the ache in his loins wrestles with the voice of conscience. "That's not the point . . . (*pause*) . . . Yes I want you but I can't get Eva out of my mind."

"But you're not in love with her," Rachel replies quickly. "You told me that yourself . . . and besides, she needn't ever know."

"Well, if she asks me if I met anyone interesting, I would feel obliged to tell her about you. I don't think we've ever lied to each other . . . and I don't want to start now. Given the way she feels about me, the truth is bound to . . . "

Rachel (*interrupting*): "Kiss me."

When Rafer hesitates, she leans forward, wraps her arms around his neck and presses her lips to his. The strength of her grip renders all thoughts of resistance futile. When he closes his mouth, she forces it open with her tongue. Gradually his hands slide up her back to her neck then to her head as he pulls her tight. The heat of her flesh inflames his own body, sending waves of desire pulsing through his groin.

"I take it you're not married," he says, stopping to take a breath.

"Oh, but I am," she replies. "At least for now. The divorce should be final in a month or two . . . (*pause*) . . . but I already feel single again. Come, let's go to my room. We've got the whole night ahead of us."

Just as she reaches for his hand, two young boys approach from across the street, the older one holding a bird in his hand. The bird is trying to fly but keeps toppling over. The boy says something in Hebrew as he holds the bird up to Rafer for inspection.

Rachel (*visibly frustrated*): "He says the bird smashed into a window nearby and hurt itself. He wants to know if we will take it. Shall I tell him to take it to a vet?"

Rafer (*kneeling*): "Here, let me take a look." As he opens the boy's hand all the way, the bird becomes alarmed, wobbles to one side and falls to the ground. Gently Rafer puts it back in his hand and begins stroking its back. To everyone's surprise, it stops fluttering and closes its eyes.

Rachel (*agitated*): "Rafe, let's go. The bird is going to die no matter what we do. I've seen it happen before."

Rafer looks up at Rachel. "Let's at least give him a chance."

Rachel sighs. "What are you going to do?"

Without answering, Rafer sits down on the curb, still holding the bird in his hand. He strokes the bird's back a few times, then closes his own eyes half way. When nothing further is said, the two boys lose interest and go on their way. Rachel is about to continue her questioning when she sees that Rafer's eyes are almost closed. Unwilling to risk getting her skirt dirty on the curb, she leans back against the lamp post and waits. A half an hour passes without anyone's moving. Then, suddenly the bird opens its eyes, flaps its wings several times and flies to the branch of a nearby eucalyptus tree. After resting for a minute, it takes off again, this time flying across the street into a neighbor's garden.

Rafer rises from the curb and smiles as he follows the bird's flight into the trees.

Still scowling, Rachel asks, "What are you, some kind of miracle worker?"

Rafer shakes his head. "Who knows? He might have recovered without my help. Sometimes all they need is a little time and a safe place until their healing mechanisms kick in."

Rachel: "Well, what were you doing all that time there on the curb? You looked like you were in some kind of trance."

Rafer: "Yes. It was a trance. I've had a little success meditating with human patients and I thought it just might work with an animal."

Rachel: "What do you mean when you say 'a little success'?"

Rafer: "Down in Mexico I worked with a young girl who was dying of leukemia . . . her parents had asked me to sit with her in the hospital. She recovered completely, and everybody, including the doctors, seemed to think the meditation helped. And then there was a woman with arthritis . . . ."

Rachel (*voice rising*): "Wait a minute. You say that this dying girl recovered after you meditated with her. What about the doctors. Couldn't she afford the usual treatment?"

Rafer: "The doctors tried everything they could think of . . . radiation, chemotherapy, medication . . . even surgery. But nothing seemed to work. I wasn't called in until they had all given up on her."

Rachel (*shaking her head*): "I don't get it. Why in the world would meditation work when all the usual treatments failed? I hate to say it, Rafe, but this is starting to sound a little fishy."

Rafer: "I understand. It takes some revisions in the way we think the world works . . . but you can't argue with the facts. We recently completed an experiment in Boston where terminally ill patients were divided into control and treatment groups. The results are really exciting. For one thing, patients who . . . ."

Rachel (*interrupting*): "So you really do believe in this kooky stuff. My God, Rafe, I took you for an educated man. It's hard to believe that someone with a Ph.D. has fallen for such nonsense. Wow, was I mistaken."

Sensing that the evening is drawing to a hasty close, Rafer says, "It appears that we have different opinions about some things. That's O.K. I just hope it doesn't interfere with what you agreed to do at tomorrow's session . . . you know, the children swapping idea."

Rachel (*pulling her jacket tight*): "That's entirely different. I still like the idea and will present it like we agreed. I think it best, though, that we call it a night while we're still good friends. We are, aren't we?"

Rafer goes to hug her. "Of course. I'm just sorry we couldn't agree on this other thing."

After a brief hug, Rachel backs off and turns to leave. "Will I see you at the session tomorrow Rafe? I may need some backup on the children's proposal."

Rafer waves. "I can't say for sure. It depends on the stomach. But I'll try."

34

Kashmir

As Julian predicted, the world utters a collective sigh of relief when the conference ends on a triumphant note. The new treaty not only resolves questions surrounding settlements, refugees and Jerusalem, but sets an actual date for the establishment of a Palestinian state which is to include both the West Bank and Gaza. The global media is ecstatic. In the newspapers, on TV shows, and throughout the online blogosphere President Burrows is lauded as a diplomatic genius whose persistence and keen understanding of the issues helped to cut through layer after layer of animosity, allowing the delegates to act on their common desire for peace. According to some reports, he is now the leading candidate for both the Nobel Peace Prize and Time's Man of the Year. The significance of his achievement is elevated even further when, to the surprise of many, the new treaty is ratified by the Israeli Knesset and both Palestinian parliaments. An agreement on the Children's Exchange Program is widely seen as a guarantee against the possible renewal of violence. With the exception of the extremists, the world seems poised to enter a new era of peace, with the Israeli-Palestinian treaty as its model for conflict resolution. A spirit of compromise goes out from Jerusalem, inspiring leaders in every corner of the globe to come to terms with their adversaries.

Within weeks, the U.S. State Department receives an invitation from a joint Pakistani-Indian council to oversee an upcoming conference on Kashmir. The letter refers to President Burrows' recent success in Jerusalem and concludes with the hope that he can bring some of the same magic to Kashmir where Muslims and Hindus have been locked in mortal combat for over 60 years. As soon as the letter reaches his desk, Julian calls Rafer to read him the contents.

Rafer: "That's exciting, Julian. It certainly speaks well of the American role in resolving the Israeli-Palestinian issue. I assume you're going as part of the U.S. delegation."

Julian: "Of course . . . but we want you to come too. Just between the two of us, I am convinced that you had a lot to do with our success in Jerusalem. I hate to think what might have happened if you hadn't been there meditating that last day. As you know, things were pretty close to collapsing at the end of the second session."

Rafer: "O.K. But let's be honest. Meditation obviously has its limits . . . otherwise things would never have slipped during the second day. Maybe it worked on the third day; maybe it didn't. There's really no way to know."

Julian: "Granted . . . but given what you did with those patients in Mexico, there's a good chance that the meditation helped here too. From what I saw at the conference, you were instrumental in moving people to a less contentious place where negotiations could begin in earnest. If they had remained stuck in their anger, nothing would have happened."

Rafer: "Perhaps. I hope you're right."

Julian: "There's probably something else you should know about what's happening in Washington; maybe you're already aware of it from TV . . . (pause) . . . We've just had this fantastic breakthrough in Jerusalem but no one besides me is aware of the role you played in pulling it off . . . O.K . . . so a vacuum has been created which our dear President Burrows is anxious to fill. He's walking around Washington like some primped up poodle that's just been declared best in show. When he gives speeches, which he does at the drop of a hat, he comes across like a self-righteous deity who has been sent here to show us poor humans how to get along with each other. Since Jerusalem, his speech has changed; his dress is more formal, his nails manicured, his hair coiffed, his cuff links monogrammed; he even walks different . . . more deliberate now, more self-conscious . . . as if he were strutting on parade. I've always known him to be a proud man but what I see now goes beyond pride. This is pure narcissism . . . an obsession with self-image . . . an unrestrained love of himself. The only people who matter to him now are those who are in a position to praise him. This is an unprecedented erosion of values that can only end in disaster for those he's supposed to be serving. And keep in mind that he's the leader of the most powerful nation on earth."

Rafer: "Whew! You're really worked up. Are you serious? Do you really think this is going to end in disaster?"

Julian: "I can't say exactly when or where it will happen but of this I'm sure: during any upcoming negotiations he will support whatever policy promises him the most adulation, regardless of how it affects others. In Jerusalem that wasn't a problem since, beyond his opening remarks, he had very little to say. But now that he has been identified, wrongly identified I should say, as the power broker who miraculously brought Israelis and Palestinians together, people around the world are going to be kneeling at his feet, begging him to do it all over again. And that makes him a dangerous man."

Rafer: "So, tell me more about Kashmir. I've read a little over the years but not a heck of a lot. I know that the trouble started way back in 1947 when Pakistan was split off from India. At the time Kashmir was a princely state bordering both countries. Given a choice, Kashmir opted to join India, didn't it?"

Julian: "Well, yes, Hari Singh, the Maharaja of Jammu-Kashmir, a despot who had sole authority in these matters, decided to throw his lot in with India, despite the fact that a majority of his people were Muslims who preferred to join the new country of Pakistan.

When that stirred up a hornet's nest, the United Nations ordered that a plebiscite be held and the results used to determine which country Jammu-Kashmir would join. The Indians, fearful of the Muslim majority, refused to conduct such a plebiscite. In lieu of a vote, a Line of Control was established dividing Jammu-Kashmir into Indian-controlled and Pakistani—controlled sectors. In response the pro-Pakistanis sent guerrillas across the Line in hopes of destabilizing the Indian half of the region. The Indians responded with thousands of troops . . . actually today I think they have 700,000 . . . an awesome number when you remember that the U.S. has only 150,000 in Iraq . . . (*pause*) . . . And that's where it stands today . . . guerillas and terrorism on the one side; an oppressive army of occupation on the other. The two parties are no closer to a solution now than they were 60 years ago."

Rafer: "So in some ways it's not that different from the Israeli-Palestinian conflict . . . the one that just got resolved in Jerusalem. If I remember correctly, the trouble there started when the U.N., conscious of the horrors the Jews had suffered during World War II, sanctioned the creation of an Israeli state within Palestinian territory . . . back in 1948."

Julian: "The dates are eerily similar, aren't they . . . 1947, 1948 . . . with de facto partitioning in each case. Lots of differences, for sure, but similar in that they both bear witness to how deep and long-lasting human hatred can be."

Rafer: "Is there any solution on the table . . . one that will be discussed at the upcoming conference?"

Julian: "Nothing new. Residents have the same three options they had 60 years ago . . . they can vote to join either Pakistan or India . . . or they can vote to form a separate state. Surveys show that there is no clear support for any of the three, although independence seems to be gaining ground. What's holding independence back is the loyalty which many Kashmiri's continue to feel toward either India or Pakistan. They are reluctant to cut the ties completely."

Rafe: "What about making the Line of Control permanent and letting those on one side join Pakistan while the other becomes part of India?"

Julian: "There's too much diversity for that to be an appealing alternative . . . that is, lots of Muslims living on the Indian side of the Line with a corresponding number of Hindus living on the Pakistani side. Besides most people there, despite differences in religion and language, want to keep Kashmir together . . . either as an independent nation or as part of India or Pakistan. Down deep they see themselves as Kashmiris."

Rafer: "So, we're stuck . . . a stalemate . . . with no good options on the table. It makes you wonder why they're bothering to have this conference in the first place."

Julian: "Just like in the Middle East, they keep trying. No one is ready to give up entirely. No one is willing to accept that the status quo . . . terror, reprisal, and death . . . is the way things have to be. People are suffering. Some researchers estimate that close to 100,000 residents of Jammu-Kashmir, most of them civilians, have been killed in the last ten years. Most folks are afraid to go shopping. No one goes out at night unless he's carrying an AK-47."

Rafer: "So what do we do? If they're this stuck, what's the point of dragging me along?"

Julian: "I may be alone in this but I think I see a way out. India will never allow Kashmir to fall to the Pakistanis; Pakistan is equally committed to keeping it out of India's hands. That's fixed, unchangeable. The only way out is to make Kashmir an independent nation."

Rafer: "But you just said that residents continue to feel loyal to either India or Pakistan and don't want to lose those connections."

Julian: "Yes . . . but I think there's a way of getting around that. Once Kashmir is independent, it could divide itself into separate regions, sort of like Swiss cantons, each with its own language and customs . . . a federalist system where the central government maintains control over currency and foreign policy while letting individual regions control things like education, public safety and commerce."

Rafer: "Sort of like the U.S.?"

Julian: "In some ways, yes . . . but organized around religious and linguistic differences. That would allow people to retain their cultural identity without being swallowed up by either India or Pakistan. For it to work, however, people have to first cool down and stop throwing bombs. And that's where you come in. If, with your help, we can establish a peaceful atmosphere at the negotiating table, people can begin to look at the proposal rationally instead of emotionally . . . something they have been unable to do up to now. For 60 years they've been obsessed with thoughts of justice and revenge . . . and that's kept them from seeing the forest for the trees. At this conference we can at least give them a chance."

Rafer:" O.K. You've got me convinced. Even if we don't succeed politically, we'll get a chance to see the Kashmir Valley which I have been told is one of the most beautiful places on earth."

Julian: "It is. But keep in mind that Srinagar where the conference will be held is rather warm and humid in the summer despite its 5,200 feet elevation . . . so don't bother with your overcoat."

Rafer: "When do we leave?"

Julian: "Two weeks from tomorrow. I'll be at my desk in Washington. Why don't you come a day early and stay at my place? We can hop a Department limo to Dulles the next morning."

Rafer: "Hey. I'm excited . . . (*pause*) . . . Now to break the news to Eva. She wasn't too thrilled with the Jerusalem trip . . . my guess is that this one won't be any better."

Julian: "I wish we could bring her along . . . but if everybody did that it would add significantly to the expense and you can guess how the taxpayers would react to that."

Rafer: "She'll survive."

35

The Word Spreads

In his capacity as honorary chairperson, Pres. Burrows gets both to open the conference and close it. It is the latter speech that gets the most media attention. In it he briefly celebrates the founding of a new independent Kashmir state and goes on to extol the "near miraculous" way participants managed to transcend their "tribal differences" in coming to an agreement. "We have achieved something here in Kashmir that no one before has ever accomplished, not even the valiant peace-makers who overcame decades of frustration to carve out the new state of Palestine. It is as if two great armies, equally intent on destroying the other, were to meet in a furious battle where miraculously no one gets hurt. Instead they agree to talk. When the day is done, they lay down their arms, toast each other and commit themselves to everlasting peace. No, my friends, this is an event new in the annals of diplomacy. Let us salute those among us who worked tirelessly to bring it all together. If it hadn't been . . . ."

Julian (*whispering*): "Rafe, you notice how he keeps referring to the "we" that pulled this thing off? He's talking about Team U.S.A. Hardly any mention is made of what this means to the Kashmir people, what they've sacrificed to get to this point or how this will change their lives. The speech is really about him and the meaning of his contribution. It's as if he were reading from a proclamation awarding himself this year's Nobel Peace Prize. What people in the audience don't realize is that he had nothing to do with the final treaty. Absolutely zilch. If I weren't worried about losing my job, I'd burst out laughing. The guy is a disgrace to the American people."

Rafer: "He does seemed convinced that he has the magic touch. I guess you can't blame him for feeling good."

Julian: "First Jerusalem, now Kashmir. Two for two. God knows what's coming next."

In the days to come, the White House is swamped with calls to resolve intractable conflicts across the globe. First it is the president of the Republic of Georgia with an invitation to attend a conference dealing with Georgian-Russian grievances. The Georgians want the Russians out of Georgia and preferably out of South Ossetia as well . . . and they are convinced that Burrows, with his historic successes behind him, can make this happen. When asked to participate, the Russians politely refuse, citing ongoing American military support for Georgia and the likelihood of bias.

The second invitation is from a Spanish-Basque peace council charged with resolving the long-simmering conflict over Basque separatism. While Spain is willing to grant some autonomy in matters of education and policing, it is unwilling to give the Basque people what they really want . . . political independence. Recent ETA terrorist attacks on railroads and military outposts around Madrid have only succeeded in hardening the government's position. While officials insist they are continuing to search for a resolution of differences, few outside government see any chance of success.

All that changes with Burrow's "miracles" in Jerusalem and Kashmir . . . hence the invitation to join a peace conference to be held at a neutral site, probably somewhere in southern France. With visions of yet another feather in his cap, Burrows hastily agrees and sends Julian to make arrangements. Outside Washington, murmurs can be heard to the effect that the president is spending too much time abroad and not enough tending to important business at home. The Cleveland Plain Dealer goes so far as to calculate how much time (an estimated 41%) he has spent either hobnobbing with foreign dignitaries or vacationing at his estate in Montana. To fend off his critics, Burrows makes a speech on prime time television in which he defends his trips abroad, citing successes which, although they may not impact Americans directly, promise a whole new era of "peace among nations." The program features images of Israelis, Palestinians, Pakistanis and Indians, all voicing fervent appreciation of America's help; there are also pictures of prematurely-wrinkled peasant women showering him with some sort of leafy material. Concluding the program is a photo of Burrows standing with arms folded under a stained glass church window. The window shows Christ anointing a group of shepherds while their sheep graze contentedly nearby. The script at the bottom reads: "Blessed are the peacemakers for they shall be called sons of God."

The TV program is a huge success. With the country firmly behind him again, the president affirms his intention to help resolve the Basque-Spanish problem. To appease any remaining critics, the White House announces that only a small contingent from the State Department will be accompanying him on the trip. The rationale given is that this will reduce both labor and transportation costs. According to the announcement, the president intends to do his bit by leaving his wife at home.

The minute Julian arrives home from southern France, he picks up the phone and dials Rafer's number. "Did you hear the news; only the senior officers at the State Department will be heading to the Basque-Spain conference. I did my best to talk them out of it but the president is convinced that in order to keep voters happy, we have to cut back on expenses."

Rafer: "So, you won't need me after all. That's disappointing, but at least Eva will be glad . . . (*pause*) . . . Let's hope that Burrows can make it three in a row. This one could be easier than the first two since the

Basque area is so small. It can't hurt Spain all that much to give in a little here and there."

Julian: "We'll see. I'm just worried that without you there, all hell is going to break loose. I think we learned something in Jerusalem and Kashmir; if you want people to think straight, you have to get them to cool off first. And that's not easy when they've been killing each other for years. Although we can't prove it, my guess is that your meditating was critical in both Jerusalem and Kashmir; it injected a spirit of peace into the proceedings. I have my doubts the same thing is going to happen in France."

Rafer: "Let's hope for the best. One thing in our favor is the momentum created by those first two successes. Who would have predicted that two huge logjams, decades in the making, would be broken in the space of a few months? Peace is now in the air. That might cool tempers long enough to make a rational solution possible."

———

Rafer's hopes, however well-intentioned, prove naïve. When the conference ends, participants are no closer to a settlement than they were at the beginning. When Pres. Burrows is asked to give a closing speech, he declines, citing an emergency back in Washington. The media are more forthright. "Basques Walk Out" blares the Washington Post. "Conference Ends in Failure" says the Boston Globe. An article in the New York Times features a photo of Pres. Burrows leaving with his head down, scowling. His right hand is curled into a fist; with his other hand he is waving off reporters. Under the photo it reads: "No Magic This Time."

When the phone rings, Rafer rushes to pick it up, certain that it is Julian, home from the conference. He's right. Not waiting for anything more than a hello, Julian explodes, "Rafe, I told you this would happen, didn't I? It was even worse than I thought. Three straight days of name-calling and mud-slinging . . . it was almost comic. We never got to a place where the issues were discussed openly. The anger was so thick at times I was sure somebody was going to pull out a gun and start firing. From what I've heard, that's exactly what happened just a few hours after the conference ended. Two delegates were killed in the street outside the hotel. Burrows high-tailed it out of there before the fireworks started. He never even stopped to talk to the reporters, afraid as he was that America would be blamed for the failure. He was probably right. After Jerusalem and Kashmir, expectations were unrealistically high . . . so when things blew up, everybody pointed the finger at him."

Rafer: "No TV pictures this time I take it . . . you know, of him standing under a stain-glass window, looking Christ-like."

Julian: "More likely the Anti-Christ . . . with six heads and a long tail, blowing smoke out of his nose."

Rafer (*laughing*): "I suppose he'll be more cautious now about accepting invitations to play peacemaker."

Julian: "That's if he get any more. Frankly I doubt it. I think he's been revealed as a fake. What happened in France . . . or more precisely what didn't happen in France . . . confirms for me what I've thought all along . . . that our esteemed president didn't have anything to do with the breakthroughs in Jerusalem and Kashmir. It was all because of you Rafe. I really believe that."

Rafer: "Maybe. I'm not as sure as you are. It could have been other factors as well. Who knows? Without experimental controls, it's impossible to say . . . (*pause*) . . . But it looks like the conference trail has come to an end . . . at least for now."

Julian: "I'm afraid so. What country is going to invite Burrows after this debacle? And even if he gets invited, my guess is that he'd be afraid to risk another defeat. He just doesn't have the heart for it. As everybody now realizes, he's all show and no substance."

36

The Speech

In the weeks following the Basque-Spain conference, Pres. Daniel Burrows turns out to be more clever than many had thought. By playing down what happened in France and talking repeatedly about Jerusalem and Kashmir, he keeps his successes in the news and in the mind of his voters. As part of his strategy he orders Secretary of State Henrietta Coles to give a speech at the U.N. celebrating the two historic events. The "New Era of Peace" is to be her theme, with liberal references to the U.S.'s role (read Burrow's role) in resolving what were thought to be intractable conflicts. She maps out what she wants to say and sends a copy to the White House for approval. It comes back with an O.K. and a few suggestions. Among the 'improvements' are words for an opening paragraph: 'Today we face an unprecedented opportunity for peace throughout the globe. If we approach this time with love for each other, we can move forward into an era of joy and abundance; if we come instead with malice in our hearts, we are doomed to perpetuate the savagery of our forefathers. The choice is ours.' Despite the clichés, she is impressed and agrees to include the statement in her speech.

Along with other State Department staff members, Rafer is invited to attend the meeting. Julian promises to save a seat for him. In the days leading up to the talk, Rafer spends hours contemplating what he hopes Secretary Coles will say. After trips to Jerusalem and Kashmir, his own political views have expanded . . . from concern for the poor in Oaxaca all the way to speculations about the future of humankind. His general outlook is a negative one. Despite those two big successes, he finds himself dwelling on how little progress humans have made in the way they treat each other. Let's face it, he muses, war and cruelty are as common today as they were hundreds or even thousands of years ago. We've just gotten better at it . . . our planes are faster, our bombs are more deadly, our guns more powerful. In the last century we've even learned how to terrorize innocent civilians . . . first with bombing from the air and then with suicide bombs in buses and restaurants . . . (pause) . . . But in other ways we've made enormous gains. While honing our destructive skills, we've also been visiting the moon, discovering how the world began, and rescuing millions from disease and poverty. "How can this be?," he asks. "How can we come so far in some ways and remain so undeveloped in others? What can we do to redress the balance between technology and politics?" Some of the books he is reading offer an obvious solution . . . like more power sharing in the United Nations. Other writers dismiss such an idea as naïve, either because they think it is good but administratively unworkable or because it is too idealistic for the general public. At any rate, as much as Rafer is drawn to the notion of a stronger U.N, he is aware that the collective will is not there, at least not now. He continues to hope, however, that in her speech Secretary Coles will offer something new, something we can build on in our quest for a more peaceful world.

After a huge build-up in the press, carefully orchestrated by the White House, the day of the speech finally arrives. In the auditorium, Rafer first takes a seat next to Julian in the rear, then quickly excuses himself, saying that he can hear better if he sits closer to the podium. He's not quite sure why he's doing this but proceeds anyway. There are several seats still vacant in the front row; he takes the one closest to the speaker and sits down. Ms. Cole enters a few minutes later.

The first thing Rafer notices about the Secretary is that she's not going to use a teleprompter. If asked, she would probably say that she doesn't need one; she knows exactly what she's going to say. After all, the words are hers, not those of a department speech-writer . . . except, of course, for the introduction.

As the Secretary readies herself to speak, Rafer who is sitting directly in front of her, studies her face. He has seen her before but never up close like this. The face is a handsome one, not yet wrinkled despite her 48 years, punctuated by two soft yet vigilant blue eyes and crowned with gently curled light brown hair. He follows her eyes as she sweeps the auditorium, presumably looking for friends or foreign dignitaries. Her final act before speaking is to drop her eyes to the front row where she is greeted with the nods of several U.S. officials, including members of her own department. Continuing down the line, she eventually comes to Rafer whose gaze she finds uncomfortably penetrating. They lock eyes, neither one able to look away. When the crowd becomes audibly restive, she lifts her eyes and clears her throat.

As she does so, Rafer closes his eyes half-way, much the way he would if he were with a patient. This time, however, there is no patient, just a speaker with whom he feels a strange intimacy. There is no goal in mind as he settles back into his chair, no magic to perform, no dragons to slay. So why is he heading into a trance? He cannot say, other than to articulate something about a mutual but unconscious identification between two like-minded individuals. He drops his head. As the world around him gives way to the ecstasy of 'unbounded, empty space', his whole being fills with psychic energy, energy which is now available for something new. Not content to stay in a state of Oneness, he relaxes his gaze until the Secretary comes back into partial focus. By the time she starts her speech, he no longer sees her as someone totally separate from himself. The lines, surfaces and edges that normally distinguish between "self" and "other" have become blurred; all thoughts and feelings now appear to be coming from a single source. He breathes deeply.

"Today we face an unprecedented opportunity for peace throughout the globe. If we approach this time with love for each other, we can move forward into an era of joy and abundance." Her voice is clear and strong. Back in the White House where Pres. Burrows and Chief of Staff Samuelson are watching on TV, a collective sigh of relief erupts when the Secretary is seen to be following the prepared script.

At the U.N. Rafer leans back in his chair, descending deeper into trance than ever before; all thoughts have now ceased . . . at least those he is conscious of. Beyond his awareness, a subliminal transmission is gathering force, threatening to make itself known. All the despair he has felt in the days leading up to this meeting . . . despair over the world's failure to keep up socially and politically with its brilliance in technology and science . . . is stirring deep inside. While he can sense its presence, he is too deep into his trance to control it. He winces at the prospect of an unconscious transmission, both excited and fearful of what might happen next.

At the podium the Secretary pauses, the looks around. When she lapses into silence, her colleagues in the first row become alarmed that she has lost her place. After gathering her thoughts, she starts up again, "It is incredible to think that the same species that has traveled to the moon and back cannot live peacefully with its own kind. There is something dreadfully wrong here. I think we can do better. And what better way to launch our New Era of Peace than to propose a radical restructuring of the United Nations itself."

Back in the White House, the Chief of Staff leaps to his feet, "Jesus Christ . . . where the hell is she going with this nonsense?"

Pres. Burrows leans forward. "I certainly never saw any of this in what she sent us for approval. Did she send a revised version that no one showed me?"

Rafer breathes deeply, only dimly conscious that he and the Secretary have now morphed into a single entity. He looks up at her, opens his eyes and directs psychic energy at the podium. With patients in the past such energy was surrounded by compassion, a desire to help by curing disease. This time is different. The energy is just as strong and similarly infused with compassion but it is no longer driven by love for an individual but by love for humanity. It is this feeling that is being transmitted to the speaker.

At the podium Secretary Coles stops again, uncertain where to go next. Already she has strayed from her prepared text; while the words are still hers, they are taking her in a bolder direction than what she had in mind. Behind the daring words is a heightened feeling of compassion for all those who have suffered at the hands of war, whether the conflict is fueled by ideology, greed or national pride. It is this feeling, only partly her own, that now gives shape to her words. "For too long now," she continues, "we have accepted war and all its evils as a necessary part of being human. But is this really the way things have to be? Why should the same species that has given us Mozart and Shakespeare, Basho and Tagore, the Taj Mahal, the Parthenon and the pyramids of Giza remain so unalterably savage that after five thousand years of civilization we are still not safe in our own homes?" She stops again . . . unsure how she is going to answer her own question, unsure why she even asked it.

Pres. Burrows rises from his chair in disbelief. "What the blazes is going on? The woman is off her rocker. For Christ's sake, somebody stop her before she says something really crazy." From his seat on the couch, Samuelson reaches for the phone and puts in a call to Coles' Undersecretary in New York.

Meanwhile Rafer continues in his trance, only dimly aware of the subterranean thoughts being transmitted from his own psyche to the podium. He can hear the words but they are like that of a distant stream, familiar in their rhythm but too far away to see in any detail.

On stage, Ms. Coles grows bolder; it is the boldness of one who senses her actions coming from an interior source immune to the wobble of doubt. The words that find their way to her lips have a spontaneous quality about them; they are too pure, too artless to be the product of contrived thought. "I have several concrete proposals to offer," she pronounces, her voice perceptibly rising. "To correct the obvious and to many, outrageous, imbalance of power in the Security Council, I propose that the five permanent members be stripped of their veto rights. In addition, I would . . . "

Before she can continue, her words are drowned out by thunderous applause from representatives rising from their seats. Some begin shouting: "Yes, yes! It's about time! Hooray for the U.S! When the noise has finally died down, she takes a further step: "By itself, of course, that will not redress the imbalance we have now. In addition we need to offer permanent membership to several of our most populous and successful countries, namely India, Brazil and Japan. Under the restructuring plan I envisage, France's place will be taken by the European Union, thereby giving Germany, Italy and other members of that organization a greater say in global matters. The remaining seven non-permanent places on the Security Council should be filled regionally the same way they are now."

By now Pres. Burrows is apoplectic. He finally gets Willard Monroe, Secretary Coles' assistant, on the phone. "Get her off the fucking stage Willard," he shouts. "I'm already getting calls from Limbaugh and a whole assortment of right-wingers. They're appalled at this threat to American sovereignty . . . and they have a right to be. I don't care if everybody's applauding like mad; we've got our position in the world to look after it. You think we want to have a bunch of aborigines from Africa telling Americans what we can and cannot do? You're goddamn right we don't. Shoot her if you have to . . . no, don't shoot her . . . just get her off the stage. Turn off the lights, sound an alarm, tell everybody there's a bomb scare . . . anything you can think of . . . just do it!"

From his seat in the front row, Rafer can feel the electricity sweeping through the crowd. When he lifts his head, he can make out a similar energy in the Secretary's face. She is ecstatic. Her whole demeanor radiates the serenity of one who has agreed to be used as a vessel for some higher purpose. No longer does she stumble over sentences as if she were unsure the words were really her own. No longer does she question the wisdom or propriety of what she hears herself saying. It all has the truth of a spontaneous revelation. "Let me go on now to the more important of my proposals," she says, scanning the audience. "To end the cycle of death and terror that has persisted for millennia we need to deprive nations of their capacity to wage war on each other. The only way that can be done is by turning over all military planes, ships, tanks, bombs and guns to the United Nations where they will be used only at the Council's discretion and for no purpose other than to put down border incursions and other illegal activities. Under this plan all countries will contribute personnel to a new U.N. military force to be stationed at critical sites across the globe. All national armies, navies and air forces are to be disbanded, with a small portion of their extant hardware donated to the U.N. force; the rest is to be destroyed. Individual nations will be allowed a civilian police force as well as a national guard to cope with emergencies. The size of those forces will be determined by a new Department of Territorial Security operating under the authority of the Security Council."

By now the noise in the auditorium has grown to such heights that the Secretary's last words are heard only by those in the first few rows. Enough gets through, however, to ignite a rally of delirious proportions . . . one never before heard or seen in this august chamber. Many members, still shocked by what they have just heard, throw their notepads into the air; some add their briefcases, some even toss their shoes. In the ensuing pandemonium, two Secret Service agents rush onto stage and grab Ms. Coles by the arm. Within seconds, she is dragged into an adjoining room and forcibly seated in front of her Undersecretary, Mr. Monroe. Before it can progress, the planned interrogation is interrupted by loud pounding on the door as dozens of Assembly members, fearful of the Secretary's safety, demand to be let in. Wisely, Monroe whisks her out of a rear door into a limo that will take her to a hotel where President Burrows, now besieged from all sides with demands for her firing and irate beyond words, is scheduled to question her later in the day. There can be no question that Henrietta Coles' term as Secretary of State has come to an abrupt end.

By the following morning, Ms. Coles has recanted the bulk of her speech, citing extreme stress as the cause of what she agrees was the beginning of a nervous breakdown. Throughout the global media, however, her disavowal is lost in a blizzard of commentary, most of which treats the Secretary's proposals seriously. Not surprisingly, the five permanent members of the Security Council recoil at the proposals while the vast majority of smaller nations respond with wild enthusiasm. "U.S. Secretary of State Suffers Breakdown on Stage" trumpets the Beijing People's Daily; "Coles Offers Visionary Plea for Peace" blares the Santiago Post.

In Washington President Burrows takes quickly to the airwaves to apologize for the Secretary's "unconscionable behavior." To appease his right-wing critics, he publicly fires several junior staff, including Julian Pulaski, before promoting Willard Monroe to Department head. For weeks, the U.S. press is full of articles about the incident. Most say very little about the proposals outlined in the speech, preferring instead to focus on Ms. Coles' mental condition. Some go so far as to lay blame at the feet of a mysterious group of peaceniks using advanced brain-washing techniques. Others point the finger at food poisoning. Few of the critics bother to evaluate the proposals objectively.

In much of the world Ms. Coles is hailed as a visionary with the courage to speak the truth without regard to personal consequences. Her recanting is seen as having been forced on her by an administration too concerned with maintaining its status in the world to see the wisdom of her proposals. In time, Coles comes to similar conclusions herself. Ideas that seemed alien when she first voiced them begin to resonate with her deepest values. Once freed from her official duties, she begins traveling the globe, giving speeches supportive of her initial proposals, particularly the proposal calling for the transfer of all major weaponry to the United Nations. Her audiences are at once shocked and thrilled at the audacity of her ideas. They are especially receptive to her claim that progress in the way humans treat each other has not kept up with progress in science and technology. She does not hesitate to suggest a way forward. "To find the peace we all yearn for," she says repeatedly, "we must be willing to give up something dear to us all . . . our weapons. War is inevitable in a legal vacuum, that is, when there is no body of enforceable laws strong enough to prevent nations from pursuing their goals by military force. This is what we have today; it is an intolerable state, more fitting for the jungle than our civilized world. We simply cannot survive unless each nation among us is willing to subordinate its will to that of a global governing body. The recipe for peace is simple: a set of international laws and the military means for enforcing them. The sooner we enact such laws, the sooner we shall find enduring peace."

Rafer follows Ms. Coles' itinerary closely. In her speeches he finds sentiments much like his own . . . but certain questions remain unanswered. Again and again he returns to her speech at the United Nations, the one where he may have transmitted ideas from his own unconscious into the speaker. It is still a mystery. "Did I get her fired by forcing my own ideas on her," he asks, "or did I simply bring to the surface ideas of her own that in her role as Secretary of State she dared not embrace publicly?" However it happened, he is thrilled to hear not only of her speeches but the serious attention around the globe now being given to her proposals. Unfortunately back in the U.S. where her former boss, Daniel Burrows, is on the verge of being impeached, she is a tarnished woman, a rogue bureaucrat best remembered for having brought a president to his knees.

37

A Power Grab?

Zeke is opening his laptop as Doc walks in the door. "Hey guys, getta load of this," he shouts. "I downloaded it from C-span this afternoon . . . it's Secretary Coles' address at the United Nations. You won't believe this stuff. The woman is out of her mind . . . maybe psychotic . . . but that's not all. Take a look."

Thomas, Pete, Revy and Hunter gather around the computer. Doc drops his coat on a chair, then joins in as Zeke points first to the speaker and then to the people sitting in the front row. "Guess who we have here," he says, fingering a tall good-looking man with his eyes half-closed. "I wasn't sure at first . . . couldn't get a good look at him . . . but I'm sure now. It's our guy Alexander."

Hunter: "What's he doin at the U.N.?"

Zeke: "Beat's me. But sittin there in the front row he must have got an earful of the crap she was spewin about us givin up our planes and tanks and everything. You know, the stuff Burrows and his boys are fumin over in Washington."

Doc squints, then moves closer to the computer. "His eyes are half-closed like he's in some kind of trance."

Revy: "Yeah. That looks weird. I wonder why he's doing that."

Thomas: "Maybe he's bored."

Zeke: "Not with the stuff that's comin out of her mouth. The whole auditorium is goin nuts. Look at all the people standing. Some are clenching their fists . . . "

Revy: "Yeah . . . like Tiger Woods after makin a great putt."

Thomas: "So why is he takin a nap or whatever when everybody else is goin bananas?"

Doc: "I don't think he's taking a nap, Thomas. My guess is that he's up to something more serious."

Revy: "Like what, Doc?"

Doc: "I'm not sure . . . (*pause*) . . . but what he's done in Vegas and Mexico leads me to suspect the worst. Let me put it this way. Have any of you ever heard Secretary Coles suggest things like this before? I'm referring to the two proposals she made about the U.N . . . the ones everybody's talking about on TV."

Petey: "I've heard her talk several times Doc and she's never come close to sayin stuff like she did today. Nobody else has said it either. After all, what kind of sicko is goin to suggest that we turn over all our planes, ships, tanks and bombs to the U.N. where they'll be controlled by a bunch of pygmies?"

Zeke: "Pygmies?"

Petey: "You know what I mean . . . foreigners, Muslims, Hindus . . . people who believe in ancestor worship, cannibalism, and stuff like that."

Revy: "So, what do you think he's up to Doc? You think he made her say those crazy things . . . usin some kind of hypnosis?"

Hunter: "But he weren't even lookin at her? How could he put her under without lookin at her . . . you know, dangling a watch or somethin?"

Doc: "I've never seen a case or even read about one where one person succeeds in hypnotizing another without some kind of eye contact. So if he was exerting influence over her, it wasn't of the conventional kind."

Thomas: "Well, what other kind is there?"

Doc: "It's got to have something to do with the paranormal . . . a kind of thought-transmission perhaps, like telepathy in reverse. Instead of reading someone's mind, you send messages to it . . . you make the other person think what you're thinking."

Thomas: "But what if the other person doesn't agree with those thoughts?"

Revy: "Yeah . . . like Secretary Coles . . . she didn't believe all that stuff about turning over weapons to the U.N . . . at least she didn't before the speech."

Doc: "I agree . . . but there may be a deeper truth here. It could be that she harbored some ideas like that even before the speech . . . but kept them hidden, even from herself. To let them into consciousness and express them publicly would have been political suicide . . . and she obviously knew it. So perhaps she bottled them up inside where they lay dormant until Alexander came along and drew them out using powers similar to what he used to make all that money at roulette . . . ."

Revy (interrupting): " . . . and to cure all those people in Mexico."

Zeke: "Yeah. Maybe this whole idea ain't so far-fetched when you remember that he brought one kid all the way back from the dead.

Shit . . . anybody who can do that should be able to stick his ideas into somebody else's head . . . ."

Revy: " . . . whether they like it or not. It's making more and more sense . . . *(pointing to the computer screen)* Just look at the way she's lookin around, kinda bewildered . . . like she doesn't know what the hell she's sayin. And all the time he's sittin there with his eyes half-closed."

Zeke: "Yeah . . . just pourin his ideas into her pretty head. It must have been confusin as hell for her."

Thomas: "Wait a minute. If the ideas were so foreign to her, why didn't she excuse herself . . . you know, just walk off stage or somethin? Why put her whole career at risk by sayin things she doesn't believe?"

Revy: "But that's Doc's point, dummy. Down deep she probably did believe such garbage but was afraid to tell anyone. Alexander simply brought the garbage to the surface . . . ."

Thomas: "Against her will?"

Revy: "Yeah . . . against her will. That's possible ain't it Doc?"

Doc: "It would take a really powerful mind to pull that off . . . but he has already indicated that he is no ordinary human being. Remember how I got him to admit that if he were threatened, he could kill a man with his mind alone. Somebody with that kind of power should find it easy to force his thoughts onto someone else. And if the victim already has unconscious leanings that way, it should be a piece of cake."

Zeke: "O.K. Assumin that he has the power to stick his thoughts into someone else's head, the question remains why. Why is he botherin to make her say such ridiculous things? Why doesn't he just convince her that he's an irresistible hunk she wants to go to bed with . . . or something fun like that?"

Doc (*sternly*): "I think you continue to misjudge this man . . . to underestimate the seriousness of his intentions. A few weeks ago, Zeke read us something from the Bible about the Antichrist's political aspirations. If I remember correctly, this so-called Prince of Darkness will try to organize armies and navies under a single roof before taking over. What better way to do that then to have the foreign secretary of the most powerful nation on earth plant the idea that we'll never have lasting peace until every country turns over its military hardware to the United Nations? And that's pretty much what she said, isn't it?""

Revy: "Jesus! This is scary."

Zeke: "Yeah, but it all fits what's in the Good Book. Daniel 11:21 tells us that he's not going to come in like gangbusters and take over the world. No, it's going to be more subtle. Here I'll read it to you; he says the Antichrist 'shall come in peaceably and obtain the kingdom by flatteries.' By 'flatteries' I guess Daniel means talkin up the good side of people, their desire for peace and stuff like that . . . (*picking up another book*) . . . This guy Arthur Pink, the one who spent a lifetime researching the Antichrist, goes further. I quote: 'Once he gains the ascendancy, none will dare to challenge his authority. Kings will be his pawns and princes his playthings.' So maybe this Alexander character is on his way to becoming ruler of the whole goddamn world."

Doc: "And staying out of the limelight as he does so."

Revy: "What a plan . . . the guy's a fuckin genius."

Petey (*scowling*): "Hey Rev . . . watch the language . . . we have a guest, remember?"

Revy: "Sorry Doc."

Doc: "He may be a genius but let's remember that we have a powerful weapon on our side. The Bible has warned us of his coming. The writers of the Old Testament knew about all this centuries ago . . . and they put it down on paper so we could get ready. Once we are sure we have the right man, we can act to stop him."

Hunter: "How?"

Doc (*shaking his head*): "I think it's a little premature to discuss the details right now. The immediate task before us is to keep on Alexander's tail . . . watch him, follow his every move . . . until we're sure he's our man."

Hunter: "Then what?"

Doc: "Then we go after him."

38

A Radical Proposal

Stefan (*looking around*): "Have people stopped going out for lunch? There are more waiters here today than customers."

Rafer: "Could be the recession. At least some people are starting to save again . . . which, if you ask me, is a good thing. We Americans partied to long . . . spending more than we earned, going deeper and deeper into debt . . . we're in a hole now and I don't know if we can ever get out."

The waiter finally arrives to take orders.

Stefan: "Go ahead Rafe; I'm not quite sure yet."

Rafer (*looking at the waiter*): "It's a little cool today . . . I think I'll try the vegetarian chili . . . but don't go overboard on the peppers. It comes with garlic bread and a salad, doesn't it?" When the waiter nods, Stefan drops his menu: "That sounds great. I'll take the same."

Once they are alone, Stefan leans forward. "Julian tells me you've been busy changing the world. Any truth in that, Rafe?"

Rafer (*smiling*): "A slight exaggeration. The world may be changing but I doubt that it's because of anything I've done."

Stefan: "I saw you sitting in the front row at Secretary Coles' speech. Your eyes were closed. Were you sleeping or was it something else, something a little more mysterious? The reason I ask is that I remember from our previous discussions that her proposals, the ones that got her fired, sound suspiciously like those I've heard you make. Unlike you, of course, she went public with hers and that effectively ended her career."

Rafer: "I must admit they are rather radical proposals . . . radical enough to get you lynched in America. I'm just glad she had the courage to make her views known, not just to Americans but to the whole world."

Stefan (*impish smile*): "But were they really her views? I've never heard her say anything remotely that radical in the past."

Rafer: "You are suggesting that . . . what . . . out with it!"

Stefan (*laughing*): "It's just a wild hypothesis . . . but is it possible that while in your trance, you transmitted your own ideas to her . . . and that she was helpless to resist? Her strange behavior on stage, you know, the confusion, the stumbling over words, would be consistent with that."

Rafer: "Hmm . . . interesting idea to be sure. But if there's any truth in it, it certainly wasn't intentional on my part. All I remember is that I felt especially close to her that day and that the deeper I got into my trance, the more we seemed to fuse into a single being. Whether or not I transmitted any opinions to her, I can't say. It's possible I guess but as I said earlier, it certainly wasn't deliberate."

Stefan: "Well, it's all over and done with now, but it has gotten me thinking . . . about you and what other powers you might have."

Rafer: "If there are others, they haven't revealed themselves yet."

Stefan: "But have you gone looking? Have you tried other things?"

Rafer: "Like what?"

Stefan: "Well, I'm no expert in these matters, but I can't help thinking about telepathy, remote viewing, levitation . . . things like that. If you have the proven ability to heal, to manipulate a roulette wheel . . . and maybe even transmit your thoughts, why would you be restricted to those three in particular? Why wouldn't you have other abilities as well?"

Rafer (*grinning*): "Are you sure you're not a talent scout for Barnum and Bailey's?"

Stefan (*laughing*): "Actually, we are short an act between our snake charmer and the man with two heads."

Rafer: "I think I'd fit in better with the trapeze artists . . . I could pretend to fall and then fly away into the blue."

Stefan (*pausing*): "Why not?"

Rafer: "What do you mean, why not? You're not taking me seriously I hope."

Stefan (*dropping his smile*): "Why not?"

Rafer: "You already said that."

Stefan: "I'm aware of that."

Rafer (*pushing his chili away*): "Let's cut the horsing around, Stefan. What are you getting at?"

Stefan: "As I said, I think you may have paranormal abilities you haven't explored yet. Flying, or at least levitating, may be one of them . . . (*pause*) . . . Don't you at least want to find out?"

Rafer: "You actually think I could fly . . . without any wings . . . ?"

Stefan: "Or motor. All you have to do is use your psychic energy to defeat gravity . . . by directing it downward instead of across the room at a patient . . . the way rockets gain thrust at lift-off. I'm sure that's the strategy yogis use when they levitate."

Rafer (*leaning to whisper*): "Are you proposing that I should jump from the Empire State Building?"

Stefan (*grinning*): "Not really. If I'm wrong, that could do a number on your spine. Why don't we start with something a little less demanding?"

Rafer: "Like leaping off the roof of your house?"

Stefan: "Actually I was thinking of walking on water . . . it's much safer . . . as long as you know how to swim. You do swim don't you?"

Rafer: "I haven't for a while . . . but I can probably manage. It still sounds a bit wacky but it's a lot less scary than jumping off some building . . . (*pause*) . . . We don't have to go where it's real deep, do we?"

Stefan: "There's a pond not too far from my house in Weyland . . . hardly anybody ever goes there . . . especially in the early morning. You could be quite private. I don't even need to come."

Rafer: "Sounds like you've thought this all out. So, tell me. What happens if it works? Where do we go from there?"

Stefan: "Well, for one thing, we will have proved that Christ isn't the only one who can do it . . . that ordinary men and women can perform feats we have traditionally assumed to be a prerogative of the divine. Now that's saying a lot, don't you think?"

Rafer: "Perhaps . . . but where do we go with that? Once we've proved that it's possible, how do we present it to the public? I mean, a lot of people are going to see it as some sort of parlor trick, the kind of thing Houdini might have tried using invisible wires or hidden bags of helium. I don't want it to come across as a carnival act."

Stefan: "How do you want it to come across?"

Rafer (*pausing*): "I think it's worth doing if, like you said, it wakes people up to what we humans are really capable of. From a practical point of view, however, I don't see much value in learning to walk on water."

Stefan (*giggling*): "You could save time by walking to work across Boston Harbor."

Rafer (*wry smile*): "That's really helpful, Stefan. I was afraid you were going to suggest some new sport . . . like sea soccer or water hockey."

Stefan: "Seriously, I see walking on water as part of a whole set of abilities . . . some of which you've already demonstrated . . . like healing the sick, the peace thing in Jerusalem and Kashmir, transmitting thoughts at the U.N., controlling the roulette wheel at Las Vegas . . . and others you haven't even tried yet. It's the whole package that needs to be presented. When philosophers and psychologists get around to analyzing all the things you've done, questions are going to start flying about the limits of human consciousness. It should get exciting."

Rafer: "I hope I'm around to see it."

Stefan: "What do you mean?"

Rafer: "Just a feeling . . . (*pause*) . . . Let's get out of here."

39

The Pond

The next morning Rafer rises early, climbs into his hiking shorts, has some tea and toast and heads for Bradford Pond. The scene is very much like what Stefan predicted. At 6:00 A.M. there is still a veil of mist on the water obscuring the sun which, as he knows from his drive, is already above the horizon. After parking his car, he heads for the shore and settles on the grass under an overhanging maple. He removes his gray backpack and leans it against a stone. There is no one in sight. Relieved, he closes his eyes half-way and begins to meditate. The cool morning air is soothing, as are the clucks and warbles of songbirds in the woods. Over the next half hour he slips in and out of that state of Emptiness where energy for his experiment can be found. Much as he would like to remain there, he knows that some orienting is necessary for maneuvering his way onto the water. After years of meditation he has become skilled at "dialing" the right balance between emptiness and form. He opens his eyes and steps toward the water.

He is unaware that while he was meditating, a young boy, perhaps 11 or 12, skinny and slightly buck-toothed, had approached, opened his mouth to say hello, then withdrawn behind a tree, not wanting to intrude. The boy watches closely now, his fishing pole leaning against the tree, his eyes fixed on the strange man before him.

Rafer inches forward until his toes are touching the water. He takes a deep breath. As he does so, the sensation of coolness, cleansed now of all words and thoughts, dissolves into nothingness, revealing a boundless, empty space devoid of anything the mind can take hold of. All things, all objects, all forms . . . water, lake, sand, and self . . . disappear into an indescribable, unspeakable Void. At the fringes of consciousness he is aware of a dense, powerful energy building up inside him, energy that has been saved by temporarily shutting out the world. This is the energy that needs to be directed downward as he lifts himself off the ground. With a slight mental adjustment he pulls back from the Void just long enough to see where he is going . . . and steps out onto the water.

From behind the tree, the boy gasps, covering his mouth to stifle the sound. He watches, transfixed, as the man with the half-closed eyes moves out over the water, his arms at his side, his feet visible with each step . . . until his body disappears completely into the enveloping mist. Overcome with awe, the boy bolts from his hiding place and dashes through the woods toward the center of town. There can be no doubt about his destination . . . St. Agnes' Church and the comforting embrace of the man who means more to him than his own family . . . Father Steven O'Malley. By the time he reaches the church, the priests are eating their morning meal.

"You gotta come right away," he cries, bursting into the dining hall and rushing to his friend's side. As he tugs at the priest's shirtsleeves, he sputters, "There's a man out there on the pond . . . he's walking on water. I saw it . . . I really did." O'Malley, a broad-shouldered man in his thirties with receding, black hair pulled into a pony-tail, pushes aside his cereal bowl and takes the boy by the shoulder. "Bobby, what are you talking about? People don't walk on water. The person you saw must have something under his feet . . . you know, like a pontoon or something filled with air. Christ is the only one who ever walked on water. And he only did it when he saw that his disciples were in danger."

"But I could see his feet . . . they was bare . . . jis his feet. I swear it, Father. Come, I'll show you. I'm not lyin.'"

Father O'Malley sighs . . . then slowly rises from his chair. Stuffing a muffin in his pocket, he points to the door, saying, "O.K. lead the way . . . but you better not be fooling me . . . (*pause*) . . . Just in case I better get my camera."

As they approach the pond, Bobby puts a finger to his lips; his head moves back and forth as he looks in vain for the tree where he left his fishing pole. "Ah, there it is," he whispers to the priest who is just a few feet behind. Once they reach the pole, Bobby turns his head toward the water. The whole pond is now shrouded in mist. His heart sinks with the realization that if the man is still out there, they won't be able to see him. In desperation, he shifts his gaze to the small sand bar at the water's edge. His spirits leap when he sees a small backpack. "That's his," Bobby cries out, pointing to the gray pack leaning against a stone.

"That means he's still out in the water," Father O'Malley replies. Privately, he considers another possibility: the man might have drowned, even committed suicide. We'll wait, he decides; if he doesn't return soon I'll go back to the church and call the police.

Together Bobby and Father O'Malley huddle behind a huge gray beech, their eyes fixed on the pond before them. At this point there is little to see other than the mist which by now has crept to within twenty yards of the shoreline. Neither speaks as they stare into the mist, one desperate to prove his credibility, the other impatient to fulfill a paternal obligation and get back to his breakfast.

When a half hour passes without anything happening, Father O'Malley reaches into his pocket, breaks his muffin in two, and offers half to his young friend. They begin talking in whispers. "How d'ya think he does it?," Bobby asks. "Maybe he's a magician or somethin like that."

Father O'Malley: "Like I said earlier, Bobby, he's probably wearing some kind of footwear that keeps him from sinking, although it's hard to imagine anything that strong. You say he's pretty tall . . . so there's a lot of weight there. I can't think of any material buoyant enough to keep him on top of the water."

Bobby: "So how did Jesus do it?"

Father O'Malley: "There's no ordinary explanation; that's why we call it a miracle."

Bobby: "Was he tryin to get somewhere . . . or what?"

Father O'Malley: "I don't think he intended to go anywhere. According to the Gospels he had just finished feeding thousands of followers with a few loaves of bread and a couple of fish. He told his disciples to get back in their boat and return to the other side of the lake while he stayed on land with the crowd. Soon afterwards a terrible storm came up and threatened to swamp the men out on the water. When Jesus saw his disciples struggling with the waves, he became concerned and began walking toward the boat . . . ."

Bobby (*eyes wide*): "You mean on top of the water?"

Father O'Malley: "Yes. But the men thought it was a ghost coming toward them and got frightened. Jesus was aware of this and reassured them that he was not a ghost. Peter, Christ's favorite, said, 'Lord, if it's really you, tell me to come to you on the water.' Jesus told him to come and Peter walked to him on the water . . . but just then a wave came up and he panicked. As he began to sink, Jesus caught him by the hand and helped him back in the boat. Then he scolded him for his lack of faith."

Bobby: "You mean Peter wasn't sure he could do it . . . and that made him sink?"

Father O'Malley: "Something like that, yes."

They fall back into silence, eyes on the mist. When another ten minutes go by without anything happening, Father O'Malley takes Bobby by the wrist and whispers, "I've got work to do back at the church. I really shouldn't stay any longer."

Bobby: "Just another few minutes, please. I know he's still out there, somewhere."

Father O'Malley: "O.K. Five more minutes and then I have to leave."

Several minutes pass in silence. Suddenly the boy grasps the priest by the arm. "Look," he cries, pointing. "There's somethin there in the mist . . . somethin spooky. It's comin toward us." Without answering, the priest continues staring out into the pond. "Yes," he whispers. "There *is* something there." To get a clearer look, he moves out from behind the tree, his eyes fixed on the indefinable shape lurking in the mist, about fifty feet from shore. Bobby follows suit, emerging from the other side of the gray beech.

Still not sure what he sees, the priest creeps several feet forward, craning his neck toward the amorphous shape. At that moment a breeze comes up from the East, blowing the mist back toward the center of the pond. Stepping out of the haze is the figure of a man, a tall sandy-haired man wearing a t-shirt and shorts . . . a sight not that unusual perhaps, particularly if he had been wading or even fishing. But in water at least two or three feet deep, this man's feet are clearly visible as he moves along the surface. He is walking on water. Despite his young friend's claim, this is not at all what Father O'Malley expected to see. His years as an acolyte, the endless nights spent reading, praying and memorizing his catechism have not prepared him for what stands before him now. As the figure comes toward him, he suppresses an instinct to rise, to run, to flee the unknowable . . . and falls instead to his knees, weeping, his hands closed in fearful supplication.

"The camera," Bobby whispers, "it's in your pocket." When the priest fails to respond, the boy crawls over to his side and pulls the camera from his jacket. Initially, he fumbles with it, pressing the wrong button. Finally, with a nod to his still paralyzed mentor, he begins taking shots in rapid succession until the man reaches shore. When the target of his curiosity picks up his backpack and disappears toward the parking lot, the boy gives his friend a nudge. "He's gone, Father. Shall we go back and tell the others what we jis seen?"

Slowly Father O'Malley opens his eyes and looks around. He shakes his head. "Did we just see a man walking on water? Tell me, Bobby, was I hallucinating or did it really happen?"

"Oh yeah . . . it really happened Father. I got it right here (*holding up the camera*). "Ya wanna see?"

Gently, O'Malley takes the camera from his young friend, turns it around and hits the memory button. The last picture taken shows a man leaning over and picking up his backpack. Bobby, who's looking over his shoulder, shouts, "No. Go back a few more . . . where he's standin on the water." O'Malley hits the backup button twice . . . then gasps. In this shot, Rafer is stepping out of the water onto dry land. "Lookit," shouts the boy. "There's nothin on his feet, Father. No shoes, no skis . . . nothin."

O'Malley begins shaking. To keep from falling, he leans over and places his palm on the grass. As he shifts his body, the camera drops to the ground. Sensing the priest's distress, Bobby picks it up and shoves it in his pocket. For several minutes he waits for his friend to speak. As they sit in silence, the mist slowly retreats to the center of the pond where it is consumed by the rising sun. The water, once hidden beneath a shroud of vapor, shines now with the sparkle of newly-polished glass. "Father," he whispers, "we gotta go back and tell everybody what we jis seen."

The priest rises slowly. With the boy's help, he makes his way back into the woods and onto the trail leading to the church. Drunk now with a vision too strong for a constitution forged in the smithy of Jesuitical reason, he stumbles his way along the path, alternately falling and rising until they reach the doors of St. Agnes. Once inside, he falls into the arms of Father Delgado, the head parish priest. Still shaken and at times incoherent, O'Malley sputters out the story of what happened at Bradford Pond. Not surprisingly, his tale is met with disbelief. Father Delgado goes so far as to smell his breath, fearing a relapse into old drinking habits. Sensing his superior's suspicions, O'Malley reaches into his pocket for the camera. "We have pictures of him," he shouts. "It's right here . . . (*fumbling*) . . . oh God, it's gone. Bobby must have it . . . yes . . . we've got to find Bobby." As the young priest grows more agitated, Father Delgado's smile morphs into a frown, then a sneer. "We can talk later, Steven," he replies, his tap on the shoulder no less unctuous than his words. "Let's wait until you've calmed down a bit."

Still in the church doorway, Bobby turns for a last look at his friend, then races home to his mother, the camera still jammed into his pocket. Bursting into the kitchen, he blurts out the story of the "man who wuz walkin on water." When his mother responds with raised eyebrows and a wrinkled nose, he pulls out the camera and begins thumbing through the images. "Lookit, Mother," he persists, shielding the camera from the overhead light, "Here's me and Father O'Malley behind the tree . . . and that's the guy there comin out of the mist. His feet are on top of the water." The mother leans over to look more closely . . . then steps back gasping. The boy's father, who has been watching a baseball game in the living room, hears the voices and rushes into the kitchen. "What the hell you two talkin about? Somebody walkin on water . . . you crazy or somethin. Gimme that goddamn thing," he bellows, reaching for the camera. When pressing buttons at random fails to produce any images, he turns to his son who is cowering in the corner. "How do you work this contraption? Show me."

When he sees the image of the man coming out of the mist, his feet clearly visible above the water, he slaps his thigh and shouts, "Holy Christ. How the hell does he do that? He's gotta be some kinda magician . . . maybe workin out a new trick. That's probly why he picked this pond, figurin nobody will see 'im so early in the morning. But you did see 'im, didn't you Bobby . . . it's too bad you had ta go get your priest friend involved. But maybe we can still get somethin out of this . . . you know . . . get our names in the paper or even make some money offen it."

Bess, the mother, stirs from her seat at the table. In a voice barely audible, she says, "Maybe he's not a magician . . . he could be more than that ya know."

The father points his finger as if accusing her of infidelity. "You're not gonna give me more of that religious crap, are ya?," he hollers. "Go see those perverts at St. Agnes if you wanna talk nonsense. For me, I'm takin these here pictures down to the newspaper to see if they'll give me anything for 'em." He turns at the door, "Go ahead and eat dinner by yourselves . . . I'll be droppin by Tony's for some spaghetti and a drink or two."

40

A Phone Call

Later that evening, an hour after dinner, the phone rings. Rafer, who is closest to the phone, picks it up, fully expecting yet another sales pitch or plea for some charitable cause.

"Hello."

"Hey, Rafe . . . it's Stefan. I see that things went well this morning at the pond."

Rafer: "What do you mean . . . I mean, how do you know? I haven't told anyone besides Eva."

Stefan: "It's all over town my friend . . . first appeared in the newspaper . . . with four pictures of you coming out of the mist, walking on water . . . beautiful shots I must say, although your face is not that clear. The headline in tonight's Globe says, 'Hoax or Second Coming?' Apparently some kid saw you and went and told his local priest. Together they took several pictures of you just as you came ashore. Now the TV people have gotten in on it . . . interviewing the boy and his father. So far, though, the church authorities won't let them interview the priest who saw you at the pond."

Rafer (*breathless*): "Oh my God . . . I had no idea. I thought I was all alone . . . (*pause*) . . . What's going to happen now?"

Stefan: "I'm sure of only one thing . . . everybody wants to find out who the hell you are. Unless you're willing to have your whole life raked over the coals, you better stay close to home . . . and let Eva answer the phone. So far it seems like there are at least two camps out there . . . on the one hand you've got the skeptics who figure you're some kind of magician who was out on Bradford Pond practicing his latest stunt. No big deal."

Rafer (*with anxiety rising*): "And the others?"

Stefan: "Then there are the pious folks . . . the ones who are desperate to believe that you are something more than human . . . a god perhaps who has come to relieve them of their suffering . . . (*pause*) . . . Oh, there may be one more group. I was checking out talk-radio an hour ago when I heard a caller suggest that you might even be the Antichrist, you know, the one the Bible says has been sent by the Devil to destroy the world. A real crack-pot . . . I was surprised they even let him speak."

Rafer (*breathing faster*): "The Antichrist. My God, what will they think of next? . . . (*pause*) . . . Maybe it's a good thing I don't have to go to work . . . (*pause*) . . . As of right now, they don't even know my name, do they?"

Stefan: "I don't know how they could. They have the pictures and probably an eyewitness description from the boy . . . but as long as you're not in some FBI mug book, you should be safe."

From the living room, Eva inches toward the foyer, anxious to catch more of the conversation. She freezes when she hears Rafer say, "The Antichrist. My God, what will they think of next?" Her heart begins to race. Thanks to her uncle, she knows all about the Beast as they call him . . . but are Rafer and Stefan talking about Petey's group in Lynn? The next words she hears are even more unnerving: "Maybe it's a good thing I don't have to go to work. As of right now, they don't even know my name, do they?" There is something new in Rafer's voice . . . an alarm she has never heard before. Leaning against the foyer wall, she tries to recall her last conversation with Petey. "Be careful," he said, "he may not be the man you think he is; he might be the Beast the Bible talks about, the Devil's own son sent to do battle with Christ." More than once now he has warned her that this man called Rafer Alexander, the man she is in love with, could be secretly preparing to unleash a global campaign of war, terror, disease, fire, floods and famine that will destroy God's world and restore the Devil to his rightful place as King of All Nations. Her thoughts turn to the newspapers and TV. "Will Petey's group be able to tell from the pictures that the man who walked on water is Rafe? Although they've never met him, they've seen photos of the two of us in Mexico. Mom says they're following his every move. She says that with each miracle they've become more convinced that he's the Beast prophesied in the Bible. What happened today is sure to eliminate any lingering doubts." She shakes her head, unable to get clear about her feelings. "So what is it that I'm afraid of?," she asks, turning back to the living room. "Am I afraid that Rafe's life is in danger . . . or that he is not the person he says he is?" Before she can answer her own question, Rafe puts down the phone and comes looking for her. The look on her face is unusual enough to prompt a question. "Is something wrong, Evie? You look like you've just seen a ghost." "Maybe . . . I'm not sure," she whispers, averting his glance.

41

The Decision

Zeke waits until everyone is seated before speaking. "After those pictures in last night's paper, does anyone doubt that this guy Alexander is the man we're lookin for?"

Thomas: "You couldn't see much of his face but everything else fits. I mean, who else in the world could do what he did?"

Revy: "I agree. The guy in the pictures is tall and slender, jis like the guy who did all those healins in Oaxaca. It's gotta be the same guy."

Petey: "What do ya think, Doc? Is this our man? Is this the Antichrist who's here to do us all in?"

Komerov shifts uneasily in his chair. "Well, I think this last stunt of his is all the proof we need. Like Thomas says, who else in the world could walk on water except Christ? He's already done things that normal humans are incapable of . . . like manipulating the roulette wheel in Vegas, all those healings in Mexico, doing it again here in Boston, working political miracles in Jerusalem and Kashmir, getting Secretary Coles to say things at the U.N. so radical that the President had to fire her. No, despite his ordinary looks and conventional demeanor, this man is not one of us. He cannot be considered a normal human being by any stretch of the imagination. Whether he's the Antichrist who's come to destroy us may still be debatable but everything seems to point in that direction. I think we have our man."

Petey: "Well said Doc . . . but what do we do now? We can't jis sit back and let 'em go ahead with his plan."

Thomas: "I think it's interesting how people are already lining up either for or against him. From what I've read, there are two camps out there . . . those who say he's just a magician out practicing his latest stunt . . . and those who see him as the Second Coming of Christ. The Catholics aren't sayin much until the Pope tells them what to do, but the Baptists and Church of Christ folks are convinced this guy is Christ himself."

Zeke: "But there are other people who think the photos are fakes . . . you know, altered. That's pretty easy to do these days with the latest software."

Petey rises to talk. "What gets me is that nobody sees this guy as the monster he really is. Like Thomas says, they think he's either a magician or Christ himself . . . that's a bunch of baloney. C'mon, if he was Christ, do you think he'd be wastin his time playin roulette out in Vegas?"

Hunter: "Or sleepin with your niece . . . (*pause*) . . . Is he bangin her?"

Petey (*scowling*): "I don't know for sure. My sister Aggie says they have a weird sorta relationship . . . so maybe not . . . (*pause*) . . . The point is that people haven't woke up yet to who this guy really is. They jis don't get it."

Hunter: "So yir sayin it's up to us, right? We're the only ones who know who he really is . . . so it's up to us to take 'im down."

Komerov (*squirming in his chair*): "I think we have to approach this question carefully. If we rush, we could end up doing the wrong thing."

Hunter: "Lookit. I've already got a plan worked out for takin 'im down. When my grandpa died he left me a 9mm Luger he stole from the Krauts at the end of the war; I know it still works cuz I . . . ."

Komerov (*hissing*): "I don't want to hear the details. If you tell us what you're going to do and we don't call the police, then in the eyes of the law, we're accomplices. If you're caught, we could all go to prison."

Hunter (*smiling*): "Don't worry, Doc. With my plan, nobody is goin to catch me."

At this point, Komerov rises and heads for the door. "I don't feel good discussing this any further." He opens the door and turns to face the group, "This is probably going to be my last meeting. But thank you for all your support. Goodbye."

Hunter (*looking around*): "What's he chicken or somethin?"

Petey: "He's jis bein cautious . . . like we should all be. We're takin a big chance here. Like Doc said, this is no ordinary guy . . . if we screw up he could make mincemeat out of us . . . (*pause*) . . . and if we take him down and get caught, the police could slap us in the jammer for good."

Hunter: "You sayin we should let 'im go?"

Petey (*scowling*): "No, I ain't sayin that. I'm sayin we gotta be careful, that's all. But I don't think we have a choice. We have to go after him. Nobody else seems to know who the fuck they're dealin with. They think he's jis another Houdini . . . or maybe that the Lord sent 'em here to prove somethin to the atheists. Can you imagine Christ botherin to come all the way down here jis to take part in an experiment?"

Thomas (*laughing*): "The Baptists are crazy if they think he's the same man who fed 5,000 hungry people with a single loaf of bread? Sorry, not this bird. He's too busy makin millions at the roulette table with a gorgeous broad at his side to worry about stuff like that. If he's Christ, then I'm the Man in the Moon."

Petey: "O.K. Are we agreed then that he's gotta go down? I mean, somebody's gotta stop him before all hell breaks out. Like Doc said, nobody except Christ himself has the power that this guy Alexander has. And he's evil. Those Baptist jerks out there who are ready to bend down and kiss his ass don't seem to realize how close we are to seein the whole fuckin world go up in flames. We gotta stop him before he lights the match. If we don't stop him, who else is goin to do it? It's up to us, ain't it?"

Hunter: "Yeah. I like what yir sayin Petey. Now, I jis need to know this guy's routine. You know, where's he live, when's he go to work, what kinda car does he drive?"

Petey: "He lives somewhere in Back Bay, but I ain't never been there so I can't give you the address. As far as work, I don't know if he even has a job. All I'm sure of is that Evie says they're headin for Mexico in a few weeks to work on some kinda charity project. Like I told ya, some bozo give them big bucks after Alexander cured him of cancer."

Hunter: "That's O.K. It jis means I have to do a little research. But don't worry . . . I can do it."

Petey: "O.K. But I don't want Evie mixed up in any of this . . . (*pause*) . . . I think I'll call my sister and ask her to invite Evie to come out for a little visit. That should get her outta the way while we settle things here."

Later that evening Komerov arrives home to find Greta in the living room reading. His agitation is evident from the way he slams the front door. "The meeting didn't go well?," she says, dropping the magazine to her lap. Instead of sitting, he paces back and forth, searching for the right words. "It wasn't too bad . . . just some disagreement about details . . . (*pause*) . . . I think I've gotten about as much as I can from the group. I doubt that I'll go back."

Greta is no fool. In the 20 years they have lived together, she has gotten good at catching him in a lie. The symptoms are familiar: he fidgets; he paces; his breathing is faster; he avoids looking at her when he talks. She decides to take the plunge. "So, what was the disagreement about?"

Komerov: "Nothing really . . . just a difference of opinion about this man Alexander . . . you know, the one we've talked about before. Some of the guys there think he's the one whose picture was in the paper, the one who apparently walked on water up at Bradford Pond."

Greta drops the journal to the floor. "And the others?"

Komerov: "They aren't so sure. They say it's too hard to tell from the photos."

Greta: "The ones who think it was Alexander . . . how did they react?"

Komerov: "What do you mean?"

Greta: "You know, did they think it was a miracle; were they excited to read about it or were they alarmed in some way?"

Komerov (*still pacing*): "Alarmed? Why would they be alarmed?"

Greta: "Well, you've already told me that some of them think Alexander could be the Antichrist prophesied in the Bible. If they're worried that this man is already here among us, it could be pretty upsetting to see a picture of him walking on water in a nearby pond, don't you think?"

Komerov: "I hadn't really thought of it that way."

Greta (*eyebrows raised*): "How *did* you think of it, then?"

Komerov: "I think I got tired of hearing about Alexander; it was boring. So I got up, said goodbye, and left."

Greta: "Did the others leave at the same time or did you leave by yourself?"

Komerov: "I left by myself. The others might have left right afterwards . . . I really don't know . . . (*pause*) . . . I must say I don't appreciate begin grilled like this. (*heading for the kitchen*) I get the feeling you're accusing me of something."

Greta: "I'm just interested in why you're giving up on the group. I thought that you enjoyed going there every Tuesday night . . . (*pause*) . . . Is it just a coincidence that you're leaving right after those pictures appeared in the paper?"

Komerov opens the refrigerator, takes out a beer, then turns back toward his wife. "Probably not. After all, it was the pictures that got them discussing Alexander at such length. I listened until I couldn't take any more. That's when I left."

Greta: "So, some of the people there thought Alexander was the one walking on water. That's interesting. What did they want to do about it?"

Komerov (*still pacing, beer in hand*): "I don't know."

Greta: "For goodness sakes, George, if they're convinced that he's the Antichrist, they must have discussed what to do next. They're not just going to sit there and forget about the whole thing, are they?"

Komerov: "Like I said, they talked a lot about him . . . ad nauseum in fact . . . but I left before they came to any decision."

Greta: "You mean there were conflicting proposals?"

Komerov: "You could say that, yes."

Greta: "And what were some of the proposals?"

All George wants at this point is his wife's support. More than anything, he wants to hear her say that he did the right thing by leaving . . . but then he would have to tell her what Hunter said about the gun in his attic. If he tells her, what will she do? She seems to like this guy Alexander a lot . . . talks about him in almost romantic terms, but does she like him enough to warn him about Hunter . . . or go to the police? It's not worth the risk, not by a long shot. But how can he relax . . . how can he even sleep tonight . . . if she doesn't make him feel good about leaving? She's done it for over 20 years. Without question, it's her support that's kept him going through one crisis after another, the last one being that interview where he was taken in by a magazine writer. Oh, how he needed her then. Being laughed at by his colleagues, made the brunt of jokes by his neighbors, even ridiculed on the pages of the Boston Globe . . . it would have been impossible to get through it all without her reassurance not only that he had acted professionally but that the world would eventually wake up to the fact that he had been right all along. He decides to compromise.

Komerov: "Well, I was afraid that someone might suggest something violent, so I got out before they could say it. I just didn't want to hear anything that could get us into trouble . . . (*pause*) . . . That was the right thing to do, wasn't it?"

Greta: "You mean violence against Rafer?"

Komerov: "Yes."

By now it is clear to Greta that George is hiding something important. His weak attempt at deception can only mean that an attack on Rafer was not only discussed but agreed upon by the others. He obviously left because he was afraid of the consequences. As he paces, she fights to conceal her alarm. Now it is her turn to lie.

"I think you did the wise thing, George. And it's probably best if you don't go back. They sound like a strange lot, with all that talk about an Antichrist and the Devil. You never know what people like that might do. I'm glad you left. (*Extending her arms*) Come now, it's time for bed."

42

The Warning

At the airport, Eva turns for a final kiss before boarding the plane to Las Vegas. The kiss is brief, not much more than a peck. Ever since her mother called, inviting her home for a visit, Eva has been frightened. From the way Mom talked, it's obvious that something dramatic is in the works. What that might be is not clear, but it's certain that Petey doesn't want her around when it happens. If Agnes has learned anything from her brother, she's keeping it to herself. To Eva, the timing of her invitation, even the tone of her mother's voice, suggests that it has something to do with what happened at Bradford Pond. Exactly what that might be remains a mystery, but it's enough to make her heart beat faster.

Back home, Rafer is no sooner settled in his living room chair when the phone rings. It's Greta. "Hello, Rafe, it's Greta . . . you know, Greta Komerov. How are you?"

Rafer: "Just fine. Nice to hear your voice, Greta. What's going on?"

Greta (*breathing quickly*): "I'm worried, not so much about me but about you. But it's not something I want to discuss over the phone. Could we get together for lunch somewhere . . . as soon as possible?"

Rafer: "Of course. But why not come over to my place. Eva has gone home to visit her mother, so we can be completely alone . . . (*pause*) . . . You sound alarmed. May I ask what the general topic is?"

Greta: "I'd rather wait, if that's O.K. with you. I'll tell you everything when I get there. I know you live in Back Bay but what's your street address?"

Rafer: "512 Beacon St . . . between Dartmouth and Exeter. What day is good for you? I'm home most of the time now."

Greta: "How about tomorrow . . . at 10:00A.M.?"

Rafer: "Wow. This does sound urgent . . . (*pause*) . . . Does it have anything to do with George and the Medical School?"

Greta: "As I said, I'll share everything with you when I get there. O.K.? See you at 10:00."

In the hours leading up to the proposed visit, Rafer struggles to make sense of Greta's call but fails to come up with an answer. A look of bewilderment is still on his face when he opens the apartment door. Greta, never known for her stylishness, has outdone herself to look attractive. The ornate floral dress she has chosen does little, however, to conceal the uncomely dimensions of her frame. Her rakish hat, bought only yesterday, sits incongruously on top of her limp, black hair. Even to Rafer, it is obvious that she has applied mascara excessively and without any attention to detail. Although he would never say it, the dark, purple glow of her lips seems more fitting for an aging harlot than a university professor's wife. He pauses for a second to digest the scene, then takes her hand and welcomes her inside. She accepts his offer of tea and takes a seat in the living room.

Rafer (*serving the tea*): "You said you were worried about something . . . something involving me in particular. I've racked my brain but so far I haven't come up with anything that makes sense."

Greta takes a sip of her tea and puts the cup back down. "That was you in the papers the other night, wasn't it? You were the one who walked on water over at Bradford Pond."

Rafer (*rising and going to the window*): "Yes. How did you find out?"

Greta: "George has been going to this group up in Lynn every Tuesday night. I think I told you about it some time ago. What I didn't tell you is that it's a group of evangelicals . . . I would not hesitate to call them fanatics . . . who believe that a Biblical prophecy is about to be fulfilled."

Rafer (*turning to face her*): "And what prophecy is that, may I ask?"

Greta (*sighing*): "That a man with supernatural powers will be sent to earth to destroy God's handiwork . . . a man sent by the Devil himself. After setting the globe on fire, starting wars, and unleashing deadly viruses, this man, known in the Bible as the Antichrist or the Beast for short, will meet God at Armageddon in a final battle for world supremacy."

Rafer (*smiling*): "And who's supposed to win?"

Greta: "God, of course. But the Antichrist will wreak incredible destruction on the earth before he goes down."

Rafer: "And George actually believes this stuff?"

Greta: "That's a sorry tale in itself. Whether he's conscious of it or not, he's always on the lookout for some outlandish prediction . . . something that few people have any faith in but which nevertheless causes a big stir . . . like the psychic's prediction that an earthquake will send California tumbling into the Pacific . . . or, and this was earlier, that the world will come to an end in the year 2000. He then throws his weight behind it, hoping that if the prediction comes true, he'll be seen as a prophet comparable to people like Jeremiah and Isaiah in the Old Testament."

Rafer: "So where do I come into all this, if at all?"

Greta takes a deep breath. "You are the Antichrist who has come to destroy us. At least that's what the members of George's group believe. I think they discussed the possibility for months but weren't convinced until they saw a picture of you walking on water. Now they're sure."

Rafer (*laughing*): "That is so far out as to be funny."

Greta (*shaking her head*): "It's not funny at all, Rafe. Although George tried to hide the truth from me, it's clear from what he said that they mean to do you harm . . . even kill you. Your life is in danger, Rafe . . . now . . . right now . . . today."

Rafer rises and goes into the kitchen. "Want some more tea, Greta? I have some biscuits I could throw in too." Greta follows him into the kitchen and takes a position on the opposite side of the cooking island. She stands without saying a word, her eyes riveted to his every move. When he comes around to the sink, his shoulder accidentally brushes against hers, sending an unfamiliar sensation rippling through her groin. Yielding to instinct, she reaches out to touch him, then pulls her hand back before he can notice. With a plateful of biscuits in one hand and a pot of tea in the other, he heads back into the living room. "Aren't you frightened?," she asks, just a step behind.

Rafer: "Not really. I suppose I should be, but the feeling just isn't there."

Greta waits for Rafer to pull up a chair, then sits down at the close end of the couch. "What *are* you feeling, Rafe?"

Rafer (*sighing*): "Sadness more than anything. Sad that those people in Lynn could believe such nonsense . . . sad that anyone could be so wrong about me."

"Greta: "I agree. But aren't you going to do something about it? George didn't say it exactly, but I think they're planning to come after you . . . soon."

Rafer: "What in the world are they thinking?"

Greta: "I just told you what they're thinking. They think you're the Antichrist prophesied in the Bible."

Rafer (*shaking his head*): "But that's so hard to believe . . . (*pause*) . . . Everything I've done so far . . . the healings in Mexico, my work for the State Department, the new fund I've set up in Oaxaca . . . it's all come out of a desire to help people, not destroy them. Isn't that obvious?"

Greta: "Not to the group in Lynn. If you read certain chapters of the Bible, as I did the other night, you'll see that this so-called Antichrist is very clever, clever enough to mask his evil intent with good works . . . acts that appear to be motivated by compassion. Then, once everyone is convinced that he's here to help us, he's going to lower the boom. Wars will erupt, plagues break out, millions will die of hunger as locusts sweep across the land ravaging crops in their wake. It's not a pretty scenario."

Rafer: "No, it's not pretty . . . it's not even rational. Look Greta, I appreciate your concern, but I'm not about to change my ways because of what some Neanderthals up in Lynn think. That would be giving in to the kind of hysteria that led people to burn witches in Salem . . . which, interestingly, is right next to Lynn."

Greta (*grinning*): "Maybe there's something funny in the water up there."

Rafer (*smiling*): "Either that or they've been reading too many comic books."

Greta (*biting her lip*): "So you're not going to do anything to protect yourself?"

Rafer: "I'm not going to let them scare me into hiding."

Greta nods and reaches for a biscuit. "That's not what I hoped to hear, but I'll respect your decision . . . (*pause*) . . . I must confess though that I'm curious as to why you're not afraid. After all, with these people in Lynn following your every move, your life could be at stake."

Rafer sets down his cup. "If this had happened years or even months ago, I might have reacted differently. The way I look at the world seems to be changing. It's hard to say exactly what is different now, but it's got something to do with my feelings about death." As the subject of dying comes up, a new, more pensive look creeps across Rafer's face. It is the look of a young boy brooding over the loss of a much-loved pet . . . tender, resigned, but baffled by the mystery of it all. Greta is quick to notice. She has all she can do to keep from reaching out and taking him in her arms. More alarming is a rekindling of the warmth in her groin. Rafer is unaware of the change.

Greta (*softly*): "I'm listening."

Rafer: "Up to recently I was afraid of dying, just like anyone else. Among other things, I wanted to live long enough to complete the projects I had started, like the work in Oaxaca. None of that really changed until a few months ago when I sensed my meditation going deeper."

Greta: "I thought it was already pretty deep, Rafe."

Rafer: "In a sense, yes. Over the last year or two I've gotten very familiar with the Void . . . you know, that boundaryless, empty space I sometimes talk about. At first, I thought it was the end of the line, the point beyond which you just couldn't go. It is clear now that I was still clinging to my old sense of self. Whenever I experienced the Void, it was always embedded in some object out there . . . a cloud, a tree, another person, something outside myself . . . but never inside me. So it's no wonder that I was still afraid of dying. Despite the new vision, I was still a separate, mortal self looking at the Void from the outside."

Greta: "But you say it's different now?"

Rafer: "Starting a few months ago, I began to see the Void in myself as well as in the objects around me. That changed everything. It changed the way I see myself; it changed who I think I am. While I remain Rafer Alexander, an individual with a name, a history, and a consciousness separate from anyone else's, that identity has been relegated to the sidelines, pushed off stage so to speak. At center stage now is a new awareness that transcends both subject and object. It catapults me to the very ends of the universe. I am the Void itself."

Greta leans closer, torn between a desire to hear more about this vision and a longing to be kissed and held. In her uncertainty, she loses her balance and falls head first into his lap. Rafer doesn't move. "Oh darling, I'm sorry," she cries, as she wriggles to get free. Back on the couch, she shakes her head in disbelief. "Was that me talking? I can't believe I actually said that. Please forgive me, Rafe. I must be losing it."

Rafer (*grinning*): "No harm done. It's probably this new tea I bought on Newbury Street last week. I was getting tired of the same old stuff so I asked the sales clerk for something *exotic*. Maybe she misheard me."

Still embarrassed by her slip, Greta moves to resume the discussion. "So what does it mean when you say that you *are* the Void rather than looking at it? How does that new awareness make you feel?"

Rafer: "Well, when I saw the Void as something embedded only in objects out there, I continued to see myself the way anybody else would . . . as a person who is born, grows old and eventually dies. But I no longer look at it that way. Yes, Rafer Alexander is growing old and will someday die . . . but that's not who I really am."

Greta: "And you are . . . ?"

Rafer: "Call it what you want . . . the Void, a Universal Energy Field, Cosmic Consciousness . . . there's really no name for it. It's vibrant yet has no lines, shapes or colors in it. Because it is without form, it can't be considered either a subject or an object. At best, you might call it a Presence. The poet Wordsworth, who apparently experienced something similar, referred to it as 'Being.' What's important here is that it is not a thing; therefore it has no beginning or end. Because it has no form, it undergoes neither birth nor death. So, if that's who I really am, there is nothing to be afraid of. Rafer Alexander, that fellow off in the wings, will surely die . . . but he is no longer my primary identity . . . (*pause*) . . . I don't know . . . does any of this make sense?"

Greta sits back on the couch, her spine erect. "It does, Rafe, not because I've experienced what you're talking about but because I've read about it in books on philosophy. Your view of death comes pretty close to what the Buddha said in some of his sutras. In the West the author who sounds most similar is Paul Tillich, the German theologian who taught at Harvard for a few years before he died."

Rafer: "I've never read his stuff. What did he say?"

Greta: "What you're calling the Void or Universal Energy, he called the 'Ground of Being' . . . but I think he meant pretty much the same thing. You can't describe it because it's beyond language, beyond thought. Sometimes he referred to it as the God beyond the God of theism . . . a 'ground' or 'power' which makes all things possible but is not a thing itself."

Rafer: "That does make sense. Our traditional view of God is very limiting. It treats God as a subject over and against the objects (the world) He has created. It drags God into the world of things and makes him a sort of person, someone with feelings, someone who rewards and punishes others, a ruler who makes judgments according to his ideas of right and wrong. The idea of a personal, loving, all-powerful God is very comforting but in my opinion, it has more to do with wish-fulfillment than reality. Tillich's Ground of Being, the God *behind* the God of theism, makes more sense. It transcends any notion we might have about God as a person, as a Creator who stands apart from his creation."

Greta: "But if this Ground is not a thing or object, just what is it?"

Rafer: "You can't describe it; the best you can do is to point to it using symbols or metaphors. For example, take the phrase 'undifferentiated energy.' It's purely symbolic in that it points to something beyond language . . . what Korzybski called the realm of the 'unspeakable.' So, what is it exactly? It is what I experience when I go into a trance, leaving the world of lines, shapes and colors behind. It is the I AM THAT I AM which lies embedded in all objects and makes their existence possible . . . (*pause*) . . . I suppose it's as close to 'ultimate reality' as we can get."

Greta: "Do you see it as something physical?"

Rafer: "It has to be, even though it has no observable form. If you call it 'spirit', then you have to deal with the problem of how physical and spiritual realities interact. How, for example, can something spiritual or non-physical impact an object made of iron or steel?"

Greta: "This is all very abstract . . . which is O.K. with me. I like to play with concepts, like I did in my master's thesis. But the emotional part of me has a different kind of question. How has this vision of yours . . . this seeing into the Void or Tillich's Ground of Being . . . affected the way you feel? From what I've read in the Buddhist literature, it's got to be a mind-altering experience. Is that true for you?"

Rafer rises from his chair and heads for the kitchen, empty cup in hand. When he returns, he remains standing by the window. There is a new softness in his voice. "It took place in stages. When it first happened, I found myself gasping, 'God, oh God' as objects around me disappeared into emptiness. But I was still there, watching the show as it unfolded. Later the vision went deeper until I too disappeared into nothingness. It was if I had been released from a

THE RELUCTANT SAVIOR

cage, a cage where I had sat for years, trapped behind bars of ambition, defensiveness, and self-doubt. In a flash, all that disappeared, leaving a world of pure, empty space where there was no ego left to worry about. If you had asked me who I was, I would have answered, "I am no longer an isolated self, I am no longer Rafer Alexander; I am the undifferentiated Energy or Space that is embedded in all things . . . I am the Self, the One. In itself, that was life-altering enough, but more recently things have changed again. These days I no longer ask, 'Who am I?'; the question no longer makes any sense. It's unanswerable because there's no 'I' left to say what it is or isn't. When I look inside, I see neither a little self nor a big Self . . . just 'undifferentiated energy.' And that's why I'm not afraid of dying. There is no one left to die."

Greta: "But you said a little while ago you were still Rafer Alexander . . . and that's a self of some sort, isn't it? So, isn't that self afraid to die?"

Rafer: "True . . . there is still a conventional self off in the wings somewhere, but it's no longer center stage . . . no longer something I dwell on. When I'm not meditating, I'm aware of it but pay little or no attention to it. During meditation it ceases to exist altogether."

Greta (*smiling*): "Forgive me for being such a pest . . . George hates it when I'm this way . . . but I'm still curious. To be aware of this Ground or Undifferentiated Energy you talk about, you have to have a physical body, don't you . . . a brain, a nervous system and so on? What I mean is that when you die . . . when Rafer Alexander dies . . . there won't be anyone left to *know* anything . . . including the fact that this Ground will go on forever. So, what's so great about tapping into this Void if there's no self of any kind left to enjoy it?"

Rafer (*laughing*): "It does sound weird, doesn't it. But it's true. When the body dies, there's no individual consciousness left to know either that this body is dead or that the Ground formerly embedded in that body still exists. However, it *is* something you can come to know *before* you die . . . that is, at the time of your enlightenment. And knowing that the Ground embedded in your mortal body can never die is what brings peace."

Greta smiles, then reaches for the last biscuit. "I've often wondered why the enlightenment experience was so wonderful. I can see now that it's all about transcending your ordinary identity, with leaving all thoughts of the self behind . . . (*pause*) . . . You're making me very envious, Rafe. I just wish I knew how to get there."

Rafer: "Anybody can do it, Greta. I think it happened to me because of the plane crash that killed my brother and parents. Losing my family apparently undid the bonds that held me together as a person; it unraveled the fabric that defined who I was and what I was supposed to become. Above all, it severed my ties to my mother, the person who had spent most of her life molding me in her image. At first her death forced me to carve out a new identity of my own; later, it made it possible to give up the need for an identity of any sort. (*Smiling*) Mind you, I'm not recommending this as a path to follow . . . it's just the way things happened to me. There are many paths to enlightenment, some featuring meditation while others call for devotion, compassion or ascetic denial. What they all have in common is a loss of self."

Greta (*rising*): "It's probably time for me to go, Rafe, I don't want George to worry. Just one other question: what about desire? Do you desire anything for yourself now?"

Escorting her to the door, "Not really, Greta. I used to dream about having a house on Nantucket and learning to sail . . . or perhaps owning a small airplane. I even had thoughts of becoming an economic advisor to the White House. But those dreams are gone now. I just don't think about them anymore."

Greta: "But what about the little things . . . clothes, food, furniture . . . things like that? Aren't there things you still want?"

Rafer: "Now and then something like that comes up . . . but it's never urgent. There are certainly things I still need but hardly anything that I want. There's only one major desire left that I'm aware of . . . the desire to put whatever gifts I might have to good use. Healing is the first thing that comes to mind. Helping to bring a sick or disabled person back to health is the most satisfying thing I can think of."

At the door Greta stops and turns to face her host. Her lips are trembling. "Could I have a little kiss, Rafe. Eva wouldn't mind, would she?"

Rafer smiles. "I don't see why she should."

When Rafer offers his cheek, Greta reaches up with both hands, turns his head to face her own, then places her lips squarely on his. Her heart leaps when he does nothing to get away. The kiss lasts until a tenant in the next apartment can be heard coming up the stairs.

With a final call to "Be careful," Greta steps out into the hall, her cheeks still afire with longing. At the landing, she turns to wave a final goodbye. It is too late; Rafer is already inside.

43

Hunter's Turn

Public demand to know more about the Man Who Walked on Water spreads quickly. In response, both Boston newspapers put out a request for information. When several readers call in guesses, reporters check out telephone and motor vehicle records; when justified, they conduct follow-up interviews. The first four calls at the Globe turn out to be false leads. The fifth, however, comes from a broker at Kidder-Homans where Rafer worked after getting his Ph.D. The description given by the caller seems to fit the picture in the paper. Once the reporters have a name, the rest is easy. A glance at the telephone book provides the desired address.

When Rafer opens the door, the reporter is the first to speak. "Hello. I'm Gary Summers from the Boston Globe." He holds up an enlarged picture showing a man in hiking shorts coming ashore at a small lake. An enveloping mist hangs over the water behind him, his feet clearly visible on the surface. "Is this you, sir?"

Rafer hangs his head. Before he can reply, a photographer steps out from the shadows and snaps a picture. Too late, Rafer raises his arm to cover his face. With his victim still recoiling, the photographer aims his camera at the interior of the apartment and snaps another shot. Nonplussed, Rafer slams the door shut and retreats into the living room.

The headlines that evening trumpet the news: 'Identity of Miracle Man Revealed: Local Man Admits to Walking on Water.' The article goes on to describe Rafer in excruciating detail, his height and weight, the color of his hair and eyes, the sound of his voice, even the style of his living room furniture. A little research quickly reveals his past association with Kidder-Homans as well as his previously-publicized healings in Mexico, including his success in treating billionaire Carlos Santana. Thousands read the story; still others see the interview reported on television. Not surprisingly, the city is mesmerized with the discovery that the first man since Jesus Christ to walk on water is a fellow Bostonian. Some descend on his apartment in Back Bay hoping for a glimpse of the young Messiah; others, of a more secular persuasion, arrive with offers of a Broadway stage contract. Barnum and Bailey sends one of its top executives to propose a nationwide tour with the water stunt as its featured act. Within minutes the street in front of his apartment is filled with paparazzi jostling for a position near the front door.

Up in Lynn, a scruffy, unshaven loner in overalls erupts with a 'whoop' when Alexander's face and name appear on his TV screen. "Ah," he shouts to the German shepherd at his side, "There it is! Everything I need . . . name, address, even the color of his hair and eyes. The Lord has gotta be in on this. Yes sir, He's tellin me to go do it . . . (*reaching down to pet the dog*) . . . What d'ya say, girl . . . is it time to go ahuntin?"

The next morning Rafer rises early, grabs a cold muffin from the cupboard, and heads out onto Beacon Street. To conceal his identity he wears a baseball cap and dark sunglasses. He looks West, then East . . . breathing deeply when he sees that he's alone. As he walks toward the Common, he has no goal other than to be by himself . . . and perhaps to mull over some of the things Greta said. Walking quickly now, he is too absorbed in his thoughts to see a man in a pick-up directly across the street.

Hunter has been sitting there since 5:30 . . . plenty of time to think about the day's plan. With an eye on the opposite sidewalk, he nestles his beefy frame down into the driver's seat, his broad-rimmed Australian shepherd's hat pulled down to cover most of his face. To a passerby the only thing showing is a fuzz-covered chin and a sparse, blonde mustache. With the fully-loaded Luger tucked into his belt, he's free to let his thoughts roam. Not surprisingly they drift back to childhood.

An image of his father is the first to appear . . . a large man, 6'2", 230 pounds, heavy black eyebrows, lips that curl menacingly to one side, and a perpetual scowl on his acne-pocked face. Back then the family lived in Everett, a blue-collar town just outside Boston where father was a security guard at a local milling factory. It was a mean existence, no friends to speak of, no money for things like television, nothing to do but shoot baskets by himself at a rusty hoop across the street. One thing was for sure . . . it was best to stay out of the house when the old man was at home. Crossing him, especially when he was drinking, was an invitation to trouble. The slightest mistake . . . like forgetting to take out the garage or leaving a light on . . . could get you whacked in the face. "No matter how hard I tried," he recalls, "I couldn't please the guy. He was like a bomb ready to explode if I said the wrong thing or looked at him the wrong way. What the fuck . . . of course I said things I shouldna said and done things I shouldna done. So he made me his favorite punching bag. He despised me, maybe even hated me. I know I hated him."

Smiling now, Hunter recalls the day when everything changed. He was 13 then, big for his age and strong but not much of a fighter. His days were filled with fear of a man who was committed to turning his son into a replica of himself . . . tough, powerful, and intimidating in his behavior. For 13 years it hadn't worked; in his father's eyes Hunter was still a mouse, constantly preyed upon by his classmates, easily reduced to tears, anxious to avoid fighting at any cost. At school he was ridiculed; at home he was loathed. Despite his mother's occasional protests, life was unbearable. And then one day in September it all changed.

His father was home that afternoon, getting ready for work when he heard some boys yelling outside. The voices were unfamiliar; Hunter's was not one of them. Dropping his jacket, he rushed out the front door and onto the walk. There was Hunter crouched behind a small maple tree, dodging stones from two younger boys, one of which he recognized as Jimmy Sciani, a neighbor. As soon as Hunter saw his father emerge from the house, he ran toward the door, seeking refuge from the barrage. What he met was not the protective embrace he longed for. Oh, no, he recalls now with a sneer; it wasn't that at all. With eyes blazing, father took him by the arm and shoved him back toward the sidewalk, yelling, "Go get 'em. You're bigger than they are; hit 'em with your fist. Beat the shit out of them . . . you can do it Hunter. You can do it."

He sits back in the truck now and lights a cigarette. Through the swirling haze he sees the incident played out like an old home movie. "Perhaps it was 'cuz he said my name," he reflects. "That made it different somehow . . . more personal . . . more like he was on my side for once. I dunno. All I'm sure of is that I felt somethin new . . . almost like I was the father this time . . . pissed and wantin to swat these pesky little bugs . . . make 'em hurt, maybe even kill 'em. Yeah, I went back to those kids and did exactly what Daddy told me to do . . . I whipped 'em real good, both of them . . . hit 'em right in the face . . . one after the other . . . until they ran home with blood shootin outta their noses. The old man stood there watchin me the whole time. He was real proud of me that day . . . you bet he wuz."

He breaks into a laugh. "Those two punks left me alone after that. So did the other kids at school. Suddenly everything was different. If somebody fucked with me, I'd go after 'em jis like I did with the Sciani kid. And I liked it. No, I loved it. I even went outta my way to pick fights with kids I didn't like. Nobody could hurt me after that . . . I mean nobody. Yeah. It felt real good to be top dog for once . . . to have kids afraid of me . . . to see the little pricks move outta the way when I come down the hall. They was all afraid I was goin to bash 'em . . . and I would've . . . if I felt like it . . . (*pause*) . . . O.K., so I did have a little trouble with Mother. She said she didn't like who I wuz becoming . . . that I wuz fillin up with hate and anger like my Daddy. She tried preachin churchy stuff to me; I listened but it didn't change nuthin."

As Rafer turns East toward the Common, Hunter checks the Luger, opens the truck door and steps out on the sidewalk. With hands in his pockets, he follows from the opposite side of the street, 20 feet behind his quickly-moving prey.

As the sun comes up, Rafer cuts through the Common and heads for the waterfront. Early risers are already trickling across the open spaces of Government Center on their way to work on the docks. When he feels his stomach rumbling, he enters Quincy Market and stops at an English bistro advertising crumpets and scones. He is the very first patron of the morning. Seated in the corner with an eye on passersby, he orders scrambled eggs and a boysenberry scone. When the waiter is slow to arrive with his meal, he closes his eyes and slips into a trance. Lost in a world without form, he fails to see a man in dirty overalls and leather jacket stop at the window and shield his eyes from the sun. Apparently satisfied, the man moves on, taking a seat on a bench in the middle of the walkway that runs between the two rows of stores.

Awakened by the waiter's return, Rafer nods his approval and begins buttering his scone. Outside, the corridor is filling with pedestrians, some of whom stop to read the ad on the café window. As he scans their faces, his attention is drawn to a large man sitting on a bench behind them. The man is neither eating nor reading. From the unwavering position of his head, it is clear that he has little interest in studying his fellow pedestrians. His eyes are focused instead on the café window, as if he were trying to read the scone ad from a distance. From his corner table Rafer stares back, trying to locate the man in his bank of memories.

He eats slowly. There's no rush now . . . nothing that has to be done today. His thoughts drift to Eva out in Vegas with her mother. "Do

I miss her?," he muses. "Perhaps. She is certainly enjoyable to be with. We seem to have grown even closer after launching the Oaxaca Fund together." He pauses. "But there was something strange about her expression before she left. Some kind of fear . . . she didn't say what . . . but fear nevertheless. Hopefully a week with her Mom will settle her down."

He stays until he can see the book store across the way open its doors, then pays his bill and leaves. Outside, sunlight has illuminated the white cupola on top of Faneuil Hall, drawing the walkway out of darkness. Careful not to appear too curious, he looks around for the husky man on the bench. The bench is empty. Relieved, he walks across to the book store and enters. The store is small but appears to have an interesting assortment of books. Finding nothing of immediate interest, he goes to the counter and asks the clerk for material on the Antichrist.

"I think we have one such book," the clerk responds, walking over to a table on the far left. "Yes, here it is . . . The Antichrist by Arthur Pink. I'm afraid it's the only one we have but you may find it useful . . . (*pause*) . . . May I ask the nature of your interest. Are you doing research or . . . ."

Rafer: "Just curious. I heard something about it recently and want to learn more." As he thumbs through pages on the 'Genius and Character of the Antichrist,' the front door opens and closes again. A customer enters and walks over to the magazine section. Rafer pauses for a minute, then turns to look. It is the burly man in the brown leather jacket. He turns back to the book and reads a few more pages. Smiling, he addresses the clerk who remains standing nearby, eager to help if asked. "Do people really buy books like this? I've only read a few pages but it sounds pretty weird."

"Oh yes," comes the reply. "We've sold several already this month." The clerk steps closer to look at the page Rafer is reading. "That stuff on the character of the Antichrist is pretty good but I think you will find the next chapter, the one on the Career of the Antichrist, even more interesting. It tells exactly what he's going to do when he gets here."

Rafer nods approvingly. "And when is that supposed to happen?"

The clerk looks around the store, then whispers, "It's hard to know for sure but some say he's already here."

Rafer (*grinning*): "And what makes them say that?"

The clerk throws up his hands. "I'm no expert on the subject but just look around. There are signs everywhere . . . global warming, wars in the Middle East, AIDS, famine in Africa, floods in Pakistan, a depression coming here in the states . . . all the things the Bible talks about. Maybe he's already started his dirty work. It makes sense, doesn't it?"

When the clerk begins to study his face, Rafer gets nervous and prepares to leave. The clerk follows him to the door, hoping to get a better look. "You aren't the guy in the newspapers, are you?," he whispers, careful not to let the other customer hear. Rafer pulls his cap tight and says nothing. The minute he is gone, the other customer moves over to the table where Rafer was standing. Reaching down, he picks up the still open book, flips through a few pages, then closes it. Out loud, he reads the title on the cover: "The Antichrist." His lip recoils into a sneer. "Of course. What else?"

Half-way down the street Rafer turns to see if he is being followed. The clerk has gone back into the store but someone else is coming out. It is the man in overalls and leather jacket.

Hunter smiles when he sees Rafer turn to look at him. His quarry has the look of a cornered rabbit . . . or so it seems to the man with the Luger in his belt. Secure now in the knowledge that he has the right person, Hunter moves swiftly, careful to leave 20 feet between him and his target. As predator and prey make their way to the harbor, Hunter allows his mind to drift. Sweet memories of his first year in middle school arise, the year when his life of misery suddenly turned around. With one eye on Rafer, he replays a favorite scene. He is coming down the hall at school; students are rushing to get to their next class. As he approaches a cluster of classmates, he expands his chest and screws his face into a menacing glare. The girls scatter to their lockers; the boys begin walking faster. He steps up his pace as the boys race away down the hall, turning their heads periodically to check his whereabouts. Just as he is about to grab them, they dash into a classroom and the safety of a teacher. He stands in the doorway as they cower behind their desks. Wordlessly he lip synchs his threat, "You little shits; I'll get you next time."

"What a great year that wuz," he muses now, checking on his quarry a half a block ahead. "Those punks wuz so scared of me they played sick just so they cud stay home." He chuckles. "I loved to make 'em run . . . jis like rabbits . . . then bash their heads in when I caught one. Best of all, Daddy loved to hear about it when I got home that night." Just then, an image of his father's casket arises, bringing tears in its wake. He nods as if in salute. "I guess he'd be pretty proud of what I'm doin today."

Together hunter and hunted inch their way along the waterfront . . . past Long Wharf and Rowes Wharf . . . then across the bridge to Seaport Blvd and into the world of docks and container ships. There are many people on the sidewalk now, probably heading for work . . . lots of cars in the street too. The smell of fish is hard to avoid, especially when a breeze blows in from the east. Over at the water's edge a hotel window welcomes the warming light. It's a new day; the whole city is coming alive.

Rafer turns into Lake Street, drawn by the sound of kids playing baseball. Just ahead at the corner of Fire Alley he comes to a playground where a few kids are having a game. They must really love the game to get up this early, he muses. He stops to watch. The boys are between 12 and 15 . . . with six players to a side . . . a pitcher, catcher, first and third basemen, and left and right fielders. It reminds him of the sandlot back in Babylon, New York where he grew up. He takes a seat in the metal stands behind home plate. A woman in her sixties, probably someone's grandmother, has been co-opted to call balls and strikes. There are no other adults around. His back is now to the sidewalk, making it impossible to see Hunter who is watching his every move from the sidewalk.

When barely an inning has passed, the catcher takes a fastball on his fingers and yells out in pain. Once it has been determined that his thumbnail is split, he removes his mask and pads and prepares to leave the field, one hand holding onto the other. At this point the pitcher, who is the boy's brother, calls out to Rafer in the stands. "Can you catch for us?" Rafer pauses, then nods a hesitant yes and comes down onto the field where he is handed the catcher's mask and glove. The pitcher reassures his brother that he will bring the equipment home later. After taking a few warm-ups tosses, Rafer signals his readiness to resume play.

The first batter draws a walk and with no second baseman in his way, steals second. The next batter gets a hit to right field, sending the first batter around third, heading pell-mell for home. At the plate Rafer braces for the throw and a possible collision. Just as the runner goes into his slide, a shot rings out; the boy screams, clutching his right arm. Rafer turns around, sees a man's shadow under the stands, then yells to the pitcher. "Run to the nearest store and call 911." With a quick look under the stands, he picks up the injured boy and heads for the sidewalk. The pitcher yells back that there's a police car up there, parked just a few yards from playground. Rafer turns to look. There are two policemen in the car, eating donuts, apparently taking a break from their waterfront patrol. The cop behind the wheel leans forward when he sees a boy running toward him; not far behind him is a man carrying a small boy in his arms. Both policemen jump out of the cruiser.

As he makes his way up the embankment, Rafer senses a figure moving under the stands. Instinctively he turns his back, shielding the boy from danger. "You're going to be alright," he whispers. "Just don't move." As both cops scramble down the embankment, a second shot rings out, hitting Rafer squarely in the back. He stumbles, then falls forward as a third shot strikes his neck. The cop who was driving races to Rafer's side while his partner scans the bleachers, looking for the source of the shots. When he spots Hunter under the stands, he begins firing immediately. A bullet strikes Hunter in the left shoulder. With his right hand he rips away his shirt to expose the wound. As blood squirts from the hole, all thoughts of running disappear. Within seconds, fear gives way to a screaming rage that sends his whole frame trembling. In his mind's eye, he sees two boys rushing toward him, throwing rocks, laughing as they drive him back to his house. Out of the corner of his eye, he sees his father watching from the porch. He stops, hiding behind a tree in the front yard. Father comes running from the porch, shaking his fist, pointing to the two boys and yelling, "Go get 'em, Hunter. Beat the shit outta them." As those magical words return, a familiar seething fills his chest.

Emerging from the stands now, he advances, roaring with the fury of a wounded grizzly. "No more," he shouts, "I'll grind you little pricks to dust." He fires first at one cop, then the other. The closest officer collapses to his knees, grasping his leg while shooting with the other hand. There is no stopping now. From just ten feet away both cops fire bullet after bullet into the advancing hulk until it falls to the ground, gasping. As the Luger slips from his hands, the man in the leatherjacket sputters a final epithet, "You bastards, I'll teach ya ta mess with me."

While the cop with the wounded leg remains beside the dying assailant, his partner rushes back onto the field. Carefully prying the boy loose from Rafer's limp hands, he carries him up to the cruiser and places him in the back seat, then returns to get Rafer whom he slides in next to the boy. Calling police headquarters on the way, he turns the cruiser around and speeds off to Mass. General.

In the back seat, Rafer is dimly aware of the boy next to him. As the cruiser races up the boulevard, siren wailing, he drifts in and out of consciousness, his awareness flickering like a candle in the wind. Out of the flotsam and jetsam of remembered faces, the image of his mother suddenly appears. "You did just fine, Rafe," she whispers from her snowy grave. "The world will remember you for all the great things you did." He winces, then raises his head, desperate to correct her.

His mouth opens, "But that's not . . . "

The words will not come. Like minnows caught in a frozen stream, they lie trapped in the interstices of his brain, buried under layers of splattered flesh and oozing blood. He slumps back against the seat as pain sweeps through his body, obliterating all thought. A few seconds pass before her voice returns, more urgent in its pleading. "I said you could do anything you put your mind to . . . and you did. You've made us all proud of you, Rafe." He lifts his hand in protest but she is not listening. "Few men have ever achieved as much as you have," she continues, beckoning him closer. "Come, let me hold you now."

He closes his eyes, too weak to respond. In the approaching darkness, her image begins to fade, receding slowly into the distance until it vanishes altogether. All that is left now is the pain. Desperately he searches for the Void, that voiceless Space where all sense of self, all feelings, thoughts, memories and fears are dissolved in the eternal emptiness of Being, where pain is unknown and peace is everlasting.

The boy is awakened by a sudden spasm from the man lying next to him. Still holding his bleeding arm, he leans over to look. When he sees the man smiling, he whispers, "Are you O.K., Mister?" Getting no answer, he repeats the question, his eyes still riveted to the man's face. An ominous silence follows, broken finally not by the man next to him, but by the policeman who has been watching through his rear-view mirror, "He's gone, kid," the cop mutters matter-of-factly. "There's nuthin you can do for him now."

At the hospital, the boy is sent immediately to the operating room. The attending physician checks Rafer's pulse, pries open his eyes, then pronounces him D.O.A. "That isn't the guy in the newspapers the other night, is it?," a porter asks his partner as they wheel the body away.

"You mean the one who walked on water up at Bradford Pond?"

"Yeah, that's the one. How the hell did he do it, anyway?"

"Beats me. Probly was using wires or somethin."

44

A Farewell

In the days that follow, all the newspapers, both local and national, carry stories of Rafer's assassination. "Mystery Man Shot in Playground" blares the Globe in an early article based on a police report and interviews with the victim's former associates at Kidder-Homans. On the second day additional material is provided by the priest at St. Agnes who is finally given permission to tell what he saw at Bradford Pond. Although the pictures of Rafer walking on water are shown repeatedly on evening television, few details are given regarding his background, family or religious affiliation. To some viewers, particularly those who believe the Mystery Man to be a reincarnation of Christ, the trickle of information is tantalizing to the point of despair. Others, less inclined to spiritual interpretations, see the murder as the probable act of a deranged colleague, perhaps a fellow performer envious of Rafer's "miracle" stunt at Bradford Pond.

Early attempts to link Hunter with any co-conspirators fail to reveal anything incriminating. Without evidence to the contrary, detectives continue to view Hunter as a lone wolf assassin who tracked his prey from Beacon St. to the waterfront playground where he shot him from beneath the stands. Because no obvious motive can be found, the door is left open for further investigation.

Stefan, who volunteers to give the funeral oration, immediately calls Eva in Vegas to give her the news. As he pours out all the known details of the murder, Eva collapses into a chair, both outwardly shaken and inwardly torn by questions she dare not ask. She promises to return immediately.

It is not until Petey calls later in the morning that those questions make their way to her lips. "I know your group didn't like Rafer," she says, "but you didn't kill him, did you?" As she waits for his answer, she rubs her lower lip to stop the bleeding.

"It's best if we don't talk about that stuff, Evie. The police are lookin into it and so far it looks like some nut with a grudge against Alexander did it. Just to be on the safe side, though, it'd be better if you didn't say nuthin about me or our group in Lynn . . . you know, in case the cops call you. No sense in muddyin up the waters . . . if you get my meanin."

Eva (*fighting back the tears*): "I think so, but I still don't understand. I'm really confused. Is he . . . or was he . . . the person you talked about . . . the one mentioned in the Bible? Or was he more the way I saw him . . . a lovable person with a big heart and a soft place for children and . . . ?"

Petey (*interrupting*): "Yeah, and somebody who could rack up millions at roulette, cure people nobody else could save . . . and bring kids back from the dead. Lookit Evie . . . maybe he was lovable at home and maybe he liked kids but he did other stuff no ordinary person could do. To me, that makes him dangerous. Just think . . . what if you said somethin to cross him and he got mad at you . . . what then . . . you think with his powers he woulda jis snarled a little and walked away? C'mon, be sensible girl."

Eva: "I don't know, Petey. I can't figure it all out."

Petey (*softly*): "You probly need a little time . . . that's all, honey. But for now, mum's the word, O.K.?"

Eva (*sighing*): "O.K."

Petey: "Call me when you get back to Boston."

That evening Petey calls an emergency session of his Lynn group. Zeke, Thomas, and Revy are all there; to no one's surprise, Doc fails to show. The mood is somber . . . with none of the horsing around that usually precedes formal business. Petey is the first to speak. He clears his voice, then nods solemnly. "Things have worked out pretty much the way we hoped they would. We don't have to go around braggin about it but we jis saved a lotta lives, maybe the whole fuckin enchilada. Someday people will get around to thankin us for it . . . but right now we gotta keep our traps shut. No mention of this group to anyone . . . I mean anyone . . . wives, lovers, parents . . . anyone. It's goin to be temptin to tell people we had this guy pegged from the very beginning . . . but yir goin to get our throats cut if you talk. Right now, nobody outside this group knows we've been keepin tabs on Alexander."

Thomas: "What about your sister out in Vegas?"

Zeke: "Yeah . . . and your niece, Eva. You warned her about Alexander, didn't you?"

Petey: "There's nothin to worry about there. I talked to them both yesterday and they promised to keep their mouths shut . . . (*pause*) . . . Now . . . I've got a funeral lined up for Hunter at church next Friday at 10:00 A.M.; it'll be announced in the paper tomorrow. It took a little arm-twistin but Reverend Peters says he'll do the honors . . . even though he can't remember ever seein Hunter at one of his services. I explained that Hunter was scared of crowds and liked to do his prayin by hisself."

Thomas (*laughing*): "O.K., but what if somebody asks us if we know Hunter . . . what do we say?"

Petey: "You mean, at the funeral?"

Thomas: "Well, anytime. Say a reporter calls wantin info on Hunter for a newspaper article. How much do we tell him?"

Revy: "That's pretty obvious. Tell 'em personal stuff . . . hobbies, favorite TV programs, and stuff like that . . . just don't say anything about this group or the things we talk about here."

Zeke: "Right. And above all, don't mention the Antichrist. We don't want no one to know we've been tracking Alexander for months; if they find out, they'll want to why we were doing it and what plans we had for getting rid of him."

Thomas (*shaking his head*): "Lookit, I don't want to spoil the party, but are we sure we got the right guy? I mean, we never got final proof, did we?"

Zeke (*smiling*): "Ah Thomas . . . always the doubter. What kind of proof would convince you?"

Thomas: "Well, maybe something in the Good Book that points specifically to Alexander . . . you know, his name or the way he died, the date or place of his death . . . a sign of some kind."

Zeke (*thumbing through the Bible*): "Hmm. Maybe this will this satisfy you. This is what Revelations has to say about the way the Antichrist is going to meet his doom. Here it is from chapter 20, verse 10: 'And the Devil that deceived them was cast into the *lake of fire* . . . and shall be tormented day and night forever and ever.'

Thomas: (*squinting*): "So?"

Zeke: "What d'ya mean, 'So?' Don't you read the newspapers, dummy? Alexander was shot at a playground near the waterfront and . . . ."

Thomas: "Yeah, I read that . . . but so what?"

Zeke (*taking a deep breath*): "The playground was at the corner of **Lake St.** and **Fire Alley** . . . (*pause*) . . . Does that ring a bell? . . . (*pause*) . . . No? . . . Didn't you hear what the Bible said about the **Lake of Fire?** . . . (*pause*) . . . Do I have to read it again?"

Thomas (*shouting*): "Jesus Christ! I get it now."

Zeke: "Good. There's your proof. It's clear from Revelations that God and His Son were behind this whole thing . . . tellin us what to do from the very beginning. We just did what they wanted us to do."

Petey: "Nice work, Zeke. That little quote should take care of any doubts we mighta had. We definitely got the right guy . . . (*pause*) . . . now I don't wanta hear any more questions about that, O.K.?"

In the days that follow, Boston and Lynn police follow up a wide variety of leads. That includes talking to Hunter's family and neighbors as well as eyewitnesses to the crime scene. During an interview with Hunter's mother, she casually mentions the Lynn group he attended on Tuesday nights. When cell phone records reveal the names of the three surviving members, all are called in for interrogation. Revy, Zeke and Petey admit to nothing other than curiosity as to why Hunter did what he did. Petey goes so far as to suggest that the murder could have been caused by "nerves" left over from feelings toward his father. When asked why Hunter chose to take those feelings out on Alexander in particular, Petey throws up his hands, indicating that, at least in his opinion, the choice of targets was purely random.

Under the pressure of repeated questioning, however, Thomas breaks down, is granted a plea bargain, and admits the group has been following Alexander ever since they learned about his phenomenal success in Vegas. "Everybody else in the group was convinced he was the Antichrist, you know, the one sent by the Devil to destroy the earth. I was the only one who had any doubts," he claims. When threatened with the possibility of life imprisonment, he tells them what they want to hear: "So yes, we planned to kill him before he could unleash his demonic powers on everybody." In his testimony he avoids including Komerov on grounds that Doc left before the actual plans were discussed. Thanks primarily to Thomas's testimony, Petey, Zeke, and Revy are all indicted on charges of accessory to murder. Their trial is scheduled for December.

Shortly after hearing of Rafer's death, Greta slips into a deep depression, unable to either eat or sleep, refusing all attempts at consolation by a husband she knows to be somehow implicated in the murder. From her bed, with nothing more than an unblinking glare, she silently condemns him for his role. George, standing anxiously at her side, interprets her wordless reserve as a sign of conjugal loyalty and a promise to remain quiet. It is only later when she is alone with her thoughts that she gives audible vent to her despair. With the image of that final kiss at Rafer's door vividly before her, she sighs, then asks herself a forbidden question . . . one that for years has remained hidden in the remote corridors of her psyche. "Yes, my husband needs me . . . as confidant, mother and cheerleader . . . but don't I deserve more from life than that? Don't I deserve something for myself?" For the first time in 20 years, she considers the possibility of divorce.

As he wished, Rafer is cremated and his ashes placed in an urn prior to being cast on the waves somewhere out beyond Boston Harbor. With no family to consult, Stefan makes the funeral arrangements on his own, keeping in mind Rafer's personal beliefs. After talking with Eva, he negotiates to have the service conducted at the Arlington St. Church, a landmark Unitarian organization with a humanistic philosophy close to Rafer's non-theistic ideas. In place of a casket, an enlarged photo surrounded by flowers is placed up front at the head of the nave. On the day of the service, every pew in the church is filled with worshippers . . . a few grieving for the friend they miss, most just eager to learn more about who he really was. The front row, typically reserved for family members, is occupied by the handful of people who knew him best . . . Stefan and Julian Pulaski, Eva, two men from Kidder-Homans, a cousin who had invested on Rafer's advice . . . and a small delegation from Mexico headed by Carlos Santana's daughter.

A recording of the dirge from Beethoven's 7th symphony comes to an end just as the last guests arrive. From her seat in the first row Eva stares at the photograph, still struggling to make sense of her feelings. "Did I love him?," she muses, "Oh yes," comes the immediate answer. "But did I also fear him?" She pauses. "Perhaps," she adds, more softly this time. "To be honest, I was never really certain who he was." She looks around at the other guests. "Is it possible to love someone you have doubts about?" She turns back to look at the photo. "Is it possible," she asks, "to love someone who might not be the person he says he is?" She shakes her head in frustration as trust and doubt wrestle inside her. In one ear she hears Rafer describing the smile on a young girl's face as she emerges from the store with her new pair of shoes. His voice is warm and bright, matching the sparkle he sees in the girl's eyes. In the other ear she hears Petey's chilling reminder: 'What if he gets mad at you some day; you think with his superhuman powers he'd just snarl and let it go at that?' Still staring, she shakes her head again, unable to make sense of it all.

When Stefan climbs to the pulpit, all chatter ceases. As befitting the occasion, he is dressed in a black business suit and vest. All tears have been wiped from his slightly wrinkled cheeks, all personal grief subordinated to the demands of the moment. In the ensuing silence, the aroma of incense, burning invisibly in the corner, creeps into the nave, drawing all petty thoughts and concerns into its mindless web.

He looks out onto the huge audience, searching for faces he knows, then lets his eyes come to rest on Eva and Julian in the front row. "Our central question here today would appear to be a simple one: who was this man called Rafer Alexander? This is what we all want to know, isn't it? Before we can cherish his memory, we need to know who he was. Was he simply one of us . . . a fellow human being . . . or something else . . . something more than that? He certainly accomplished things that none of us here could hope to equal . . . but what exactly were they? There are some who would dismiss them as magical tricks, stunts of the sort we might encounter at a carnival or circus. They are quick to cite the case where Rafer was seen walking on water. Now, I can assure you this was no circus stunt; it was in fact an experiment I suggested to him earlier in the week, an experiment designed to see what paranormal abilities he might have in addition to those we already knew about. While he was hesitant at first, I finally convinced him that it was in the interests of science to see if such a thing could be done. Our plan was to follow up the demonstration with a formal experiment under controlled conditions comparable to the hospital study conducted last year here in Boston." A rustling sweeps across the church as listeners recall the healing study that was featured in newspapers and television.

"There are others in our city who take quite the opposite view of Rafer's actions. I refer to those who see him through the veil of their religious beliefs . . . in other words, as a personification of the divine, in particular, as the Second Coming of Jesus Christ. In light of all the miraculous things he did . . . like the healings in Oaxaca, bringing the Lorenzo boy back from the dead, the curing of Carlos Santana, and his less publicized work in Jerusalem and Kashmir . . . it is no wonder that some regard him now as a divine being. But this is not at all what Rafer would have wished. In talk after talk he reaffirmed to me that there was nothing divine about him at all. He didn't even believe in the concept of divinity.

"So, let's get back to our original question: Who was this man Rafer Alexander? If he wasn't a clever magician capable of convincing sick people they were actually healthy . . . and if he wasn't the incarnation of Christ or at least a figure saintly enough to defy gravity . . . then who was he? . . . (*pause*) . . . I can hear Rafer's answer now: 'He was one of us.' Yes, that's precisely what he would say, and it's true. In most respects he was an ordinary human being . . . he grew up in a small town, got good grades in school, was ambitious, entered the world of finance, made some mistakes in the stock market, lost his family in a plane crash, and had a setback in love . . . a life that may have been dramatic in some ways perhaps but hardly the stuff of legend. What set him apart from the rest of us was his ability to heal, whether that meant curing a physical disease or healing the conflict between two warring parties. He would be the first to say, however, that there was nothing unique about this ability. I remember his precise words at lunch one day: 'All humans are capable of doing what I've done.' In other words, he didn't see himself as all that different from the rest of us. He may have performed some extraordinary deeds but he refused to see them as signs of divine intervention, that is, as miracles. To Rafer they were nothing more than the acts of a caring individual doing his best to help others.

"So that's his real message. We all have the ability to do the things he did . . . curing disease, resolving conflicts, even walking on water. If that sounds a little hard to believe, it is because we insist on clinging to an outmoded and restrictive idea of human nature. If we are to honor Rafer's memory, we must expand out notion of what ordinary humans can do. We must give up our knee-jerk reaction to events that appear to violate science . . . a reaction which leads us to label something like non-medical healing as a miracle and attribute it to divine intervention. Rafer would have us believe there is nothing divine about such events; they are the work of a human mind brought to razor-sharp focus by meditation. He can say that with conviction, of course, because he had the personal experience to prove it.

"It is obvious that Rafer took great pleasure in healing others yet he never asked for recognition, never once bragged about his accomplishments. So, you might ask, why did he do it? Why did he spend so much of his time rescuing strangers from death and showing bitter enemies the way to peace? . . . (*pause*) . . . What could it possibly be other than love . . . the kind of selfless love conveyed by the Greek word *agape* . . . a love for others without any thought of personal gain, either emotional or material. This was his only motive, if you can even call it a motive. It is no coincidence, of course, that this kind of selfless love and the ability to heal are typically found in the same person. According to Rafer, they both arise when meditation dissolves all sense of self-separateness . . . a process that releases a kind of energy that can be transmitted to others where it is used to restore health.

"Because he was unafflicted with the many character flaws we associate with ego . . . I'm thinking of things like jealousy, envy, greed, pride, and the like . . . he could sometimes come across as unemotional. To those who knew him well, however, he was anything but cool. The passion was always there, but it was never about things he wanted for himself. You could see it most clearly in his love for children. I don't think I've ever heard him more enthusiastic than when he was describing what it was like to take a horde . . . and a horde is probably no exaggeration . . . of Oaxacan kids to the store to buy them new shoes. Back home I have a photo of him coming out of the store with 10 or 15 kids hanging onto his arms and legs . . . holding their precious boxes snuggly against their chests. His face was aglow, his smile broad and radiant as he guided them out the door and into the plaza. That's who he was; that's the way I'll always remember him.

"Now, if anyone would like to come up and say a few words about Rafer, this is the time to do it." Two people come forward, Graham Edwards from Kidder-Homans and the golfer Charlie Haffner. When both have finished, Stefan looks around, then looks down at Eva who quickly turns her head, averting his gaze. He waits for a minute until he is sure that no one else is coming up, then with a nod of his head, signals for the playing of the last movement of Beethoven's Symphony #9 . . . the Ode to Joy. As the audience rises, the sound swells, filling the huge church to its rafters. Inspired by Stefan's words and stirred by the music, the guests file solemnly toward the door, many with heads down, some with moistening eyes. After complimenting Stefan on his speech, they step out onto the street and head for home. When the church is finally empty, Stefan looks around for Eva, sees her jumping into a cab, and yells a startled goodbye. She waves briefly before disappearing down Arlington Street. "Logan Airport, please," she says to the driver, clutching her purse and the plane ticket inside. As the cab heads into the tunnel, she scans the traffic, first one side then the other, waiting for her heart to slow down. Her thoughts return briefly to the ceremony, then leap ahead to Mexico. As sole manager now of the Oaxacan Fund, there are decisions to be made, people to meet, so many arrangements to make . . . the opportunity of a lifetime, yes, but is it more responsibility than she can bear? Still clutching her purse, she pictures Rafer first at the zocolo, then in the shoe store, finally at the hospital. Silently she nods her head. "I know what he would do if he were still alive. I'll just try to do the same thing."

After crossing the Commons, Stefan is about to pass the First Baptist Church on Tremont St when he sees a large group of people on the sidewalk just outside the church. On closer inspection they appear to be part of an overflow crowd listening to a sermon through open doors. Stepping nimbly between cars, he crosses the street and stops to see for himself. From deep inside the cavernous hall, the voice of a man, presumably the pastor, comes spilling out onto the sidewalk. "Let us be clear about one thing," he booms, "This man called Rafer Alexander was no ordinary man; nay, He was Christ once again incarnated in human form." His voice rises. "Oh Lord have mercy on us. We . . . God's own children . . . have done it again. We have murdered the very Son who was sent to save us from our sins." His voice falters. "It is clear that we are still not ready for God's promised kingdom, not worthy of His love. The only thing we . . . ."

As Stefan continues down the street, the pastor's voice grows quiet, disappearing finally in a vortex of honking cars. He shakes his head. "How can it be?," he asks. "After all Rafer has said about himself . . . about the powers that lie hidden inside all of us . . . they still don't get it. When are they going to realize who we humans really are?"

Edwards Brothers,Inc!
Thorofare, NJ 08086
04 November, 2010
BA2010309